Emma Blair was born in Glasgow and now lives in Devon. She is the author of twenty-nine bestselling novels including *Scarlet Ribbons* and *Flower of Scotland*, both of which were shortlisted for the Romantic Novel of the Year Award.

For more information about the author, visit www.emma-blair.co.uk

Emma Blair

HESTER DARK

PIATKUS

PIATKUS

First published in Great Britain in 1984 by Arrow Books Limited
This paperback edition published in 2009 by Piatkus

A CIP catalogue record for this book
is available from the British Library

ISBN 978-0-7499-4262-5

Printed and bound in Great Britain by Clays Ltd, St Ives plc

Papers used by Piatkus are natural, renewable and recyclable
products sourced from well-managed forests and certified
in accordance with the rules of the Forest Stewardship Council.

Mixed Sources
Product group from well-managed
forests and other controlled sources
www.fsc.org Cert no. SGS-COC-004081
© 1996 Forest Stewardship Council

Piatkus
An imprint of
Little, Brown Book Group
100 Victoria Embankment
London EC4Y 0DY

An Hachette UK Company
www.hachette.co.uk

www.piatkus.co.uk

PART ONE
Her Mother's Image

1

Hester sat on the edge of her seat staring out the window at the uninviting, grey expanse beyond. She was appalled.

Her lower lip trembled and the inside of her throat tightened at the thought that she would be living here, that this was now her home. She hadn't quite known what to expect of Glasgow. Her mother had rarely spoken about it. But whatever it was she'd vaguely imagined, it certainly wasn't this.

The train juddered to a halt in the centre of a bridge over what she knew must be the River Clyde. A filthy river, black and ominous, that flowed coldly and silently on its way.

The carriage shuddered suddenly under her, while ahead the engine gave a long piercing wail. It started to rain, full-bodied drops that fell splashing in a million soft explosions.

'Typical Glasgow weather,' a woman further along the carriage commented.

Her companion, another middle-aged woman, nodded vigorously so that her huge bosoms bounced up and down despite the obvious corset she was wearing.. 'Aye. Wouldn't you know it,' she replied.

The train started moving again, very slowly running into the station that lay beyond the bridge.

There was a sooty smell about the station, and the overall impression was one of dirt and grime. Just like the squalid tenements Hester had glimpsed a few minutes previously and which had so appalled her.

The train stopped and the carriage quickly emptied. The woman with the bosoms paused in the doorway to give Hester a friendly smile.

'Are you all right, hen?' she asked.

Hester returned the smile, trying to look confident, which she wasn't at all. 'I'm being met by my aunt and uncle,' she replied.

The woman nodded. 'That's fine then,' and stepped down onto the platform to join her travelling companion. Arm in arm they disappeared into the throng.

Although she was tall for fourteen, Hester still had to climb up on the seat to reach her small case on the rack above. She nearly lost her balance as it came tumbling down but a quick jiggling of her feet saved her from falling over.

Clutching her case she stepped down onto the platform, and stood there waiting in accordance with the instructions in her uncle's letter.

The crowds had thinned now as she glanced about. She felt dreadfully conspicuous and not just a little lost. There were butterflies in her stomach and the insides of her thighs were trembling ever so slightly.

So this is Scotland, she thought to herself. So far she didn't think much of it.

'Miss Hester Dark?'

She turned to find herself staring at a young man of average height wearing a grey chauffeur's uniform. His hat was in his hand and there was a polite smile on his face. His hair was a sharp red colour, his eyes a piercing blue.

'I'm she,' Hester replied.

The young man took her case. 'Is the rest of your luggage in the guard's van?' he asked.

'Yes.'

'I think the best thing would be for me to put you in the car and then I'll collect them. I presume they've all got your name on them?'

Hester nodded.

'I thought my aunt and uncle were coming to meet me?' she said, as they started for the car.

'The Colonel's at work and Mrs Oliphant is busy

preparing for your arrival,' the young man replied, reassuring her with a smile.

Hester cast her mind back over her uncle's letter. Now that she came to think of it, what he'd said was that she would be met. Not that he and Aunt Sybil would be doing the meeting. She'd just assumed that.

The young man ushered her into the car and, after making sure she was comfortable and having inquired how many cases there were and what they looked like, hurried back toward the train.

It was a beautiful car Hester thought, by far the grandest she'd ever been in. She'd known her Uncle Will was rich, though not how rich. Curiously, her father had sometimes spoken of his brother-in-law's wealth, but her mother had never said a word.

Her musings were interrupted by the return of the young man with her two large cases. He stowed them in the car's boot and, that done to his satisfaction, took his place behind the wheel.

Hester blinked as they emerged from the bowels of the gloomy station into the fragile daylight. It's a grey city, she thought to herself as the car sped on its way. The sky overhead was grey, as were the pavements beneath them, the buildings and the streets. Even the thin, pinched faces of the majority of people they passed were tinged with that colour.

A sour feeling chased the butterflies from her stomach. For the first time since starting out, she felt dreadfully homesick and would have given anything to be back in her beloved Bristol.

Despite trying to hold them back, the tears rushed into her eyes. She lowered her head and dabbed at them with the scrap of handkerchief she'd tucked up her sleeve.

'Are you all right, Miss Dark?' the driver inquired gently.

She looked up to discover him staring at her through the rear-view mirror. He was plainly concerned.

'Yes, thank you,' she replied huskily.

'Would you like me to stop?'

'How long till we reach my uncle's house?'

'Ten minutes.'

That would give her time to recover herself, she thought. 'Just go on,' she finally answered. And, blowing her nose in her hanky, sat further back in the plush, leather seat.

They drove for a few minutes in silence, and then the chauffeur said, 'By the way, my name's Tam Ritchie. I was engaged earlier this year by your uncle. I'm daft on cars. Always have been.'

He was obviously trying to cheer her up, and she appreciated it. His reflection in the mirror bore a genial, homely grin.

'I'm pleased to meet you, Tam,' she smiled back, wondering immediately if she was being too familiar with a servant. She didn't really know. They hadn't had servants at home, or anything at all grand. How she wished she were safe in her mother's kitchen, setting the table for their simple tea.

'Did you have a nice trip up from England?' he asked politely.

Brushing away a few stray tears, Hester decided she might feel better talking. And so she did. She told him all about the long and arduous journey from Bristol, the funny conductor who had never stopped singing, and the beautiful countryside they'd come through.

Tam turned the car into an impressive street of tall, stately houses. Like the rest of the city, or all that she'd seen so far, they were built from grey stone.

'Here we are,' said Tam drawing the car up to the kerb. Switching the engine off, he hurriedly got out to come round and open the door for her. He assisted her out by holding her elbow.

So this was her new home, this grand and imposing house with its polished knocker, its many windows and unwelcoming entrance.

They climbed a dozen flagged steps, bounded on either side by intricately worked wrought iron railings. Tam pulled the bell which echoed within the rambling depths of the house.

'I'll take the car round the back and bring your luggage in from there,' Tam said. He flashed her a last brief smile and then was hurrying back down the steps to the vehicle he so obviously cherished.

Hester was sorry to see him go. He'd been the first friendly face in what was to her the great unknown. As she heard footsteps hurrying towards the door, she prayed it wouldn't be the last friendly face.

The door was opened by a shy-looking maid about her own age.

'I'm Hester Dark. I'm expected,' Hester blurted out.

The girl made a small curtsey. 'Please come in, Miss.'

The hall Hester entered had a forbidding air about it. It was immaculate, high ceilinged and cold. The smell of wax polish assailed her nostrils.

'If you'll follow me,' said the girl.

Hester shivered. It was as bitter in the house as out, and grey in its feeling if not in its colour. Her shoes made clacking sounds on the highly polished floor.

Oh Ma, she cried inside herself, oh Ma. For a second, the image of her beloved mother's face floated before her eyes as though about to lean forward and kiss her.

Hester followed the girl up the carpeted staircase with growing fear. On the second floor, the maid stopped before a heavy wooden door and knocked.

'Come in!' a female voice called out.

Hester knew that the voice must belong to her Aunt Sybil whom, like her uncle and the rest of their family, she'd never met. She put her best smile on and took a deep breath as she entered the room.

Aunt Sybil was a tallish, thin, plain woman with a beaky nose. Her eyes were like a bird's, beady and fierce.

Rising from in front of the fire where she'd been sitting, she stared at Hester with curiosity but not real interest. Her gaze devoured Hester from head to foot.

'So.' Aunt Sybil breathed, 'you're Mary's lass.'

11

Hester had been expecting a clasp to the bosom or a kiss on the cheek, or both. She was obviously going to get neither.

'I'm pleased to meet you, Aunt,' she stammered.

'I've already rung for tea and sandwiches,' Aunt Sybil replied, ignoring her niece's unease. 'After which I'll have you shown to your room where I'm sure you'll want to rest for a while. You can join us at dinner which is at eight o'clock. We dress, of course.'

Hester's reply was a nod. She wanted to cry again, but this time managed to stifle the tears. She felt so lost, so alone. So unloved. But she wouldn't let this woman see her weep.

They sat. Aunt Sybil regarded Hester thoughtfully. 'A terrible business about your parents,' she said at last, watching Hester closely.

'Yes,' Hester replied in a quiet voice.

'Especially your mother.'

Hester stared at the carpet.

'An orphan at fourteen. A tragedy,' clucked Aunt Sybil.

Hester bit her lip. Her father had been dead for two years now. She'd come to terms with that, and to live with it. But it was only a fortnight since her ma had. . . had. . . .

'Pills wasn't it?' Aunt Sybil said in what was almost a hiss.

'Yes.'

'Poor Mary,' cooed Aunt Sybil, with what passed in her for sympathy. 'I suppose it was your father being killed that turned her mind?'

Somehow, she forced her voice to answer. 'She was never the same after Da died. She just sort of went to pieces.'

'She was quite mad then at the end I take it?' Aunt Sybil's voice almost seemed to smile.

Hester cringed. Was her aunt being deliberately horrible to her? Or was she being oversensitive?

The truth was, she found it terribly difficult to discuss her mother's death. Her entire insides became a great raw wound whenever the subject was broached.

She kept her eyes averted from her aunt's. She didn't want her to see how totally devastated she was. The last thing she wanted was pity. Especially from this woman with her fine clothes and finer airs.

'Well?' Aunt Sybil urged.

Hester gulped and then cleared her throat. 'Deranged, the doctor said,' she whispered hoarsely.

Aunt Sybil sat back in her chair and made a pyramid with her hands. Her face was a stone mask from which her eyes shone like two black gems. She seemed satisfied about something.

'Do you know much about us?' Aunt Sybil changed the subject.

'Not a lot. I know I have two cousins, both older than I. And that Uncle Will owns a newspaper. Apart from that very little.'

'Billy is sixteen and Christine fifteen. They're both at school now, but will be back late afternoon. They've been looking forward to your arrival.'

Finally, the tea appeared. The sandwiches were dainty cucumber ones. Hester was ravenous and ate most of them. Outside the rain increased, hitting the tall windows like pebbles.

She wondered what Billy and Christine were like. Would they be like their mother? She hoped they were nice. Life was going to be awfully difficult if they weren't.

And what sort of man was Uncle Will? A lot like her mother, she hoped and prayed. As she'd been hoping and praying ever since the letter had arrived to say she was to travel north to stay with the Oliphants.

'I believe a neighbour looked after you until now.'

'Mrs Egbert who lived next door. She and Ma were great friends. It was Mrs Egbert who arranged the funeral and everything.'

13

Aunt Sybil gave a thin smile. 'Mrs Egbert may have arranged it, but it was your Uncle Will who *paid* for it. I hope you appreciate that?'

'Yes, Aunt Sybil.'

Aunt Sybil nodded, then delicately sipped her tea. 'Was there a Mr Egbert?' she asked suddenly.

'Yes.'

'And what did he do?'

'He worked on the docks like my Da.'

Aunt Sybil looked vaguely disapproving, as though someone had walked on the carpet in muddy boots.

'He was a nice man and she a nice woman,' Hester said defiantly. If she'd had her way she'd have stayed with the Egberts rather than come to live with her aunt and uncle. She'd pleaded with the Egberts to keep her, but it was impossible. Much as they would have liked to take her in, with eight children of their own to feed and clothe their money was already stretched. One more mouth was just beyond them. Anyway, Mrs Egbert had argued, it was only right and proper that Hester went to the Oliphants. They were blood relatives, after all. Her uncle was her mother's brother, it was what her mother would have wanted.

Aunt Sybil poured more tea. 'You'll no doubt miss Bristol to begin with, of course. But I think you'll come to find that Glasgow has a great deal to offer,' she said.

Hester smiled, but didn't reply.

They chatted about this and that for a little while longer, then Aunt Sybil took her upstairs and showed Hester her bedroom where her clothes had already been unpacked and put away.

The room surprised Hester. For some reason she'd been expecting something dreary and tucked out of the way, but this room, though out of the way, was anything but dreary.

She thought it delightful. There was a double bed and bright paper on the walls. There was a fireplace in which a large fire now roared and, covering most of the floor, a thick, fluffy carpet.

Hester sat at the dressing table and gazed at her reflection in the mirror. She was drawn and pale, not at all as she had been only a few weeks ago. Her eyes were strained-looking and ringed with dark circles.

She rose from the dressing table to touch the back of a comfy club chair close to the fire.

'Well?' Aunt Sybil asked.

Hester gave her aunt a grateful smile, wondering if she hadn't misjudged her. 'It's lovely,' she sighed.

A middle-aged maid with an Irish accent appeared at the door and announced that the young miss's bath was now ready.

'I thought you'd like one,' Aunt Sybil explained.

'Oh, yes please!' Hester exclaimed.

Aunt Sybil gave her directions to the bathroom and then said she would leave her alone now. She expected Hester to be downstairs dressed at seven-forty-five. She would arrange for her to have a call at six.

After her aunt had gone Hester closed the door and leaned against it. Her eyes swept over the room, taking everything in.

The room had a calming, soothing effect on her. How grand it was! Nothing at all like she'd been used to back in Bristol where home had been a terraced two up and two down. Her room had been barely quarter the size of this one and nowhere near as luxurious.

She crossed to the bed and sat on it, exclaiming with delight as she literally sank into its deep, soft mattress.

What a curious mixture she told herself. Her aunt cold and somewhat distant and the rest of the house chilly and gloomy. And then the sheer heaven of this room, which was so warm, friendly and comforting.

Rising from the bed she took off her travelling clothes and put on her dressing gown. Outside in the hall she followed her aunt's directions and had no trouble finding the bathroom.

The tub was enormous with steam lazily rising from the scented water within. She saw that bath crystals had been added to the water which had turned it deep green. A thick towel lay on a wooden chair nearby.

She sighed with pleasure as she slid into the water. She stared up at the magnolia painted ceiling high overhead.

'Glasgow,' she mused aloud. An ugly name for an ugly city. For a long time, she lay half sleeping wondering what it had in store for her.

'Come in!' Hester called out in reply to the knock on her bedroom door. It was a few minutes to six and she was just completing dressing.

She turned round when she saw it wasn't a maid who entered. There was no mistaking who the girl must be. Slightly shorter than Hester, she was skinny as a stick and had her mother's plain face and sharp nose.

Hester smiled. 'You must be Christine.'

'Mother said you would still be in your bed.'

'I couldn't sleep. It's all the excitement, I suppose.'

Christine nodded and advanced into the room a little further, studying Hester carefully. 'You're very pretty,' she pronounced almost grudgingly.

Hester flushed. 'Thank you.'

Hester held out her hand towards her cousin which, after a moment's hesitation, was taken. Solemnly they shook. Hester, who had had fantasies about Christine being the sister she had never had, wanted to clasp Christine to her, but the other girl's manner forbade that.

'You'll be coming to my school,' Christine announced in her abrupt way.

'Oh, that's nice,' mumbled Hester, not knowing what else to say.

'It's called Maybank. I think you'll like it. It's the most expensive girl's school in Glasgow.'

'The school I went to before was just an ordinary one. I hope I'll fit in.'

Christine raised an eyebrow. 'You'll just have to.

16

Father would never allow you to attend a common school now that you're living with us. It would reflect badly on him, you see.'

'Yes,' Hester said slowly, 'I guess I do.'

'You'll have to get a uniform first, mind you. Grey and red it is. Rather pretty, in a subdued way,' Christine said, looking at her cousin with disapproval.

The doubts she'd had earlier came flooding back. 'I hope you don't mind me coming to stay here?' she said, the hint of a tremor in her voice. How she'd hoped Christine would like her! 'I had nowhere else to go.'

Christine looked through her as though she hadn't spoken. 'Your father was an American, Mother said?'

Hester nodded. 'Yes. He came from Boston.'

'And wasn't he a seaman?'

'Until he met my mother and they went to live in Bristol. There he worked on the docks.'

'You don't mean as a common labourer?' Christine was clearly shocked.

Hester's mouth pursed on hearing the scorn in her cousin's voice. 'He started off as one. But after a while they made him a foreman,' she said defensively.

Christine was unimpressed. 'Your parents were very poor, Mother said?'

'We never went without,' Hester replied quickly.

'I just hope you don't let me down at school, that's all,' Christine said suddenly. 'I'll hate you if the girls laugh at me because of you.'

What could she reply to that? Her cousin's words made her dread the thought of going to Maybank. 'I'd rather hoped we were going to be friends,' she answered bravely after a short pause.

Christine's small, incessantly watchful eyes bored into Hester's. 'Perhaps. Perhaps not,' she said archly, and turning on her heel swept from the room.

Hester sat in the club chair and gazed into the remains of the fire, shaking and feeling sick.

In the glowing embers she saw first her father's face

and then her mother's. 'Oh Da! Oh Ma!' she whispered to their ghosts. New tears sprang into her eyes, and the old pain burned in her heart.

She remembered the countless Sundays her Da had taken her along the banks of the Avon, or out into the country. The many games they'd played together. The marvellous times they'd had. The great love she'd had for him and he for her.

Then there was Ma. Ma whom she'd idolized, who was not just her mother but her best friend. Ma who'd never been the same after Da had been killed.

It had started with Ma not doing the housework as much, or as well, as she always had. A little after that Ma's appearance had begun to deteriorate, and she'd forget what she was doing or even saying.

Hester could still remember the first night she'd woken to hear her mother sobbing her heart out in the bedroom. From then on it was a rare night that passed when Ma didn't cry.

Hester wiped her own tears away and gulped in a deep breath to try and steady herself. Glancing at the clock, she realized she'd been lost in her dreams longer than she'd thought.

Using the jug and basin in the corner to wash away all signs of her tears, she walked to the door as though she was going to her execution.

'I'm Billy and it's marvellous to meet you and have you stay with us.'

Billy wasn't at all like Aunt Sybil or Christine. Not only was he friendly but charming as well.

A great deal of Hester's depression lifted from her when he kissed her on the cheek and squeezed her tightly. This was more like it. This was as it was meant to be.

'It's marvellous to meet you too,' she replied with real feeling.

Billy, eyes twinkling, held her at arms' length and

studied her. 'I must say I never expected you to be such a cracker,' he said admiringly.

'Billy!' Aunt Sybil snapped.

'Well she *is*, Mother.'

Christine sniffed and glowered.

'It's very kind of you to say so,' Hester said.

'Beauty is only skin deep,' Christine hissed, but not quietly enough for her brother not to catch it.

Billy burst out laughing which infuriated Christine and made her turn away blushing.

'Your father's late,' said Aunt Sybil as the ornate Grandfather clock in the corner chimed eight.

'How unlike him,' commented Christine.

'It is, indeed. Something very important must have come up to detain him at the office.' Aunt Sybil called the maid and gave instructions that dinner was to be held for half an hour.

'Cook will love that,' Billy grinned mischievously.

'Cook's likes and dislikes hardly enter into it,' his mother sniffed waspishly.

Billy was a good looking young man who, at sixteen, was starting to fill out in the chest and shoulders.

Hester and Billy drew apart, chatting together animatedly. She told him about Bristol, and he told her about Glasgow. She liked the easy, friendly, manner he had about him. At last she'd found an ally.

All conversation in the room suddenly stopped when the door burst open. The man who entered was exceptionally tall for a Glaswegian. He was well built, with a great, leonine head, topped by a shock of dark auburn hair which he wore swept straight back from the forehead. The eyes were green and filled with the mystery of Celtic mists. She guessed him to be about forty.

Hester stood and unconsciously smoothed down the front of her dress, deciding it best not to speak until spoken to.

'Good evening dear,' said Aunt Sybil. Going to her husband's side, she pecked him on the cheek, immediately recoiling. 'You've been drinking,' she accused.

'Just a few drams,' he replied. His voice was rougher, less cultured than those of the rest of his family, but it was a good voice; strong, firm and resonant.

Aunt Sybil's eyes went from his to Hester. For one fleeting moment Hester thought she saw the slightest hint of malice in that levelled gaze – but she couldn't be sure.

'Your niece, Hester,' Aunt Sybil said.

Uncle Will stared at Hester long and hard, as though lost in a world of his own.

'Dearest?' Aunt Sybil prompted.

Slowly, Uncle Will crossed the room to stand in front of Hester. There was a trace of perspiration on his forehead and his breathing was heavy and strained.

'The spit of your mother,' he said slowly, like a man coming out of a trance. He reached out to touch Hester's hair, which was the same coal black her mother's had been. He nodded to himself. Remembering.

'People have always said we were very alike,' Hester replied shyly.

Uncle Will grunted.

Aunt Sybil's now veiled eyes went from him to Hester and then back again.

'We'll talk about your mother later,' he said abruptly, his words just noticeably thick with emotion. Then added, 'In the meantime, welcome to our home, lass. It's good to have you with us. I only wish the circumstances had been different.' He then stooped to give Hester a fatherly kiss on the forehead and cheek.

'Thank you for taking me in, Uncle,' Hester whispered.

'Was there trouble at the office, dear?' Aunt Sybil inquired.

'Not really.'

'But you're late?'

'That's because I stopped off at a pub on the way home.'

Aunt Sybil's smile thinned instantly, and again her gaze swung to Hester and away again.

'Get me a dram, Billy,' Uncle Will said. Tearing his gaze from Hester, he made his way to the fire where he briskly rubbed his hands. 'It's still teeming out,' he said to no one in particular.

Hester watched the amber liquid vanish down her uncle's throat. He was a powerful man and she felt naturally drawn to him, like iron to a magnet. And yet there was something about him which made her uneasy. Scared her even. But she didn't know what it could be.

'How was your day?' Aunt Sybil inquired.

'Fine. A few problems late in the afternoon, but I got them sorted out before I left.'

At a sign from his father Billy took the glass and refilled it. Uncle Will carried it with him when they all trooped through to the dining room.

During the meal Hester was aware of her uncle glancing surreptitiously at her from time to time. Nor was this attention lost on Sybil, who watched her husband's face continually.

It was a strange home-coming meal, Hester thought. Instead of being happy and excited it was overhung with a black, oppressive atmosphere. Uncle Will seemed morose and lost in himself, his face a dirty white colour and the perspiration that had dotted his forehead when he arrived was even more pronounced.

Christine was sullen and only spoke when directly addressed. Billy, on the other hand, the one exception, chattered nineteen to the dozen. He managed to squeeze a number of smiles, and even a laugh, out of Hester before the meal was over.

Back in the drawing room Uncle Will went directly to the whisky decanter and poured himself a triple. Indicating that they should all sit, he took a chair in front of the fire that gave him a clear view of Hester.

'Now,' he said slowly, addressing her. 'Let's start at the beginning. Tell me exactly what happened to Robert

Dark. Your mother wrote at the time to say he'd died, but didn't give us any details.'

There was something here. An undercurrent of some sort. She'd felt it ever since her uncle's arrival home. But she didn't know what it was. Unless . . . there had been disapproval in her uncle's voice when he'd spoken her father's name.

'Didn't you get on with my father?' she asked bluntly, in what Robert Dark himself would have said was a good, forthright, New England manner.

Uncle Will regarded her from behind hooded eyes. He tipped his glass and the whisky vanished. 'Your father and I. . . . well . . . let's just say we had our differences. But I respected him. He was always a good husband to your mother.'

She lowered her head to stare at the carpet. Her voice trembled when she at last spoke. 'Two years ago, nineteen-seventeen,' she said. Her chest seemed to be on fire. 'It was a Tuesday. I remember that quite clearly. He saw me off to school as he always did, waving to me at the crossroads where he turned right and I went left into the school. He used always to walk a little way along that road and then turn and wave and I would wave back. Then . . . that afternoon . . . Mrs Egbert was waiting for me in the kitchen. There's been an accident, she said. Your Da. Word came an hour ago. Your Ma's gone to the hospital and says you've to wait here till she gets back. But I didn't understand. I thought he would be all right. . . .

'Mrs Egbert made me some tea and then I did my homework. It was nearly six when Ma got back. I knew the moment I saw her face. It was all red and swollen from crying. But it was more than that. There was just something there that told me. He's dead, I said. And Ma just nodded and sat beside me at the table.' Hester stared at the floor, her eyes bright with unshed tears.

'I couldn't believe it. It was all so unreal. Mrs Egbert

made a pot of tea for Ma, but she couldn't drink it. It stuck in her throat she said. I asked her how Da had died, but all she said was that it was an accident. She wouldn't tell me more.'

Hester wrung her hands together, the memory of that day and what had happened since making her feel all tight and empty inside.

'Did you never find out?' asked Aunt Sybil.

'Yes,' Hester gasped. 'One of the lads at school told me a few months later. He'd heard his parents talking about it and that was how he knew. Da had been inspecting a faulty winch when someone had accidentally turned it on. There was a chain on the winch which wrapped itself round my Da's arm. It tore it right out by the roots. He was dead long before they got him to the hospital.'

'My God!' said Aunt Sybil softly.

Christine sat staring at Hester, her eyes bulging and an expression of horror on her face.

Billy's mouth hung open.

Uncle Will rose and poured himself more whisky. At the decanter he said over his shoulder, 'Robert Dark certainly didn't deserve that. That's a terrible way to die.'

'Yes,' Hester agreed quietly, feeling as though she had just lived through it all again.

Uncle Will sat again, and his mood became even more intense. 'Now tell me about Mary,' he said.

Hester ran a hand through her hair, wanting to go on, and not wanting to. 'After Da was killed, Ma just went to pieces. When I was at school she'd sit at home staring out of the window for hours on end. And it was more or less the same when I got home. Sometimes she'd make a meal but more often than not she wouldn't. She lost complete interest in everything. It was as though she just gave up.'

Hester stopped suddenly, not daring to meet their eyes. She felt numb all over.

'Did she ever say anything about all this?' Uncle Will asked.

'Sometimes, when she was really beside herself, she'd

rave on that it was all her fault. That my Da had paid for what *she'd* done. It was the grief, Mrs Egbert said. She blamed herself. She loved him so.'

Uncle Will's eyes were filled with pain. 'Your mother never did anything to be ashamed of,' he replied huskily.

Gathering all her young strength, Hester went on. 'She'd been seeing the doctor for some time and he gave her some pills and powders to quieten her down . . .'

'Was it these pills. . . ?' He left the question incomplete, the words he did utter coming reluctantly.

Hester nodded sadly. 'She must have saved them up for weeks.'

Minutes went by and the only sounds to break the silence were the steady ticking of the Grandfather clock in the corner and the crackle and occasional hiss of the fire.

Hester glanced up and was shocked to see the effect her words had had on her uncle. He seemed to have shrunk to half his normal size and his face looked at least twenty years older.

'Poor Hester,' murmured Billy.

'Mrs Egbert and I thought you might have come to the funeral,' Hester said to her uncle.

Uncle Will roused himself to stare at Hester through tortured eyes. 'Naturally I considered going,' he said in a cracked voice. 'But when it came down to it I couldn't. Mary and I were very close you see. I just couldn't bear the thought of watching her being buried.'

He was obviously sincere, and yet his words surprised Hester. She'd had no idea he and her mother were particularly close. Her Ma had rarely mentioned her brother, and corresponded with him even less. Most of the little she did know about the Oliphants came from her father.

'Were there many at the funeral?' Uncle Will asked.

'About a dozen neighbours from round about. Plus a few friends of my Da's from the docks. And me of course.' She added that last bit almost as an afterthought.

'I think you've been very brave,' said Billy.

Hester flashed him a grateful smile. Already she'd become extremely fond of him.

Uncle Will rose and stalked across to the whisky decanter which, after pouring himself yet another, he brought back with him to his chair, setting it down between him and the fire.

'I think you should get along upstairs now children,' Aunt Sybil said. It was not a suggestion.

Christine pulled a face and Billy groaned.

'Now then, no arguments. You've both got school in the morning. Get along with you and I'll be up later to say goodnight.'

Christine and Billy rose, as did Hester.

'There's no need for you to go yet, lass,' said Uncle Will. 'Sit and talk with us a wee while longer.'

'I'll see you tomorrow afternoon then. When I get back from school,' Billy said to Hester.

'I'll look forward to that,' she replied truthfully.

Hester turned her attention back to Uncle Will to find him staring at her. A stare that seemed to penetrate to the very depths of her being. She shivered.

'Are you cold?' asked Aunt Sybil.

'No. Just . . . well I suppose it's been a long day. And an eventful one.'

'Perhaps you should. . . .'

'No, no.' I'll enjoy staying up for a little while yet. It gives me a chance to get to know you both better.'

'And we you,' Uncle Will said softly.

Producing a silver case from which he took a long, thick cigar, he made a ritual out of trimming and then lighting it.

'Your mother used to like the occasional cigar,' he said suddenly, almost as though talking to himself.

Hester blinked.

'Small ones of course. Not big fellows like these. I used to buy them in especially for her. She never smoked them in company, not wanting to shock people. But on nights like this, when we were alone before a good fire, she'd indulge herself.'

Hester couldn't imagine her mother smoking a cigar.

Aunt Sybil had positioned herself roughly halfway between Hester and Uncle Will. She was further away from the fire than they and formed the apex of a triangle. As each spoke her gaze went from one to the other, like an umpire in a tennis match.

'She never smoked at all in Bristol,' Hester said.

'I'm not surprised. Robert Dark was always a very righteous man. No smoking, drinking, gambling or any other vice.' And having said that his mouth twisted slightly up at the corners, as though he was laughing at some secret joke.

'What were the differences between you and my father?' Hester asked.

Uncle Will took a long pull at his glass, then clamped his teeth round the end of his cigar. When he finally spoke it was without removing it.

'I didn't agree with Mary marrying him.'

'Because he was poor?'

'No.'

'Then why?'

'I suppose I took an instant dislike to him. It broke my heart when he took Mary down to Bristol.

'They were extremely happy together,' Hester stated.

'So I heard.' After a moment's pause, he went on. 'When they married I offered them a substantial amount of money, your mother had none of her own you see, but Robert Dark turned it down. He said he didn't need any money to support his wife. That was another thing I disagreed with. Noble sentiments no doubt, but your mother was used to finer things in life. She shouldn't have had to go without.'

Hester lifted her chin and sat up straighter. 'Ma always said *things* weren't everything. That there was a great deal more to life than mere material possessions.'

Uncle Will quickly finished his drink and refilled his

glass again. Since returning from dinner, he'd done considerable damage to the contents of the decanter. His face was very flushed and his speech decidedly slurred.

Aunt Sybil said, 'I don't think this is the sort of conversation the child should be subjected to on her first evening here.'

'Why not?' he growled.

'If you don't know then there's little point in my trying to explain it to you.'

He glared at her with something between fear and hatred.

'Why do you always call my father Robert Dark?' Hester asked.

'That was his name wasn't it?'

'Yes. But you never just call him Robert.'

'From the day I first met him I've called him Robert Dark. I don't really know why.' He glanced across at his wife. 'It doesn't matter.'

'I loved him,' Hester said simply.

An expression of contriteness immediately came across Uncle Will's face. 'Of course you did, lass. And it's only right that you did. I'm not trying to come between you and the memory of your dad. Nor am I speaking bad of him in any way. He was an honourable and upright man. No one could ever question that. We were just a bit like oil and water I suppose.'

'A conflict of interests you might say,' Aunt Sybil interrupted with a tight smile.

For the first time, Hester realized that the atmosphere between her aunt and uncle had become electric. If the air between had crackled she wouldn't have been surprised.

Wanting desperately to be on her own, Hester said that if they didn't mind she thought she really should go to bed now. Aunt Sybil immediately agreed, saying she would accompany Hester up the stairs.

Hester stood up. 'Goodnight, Uncle Will.'

He regarded her for a long moment. 'Just you understand, you're most welcome here lass. From today on this is your home. You're one of us.'

'Thank you.'

'The spit of your mother,' he said shaking his head in disbelief. 'Her absolute image.'

As she closed the door behind her and Aunt Sybil, she saw that he was staring after her. Even at that distance she could see the terrible, tortured look in his eyes.

Once in her room she sat on the edge of her bed to think about her new home. She didn't know what to make of her uncle. She knew she liked him, but it seemed impossible that he hadn't got on with her Da. Everyone had got on with her Da. Everyone except Uncle Will, it would seem.

She undressed slowly, slipped on her nightdress and, having first turned off the unfamiliar electric light – they'd had gas at home – got into bed where she lay watching the flickering shadows cast by the fire on the walls.

The next thing she knew she'd come to with a start and realized she must have dozed off. A glance at the fire, which had now died down and collapsed in on itself, told her she'd been asleep for a couple of hours at least.

What had wakened her? She hadn't had a nightmare – she hadn't even been dreaming.

She was about to turn over and snuggle down, when she heard the measured tread of feet walking away from her door. There was no question that the footsteps belonged to a man. Billy? Uncle Will? It had to be Uncle Will. Probably just checking that everything was all right with her.

That thought gave her comfort and brought a smile to her face. Within seconds she was asleep again.

'Time to get up, Miss,' said the middle-aged maid, gently shaking Hester's shoulder.

Hester yawned and sat up. 'What time is it?' she asked.

'Seven o'clock, Miss.'

Hester swung her legs out of bed, exclaiming with the cold.

'Would you like me to help you dress, Miss?' the maid asked.

'No, thank you. I'm quite used to doing it by myself.'

'Anything you want, Miss, just ring and I'll come,' she said, indicating the brass bell pull near the bed.

'What's your name?' Hester asked.

'Kathleen.'

'Then I'll do that should I need you, Kathleen.'

Kathleen's reply to that was a brief curtsey.

On arriving at the breakfast table, Hester discovered that Uncle Will and Billy had already gone. She was informed that it was their custom to take breakfast during the week earlier than the women, since they both had considerable distances to go.

'Ritchie, the chauffeur, drops off your uncle first and then takes Billy on,' Aunt Sybil explained as Hester tucked into delicious scrambled egg. 'He then comes back for Christine. Only today, I've decided, he'll be picking up the three of us as I intend seeing the headmistress about your enrolment. We'll also be going to my dressmaker's.'

'You're having some new clothes made?' Hester inquired politely.

'No. you are.'

'But I already have. . . .' Looking down at her old, faded dress.

'Quite unsuitable,' interrupted Aunt Sybil. 'You're to have a complete new wardrobe. Your uncle says so.'

'That's very kind of you both.'

'Well, we can't have you walking around looking like the proverbial country cousin, now can we?' Aunt Sybil replied a trifle acidly.

Hester gnawed her lip. Ma had made most of her clothes including the dress she was now wearing. She'd

29

thought she looked very smart in them before she came to Glasgow.

'We'll also have to buy you a school uniform, which we'll get in Paisley's. Best shop for that sort of thing,' her aunt went on. Adding, in almost a winsome tone, 'We must have you looking your best. You're such a pretty thing, really.'

Christine's mouth became tight and she glared at Hester. It seemed most unfair to her that her cousin should be so attractive when she was so plain.

The fact that she was unattractive had always rankled with Christine. When she was young she'd told herself that she'd change when she grew up; that she'd be the ugly duckling who turned into a swan. But now she'd come to accept the fact that that was seeming less and less likely. Plain she'd been born and plain she'd stay – barring miracles.

Acceptance of that had been hard enough, but now here was Hester in her own home as a constant reminder of what she would never be. For Hester was already a swan. A swan who was obviously going to grow more and more beautiful as time went by.

Jealousy of her cousin had been born in Christine on meeting her. That jealousy now began to deepen and intensify.

The car was waiting for them out front. Hester was pleased to see Tam's friendly face again. When neither Aunt Sybil nor Christine was looking, he gave her a conspiratorial wink.

Maybank was only a short drive away. It was a large, Gothic building which looked rather like a middle-European castle. Inevitably, it, too, was made of grey stone.

Tam parked the car outside the front gates and they all got out.

'You run along now, dear,' said Aunt Sybil to Christine, giving her a swift peck on the cheek.

Christine hurried on to join up with some of her friends heading for one of the building's many entrances.

'You'll like it here,' Aunt Sybil said, with finality. Steering Hester in the direction of the main entrance, she continued, 'Very high standard. And, of course, only girls from the best families attend.'

What girls she'd seen so far looked a right snotty bunch, Hester thought. And as for the place itself, it was not only cheerless inside, but the cream tiling that was everywhere reminded her of a public toilet. She had to stifle a giggle at the thought. She turned her head away when her aunt shot her a reproving look.

'How pleasant it is to see you,' the grim-faced headmistress said when Mrs Oliphant and Hester entered her office.

'And it's good to see you, Miss McSween,' Aunt Sybil replied, in her most gracious manner.

Miss McSween gestured to a chair in front of her desk where Aunt Sybil now sat. Then, completely ignoring Hester, Miss McSween walked round behind the desk and sat herself facing the older woman. Hester was left standing with a half smile on her face that was rapidly turning into a grimace.

Miss McSween had white hair, tied back in a tight bun. Her eyes were flint-hard and a pale blue in colour. Her skin was thick and leathery. There was something mannish about her which was strange to Hester, who had known only her Ma's softness and femininity.

'Is there some problem at home with Christine?' Miss McSween asked.

'No, no, everything's fine with her. As it is at school I trust?'

Miss McSween gave an icy smile that was ever so slightly patronizing. 'Of course,' she replied, as though it was absurd anyone could think otherwise.

Aunt Sybil nodded. 'Why I've come to see you is about this young lady here. My husband's niece, newly arrived from Bristol. We wish to enrol her at Maybank.'

'Ah!' exclaimed Miss McSween softly, turning her attention to Hester for the first time.

'Her mother has just died leaving her an orphan. She'll be staying with us from now on in.'

'An orphan? How sad,' Miss McSween said slowly, as though Aunt Sybil had said that Hester had a cold.

Hester dropped her gaze to the floor. She was cringing inside from embarrassment and an unreasonable sense of shame.

'Look up, girl.'

Reluctantly, Hester raised her eyes to meet Miss McSween's.

'Of what did the mother die?'

The question caught Aunt Sybil off guard. 'She, eh . . . eh . . .'

Hester bit her lip, and the pain helped steady her. Her embarrassment and shame had become even more acute. She wished herself anywhere but in that office.

'Hester's mother committed suicide,' Aunt Sybil said in a nervous rush.

One of Miss McSween's eyebrows shot up. 'Dear, dear,' she murmured.

'It was all very unfortunate.'

'I'm sure.'

'She was mentally ill, poor thing.'

'And the father?'

'Killed at his place of employment two years ago.' Hester saw that Aunt Sybil had begun to sweat, and knew she was dreading being asked what her Da's job had been. 'Her name's Hester Dark,' Aunt Sybil added hurriedly.

'Dark? Is that an English name?'

'Actually, Robert Dark was American.'

'An American!' Miss McSween nodded as if that explained a great deal if not everything.

'I would like her to start on Monday, if that's possible. The quicker she's settled in the better, I think,' Aunt Sybil said.

'Quite,' agreed Miss McSween. She gestured Hester to

32

come closer to her desk. 'Now child what sort of school were you in at Bristol?'

Miss McSween made several notes in a black folder while Hester answered her many questions. 'We'll start her in the second year and see how she does,' she said to Sybil Oliphant when she was done. 'She may need extra tuition. After being at a council school she's hardly likely to be up to the Maybank mark.' She smiled thinly. 'But we'll see.'

'That's settled then,' said Aunt Sybil with obvious relief, rising to her feet. 'We're on our way now to see about a uniform.'

'Excellent.'

Hester was glad to escape Miss McSween's office and the headmistress's stern presence. She hadn't taken to the woman at all. There was something about Miss McSween that made her flesh crawl.

Miss McSween's parting words to Aunt Sybil had been for her to give Miss McSween's regards to the Colonel. That was the second time Hester had heard her uncle referred to by that title.

'Was Uncle Will in the war?' she asked as the car sped on its way into the centre of Glasgow.

'Indeed he was,' Aunt Sybil replied proudly.

'My Da wasn't,' said Hester. 'He was in what's called a reserved occupation.'

'Yes, he would have been.'

'What did Uncle Will do in the war?' Hester prompted.

Aunt Sybil's eyes took on a far away, almost dreamy look. 'He went in as a captain and ended up as a lieutenant colonel in charge of his own regiment., The King's Own Scottish Lowlanders. If the war had gone on any longer he would've ended up a full colonel in charge of a battalion.'

'Did he win any medals?'

'Oh, yes. When he was a captain he won the Military Cross. Only the Victoria Cross is higher than that.'

Her uncle must be an extremely brave man, Hester

thought. 'What did he do to win the Military Cross?'

Pride and love bathed Aunt Sybil's face. 'He refuses to talk about it. But I winkled it out of one of his army friends,' she confided.

Somehow, the love shining from Aunt Sybil's face like a beacon momentarily transformed it. The plainness of her features softened and were almost attractive; her eyes were large and luminous.

Aunt Sybil went on. 'He led four attacks on the same morning. He was the only officer to return alive each time. After the fourth he went back into No Man's Land to rescue his CO whom he thought was wounded. As it turned out the CO was dead from a bayonet wound. Will was about to return to his trenches when he was jumped by three German soldiers. He killed all three of them in hand-to-hand combat. After that he rescued an English soldier who'd got entangled in the wire. When he reached the trenches he was carrying the boy draped over his shoulder. He was promoted to major that afternoon.'

Hester listened to all this in awe.

'There's not a day goes by that I don't thank God for sending him home alive and all in one piece,' Aunt Sybil added in a whisper. 'So many fell. So many, many.'

They were silent after that, each lost in her own thoughts, till the car reached Jamaica Street where the outfitter's was.

It didn't take Hester long to be kitted out, and after they drove to Aunt Sybil's dressmaker who had a small shop just off the Trongate.

Their business there took a great deal longer than at Paisley's. Mrs Rosenbloom, the plump proprietress, took endless pains over measuring Hester from head to toe. After that, cloths and materials had to be chosen, and styles discussed.

At the end of it, Hester was exhausted. Aunt Sybil suggested that Hester go out and sit in the car to recover herself while she stayed behind to sort out final details with Mrs Rosenbloom.

Tam opened the car door for her and she slid inside. 'Will she be much longer?' he asked.

'Five or ten minutes. But it could be more.'

Tam grunted and climbed back into the driver's seat. Reaching behind him he slid open the glass communicating panel.

'Terrible looking place that Maybank. I'm sure the French Bastille, where they kept all yon prisoners, must look just like it,' he said.

Hester laughed. 'It does give that sort of impression,' she agreed. 'You should see the headmistress.'

'When do you start?'

'Monday.'

'I'll be driving you and Christine together then.'

How incredibly posh, going to school by car every day. She would feel quite the lady.

'Do you live in the house as well?' she asked.

'Oh, aye. Below stairs with the rest of the servants. I'm on call twenty-four hours a day you see.'

'Surely Uncle Will doesn't get you out of bed once you're in it?' she asked, genuinely shocked at the thought.

'Not very often. In fact only twice so far. But it's part of my duties to get up if called.'

'Where would Uncle want to go at that time of night, or the morning?' she asked.

'The paper, Miss. Occasionally things happen which need the Colonel's personal attention.'

'What's his paper called?' she asked.

'*The Glaswegian*. Haven't you seen a copy of it yet?'

'There was one on the breakfast table,' she remembered. 'But I didn't realize it was Uncle's.'

'It's a fine paper, Miss. I read it every day without fail.'

'Because it's my uncle's?'

Tam chuckled. 'No, no. Because I like the paper for itself. If I didn't I'd buy one of the others.'

'You said yesterday that you were daft on cars?' she said.

'Aye, I am that. Always have been. Couldn't wait to get my licence.'

'You'll be happy being a chauffeur for the rest of your life then?' she asked curiously.

'Now I didn't say that. My biggest dream is . . . well, to have my own garage. Tinkering with cars from morning to night. That would be my idea of heaven right enough.'

'Do you think you'll ever get this garage?'

'I don't see why not. I've always believed that if you want something hard enough the chances are high that you'll get it in the end. And I want my own garage more than anything.'

'What does Mrs Ritchie think about it?'

Tam laughed. 'I'm not married, Miss. I haven't even got a lassie.'

'Have you had?' she asked, curiosity overcoming her natural shyness.

'Och, I've been out with a few. But none of them really took my fancy. Nice girls, mind. But none of them were for me.'

'I hope your dream comes true for you,' Hester said with a soft smile, suddenly wishing that she had a similar dream.

'Thank you, Miss.' There was a pause and then he said boldly, 'You're very easy to talk to. Not like Miss Christine. I can't remember the last time she spoke to me other than to give instructions. No offence meant to her, of course. It's just nice to have a chat sometimes.'

Hester decided to be honest. The servants would no doubt soon work it out for themselves if they hadn't already.

'I'm not used to chauffeurs and maids,' she confided. 'We didn't have any where I came from. My father was just an ordinary man you see.'

'But your mother was the Colonel's sister?'

'That's right.'

'So she married below herself like?'

'Some people might say that. I certainly wouldn't. Nor would you if you'd ever met my Da. He was one of the best. But what I meant was that I'm not used to having servants. I just talk to you like I would anyone else. Is that bad?'

Tam caught her eye in the overhead mirror and winked. 'I wouldn't say so, Miss. You keep on like that and you'll be popular below stairs, I can assure you that.'

'The car's beautifully polished,' she said. 'I noticed that this morning as we were getting in to go to Maybank.'

'It's done every day without fail,' Tam replied, not without a certain proprietorial pride.

'And where do you do it?'

'There's a lock-up-cum-workshop behind the house. That's where this beauty is kept and where I look after her. Drop by any time and I'll show you all the tools I have for her. If you're at all interested in things mechanical, that is.'

'I might just do that.' Hester smiled. She was finally beginning to relax. But the next second Tam was jumping out of the car and holding the passenger door for Aunt Sybil who had appeared.

'Home now, Ritchie,' Aunt Sybil commanded once he was seated, and snapped the glass panel shut.

Hester sat back in her seat and stared out of the window. Aunt Sybil was being a lot nicer to her today than she'd been on her arrival, but there was no way of knowing if that would continue.

The car sped through a slum area which both fascinated and shocked Hester. Their home in Bristol had been in a working-class neighbourhood but it had been nothing like this; nothing so bleak, so gloomy and so foul-smelling.

A long line of children, ranging from toddlers to adolescents, suddenly appeared on the pavement ahead of them. Most of them were barefoot. A few wore wooden clogs which banged as they walked; fewer

37

shoes. The clothes they wore looked like they'd been fished out of dustbins.

As the car passed them, Hester saw that they were being led by a middle-aged man who appeared to be someone in authority. 'Who are those children?' she asked, turning to her aunt with wide eyes.

Aunt Sybil turned to stare at the receding line and grunted. 'The ragged school,' she said.

'Ragged school?'

'They're the orphans who are looked after by the city.'

Hester felt her heart grow cold. 'You mean there's no one else to take care of them? No friends or relatives?'

'That's right.'

Hester twisted right round in her seat. The children were only just visible in the distance. Then the car turned another corner and they were lost to view.

'Lucky for you you had us to take you in,' said Aunt Sybil, echoing Hester's own thoughts, 'Or you might have ended up like that.'

2

Hester sat on the toilet with her head bent forward. She was between classes and had a few minutes before English Lit.

The first indication she had that there was something going on was a smothered giggle from above. Glancing up she saw four faces staring down at her over the top of the dividing partition. A hand belonging to Elspeth Simpson-Ogilvie was just disappearing back over the partition and Hester was sure it had been clutching something.

'What are you lot up to?' Hester demanded.

In reply Elspeth grinned, Violet Cochrane sniggered,

Patti Forbes leered, and Moyra NcNaughton gave a secretive smile.

These four girls formed the clique which dominated the second year at Maybank. They'd been making Hester's life a misery ever since she'd started at the school.

'Go away!' Hester said crossly.

'We prefer to watch,' replied Violet.

Hester had no intention of standing and pulling her knickers up while this foursome ogled her.

'A big bum don't you think?' said Moyra NcNaughton.

Hester flushed. 'You're all hateful!' she shouted back.

'We don't think much of you either,' Patti replied. 'And, yes, it is a big bum.'

'Absolutely *ginormous*!' said Violet, raising a laugh from her three friends.

Hester reached round and scratched a sudden itching on her back. The foursome looked at one another and snickered in unison.

The bell announcing the beginning of the class rang through the building. With a laugh and several whoops, the foursome ran from their cubicle while Hester tugged up her pants.

She arrived in class only seconds late, but still received a black look from the teacher.

'You'll have to smarten up, Dark,' Miss Hunter admonished.

Hester glanced across at the foursome who sat looking as innocent as angels. Frauds, she thought.

Miss Hunter started the lesson. Hester listened with only half an ear. She was desperately unhappy since starting Maybank. Not only the four who had taunted her in the toilet, but the rest of the year, following their lead, had completely rejected her.

So far, thank God, they hadn't found out about her background. They knew she was an orphan and came from Bristol, but that was all. She dreaded to think what they'd call her if they ever discovered that her father had been a dockie.

She was thoroughly miserable and wished she could run away. But there was nowhere to go. She was still far too young to be on her own. It would be two years at least before she left Maybank. Maybe even three or four. Just the thought made her groan.

Things wouldn't have been quite so bad if she and Christine had become friends, but Christine, realizing the way the wind was blowing, had almost completely disowned her.

Even at home Christine rarely spoke to her, and when she did it was always with an expression of contempt on her face.

Hester reached behind her and scratched again. The more she scratched though, the itchier it became. Must be a rash of some sort, she thought, and raked the spot with her nails.

Within minutes the itch had become almost unbearable. It had spread from the small of her back down over her bottom to the inside of her thighs.

Hoping no one was looking, she eased her hand up the inside of her skirt and desperately tore at the skin. She couldn't keep her backside still. Continually shifting from one cheek to the other and back again.

From nearby came the sound of a half-choked laugh. Glancing across, Hester saw that it had come from Elspeth Simpson-Ogilvie whose hand was clamped tightly across her mouth. She also saw that the other three who'd been in the toilet cubicle with Elspeth were watching her intently, their faces lit up in amusement.

Her hand clawed at her tormented flesh. And in that instant she remembered that she'd thought she'd seen something in Elspeth's hand as it had vanished back over the partition separating the cubicles.

Itching powder! It had to be. While she'd been bent forward Elspeth must have sprinkled the powder down her lower back.

'Dark will you stop squirming!' snapped Miss Hunter.

'I can't help it, Miss!' Hester replied through gritted

40

teeth. No matter how hard she scratched, clawed and tore the terrible itch wouldn't stop.

The four girls were now openly laughing at Hester's predicament. Soon most of the class had joined in.

'Control yourself, Dark!' ordered Miss Hunter, her eyes darting from Hester around the class and back again. If this wasn't stopped immediately things could get out of hand.

'I can't Miss.'

'What's wrong with you, girl?'

Hester rose. 'Please can I be excused, Miss?'

'Do you need the toilet?'

'It's not that Miss. It's something else.'

Miss Hunter didn't know what was going on. But whatever it was the Dark girl was obviously in great distress. 'Cut along then,' she said.

As Hester fled down the aisle between the desks she saw that Moyra McNaughton was nearly hysterical with laughter, and that tears of mirth were streaming down Violet Cochrane's face.

Christine gave Hester a stinker of a look as she climbed into the car. 'I hear you made a complete fool of yourself today,' she spat as the car drew away from the kerb.

'I did nothing of the sort.'

'I'm told everyone was laughing at you.'

'Some girls in my class put itching powder down my knickers. I was in a terrible state.'

'That's because they don't like you,' Christine said cruelly. 'You don't fit.'

Hester stared out of the car window. 'I'm trying my best,' she said seriously.

'I've had some wicked things said to me since you arrived,' Christine hissed. 'They're associating me with you and I hate that. In fact I hate you and wish you'd stayed in Bristol where you belong.'

Hester glanced at the back of Tam's head through

the closed glass panel. He could hear none of their conversation.

'I'm sorry if you're having a rotten time because of me,' she apologized.

Christine sniffed, one of her many irritating habits. 'I don't like being different. Spotted out in any way,' Christine said in a low, self-pitying and accusing voice.

Hester stared at her cousin. Until this moment, she hadn't realized just how weak a personality Christine was. She didn't like being different either, but if it happened she could somehow cope. Obviously Christine couldn't.

Suddenly, Hester felt almost sorry for her cousin. 'I wish we could be friends,' she said.

Christine sniffed again.

'You never let up on the boy!' Aunt Sybil complained.

Uncle Will merely glared back at her. 'He isn't a boy any more. He's a man. Or at least he should be. I certainly was at his age.'

Hester sat quietly with her head bowed. The row had blown up out of nowhere to take her by surprise. She'd never seen her uncle so angry. It was also the first time she'd realized that the relationship between Billy and his father wasn't all it should be.

'I don't like sport,' Billy said tightly.

'Too rough for you. Is that it?' Uncle Will goaded.

'It just doesn't appeal to me, that's all. It never has.'

'Billy has always preferred the academic side of things. There's nothing wrong with that,' defended Aunt Sybil.

'I never said there was,' Uncle Will replied. 'Books and the like are fine. I'm all for education. But there's more to life than just that.'

'I find sport senseless and stupid,' Billy said, anger making his voice tremble. 'Who cares about twenty-two chaps kicking a ball around a field? And as for rugger, well that's just downright vicious and nasty.'

42

'I knew it scared you. . . .'

'It does nothing of the sort! I just don't see any pleasure, or achievement, in being kicked half to death for absolutely nothing.'

'That's where you're wrong. It isn't for nothing.'

'Then what's it for? Participating, I suppose you're going to say?'

'To hell with participation,' roared Will. 'I'm talking about winning. Going out there and beating the other fellow. Proving you're a better man than he is.'

Cautiously, Hester stared at her uncle. This was a side of him she'd never seen before.

But Billy could be stubborn as well. 'I've got no great urge to prove I'm better than anyone else.'

Uncle Will shook his head. 'You're a born loser, son. I've known since you were a tot. You've no guts.'

'Will!' Aunt Sybil was more than angry, she was shocked.

'It's true, woman, and you know it as well as I do.'

'I know nothing of the sort! Don't you put words into my mouth, Will Oliphant.'

Uncle Will glared at Aunt Sybil who glared back. 'Maybe if you hadn't been so soft on the lad,' he said.

'I *wasn't* soft.'

'We disagree on that then because I think you were. When he was young you treated him with kid gloves, like he was a lassie.'

'That's ridiculous. I did nothing of the sort.'

'You spoiled him, Sybil. Through and through.'

'If you'll excuse me, I think I'll . . .' Billy started to say.

'Sit still!' his father roared. 'You'll only leave this table when I bloody well say so!'

'Will!' screeched Aunt Sybil. 'Language!'

Hester glanced across at Christine who was sitting so still and so quietly it was as though she wasn't there.

Uncle Will snorted and pushed his plate away. He saw off what was left in his glass, then refilled it. The claret gleamed in the light like freshly drawn blood.

Sybil was the first to recover. 'Anyway, the dinner table is hardly the place for such a conversation.'

'In my house I lay down the rules.'

'Your house, Will?' asked Aunt Sybil, so softly it was possible to believe that it hadn't been said.

Silence reigned while the maid cleared the table. When she was gone, Will turned his attention back to his son. 'Sometimes I wonder about you,' he said sadly.

Billy tried to meet his father's gaze but couldn't. 'What's that supposed to mean?'

'Work it out for yourself.'

'I would also like a little clarification,' said Aunt Sybil.

'Sixteen going on seventeen and never had a girlfriend. Bit strange wouldn't you say?'

Billy's face and neck turned a bright pink.

'There's time enough for all that,' said Sybil quickly.

'If you mean what I think you do, you're quite wrong,' Billy said quietly.

'So you know about such goings on then?'

Billy ignored him.

'How can you insinuate such a thing about your own son, Will?' Aunt Sybil demanded fiercely.

'Doesn't like sport. Doesn't like girls. What does he like I have to ask myself?'

'I do like girls,' Billy said.

'But no girlfriend?'

'Not yet.'

'Hmmh!'

Sybil rearranged her napkin on her lap. 'You can be very cruel at times.'

'And so can you, my dear.'

'You may be excused now,' Uncle Will said to Billy, when the girls had finished the pudding. No one else had the appetite to eat.

Billy rose and walked stiffly from the room.

★   ★   ★

It was just before dinner three days later that Uncle Will told Hester he wanted a word with her in private. She followed him into his study and he closed the door softly behind them.

'Have you ever been round a newspaper?' he asked, completely taking Hester by surprise.

She shook her head.

'Would you like to see one?'

'Oh yes please!' she replied enthusiastically.

Her obvious pleasure pleased him. 'When you've finished school on Tuesday, have Ritchie drop you off at *The Glaswegian* and I'll personally show you everything there is to see.'

Hester's eyes shone. 'I'll look forward to that,' she beamed.

'So will I,' Uncle Will answered quietly.

He rose from behind a rolltop desk, giving her a wide, welcoming smile. 'So what do you think of my office?' he asked, making a gesture that took in the entire room.

Hester stared around her, unable to hide her disappointment. 'I was expecting something more . . . well, lavish,' she said slowly.

Uncle Will nodded, then ran his hands over the very old and battered desk. In a voice that was almost a caress he said, 'I brought this with me from *The Rutherglen Advertiser*, the paper I owned before *The Glaswegian*. It was made well over a century ago and every mark on it is a piece of newspaper history and tradition.'

He took a deep breath, then slowly let it out again. 'What do you smell?'

Hester wrinkled her nose. She'd noticed the smell when she came into the building but couldn't place it.

'Describe the smell,' he said.

Tentatively, she sniffed. 'Sort of sweet, yet tangy at the same time.'

'That, Hester, is printer's ink. And to a newspaper

45

man like myself it's the very elixir of life. Now have another look at my office.'

She did.

The walls were dirty and obviously hadn't seen a lick of paint in years. There were cobwebs in the corners of the ceiling and, if the carpet had once held a pattern, it had long since disappeared under the comings and goings of countless feet.

But the more Hester stared around her, and *experienced* the office, the more she became aware of its true nature. The office might be shabby in the extreme, but its very shabbiness lent it a strange charm, and above all character. It was almost like a well-loved home.

'I can see it's getting through to you,' Uncle Will said, unable to disguise his joy. He had tremendous affection for this room, which he considered a true newspaper office. Whenever he paused to look at it afresh, it never failed to give him a thrill.

Hester nodded, it *was* getting through to her. And so was her uncle's real pride in it.

Uncle Will lit a cigar, then offered it to her. 'How about a little puff?' he teased.

'Just like mother used to?' The look he gave her made her shiver. 'Perhaps some other time,' she said.

She picked up a long strip of paper from atop a bundle of similar strips. 'What's this?' she asked.

'That's a galley proof. When a story, which we call copy, is written, it's first of all printed in separate columns, an imprint of which, or pull, is called a galley. These galleys then go to readers who go through them correcting mistakes. The galleys then go back to the printer who makes the corrections in the lead, that being the type. With me so far?'

'Yes.'

'Good. A page is then made up consisting of a number of these galleys. When that has been locked together another pull is taken. This we call the page proof.'

He leant across his desk and picked up a sheet of paper which he handed to her. 'That's a page proof.'

'And does the reader also correct this?'

'That's right.'

'And then?'

'Back to the printer who again makes what alterations, if any, are needed in the type after which the type is ready for the presses. Of course I've simplified all this for you, it's really more complicated than I'm making out, but those are the basics of what's involved in getting a newspaper ready for the street.'

Hester was fascinated. She was handing the page proof back to her uncle when her eye fell on an interesting object on his desk. 'What's that?' she asked, pointing.

The object was a long thin spike embedded in a wooden base. Pages of typewritten material were impaled on the spike.

'That's copy we've decided, for one reason or another, not to use. It's kept on the spike for reference, and so it doesn't get mixed up with any other copy, until the spike is full, when it's discarded. If you say to a newspaperman his story has been spiked, he knows precisely what you're talking about.'

For the first time Hester realized that the floor under her feet was vibrating slightly. In the distance she could hear a low hum, like some great beast growling angrily under the ground.

'The presses,' Uncle Will explained.

'Can I see them?'

'Of course.'

Hester noticed that he didn't put on his jacket or tighten his undone tie.

They went down two flights and into the back of the building. With every step the noise grew louder and louder.

They stopped in the readers' room where she was introduced and had her hand shaken by the readers and their assistants.

47

Further into the bowels of the building they went, until they came to where the type itself was produced. These machines she found on the one hand bizarre, on the other strangely appealing.

The operator of one of them asked her name which he then punched out on the keyboard. The machine clanked and hissed, squeaked and groaned. A few seconds later a small piece of typeface standing proud on an inset bar was delivered into the receptacle at the end of a slide.

'Give it a moment or two to cool,' advised the operator.

Hester glanced up at her uncle. She could see the pride and love he had for the place written all over him. He was a newspaperman through and through all right. There could be no doubt about that.

When an appropriate time had elapsed the operator picked up the typeface and handed it to Hester. 'Your souvenir,' he said.

'Here,' said Uncle Will producing an ink pad. 'Try it.'

She pressed the typeface onto the pad and then onto a piece of paper, exclaiming with delight at the result.

HESTER DARK it proclaimed.

'In Bodoni,' the operator said.

'Bodoni is the name of that particular style of typeface,' Uncle Will explained.

They visited other rooms, and in each Uncle Will went to great pains to make sure she understood what was happening there. Then it was on to the great presses themselves.

The noise was tremendous. They had to hold their heads close together and shout at the top of their voices to be heard.

Hester stared in awe at the thundering, ever-moving machinery along whose assembly belt hundreds, if indeed not thousands, of newspapers flashed before her eyes.

A few minutes was all she could stand. How could the

men she saw moving here and there put up with this mind-shattering clamour day after day?

She tapped her head, and Uncle Will, nodding that he understood, took her by the elbow and guided her back the way they'd come.

'What do you think?' he asked when the presses were sufficiently behind them for normal speaking to be possible.

She shook her head in wonder.

'Speechless?'

'No. Just trying to find the right words.' She paused for a full minute before saying. 'I think if I ever have to work I'd like to work here. Nothing has ever excited me as much as all this. I feel as if . . . as if it's my natural habitat.'

Uncle Will stared down at her, his eyes bright with pleasure. 'There's a long history of newspapermen in our family. Myself, my father, his father before him. And my grandfather had a brother who ran a paper out in South Africa. And there are two sons of his still alive there, also in the newspaper business. Maybe you've inherited the family bug.'

'What about my mother?'

The handsome face clouded. 'No. She wasn't interested.'

'Not even a little bit?'

He shook his head. 'She thought newspaper buildings dirty, noisy places and consequently kept well away.'

'But all this is so *exciting*!' Hester exclaimed.

'You and I might think so, but your mother never did. She never felt the magic.'

When they left the building half an hour later it was Hester's avowed intention to be back as soon as possible.

'Whose mother did herself in then?'

The words caused Hester to react as though a basin of icy water had been thrown in her face. She stood stock still. Then slowly turned in the direction the voice had come from.

Violet Cochrane leered at her. Behind Violet were the other three who'd been involved in the itching powder incident.

'How did you find out?' Hester asked.

'Wouldn't you like to know!' Elspeth Simpson-Ogilvie teased.

Apart from Miss McSween, the only other person at Maybank who knew about her mother was Christine. That was the answer, Hester thought grimly. Christine had gone and opened her big mouth.

'Mad, I hear,' taunted Violet.

Patti Forbes crossed her eyes and made choking noises.

'Completely round the bed when she took the pills,' smirked Moyra McNaughton.

Hester stared at her four tormentors. Her stomach was heaving, and there was a burning sensation in her throat.

'Do you think she's likely to go off her trolley as well?' Violet asked Elspeth.

'Wouldn't be surprised if she did,' Elspeth replied.

'Dark's mother was a loonie! Dark's mother was a loonie!' chanted Patti Forbes, giggling and sniggering at once.

A red rage slowly began to boil in Hester. It was one thing for them to rag her – but to mock her dead mother was something else.

'Shut up!' she screamed. 'All of you.'

'Do you think being a nutter is catching?' asked Moyra, pretending to shrink from Hester.

The other three laughed.

'I'm warning you,' Hester hissed between clenched teeth.

'Dark's mother was a loonie! Dark's mother was a loonie!' cried Patti Forbes, returning to her earlier chant.

Something snapped in Hester. With a screech she flew at Patti, catching the girl's hair in her hands and tugging it as hard as she could.

Patti yelled in real pain, and Hester felt arms around

her neck, trying to pull her away. She let go and managed to twist on her assailant, who turned out to be Violet Cochrane.

With all her angry strength, she managed to push Violet from her. Then, using the flat of her hand, she smacked Violet again and again across the face.

Suddenly arms and legs were everywhere as she was jostled, punched and kicked simultaneously.

She rolled on the floor with the foursome on top of her. She managed to get a solid punch into Elspeth Simpson-Ogilvie's ribs before Moyra began yelling, 'Teacher coming! Quick! Teacher coming!'

The four were up and away instantly, leaving Hester sprawled face down on the floor.

She felt groggy, her senses reeling. Gingerly she felt her mouth to see if she'd lost any teeth, but her hand came away unbloodied.

She looked up to find herself staring at Miss Moodie, one of the history teachers.

'Look at the state of you girl! You're an absolute shambles!'

Hester came to her knees and then to her feet. She felt as though she'd been through a mangle and then dragged through a hedge backwards.

'Don't you know that fighting is strictly forbidden and that Miss McSween always deals personally with any offenders?'

'I know, Miss,' whispered Hester, trying to straighten her clothes.

'Right then, who were those other girls I saw dashing off?'

Hester didn't reply.

'You'd better tell me, or it'll be all the harder for you.'

Several other girls had gathered round, nudging each other silently and talking with their eyes. Hester glanced briefly at them and then brought her attention back to Miss Moodie.

'Sorry, Miss,' she mumbled, staring down at the floor.

Miss Moodie shook her head and tutted in exasperation. 'If you won't help yourself, then that's your lookout. Follow me,' and, having said her piece, she turned on her heel and marched back the way she'd just come. Hester had to run to keep up. There was no question of where they were headed.

Hester sat in a small ante-room for five minutes, nursing her wounds, while the indignant Miss Moodie was closeted with Miss McSween. She looked up only when the office door was opened.

'Come in, Dark,' said Miss Moodie.

Miss McSween was sitting behind her desk, her lips pursed and her eyes glinting coldly. She might have been carved from stone. She gestured Hester to come and stand before her.

'Thank you, Miss Moodie. You may go now,' said Miss McSween evenly.

As Hester walked slowly towards the desk she heard the door click shut behind her, like the door of a jail.

The cold eyes bored into her as though reading her soul. The pursed lips pursed even more.

'You're not going to deny brawling are you, Dark? Considering the condition you're in you can hardly do that.'

Hester dropped her gaze.

'Look at me when I talk to you girl!'

Hester made herself stare into those empty eyes. She saw cruelty there. Cruelty and something else – something she didn't understand.

'Who were the other girls?'

Hester remained silent.

'Answer me!'

'I won't tell tales, Miss.'

'I'm ordering you to Dark. I won't have fighting in my school. Anyone who indulges in it has to be punished.'

'I'm sorry, Miss.'

Miss McSween rose to her full height. She was not accustomed to being disobeyed. 'I will not be defied,

52

Dark. Not by you or anyone.' She opened a drawer in her desk from which she extracted a small key.

Hester watched in fascination as Miss McSween crossed to the cupboard door and unlocked it. Hester knew what was kept in that cupboard; the entire school spoke of it in awe, and not a little terror.

Miss McSween flicked the thin cane so that it made a swishing sound as it cut through the air. 'Believe me, you'll tell me Dark,' she said unemotionally. 'One way or the other.'

No I will not, Hester reassured herself. No matter how much pain there was she would not be intimidated. She swore it. She was tired of being patronized and pushed around.

'Well, Dark?'

Hester shook her head.

A hint of a smile moved the corners of Miss McSween's mouth. 'Bend over and grasp your ankles then,' she ordered.

Hester did as she was bid. She felt totally vulnerable.

Delicately, Miss McSween took hold of the hem of Hester's skirt, pulling it back until Hester's bottom was completely exposed. Hester closed her eyes when she felt Miss McSween grasp her knickers and pull them down to her ankles where they rested against her hands.

'Five strokes is the usual punishment for fighting,' Miss McSween said smoothly. 'But in your case I intend to keep going until you tell me what I want to know.'

The cane whistled through the air, slicing into Hester's bare backside. A vicious red welt immediately appeared.

Hester rocked forward from the ferocity and force of the blow. The pain was excruciating. The knuckles gripping her ankles glowed white as the next blow landed.

Fourteen times the cane landed, Hester holding in her screams, and then, giving a soft sigh-like moan, she pitched sideways in a dead faint.

When she came to a few minutes later her knickers

were back in place and she was sitting once again in the ante-room. Of Miss McSween there was no sign.

Her bottom was on fire and felt as though it had been skinned. She groaned as she came to her feet, clutching at the wall for support. She'd have given anything for a soothing bath.

But even as she limped down the corridor she managed a triumphant smile. She'd won. She hadn't told. She'd bested Miss McSween.

That thought made the throbbing pain bearable.

'You told about my mother,' Hester accused. She and Christine had just been picked up by Ritchie and were now on their way home from school.

'So what if I did?' Christine replied sullenly.

'How could you?'

'Violet Cochrane and that bunch have been pestering me for ages to tell them about your background. In the end I just did.'

'But why? Didn't you realize how much it might hurt me?'

Christine sniffed.

'They're not even in your year.'

Christine pretended to be interested in the passing scene. 'Violet's sister Fiona is. And I like Fiona. She's a great friend of mine.'

'You mean she lets you tag along with her set. *Sometimes*.'

Christine flushed. 'It's not like that at all.'

It was all clear to Hester now. Fiona had threatened to ostracize Christine from the set of girls of whom Fiona was the undisputed leader unless Christine told Violet about her. Christine, weak as ever, had given in to the threat.

'I feel sorry for you. I really do,' Hester said gently.

Christine's flush deepened.

'You're so easily used.'

54

'I wish you'd never come to our house,' Christine said nastily.

There was no suitable reply. Hester, too, wished she had never come.

As soon as they arrived home, Christine shot out of the car without waiting for Tam to open her door.

Hester followed her stiffly into the house.

'Christine tells me you were caned for fighting. Is that true?'

Hester stared at Christine, standing triumphantly by her mother's side, smirking and looking very pleased with herself.

'Yes, Aunt Sybil.'

'But that's disgraceful! Young ladies don't fight. It's . . .' Aunt Sybil struggled for the right words, 'it's unfeminine.'

'Yes, Aunt Sybil.'

'I'm ashamed of you. Mortified. I dread to think what your uncle's going to say when he finds out. He'll give you another thrashing I wouldn't be surprised.'

Christine grinned.

'Go up to your room this instant. And don't move out of it till the morning. There will be no dinner for you tonight. Now go!'

As she painfully climbed the stairs, Hester contemplated the injustice of it all.

She was sitting in her nightgown in front of the fire when there was a knock on the door. 'Come in!' she called out, slowly standing as her uncle entered the room.

'So, what's all this about then?' he asked, and though his voice was serious its tone was kind and concerned.

In a halting voice, she told him exactly what had happened. He watched her closely, listening to each and every word.

'What I don't understand is how these girls found out about Mary,' he said thoughtfully when she was done.

55

Hester glanced away.

'Of course. *Christine*.' He took Hester gently by the shoulders. 'Well, don't you worry lass. I'll see she gets what's coming to her. You have my word on that.'

'Oh, no,' pleaded Hester. 'I don't want to get Christine in trouble. She didn't mean what she did. She just doesn't know any better.'

'All right, Hester,' he said soothingly. 'As you will. Are you hungry?'

'Starving.'

He laughed, relieved. 'As you're already in your night-clothes, I'll send Kathleen up with a tray.'

'Thank you.'

'Poor Hester, the world is awful hard on you,' he said softly, drawing her close to him, her cheek on his chest.

'Poor Hester,' she repeated.

'And poor Hester's bottom,' he whispered.

His arms held her tightly. 'So like your mother,' he said emotionally, more human than she'd even seen him. 'So like Mary.'

And then, the next moment, he was himself again, business-like and brusque. 'I'll speak to Kathleen about that tray right away,' he said, and turning left the room without looking back.

Hester was numb with shock. Had she dreamed that embrace and the passion in his words?

But she hadn't been dreaming. The scent of his cologne still surrounded her.

He and her mother had been so very, very close. He talked of little else. So like Mary, he'd said. With his hand on her shoulder, his lips on her hair. So like Mary. Surely he couldn't mean. . . .

The moment she entered the school's front gates she saw the foursome waiting for her. 'Now you're for it,' said Christine.

Hester advanced slowly. They were directly in her path. They'd have to move, she told herself. She had no intention of going around them. When she was almost on them Violet Cochrane stepped forward. 'We'd like a word with you,' she said.

'Yes?'

'We heard what Miss McSween did to you for not telling on us.'

'We want to say thank you,' interrupted Elspeth Simpson-Ogilvie.

Hester looked at them in surprise, nodding her acceptance of their apologies.

Four hands were extended in front of her.

'Welcome to Maybank,' said Violet Cochrane.

3

One night several weeks later, Hester was sitting in the drawing room, reading. Occasionally she glanced up, and every time she did so it was to find Uncle Will staring at her.

The decanter was by his chair, already half empty. His eyes were glazed, his face red.

'I'm just writing to dear Margaret Telfer who lost both her sons in the war,' Aunt Sybil announced from the table where she sat with her writing materials spread before her.

Uncle Will grunted. His eyes intent on Hester.

Aunt Sybil shook her head. 'Last time I saw Margaret she was a shadow of her former self. Those boys were her entire life.' She glanced across at Billy who was also at the table, immersed in his homework, and gave an involuntary shiver. A few years older and he would have been off to France, too. She knew she wouldn't have been lucky enough to get both him and his father back unscathed. She could still see the Telfer boys, Harry and Jack, in her mind.

As though reading her thoughts, Uncle Will said in a very quiet voice, his gaze lingering on Hester, 'I saw Harry the morning he died. I stopped just to have a few words with him. I can't remember what we talked about.'

Aunt Sybil looked at him quickly. 'You never mentioned that before.'

'No reason to.'

'What happened to him?' asked Hester.

'He went over the top and just didn't come back. They never did find his body.'

'You mean he was blown up?' Hester said.

From far away, he answered her. 'He might have been. Then again his body might have gone down in the mud. A lot of bodies were lost that way. And not always dead men, either.'

'How horrible!' exclaimed Christine.

'War is,' he replied, and making a gesture which clearly indicated the subject was closed, bent over the decanter and refilled his glass.

Hester went back to her book but her concentration was broken. In her mind's eye she kept seeing soldiers trapped in the hungry mud. Endless dark oceans of mud, stretching from horizon to horizon.

Suddenly Aunt Sybil gave a shrill scream and doubled over clutching her side.

Billy jumped up in panic. 'What is it, Mother?'

Sybil groaned, her face contorted in agony.

Instantly Billy was at his mother's side but Uncle Will pushed him away to get to his wife. 'What's wrong, Sybil?'

'Awful pain!' she gasped. 'Here.'

Will stared at the spot she was clutching. 'Is it wind, do you think?' he asked slowly.

She shook her head. 'It's a hundred times worse than that,' she said, collapsing in a moan.

Hester came to stand near her uncle. 'Could it be appendicitis?'

Uncle Will considered, his expression troubled and uncertain.

'Whatever it is she needs the doctor here and fast,' he decided as Sybil screamed again. He rounded on Billy. 'Telephone Doctor Duthie and tell him it's an emergency. Tell him to get here as quickly as he can. Say we think it might be appendicitis.'

Billy ran for the door.

'Help me get her onto the sofa,' ordered Will.

Hester and Christine helped him carry the ashen Sybil across the room to the sofa.

'Is there anything else we can do?' Hester asked.

Uncle Will bit his lip, then shook his head. 'Not that I can think. Except that we should cover her up.'

'I'll get the quilt from my room.'

'You don't have to go that far. There's a good warm travelling rug in my study.'

Hester found Billy beside the telephone, frantically leafing through his father's address book. She had just picked up the rug when Uncle Will burst into the room.

'Haven't you phoned yet for God's sake?' he roared.

Billy looked flustered and confused. 'I can't seem to find the number,' he said apologetically.

With an oath Will snatched the address book from Billy, then pushed Billy aside. 'Useless fool.'

Billy glanced at Hester, his expression one of despair. 'I was doing my best,' he mumbled. 'The number wasn't under D for doctor or Duthie.'

But his father was already talking to the doctor, and not listening to him. 'He's on his way,' he said, slamming the receiver back into place.

It was an anxious twenty minutes till Doctor Duthie arrived. During that time Aunt Sybil's condition worsened and Christine sent for water, then insisted on bathing her mother's brow herself.

Doctor Duthie was old with white hair and a yellow-

59

tinged moustache. He reeked of mothballs and liniment. 'Children outside please,' he ordered on entering the drawing room.

Hester, Billy and Christine stood in the hallway while the door was closed on their faces. They looked at one another only when the loudest and most agonized shriek yet came from within.

'She's going to die,' Christine sobbed, tears pouring from her eyes.

'Don't be soft,' Billy said stoutly. Then, to Hester, 'Do you think she is?'

'Of course not. The doctor will fix her up. You'll see.'

'I could murder a cigarette,' Billy whispered.

Hester looked at him in amazement. She hadn't known that he smoked.

'He's so unfair to me at times,' Billy complained to Hester when the house was again quiet. 'The number wasn't under D.'

'Don't worry,' she said, touching his shoulder. She was about to say more but there was a sudden urgent ringing of the front door bell. A servant scurried out of nowhere to answer it.

The door to the drawing room opened and Doctor Duthie reappeared. 'That'll be the ambulance I ordered,' he said to Billy. 'Tell the men to bring a stretcher in here.'

Billy dashed to obey. Christine cried even harder.

The two men Billy ushered through wore uniforms and were briskly efficient. Hester watched from the drawing room doorway as they gently eased her aunt onto the stretcher.

Hester stood to one side as the stretcher and Aunt Sybil went past her. Aunt Sybil's eyes were closed and she appeared unconscious.

'You go in the ambulance and I'll come on behind in my car,' Doctor Duthie said to Uncle Will. 'Now where's the telephone? I have to ring the hospital and tell them to be standing by. She'll have to be operated on immediately.'

'I'll take you through,' volunteered Hester.

'Good lass,' Doctor Duthie said approvingly.

When she returned to the hallway, Uncle Will had already gone. A clamour of bells came from outside, announcing that the ambulance was away.

'Which hospital are they taking her to?' she asked Billy.

'The Western.'

'I know she's going to die,' sobbed Christine.

'Oh, shut up!' Hester said in exasperation. She hated people who went to pieces when quite the opposite was called for.

Doctor Duthie reappeared and without a word to any of them hurried out of the door. Seconds later his car was rattling after the ambulance.

Hester and Christine returned to the drawing room while Billy went to talk to the servants. When he joined them he lit up the cigarette he'd been wanting so badly.

'Father will kill you if he catches you with that,' Christine said, her eyes red and swollen and still wet with tears.

'Well, he hasn't caught me yet. And he won't either. Unless someone tells,' he replied, giving her a significant look.

Christine flushed. She knew what he was referring to. She shot him a baleful glare but didn't reply.

'Did the doctor say what was wrong with Aunt Sybil?' asked Hester.

Billy shook his head. Christine began to cry anew.

Hester picked up the whisky decanter from the floor and placed it in its normal position. She stood her uncle's half-filled glass beside the decanter.

'I suppose there's nothing else to do but wait,' Billy said nervously.

'What will become of us if Mother dies?' wailed Christine, her eyes wide with a sort of hopeless terror.

'She won't. But even if she did we'd still have Father. Which is more than Hester had when her mother died.'

61

'I think I'll go upstairs and wait in my room. I feel a bit sick,' Christine said, standing up shakily.

'Want me to come with you?' asked Hester.

'No. I'll be all right on my own.'

When they were alone, Hester and Billy settled themselves by the fire.

'It could be hours before Father gets back.'

Hester nodded, too stunned to speak.

Billy threw his cigarette into the flames where he watched it burn. Then he moodily lit another one, his face closed in thought.

At last she broke the silence. 'I thought your father was unfair to you tonight. But it was probably just the circumstances.'

Billy dragged savagely on the cigarette. 'No matter how hard I try I never seem to be able to do anything right for him,' he said angrily.

'It can't be as bad as that. . . .'

'He hates me.'

'I don't believe that!'

'It's true. I've known it ever since I was a child.'

'But why?'

Billy shrugged. 'I don't really know. The only answer I've ever come up with is that it's because I'm so different to him. We're complete opposites.'

'I know, but . . .'

'Everything he does is big, theatrical. He adores being the centre of attention. He has real charisma, and a strange power over other people. When he wants to, he positively oozes charm.'

'And what about you?'

He smiled almost bitterly. 'Me, I'm quiet and shy. I hate a fuss. I hate to take chances or bring attention to myself. I'm a follower, I guess. We have completely opposite natures.

'You couldn't get two people more unalike. The archetypal chalk and cheese.'

'I went to the paper recently,' Hester said thoughtfully. 'I thought it was the most fabulously exciting place I'd ever seen. I'd love to work there.'

'You're welcome to it.'

'Don't you want to be a reporter?'

Billy laughed. 'A reporter? Fat chance you'd ever have of becoming a reporter. There are no women reporters. Not in Glasgow, anyway.'

Hester was undeterred, but said nothing. Instead, she asked, 'Will you start in the paper directly you leave school?'

'Father wants me to. But I want a university education first. Mother agrees with me.'

'Your father says the newspaper bug runs in our family. Haven't you got it, too?' she asked.

Billy smiled cynically. 'It's a good industry and one I'll enjoy being in,' he replied.

'That doesn't answer my question.'

'If you mean do I have the all-consuming passion for newspapers that *he* has, then the answer is no. He lives and breathes them, which I'll never do.'

Hester looked at him sadly. He was so unlike herself as well. She and Uncle Will were both creatures of fire, but Billy, she was now coming to realize, had a lot of ice in him.

Hester woke when her uncle entered the drawing room. She and Billy had fallen asleep in the armchairs.

'How's Aunt Sybil?' Hester asked as Billy came groggily awake.

Uncle Will looked completely exhausted. There were bags under his eyes and far more lines on his face than normal. He picked up the glass of whisky he'd left earlier and swallowed its contents in one gulp.

'You were right,' he said turning to face Hester and the anxious Billy. 'It was her appendix. The surgeon told me after the operation that it was only a whisker away from bursting. If that had happened we'd probably have lost her. But as it is she's going to be fine. She was extremely lucky.' He smiled 'We all were.'

'How long will she be in hospital?' asked Billy.

He poured himself another whisky as he replied. 'Two weeks at least. Perhaps three.'

'When can we go and see her?'

Uncle Will ran a hand over his face. 'I didn't think to inquire about that. I'll be returning to the hospital first thing in the morning. I'll ask then.'

Hester glanced at the Grandfather clock in the corner. 'What about school?'

'I think the three of you can have the day off. But it's back the day after.'

'I'll go and tell Christine,' Billy said. 'She was supposed to be waiting up in her room. But I've no doubt she fell asleep, too.'

When Billy had gone Hester said, 'I'll away to my bed now. Unless there's anything I can do for you?'

Uncle Will stared at her over the rim of his glass. 'No, there's nothing. You run along.'

At the door she paused, 'Goodnight.'

'Goodnight, Hester.'

She waited, thinking he was about to say something more, but he was lost in his thoughts.

She had only taken a few steps in the direction of the stairs when behind her she heard the chink of glass on glass which told her he was back at the decanter.

Once in bed she couldn't sleep, her mind racing with all that had happened. Over an hour after having said goodnight to her uncle, she heard his footsteps in the corridor outside. As had happened before they approached her door and stopped.

Her heart was thumping with a feeling she couldn't explain.

For what seemed an eternity he remained there. Then there was the creak of shoe leather, and his footsteps receded back towards the stairs.

* * *

Several nights later the footsteps came again. But this time they didn't go away.

Hester's eyes were glued to the door. Through the darkness she felt, rather than saw, the handle turning. Slowly, the door creaked open.

He was carrying a candle and wearing a dressing gown. For a moment or two he stood framed in the doorway, silently watching her. She knew from the way he swayed slightly that he must be drunk.

She pretended to be asleep. He'll go away, she tried to convince herself. Please God, make him go away.

But God in His Heaven wasn't listening to her plea. Uncle Will stealthily entered the room, closing and bolting the door behind him.

He came to her bedside standing there quietly as though he might be seeing her for the last time. Then, reaching across the bed, he placed the candle beside her water. Gently and softly he began to stroke her face.

She opened her eyes, amazed by her own lack of fear, by the power she suddenly realized he had over her.

His eyes bored into hers, speaking of things she could feel but not understand.

The breath caught in her throat as his hand slid into the open neck of her nightgown to stroke tenderly her young breast.

'Uncle?' she whispered, unsure herself if it was a plea to be released or held.

'I won't hurt you, lass. That's the last thing I want to do.'

His other hand turned down the covers, and pulled her nightie up to her waist.

'So like Mary,' he whispered. 'So like her.'

Carefully, and very gently, he placed his hand on her, his fingers warm on her silky skin.

It was the first time a man had ever touched her. Yet it didn't seem strange or ugly. Suddenly she was overwhelmed with her own loneliness, the lack of love that had been swallowing her since her mother died. Oh

God, she thought, I need someone to love and hold me.

He stood up straight and undid the belt of his dressing gown which fell open to reveal his nakedness. She felt as though his body was pulling her to itself like a magnet, that she had to touch him.

He climbed into bed beside her, his arms around her, his hands all over her. Her body felt electric, her mind could think of nothing but the comfort and excitement of his nearness.

His mouth found hers. Though her brain didn't understand what was happening, her body knew.

He was an expert and passionate lover. She had never imagined such feelings or sensations. Had never dreamed they might exist.

When it was over, he lay with his face buried in her hair. 'I've dreamed of loving you since the first moment I laid eyes on you,' he whispered. 'I haven't been able to get you out of my thoughts or my dreams.'

'Is that why you started drinking so much?' she guessed, her hands still holding him.

'Yes.'

'I think you'd better tell me about you and my mother now,' she said quietly, realizing that she felt like a woman now and not a girl.

And he told her. How close he and Mary had always been. How they had done everything together and were seldom out of one another's sight.

'And when did you first . . . first . . . ?'

'Make love to her?'

'Yes,' Hester whispered.

'When she was thirteen. I was sixteen at the time.'

'But why?'

'We were madly and desperately in love. It's not supposed to happen between brother and sister, but it does. It did to us.'

'And no one ever found out?'

'God Almighty, no! We were very careful.'

66

'If my mother loved you as you say then why did she marry my father?'

He smiled into the darkness, his voice heavy with remembering, 'Out of revenge.'

'Revenge?' She pulled away from his embrace to turn and face him.

'Mary and I made a pact when we were still very young. We'd go on just as we had been. Two single people living at home. And when our parents finally died no one would question it if we continued to live in the same house together.'

Was the Mary he was talking about really the same woman she'd known as her mother? Her mother had been so normal, so ordinary.

'One day, I met Sybil. It was obvious that she found me attractive.'

'And did you like her?'

He laughed, but it was not a happy sound. 'Sybil couldn't hold a candle to Mary in either looks or personality.'

Hester frowned. 'Then why did you marry her?'

Within the silence of the night was another, private silence. At last he choked out 'Money'.

'But I thought you had money?'

'I owned *The Rutherglen Advertiser* and it brought in a nice income. Not a tremendous amount, but a fair return considering its size. We were comfortable.'

'But you wanted more money?' He had never seemed like a greedy man.

His eyes were dark in the candlelight. 'Money was only the means to an end. I wanted a big city newspaper. I wanted it so badly it hurt.'

'Which you bought with Aunt Sybil's money?'

'Yes. I took over *The Glaswegian*.' He stared into the night. 'I got what I wanted. But I had to pay the price.'

She laid one hand on his, but he still stared ahead.

'I'll never forget the look on Mary's face when I told her Sybil and I were getting married.'

67

'Did you tell her why?'

He nodded, the memory of that time as vivid as if it had just happened.

'What did she say?'

'She said she'd known I was ambitious but had never before realized just how much. She said she felt sorry for me. And that I'd regret what I was doing for the rest of my life.'

And have you, she wanted to ask, but the tortured look in his eyes when he finally turned to her made her stop herself.

'And she was right. Losing Mary was worse than anything I could have imagined. When she went out of my life part of me died. I was never the same after that.'

'And yet the choice was yours.'

'Yes,' he whispered. 'There have been two great loves in my life, your mother and newspapers. I sacrificed one for the other.'

'Was it worth it?'

'It's difficult for me to explain just how much *The Glaswegian* means to me. Owning and making a success of a big city newspaper has given me the sort of fulfilment I always craved. The sort of fulfilment I could never have got from a penny-ante paper like *The Advertiser*.'

They lay in silence, his head against her shoulder while the house slept on. 'How did my father come into all this?'

'If you mean how did Mary meet him, I've no idea. He was an American seaman ashore in Glasgow. Somehow they met and the next thing I knew they were married. I hadn't reckoned on her doing that. I think, at the back of my mind, I had always hoped that she'd forgive me Sybil and that, sometime in the future, things would be the same between us.'

'So marrying my father was a revenge?'

'Yes. Although, she never admitted it to me.'

'But she was always so devoted to my father. Surely she loved him?'

'It could well be she came to. He was a good man and he certainly loved her. There was never any doubt about that. But if she loved Robert Dark, I'm also certain that she never stopped loving me as well. I had one letter from her after Robert was killed. I know she blamed herself for his death. That she believed he'd been taken from her as a punishment for our love.'

He leaned from the bed, groping in his dressing gown for a cigar. Biting off the end, he lit it from the candle.

'May I?' Hester asked, smiling both shyly and daringly.

He smiled as he handed it to her, laughing when the first puff caused her to splutter and choke.

'It's horrible,' she gasped, handing it back.

'You have to persevere.'

'Does Aunt Sybil know about you and my mother?'

Uncle Will regarded his cigar. 'She suspects, but has never been able to prove it. There were some letters she found that Mary had written to me once – and there were some poems from me to her.'

'You write poems?'

'Only to Mary. Rather poor ones, I'm afraid. But she liked them. I know Sybil suspects there was something between us – something more than just a normal brother and sister relationship. That's why, I suppose, she's always been jealous of Mary. What she does know for certain, though, is that Mary and I had something she and I will never have.'

'She was very cold towards me the day I arrived. I've always felt she didn't want me here.'

'She was very much in two minds about you coming to stay with us. On the one hand she felt it our duty to take you in. On the other, well you were Mary's child. It was an awful shock to her to see you were so much like Mary.'

'Was it a shock to you?'

69

'No. I think I'd always had an idea of what you would be like. Mind you, I wasn't expecting to be faced with Mary's double but I was expecting you to be like her.'

He touched her cheek, tracing the outline of the bone. He leaned forward and kissed her tenderly on the mouth. 'I loved your mother very much,' he whispered.

'But I'm not her.'

'You are to me.'

There was a pause in which she wondered if she had known from the start that this would happen, that they would lie like this.

'It was like the end of the world when she went to Bristol,' he said hoarsely, far away again. 'It never crossed my mind she'd leave Glasgow and that I'd never see her again. The day she and Robert left for the south I sat in my office the entire day, staring straight ahead of me. I saw nothing. I heard nothing. I was completely numb.'

She could see the turmoil in his heart reflected in his eyes. She could imagine all he'd been through inside him, over and over.

'Do you remember the other night I was talking about the war?'

'Yes.'

'During it I acquired something of a reputation for bravery.'

'So Aunt Sybil said. She's very proud of you.'

'Is she now? But what she didn't tell you was that in the middle of all that blood and waste, I began to brood on Mary. In the end I wanted to die. I wanted relief from all the anguish I'd inflicted upon myself. I wasn't really brave, you see. What I was actually trying to do was get myself killed.'

He smiled grimly at the memory. 'You had to laugh. There were all those men, millions of them, desperately wanting to live and being killed. And then there was me, wanting to die, and bearing a charmed life.'

'And do you feel that way still?'

'Since coming home I've got my other great love, the paper, to sustain and keep me going,' he replied, beginning to move his hands along her body. He rolled back on top of her. 'And now I've got you,' he smiled.

She came lazily out of sleep, yawning and stretching. Light streamed through the window. Somewhere beyond the house, a bird was singing.

And then she remembered and realized the full enormity of what had happened the night before.

Her first impulse was to throw on her clothes, pack a suitcase, and flee. Just get as far away as she could from this cold, gloomy house and its dark secrets. But where could she go? There was no one to whom she could turn. Apart from the Oliphants, she was all alone in the world. Alone. And then she remembered something more than the guilt, the confusion, and the shame.

Last night, for the first time since she was orphaned, she didn't feel alone and unloved. Last night for the first time since arriving in Glasgow she felt safe and cared about, felt that she meant something to someone. A woman now in many ways, Hester was still, in others, a girl. And she wanted her uncle's love.

Silently, in her beautiful room with the sun shining on her, Hester began to weep.

The idea had come to Hester during the early part of the afternoon and had been buzzing round in her head ever since.

She pulled the flush chain, then washed her hands. She was in Mrs Rosenbloom's, the dressmaker's, being fitted for some new clothes, she was growing so quickly.

On finishing at Mrs Rosenbloom's, Hester was going to visit *The Glaswegian* again at Will's suggestion. It was thinking about this visit which had sparked off her idea. An idea she was extremely excited about.

She was humming as she let herself out of the toilet, and ran slap-bang into Mrs Rosenbloom and a very handsome man in his late twenties or early thirties.

'Now who's this?' the man asked teasingly on seeing her.

'Rory, I'd like you to meet a client of mine, Miss Hester Dark,' Mrs Rosenbloom said in her formal way.

'How do you do,' Hester smiled.

'A lot better for having met you,' he grinned.

'Watch him, he's got an awful reputation for the ladies,' Mrs Rosenbloom warned mischievously.

'It's all lies,' he denied, a twinkle in his eye.

Mrs Rosenbloom went on. 'Hester, meet a very old, and dear, friend of mine, Rory McNeill, The Right Honourable the Viscount Kilmichael.'

'At your service, Miss Dark. And please call me Rory.'

'Oh!' she exclaimed. 'I've never met a Right Honourable before . And *you* may call me Hester.'

Rory laughed. 'I'll do that,' he winked.

'I must be going. My uncle's expecting me,' Hester said.

'I only popped in for a moment, so I'm just off as well. May I give you a lift?' Rory asked.

'I don't want to trouble you. . . .' she began hesitantly.

'No trouble at all! There, that's settled then.'

'I'll see you both out,' said Mrs Rosenbloom. 'You take good care of her now.'

As they walked to the car Hester wished she wasn't in school uniform, like a child. Something sophisticated would have been far far better for riding with a Right Honourable.

Once in the car, a sleek sports model, there was too much noise to speak without shouting. Not until the car drew up to a screeching halt outside *The Glaswegian* did they speak.

'What does your uncle do here?' Rory asked, switching off the engine.

'He owns it.'

Rory pulled a face. 'I'm impressed.'

'It's a good newspaper, don't you think?'

'I've never read it, I'm afraid. I'm a *Times* man myself.'

'Then you should. Broaden your outlook.'

'And how do you know my outlook isn't broad enough?' he asked, a teasing tone in his voice.

'Is anyone's ever?'

He laughed, realizing she'd picked up his real meaning. 'I'll buy it starting tomorrow,' he conceded, getting out of the car.

Taking her hand, he helped her to her feet. 'It's been a pleasure meeting you, Hester,' he said.

'And I enjoyed meeting you.'

'Goodbye then.'

'Goodbye.'

As she walked into the building she heard him roar off behind her. Now that's the sort of man I'd like to marry she thought as she rode up in the lift. Handsome, urbane and no doubt, stinking rich. Everything a woman could want.

Then the idea that had so excited her all afternoon came back and she promptly forgot about Rory McNeill, The Right Honourable the Viscount Kilmichael.

Will rose from behind his rolltop desk as she entered his office. 'How did the fitting go?' he asked, coming to give her a fatherly embrace.

'Fine. The new clothes are going to be very nice. You'll like them.'

'Excellent,' he answered, his eyes devouring her.

On the way up she had savoured the smell of printer's ink, the distant clamour of the presses music to her ears. Again she'd experienced the overwhelming sensation that a newspaper building was where she belonged.

'Can we chat?' she smiled.

'Certainly. What about?'

'*The Glaswegian*.'

He returned her smile. 'One of my favourite subjects.'

'I know.'

'Anything in particular about the paper?'

She watched him trim and light a cigar. After which he sat back in his chair and put his feet on the desk.

'Why is your newspaper more successful than the other city dailies?' she asked.

'Several reasons. To begin with, I didn't aim for the upper end of the market. Prestige is all very nice but the readership there is far smaller than at the centre which comprises by far the largest readership of all. In other words, I went for the upper working class and lower middle. In Glasgow there are far more newspaper readers in that section of society than all the others put together.'

His eyes took on an evangelical fervour as he spoke. Nor did it escape Hester's notice that his voice was as rich and full of passion as when he was making love to her.

Again and again he snatched the cigar from his mouth, using it to stab the air whenever there was a particular point he wished to stress.

Hester listened in genuine fascination.

'Give the public what they want and in the fashion they want. If there's a secret to having a popular newspaper that's it,' he said. 'And to give it to them get the best money can buy. Men as well as machines. Never stint on either. To do so is a terrible mistake, believe me. If there's a journalist working for another paper whom you admire, then poach him. Find out what he's earning and offer him more. He'll pay his way by keeping the readership up. The good ones always do.'

He'd been talking so much his cigar had gone out. He now paused to relight it.

Hester knew this was the moment to strike. 'I'd like to ask you a favour,' she said.

'Name it.'

'It's about *The Glaswegian*.'

'Yes?'

74

Taking a deep breath, she boldly announced what she had decided. 'I want to work here during the summer holidays.'

He regarded her closely, an amused expression on his face. 'Do you indeed!'

'Yes, I do.'

He shook his head. 'I'm afraid a newspaper office is out of the question for a young girl like yourself.'

'Why?'

'Because newspapermen are rough. And I don't mean that in the physical sense. Perhaps abrasive would be a better word. They use appalling language, to begin with, the sort no niece of mine is going to be subjected to.'

'You mean they swear a lot?'

'Precisely.'

She laughed. 'I think I'd survive that. You forget I was brought up amongst dockie families where swearing isn't exactly unheard of. I'm sure they wouldn't come out with anything I hadn't heard before.'

But Will was adamant. 'They can be uncouth in the extreme. Especially when they've been drinking. Which for the vast majority of them seems to be most of the time.' He threw his hands in the air. 'It's a man's world Hester. My niece, and a girl who attends Maybank, doesn't belong there.'

'Please?' she pleaded.

'No!'

'*Pretty* please?'

'No. And that's final.'

'You're being old-fashioned, reactionary and short-sighted.'

'I'm being nothing of the sort. I'm only thinking of your best interests.'

'You were the one who said I had the family bug.'

'I did. And this only confirms that I was right. But because you've got it doesn't mean I'm going to agree to you coming to work on the paper. Anyway what would you do?'

'I could write down copy that comes in over the telephone.'

'Men do that.'

'There's no reason why a woman can't.'

'You're not a woman. You're a girl.'

'That's not what you say at night.'

'That has nothing to do with this.'

'I want to learn the newspaper business,' she stated firmly.

'It's impossible.'

'Nothing's impossible. You told me so yourself.'

He broke down and smiled. 'You've got a lot of spunk, Hester. I can't deny that. And I admire it. Oh yes! I admire it all right.'

'But you won't give me a summer job?'

'Believe me, I know what's best.' From the tone of his voice, it was clear that the subject was closed.

Hester pouted, her hopes temporarily dashed. But, she told herself, she would find a way. Nothing was impossible if you wanted it hard enough. The only trick was to find the right key with which to open the door.

'Here she is!' cried Christine excitedly. She'd been peering out of the drawing room window from behind the curtains. Hester and Billy immediately sprang to their feet, hurriedly leaving the room with Christine bringing up the rear.

Uncle Will was supporting Aunt Sybil by the elbow. She was pale, drawn and tired, and the weight she'd lost made her look like another woman. She beamed as Christine rushed into her arms, tears of happiness at being home streaming down her cheeks.

'Welcome back,' said Hester.

'It's good to be back,' replied Aunt Sybil, hugging her warmly.

Billy kissed his mother on the cheek. Then they all moved through to the drawing room where Aunt

Sybil sank gratefully into a chair by the blazing fire.

She looked terrible, Hester thought. It hadn't been so noticeable at the hospital, but here, in her own home, it was. Since the night of her collapse she had aged ten years.

'How about a wee sherry to celebrate?' suggested Uncle Will cheerily.

'That would be nice,' agreed Sybil, her eyes still misty.

'I'll do it,' said Billy, bounding over to where the drinks were kept.

'Are you hungry?' asked Christine.

Aunt Sybil smiled, but shook her head.

Hester sat quietly on the side, feeling a bit out of things.

'How about you, Father?' Billy asked.

'A dram. A small one,' Uncle Will replied, holding up two fingers. 'As it's a special occasion, you children can have a sherry if you'd care to.'

The drinks were poured and handed round. 'To your full, and speedy, recovery,' Uncle Will toasted.

Hester drank. And as she did so her eyes met his for the first time since he'd brought Sybil home.

I love you, they seemed to say.

Then they both looked away.

For three nights after Sybil's return from the hospital, Will stayed away from Hester's bedroom, but on the fourth she woke just past midnight to find him sitting on the bed beside her.

'Oh, Hester!' he whispered.

She sat up. There was a terrible need on his face, a need she intended turning to her advantage. After considerable thought it had come to her how she could bend her uncle to her will.

'Aunt Sybil?' she queried.

'Fast asleep.'

'She'll realize you've gone.'

77

'Not her. She's worn out. God, I've missed you!' and he buried his face in her hair.

He started to untie his dressing gown but she stretched out her hand to stop him. 'No,' she said.

'It's all right. She won't come. We're perfectly safe.'

'It's not that.'

'Then what is it?'

'I just don't feel like it,' she lied. She had missed him more than she had thought possible.

'Please.'

' I don't know why I should give you what you want when you won't give me what I want,' she said sulkily.

'And what is that supposed to mean?'

'I want a summer job on *The Glaswegian*,' she replied.

'That's impossible. I've already told you. . . .'

'Then you don't care for me at all, really. You're only using me.' She turned away from him, steeling herself against the longing in his eyes.

'Hester, you must understand. . . . It wouldn't be right for you to work on a newspaper.'

She gave him a soft, hurt smile. 'I thought we were above what other people consider right and wrong. Is it right that we love each other? Is it right that we go on seeing each other like this?'

She had him, and he knew it. She could see the struggle in his eyes. 'Well?'

It was rare for Will Oliphant to be bested, yet alone by a slip of a girl. Suddenly he laughed. 'All right, you win,' he conceded. 'The paper it is.' Immediately he reached for her, but she held him away.

'Promise me you won't go back on it,' she demanded.

'I promise.'

And only then did she reach out for him, shaking with relief that her own bluff had actually worked.

78

4

'Time to get up, Miss Hester. I've brought your coffee,' Kathleen said, gently shaking Hester by the shoulder.

Hester woke and a second later was out of bed. It was the Monday morning after school had closed for the summer holidays. *The* day.

On Saturday Aunt Sybil and Christine had left for Balfron, in Stirlingshire, where Uncle Will had taken a house for the summer to help in Sybil's convalescence. Originally, Billy had been supposed to go with his mother and sister, but after a great argument one night it had been agreed for Billy also to work at *The Glaswegian*.

'You say you want him to start work directly he leaves school, but when he offers to work through the summer for you you want to turn him down. I just don't understand your logic,' Aunt Sybil had reasoned.

Uncle Will had been stumped for a reply, or one that would have been convincing, anyway. Under different circumstances he would have been delighted with Billy's unusual enthusiasm to work during the summer break, but he'd been looking forward to being alone in the house with Hester.

And so it was that upstairs Billy would also be getting ready for his first ever day's work. Enthusiastic as he was, Hester doubted he was half as excited as her.

'Big day,' Will smiled when she arrived at breakfast, knowing how much she'd been looking forward to it.

'A big day,' she agreed, sitting beside him.

He reached under the table and patted her knee. 'And a big night,' he whispered.

She smiled back, beautiful in her obvious excitement.

'I would still prefer if you didn't do this, you know. It's not too late to change your mind.'

'All right then, I'll go on out to Balfron this afternoon,' she teased.

His face fell. The prospect of six weeks without Hester was intolerable.

'Well?' she demanded, unable to keep from laughing at the look on his face.

He saw then that she was only teasing. 'Minx!'

'All set for the fray, cuz?' Hester asked when Billy entered the room.

'Never more,' he replied, helping himself to a huge plateful of scrambled egg.

'I see you're not nervous,' Hester grinned.

'Why should I be? It's only a job.'

Will snorted. 'Just see you don't let me down. Either of you,' he said. Then, pointing his fork at Billy, added 'Especially you. They all know you're my son. They'll be watching you like a hawk to see what you're made of.'

Billy gave an easy smile. 'That also works both ways. I'll also be watching *them*. For as you so often say, I am the heir apparent.'

As it so often did, the antagonism sparked between father and son.

'It'll be a long time yet before you sit in my seat, Billy. Don't you forget that. I'm not an old man yet.'

'Lovely egg,' murmured Billy. And that was the end of that conversation.

Ritchie drove them to *The Glaswegian* where they got out at the front of the building. 'Today you come in this way with me. Tomorrow you go round the back with the rest of the workers. Understood?'

Hester and Billy nodded.

Once inside they were introduced to Mister McFarlane, a humourless, Presbyterian man whose face seemed set in a permanent scowl. He didn't offer to shake hands, merely grunting when told their names.

'Follow me,' McFarlane said.

'What are we starting on?' Hester asked, trotting behind McFarlane.

He regarded her sourly. 'You'll see,' was all he replied.

Hester glanced at Billy who shrugged. She'd thought McFarlane's reply sounded ominous.

They followed McFarlane through a maze of corridors until at last they reached a partitioned area at the rear of the building. Here were laid out long tables upon which men were tying up bundles of papers.

The floor of this area was covered with debris: pieces of string, torn off sheets of brown packing paper and all sorts of other gash items.

'Wait here,' said McFarlane, disappearing into the activity.

'Bundling,' said Hester. 'Could be worse.'

'Bit strenuous for a girl, I would've thought,' frowned Billy.

'I'll manage,' said Hester determinedly.

McFarlane rematerialized with two brooms, handing one to Hester and the other to Billy. 'Come this way and I'll show you where the bins are,' he said gruffly.

Walking behind McFarlane, Billy tapped Hester's shoulder to get her attention, then gestured to his broom. 'At least no one will ever be able to accuse me of not starting at the bottom,' he laughed.

Hester didn't care where she'd started. She'd started. That was all that mattered.

Ten days later found the three of them returning from work in the car with Hester staring grimly, and angrily, ahead. Her mouth was clamped shut, her eyes sparking.

Billy was oblivious to her mood, but Uncle Will wasn't. He decided to wait till later to ask what was wrong, assuming it must be something to do with work.

During dinner and for the remainder of the evening, Hester was mainly silent, speaking only when spoken to – and even then giving only curt replies. At the earliest opportunity she escaped to her bedroom.

Uncle Will came shortly after Billy had retired.

Slipping inside he closed the door behind him. He found her sitting on the bed waiting.

'Let's get it over and done with,' he said. 'Tell me what's annoyed you.'

'Billy started at the sub-editing table today.'

'So?'

Her eyes snapped fire. '*I'm* still sweeping up.'

He sat on the bed beside her and took her hand in his. 'Billy's got to learn every job there is to learn. When the time comes I want him to be able to do, or at least have a working knowledge of, every job directly connected with *The Glaswegian*. That was the way I learned on the old *Advertiser*.'

'Fine, I accept that. In fact I think it's an excellent idea. But I want to learn as well.'

'You said you'd be happy doing anything,' he reminded her.

'And so I am. But I've got a good brain in my head. I'm just as capable of learning as Billy is.'

Uncle Will sighed. 'And I suppose if I don't put you on the sub table with Billy it'll be the old crossed legs routine?'

She gave him a wicked smile. 'What a good idea!' she exclaimed.

He laughed at that. 'You're an awful girl,' he said, hugging her to him.

'Just a determined one,' she replied. 'And I join Billy tomorrow?'

'Tomorrow,' he said resignedly.

She kissed him warmly, with tender affection.

'And this,' said Uncle Will, 'is Alan Beat, without a doubt the best sub-editor in all Scotland.'

Beat was a small, craggy man with huge bristling eyebrows. When he snorted Hester immediately thought of a shaggy Highland bull.

'How do you do,' Hester said politely.

He ran his eyes over her, missing nothing, then swung on his employer. 'What in Christ's name is this newspaper coming to?' he thundered.

'What do you mean, Alan?' Will replied with a smile.

A stubby, gnarled finger was waved at Hester. 'She's a bloody lassie!'

'I know that.'

'And you expect me to teach her?'

Uncle Will began to speak, but Hester interrupted him.

'I've heard a great deal about you Mr Beat,' she smiled, drawing herself up to her fullest height.

'Have you now?'

In fact, she'd only heard of him that morning when Will had warned her, en route to work, what to expect. Throughout the industry Alan Beat had a reputation as a hard man of the old school. If she wasn't accepted by him now, then she might as well go home and forget all about a career in newspapers.

She was trying to get his measure. Wondering what her right line of attack should be. Flattery? No, that wasn't the way.

'I'll not have a lassie at my bloody table!' Beat said to Will Oliphant. 'It's flying in the face of tradition and just asking for trouble.' He snorted. 'Lassie, indeed! Whoever heard of anything more ridiculous.'

'You seem to forget I'm the boss, Alan. If I say you teach her the job, then you teach her.' Will said quietly.

A hush fell. All eyes turned to Beat.

'You're the boss all right, Mister Oliphant, but I'm also a free man. If I walk out of here today I'll have another job tomorrow. Now you know that to be true.'

'Aye, I'm sure you're right.'

'And I won't fucking teach a lassie!' Beat suddenly thundered.

Hester smiled at him sweetly. 'I always thought that people who worked on newspapers were supposed to be clever, witty and above all articulate,' she said.

83

Beat's lips set in defiance.

'Oh, well,' continued Hester lightly. 'I suppose there's the exception to every fucking rule.'

It was one of the subs who broke the profound silence that followed that remark. He started to titter; a titter that soon became a full-blown guffaw. Others joined in till the only two people not laughing were Hester and Alan Beat.

She knew she'd won when she saw his face crack into a smile.

'Will you teach me Mister Beat?' she asked, holding out her hand to be shaken.

He held back a second more. Then put his hand in hers.

'You'll do lassie. Oh, aye. You'll do just fine,' he said.

Billy was more angry than Hester had ever seen him. He sat in the car virtually shaking with rage.

'You had no right to do that,' he said.

'You made a stupid mistake,' his father replied. 'I had every right.'

'Not to tell me off like that in front of the others. You made me look . . . small.'

'And you made a damn stupid mistake.'

'And have you never done that, Father? Have you never made a stupid mistake?'

But Will didn't reply.

'I admit to the mistake, and it's right you should tell me off for it. But not in front of the others. That was unforgiveable.'

Will caught Hester looking at him reprovingly and glanced away. He knew her sympathies were with Billy on this. At the time what he'd done seemed right. But on reflection . . . perhaps he had been a bit too harsh.

Chalk and cheese Billy had said, Hester thought. Well he was certainly right about that.

She tried to change the subject with Billy who sat

silently fuming, but he wouldn't be drawn. The only reply she got was a grunt.

She noticed that when Uncle Will thought neither she nor Billy was looking his glaze flickered sideways to momentarily rest on Billy. His expression was one she couldn't interpret.

As was their custom, they met in the drawing room to await dinner being announced. Tonight Will poured two hefty whiskies. 'Here you are, Billy,' he said, handing his son one.

Billy stared, amazement and surprise written across his face. He couldn't believe it as he accepted the dram. Up until that moment he'd only ever been offered sherry, which was a woman's drink. Whisky was strictly the preserve of men.

'Slainte!' said Uncle Will, raising his glass in a toast.

'Slainte!' Billy repeated.

An apology would have been too much to expect. Will Oliphant wasn't the sort of man who made them. But the whisky was a compromise gesture. It said he now accepted Billy as being grown-up. They might not agree with one another, or even like one another, but there was now a new respect between them. He admired the way Billy had stood up for himself at last.

Will grinned at his son over his drink. 'You may as well have one of those cigarettes you've been so furtively smoking for the past year,' he said suddenly. 'Your preference is Turkish tobacco isn't it? At least that's what I keep smelling round the house.'

Billy looked dumbstruck at this.

As Will moved past Hester he managed to wink at her. She smiled back at him, touched by his odd generosity.

Looking somewhat sheepish, Billy lit up.

Hester's pencil moved quickly over the copy. Her concentration was intense as she prepared it to go down to the printer. She paused to think of a good title for the piece when sweat suddenly burst on her forehead and nausea rumbled in her stomach. Her head started to go round and round and she thought she was going to faint.

'Hester?'

The voice seemed to come from a million miles away. 'Hester?'

She looked up to see Alan Beat staring at her in concern. Like the inside of her head, his face was spinning.

'Are you all right?' Beat asked.

She took a deep breath. Then another. This steadied her a little. 'Can I go to the toilet?' she asked.

'Certainly.'

She rose unsteadily, aware that every eye around the table was on her. 'Little bit of a tummy upset,' she apologized.

'Perhaps you should go home?' suggested Beat.

'No, no! I'll be fine.'

'There's been a lot of stomach trouble around,' said Shughie McPhail, another of the subs.

'Aye. My wife's got it,' added Hector Munro, a gentle soul of a man who, because of his close-set eyes and thin shaped face, Hester had nicknamed The Ferret.

'I won't be long,' Hester said and stumbled away.

She only just made the toilet cubicle in time. Thankfully, there was no one else present.

She retched and retched until there was nothing left in her stomach and then fumbled in her pocket for the hanky she kept there, using it to wipe her lips and chin.

This was the fourth time in the last six days that she'd thrown up, but it was the first time it had happened at work. She came to her feet and stumbled to the handbasins.

She stared at her image in the mirror above the basin, smiling to herself to see how well she looked in spite of her illness. She positively glowed, in spite of the worry on her face. It was time to face the truth.

The attack had completely passed by the time she returned to the subs table a few minutes later where she found a message that she was to go up to see her uncle. It was the first time he'd sent for her since she'd started at *The Glaswegian*.

'Come in!' he called out when she knocked, waving her to a seat. He finished the editorial he was reading before glancing up and smiling at her. 'You've been doing so well since you joined us, and everyone speaks so highly of you, that I thought I'd splash out and buy you lunch at my club. What do you say?'

But Hester could not so much as smile. She'd been hoping and praying she was wrong – now she knew she wasn't. The sooner he was told the better.

'Lunch would be lovely,' she said. 'As long as I go and come back within the time of my usual break. I don't want the others thinking I'm taking advantage.'

He nodded his approval. 'Twelve-thirty to one-thirty, isn't it?'

'Yes.'

'Then meet me on the front door dead on half past twelve. They can hardly grudge you that little leeway,' he chuckled.

Precisely on the half-hour she presented herself at the appointed spot to find him already waiting. They talked about the paper as they strolled to his club nearby. He didn't notice her nervousness.

It was the first time Hester had been inside his club, and she wasn't particularly impressed. It was far too pompous and stuffy for her liking.

'How about some *escargots* to start with?' Will asked once they were seated and had the menu.

Hester nearly gagged at the thought. 'Something plain for me,' she replied, relieved when he said he'd have the same.

The wine was a Burgundy which tasted like vinegar in her mouth. 'Lovely,' she lied.

'Just the one glass, mind. We mustn't forget you're under age,' Will winked.

It was as good an opening line as any, she thought.

'Speaking of being under age. . . .' she began, her heart galloping. 'Will . . . I . . . I'm pregnant.'

He looked at her blankly, as if expecting her to add that she'd only been joking.

'I'm pregnant,' she repeated, calmer now that it had been said.

He lifted his glass and drained it.

'Are you sure?' he asked at last.

'Yes,' she replied, knowing somehow that she was.

He licked his lips. 'How can you be?'

'I don't know how. Women just know these things.'

'But you could be wrong?'

'I know I'm not. The signs are unmistakable.'

'Perhaps you've just got flu or something?'

She almost wanted to laugh. 'Flu doesn't make you feel the way I feel.'

'My God!' he mumbled and swallowed more Burgundy.

This was what he'd secretly dreaded. What he'd hoped wouldn't happen if he only didn't think about it. Now he was trapped in a nightmare.

'How far along are you?' he whispered from far away.

'I've definitely missed one period. And the one before that was peculiar. . . . I should be due for the next one any day now. I think . . . well, it must be eleven or twelve weeks. Certainly not more. Perhaps even a little less.'

His look was stern and distant. 'You haven't mentioned this to anyone else have you?'

'Of course not!' She was shocked. Was this the man she loved?

He ran a hand over his face. 'Thank Heaven for that.'

The first course arrived, a consommé. Hester stirred hers with a heavy silver spoon much lighter than her heart. She had no appetite. She couldn't speak or think. His coldness and distance terrified her.

'What are we going to do?' she managed to whisper.

'I don't know. But leave it to me. I'll make the necessary inquiries.'

She suddenly wanted to cry. She wanted her mother. Somehow she fought back the tears.

He placed his hand on hers lightly, like an uncle. 'Everything will be all right. I promise you,' he said, but his eyes were far away.

Billy yawned. 'I'm bushed. It was a busy day.'

Uncle Will looked up from the book he was reading. 'Run along to bed then. We won't be long behind you. Will we, Hester?'

'No.'

'See you both at breakfast then,' said Billy. With a backward wave he left the room.

The moment he'd gone, Will threw his book aside and crossed to Hester. It was the evening following their abandoned lunch and he'd been absent from the paper virtually all afternoon.

'How do you feel?' he asked, but was it with concern or anxiety?

'Awful,' she answered truthfully, trying to smile.

He nodded his curt sympathy. Reaching into his inside pocket, he pulled out a buff-coloured envelope and handed it to her.

There were some pills inside. A dozen.

'Three tonight. The same in the morning. If nothing has happened by tomorrow night, repeat the procedure,' he instructed her, as though still at work.

Hester's mouth was dry as she fingered the pills. 'Are they dangerous?' she asked timidly, searching his face for some sign of affection.

'The doctor I got them from swore they weren't.'

Her hand closed over the envelope, crumpling it in the palm of her hand. 'Do we *have* to do this?' she asked.

Immediately, he looked alarmed. 'You certainly can't

have this child, if that's what you mean.' His voice was harsh.

'Couldn't I go somewhere and then have it adopted after it's born?' It was something she'd read in a book once. It had seemed so romantic then.

'There's no question of that. How would I explain your disappearance to the rest of the family? They'd be bound to be suspicious. Especially Sybil. She's not a fool.'

'There must be some way,' Hester pleaded.

'There isn't,' he snapped. 'You have to get rid of it, and that's final. Can you imagine the effect it would have on my standing in the community if it ever came out that I'd had a child by my under-age niece? Christ Almighty, they'd crucify me! I'd lose everything. Everything.' He shook his head, his eyes wild. 'No! No! There's no possibility whatever of you having the child. I've got too much to lose.'

She placed her hand on her stomach. It was her imagination, she knew, but it was almost as though she could feel something. A tiny life. Her baby.

When she looked up again he was standing in front of her offering a glass of water.

'It's for the best, Hester. I assure you,' he said gently, composed again.

He must be right, there was no other way. She had to accept that, she told herself. He was a man of the world, after all. He knew best.

Opening the envelope she tapped three of the pills into a palm, closed her eyes and swallowed.

'I don't want you to come to me tonight,' she whispered, though she longed to be cuddled.

'Of course not. I understand.'

He raised her to her feet and held her close. 'You take a couple of days off work. When it happens it's best it happens here. All right?'

Even now she loathed the idea of missing even a moment from the paper. 'I'll tell the servants it's this stomach trouble that's going around. I've already told Alan Beat and the other subs that's what it is.'

She left him then and went upstairs to bed alone but sleep evaded her and she tossed and turned all night, troubled by her dreams.

Morning found her tired and exhausted, but still pregnant. She waited till the coffee Kathleen had brought her had cooled, then used a mouthful of it to wash down the second lot of pills. Picking up a novel she was halfway through, she settled back in bed.

A few hours later the pain came from nowhere to hit her a sledgehammer blow in the stomach. Then a second pain hit her, taking her breath away. She trembled as much in terror as in pain. If only she weren't alone. If only her mother were here to comfort her and stop her fear.

Reaching under her pillow she pulled out the towel she'd secreted there, and placed it between her legs, whimpering as another pain scorched her. When that subsided she felt leaden, drained.

The pains lasted for forty-five minutes, lessening in severity until the last one was no more than a twinge.

When they finally stopped completely, Hester knew that the pills had failed. She had still six more to take. Bathed in sweat and tears, and feeling dazed, she eventually drifted off to sleep. Later, Will entered her bedroom wearing an expectant look.

'Well?' he demanded eagerly.

He swore viciously when she shook her head.

The following evening, shortly before Uncle Will and Billy were due back from *The Glaswegian*, Hester rose and got dressed. She'd taken the pills the previous night and the remainder that morning. All day she'd waited for those terrible sledgehammer blows to return, but they hadn't.

'Are you sure you're well enough to get up, Miss?' Kathleen asked anxiously on meeting Hester halfway down the stairs.

'I'm fully recovered, thank you,' Hester replied.

The first time Billy turned his back, she glanced across at Will and signalled 'no'. Immediately, he became very tight-lipped, and reached for the decanter.

No opportunity arose during the remainder of the evening for them to speak privately. She knew he'd come to her later.

She was lying staring in the darkness when the door opened and he slipped into the room.

'I'm sorry,' she said as he got in beside her. So happy just to have his arms around her.

He murmured words of endearment as always, familiarly fondling her breast. He continued to caress her for some minutes, but didn't attempt to go any further. The words he spoke came automatically, without feeling. He was deep in thought, sunk in on himself.

Finally he whispered, sounding relieved, 'I'd better get back upstairs. I've a busy day ahead of me.'

It was the first time they'd been in bed together without making love. It was the first time she'd been with him and still felt alone.

Hester returned to *The Glaswegian* the next day. That Friday after work Tam Ritchie collected the three of them and drove them out to the house in Balfron for the weekend.

The house was a large rambling one with stables attached. It belonged to the Laird of Garlunzie who spent every summer in South Africa, renting the house out while he was away.

After breakfast on Saturday morning, Hester made straight for the stables, intent on having a ride. She'd made excellent progress since her first lesson a few weeks before and had now reached the stage where she was able to canter though she still wasn't allowed out unaccompanied.

One of the stable boys was saddling her mount for her when she was joined by Will, who'd changed into jodpurs and a hacking jacket. 'Thought I might come with you if you don't mind,' he said, and shouted instructions for another horse to be made ready.

It was a beautiful summer's day. The sky duck-egg-blue, the sun high and yellow as butter. Hester breathed deeply, revelling in the fresh country smells. As the horses walked on she felt extremely peaceful and content.

They crossed several fields, then made their way down a rutted track leading to a wood-covered hill, beyond which more hills could be seen. A solitary puff of cotton-wool cloud wandered lazily across the sky.

Suddenly there was a flash of movement below Hester's horse. A snake? Her horse, startled, whinnied and reared.

She could feel the horse's fear and panic, as it began to plunge forward. She cried out to Will to grab hold of her bridle. Once the horse bolted, it was unlikely she'd be able to bring it back under control.

Will was staring at her, a strange expression that was only partly fear on his face. There were a few moments in which he could have grabbed hold of her bridle, but he made no effort to do so.

Hester's horse threw itself into a frantic gallop. Hester screamed uncontrollably as they were swallowed up by the dense wood, branches grabbing at her like witches' hands. Again and again she was hit, but clinging on desperately, she somehow managed to retain her seat.

She was sobbing when they broke free from the wood. She hauled on the reins, but they might have been attached to the air. Then, at the bottom of the hill, the horse stumbled.

The next moment, she was flying through the air. I'm going to die, was the last thing she thought.

*   *   *

She came to in a large double bed to find a middle-aged woman staring at her. The woman hurried away shouting. 'Renton, the lassie's awake!'

A few seconds later the woman returned with a strange man and Will.

'I'm Doctor McLeod, you've had a nasty accident,' the man said, smiling reassuringly.

Slowly she focused her eyes. 'I remember. I came off my horse.'

The doctor nodded. 'Aye lass, you did that all right. And a bad fall it was, too. You were lucky to escape with life and limb. However, I'm afraid. . . .' He coughed, embarrassed, trying to find the right words.

She looked at Will, 'What is it?'

Will looked away.

'I'm afraid. . .' McLeod began again.

'The baby?'

He shook his head.

Hester glanced at the woman, but she too averted her eyes. Only the doctor seemed concerned.

'Where is this place?' she asked faintly.

'The village of Bouquhan. I knew there was a doctor here. You're in his house now,' replied Will.

She gazed at her uncle, trying to remember what had happened.

'You'll have to stay here for a few days,' the doctor advised.

'I'd prefer to go back to Balfron.' She wanted to escape from his wife's coldly accusing eyes. *Harlot* those eyes seemed to be stating over and over again.

The doctor shook his head. 'You're not to move out of that bed till I tell you. What you've been through would lay up anyone, but you're young and healthy. You'll recover in the minimum of time.'

Hester stared Will straight in the eye, and watched a cloud descend to hide from her his inner feelings and thoughts. She remembered how he could have grabbed the bridle. How he hadn't.

'When you're back on your feet I want you to see a specialist in Glasgow,' McLeod said.

'Why? Isn't everything all right?'

He gave her a paternal smile. 'Just to be on the safe side, you understand. That was an awful thump you gave yourself. It's best a specialist checks you over to ensure all's as it should be. For your own peace of mind if nothing else.'

'We'll get the top man,' Will assured him.

'Good,' said the doctor, a trace of harshness in his voice.

Will Oliphant nodded, then looked away. He couldn't hold the doctor's gaze, nor was this lost on McLeod or Hester.

Had the doctor guessed who the child's father was, wondered Hester.

'Now, I want you to sleep so I'm going to give you a sedative,' McLeod said. Taking a powder from his bag he tapped it into a glass of water which immediately became cloudy. 'Drink,' he ordered, handing the glass to Hester.

She stared into the white, milky depths. 'Doctor?' she whispered, her throat tight.

'Yes, lass?'

'Was it a boy or a girl?'

A sudden stillness descended on the room. McLeod hesitated, then replied smoothly, 'Impossible to say at such an early stage.'

Hester looked at the doctor, but was unable to tell whether that was the truth or a lie.

McLeod and his wife left the room but Will stayed behind. 'We don't have to worry about the good doctor,' he whispered, 'I've spun him a yarn and also arranged to pay well above his normal fee. He'll keep his mouth shut. As will his wife. He'll see to that.'

The sedative was working quickly. Already she was feeling drowsy. Underneath the bedclothes she laid her hand on her stomach. It felt so empty. So empty.

'Aunt Sybil and the rest of the family can visit you

tomorrow. But of course as far as they're concerned you only came off your horse,' Uncle Will said.

Closing her eyes Hester turned away from him.

She dreamt she was riding through the woods, racing, searching for her lost baby.

To Hester it felt as though years had passed. She gazed at her uncle, thinking if she'd been a man she would have hit him. 'I saw the specialist today,' she said at last after an evening of strained silence.

'Of course I was aware you were going to see him. I've been waiting for Billy to get out of the way so I could hear what he told you,' answered Will, closing his paper.

Billy was on his way up to bed, and could still be heard mounting the stairs. Hester's excuse for lingering on with her uncle was that she hadn't yet finished her cocoa.

Hester took a deep breath. 'Mr Smellie told me that the fall from the horse has destroyed any chances of me ever conceiving again.' She had been repeating the doctor's words all afternoon but only now did they sound real.

The dram stopped halfway to Will's mouth. He'd gone quite white. 'Oh Hester!' he exclaimed softly. 'Maybe he's wrong.'

But she hardly heard him. 'It could have been worse. I could easily have been killed,' she said numbly, again repeating what the doctor had said.

He dropped his eyes to his drink.

Suddenly, her control snapped. 'You could have stopped that horse bolting,' she shouted. 'You could have grabbed the bridle.' Her body shook with sobs.

He threw the whisky back, then quickly poured himself another.

'You selfish old man!' she wept, pushing aside his hand.

'I'll make it up to you, I swear,' he said. 'Anything at all.'

'Can you give me back the children I might have had?'

He stared at her as though she'd shot him.

'Then you can't make it up to me.'

Holding back when he could have grabbed her bridle had been his decision. Well, she'd made a decision too. She had loved him and trusted him, but it had never been her he'd cared about.

'I don't want you ever to come to my bedroom or lay a hand on me again,' she whispered through clenched teeth. 'Never.'

'Hester. . .' he began and this time held her hand. 'I know you've had a shock. . .'

'Because if you do I'll go to every newspaper in Glasgow, with the exception of yours that is, and tell them everything. Including your relationship with my mother.'

He stared at her in disbelief, appalled. 'That would ruin me.'

'Yes, I know.'

'But how can I live without you? I love you!' His lips brushed her hand.

She gave a laugh that rang with bitterness. 'You love me? You love me enough to shame and disgrace me, but not enough to save me when I might have been killed. Is that what you call love?'

'You're twisting things!'

'Am I?' she shouted, the tears streaming down her face.

'I know it was terrible what I did. I know I was wrong. But I was under so much pressure. You must understand.'

'Oh, I understand all right, Uncle Will. I understand only too well. But you had better understand, too. One hand on me from now on in, that's all it will take, and the papers will have a field day.'

He knew she meant it. His shoulders, usually so proud and defiant, dropped, then sagged. The spirit seemed to die in him. Even as he watched her sweep from the room,

97

her eyes red and moist, he could feel his heart break. And knew there was no one but himself to blame.

5

Two and a half years after her 'accident' found Hester grown into an extremely attractive young woman. Her bust was full, her waist trim, her legs shapely and long.

It was dinnertime and the family was gathered around the table. The first course, cock-a-leekie soup, had just been laid before them.

'Why are you frowning like that, Hester?' Aunt Sybil demanded. 'You've been a right misery these last few days.'

'I know why,' piped up Christine, a hint of malice in her voice. The years hadn't been nearly so kind to her. Now very tall, her body hadn't matured. Nor did it seem it ever would. Tall, thin and angular, the girls at Maybank called her the walking clothes' pole.

Hester shot Christine a warning glance which was quite the wrong thing to do as it merely spurred Christine on.

'The reason she's so upset is because she can't find a chap to take her to the school dance,' Christine crowed, exultant because she herself had a boyfriend who was to accompany her to the Maybank Christmas dance.

'That's not true,' retorted Hester.

'Yes, it is!'

Hester stirred the soup round her plate. She hated cock-a-leekie.

'Well, Hester?' pestered Aunt Sybil.

'It's not that I can't find anyone. It's just that I can't think of anyone I particularly want to take me.'

'Then go alone,' said Uncle Will.

She stared into that now permanently whisky-flushed face, a face that had shrunk and shrivelled, as had the once well-built body, and gained a dozen or so deeply etched lines that ran like furrows from eyes to cheek to chin. The auburn hair had dulled and was starting to turn grey.

'I'd prefer not to,' she replied evenly.

'Why's that?'

'It would give the other girls something to talk and laugh about.'

'Surely not!' exclaimed Aunt Sybil, somewhat naively.

Christine tittered to herself. There was still little love lost between her and Hester.

'She's more than welcome to come with Graeme and me,' Christine said sweetly.

'I'd prefer not to play gooseberry,' Hester replied softly. 'But thank you for the offer anyway.'

Billy chuckled. At nineteen going on twenty he was at Glasgow University; he and his mother's wishes having won out against his father's as he'd always known they would. He was doing well. 'And how is Specky Souter these days?' Billy asked. He and Graeme Souter had gone to school together.

'*Graeme* is in excellent health, thank you very much,' Christine replied icily.

'Pity he didn't make it into the Uni,' Billy said, goading Christine on. 'We always thought him such a swot, too.'

'He's doing very well in the family business,' said Christine airily.

'Biscuits isn't it?' Billy said. Then added, before she could reply, 'In a small way.'

Hester smiled into her soup. She knew as well as Billy that Graeme was after Christine for the money he was hoping she'd bring. If Christine was aware of that she'd certainly never mentioned it. Nor had Uncle Will or Aunt Sybil.

'Yes. In a small way,' Christine replied through gritted teeth.

'Graeme's an extremely nice chap,' said Aunt Sybil defensively. 'Christine could do a lot worse.'

She could do worse, but hardly a lot thought Hester.

She stared at Christine, then across at Aunt Sybil. If Christine married Specky Souter than it would be a clear case of history repeating itself, she thought. Uncle Will had married Sybil for her money. Now it looked like the same thing would happen to Christine.

The subject of her finding a partner for the school dance was dropped as the soup plates were removed and the next course brought on.

'I was up at the paper today,' Billy announced.

'Oh, aye?' said his father.

'Didn't come in to see you as I presumed you'd be busy and not wanting visitors.'

Both men knew what Billy really meant was that he hadn't particularly wanted to see his father nor would his father have particularly wanted to see him.

'So what took you up there?' Will asked.

'Just felt like a wander round. See what was what.'

Will grunted, knowing a lie when he heard one. Billy wasn't the type to just come in for a wander round. With Billy there was always a reason.

'Who did you speak to?'

'A number of people.'

'Oh, aye?'

'Including Mathieson Lamb. Had a long chat with him.'

Will knew now what this was about. 'Did Mathieson tell you circulation has fallen away?' he asked. Mathieson Lamb was Distribution Manager.

'He did mention it, yes.'

'And now you're mentioning it to me. Is that it?'

Billy assumed a nonchalant look. 'It's a bit worrying isn't it? According to Mathieson we're down considerably on what we were this time last year.'

'We're also down overall. Did he mention that?'

'Yes,' said Billy.

'I thought he might have done,' said his father sourly. He chewed slowly on his food. His eyes taking on a faraway expression.

Billy cleared his throat. 'Is there a reason?'

Will regarded him thoughtfully. 'Let's stop beating about the bush, son. You went in to see Mathieson specifically because you'd heard something. Is that right?'

Billy nodded.

'And you being you, were immediately concerned about your inheritance. Am I right again?'

'I wouldn't put it quite like that.'

Uncle Will smiled thinly. 'I would. You've never cared tuppence about the paper as a paper. What you do care about is that one day it'll be your livelihood.' He shook his head. 'I've said it before and I'll say it again. You've no heart, Billy.'

'Business is business, whether it's newspapers or metal washers,' Billy replied.

Will shook his head again.

'And please stop being so patronizing,' snapped Billy. 'You've certainly nothing to be patronizing about.'

Uncle Will's eyes narrowed. 'And what's that supposed to mean?'

'Circulation's down.'

'So?'

'*Why* is it down?'

'A number of reasons.'

'Such as?'

'I don't have to account to you,' Will stated quietly.

Hester's gaze was going from Billy to Uncle Will and back again. This was the first she'd heard about the drop in circulation.

'The word around is that you're not up to it any more,' Billy said.

'Billy!' Sybil exclaimed, genuinely shocked.

Anger flared in Uncle Will's face, only to die just as quickly and disappear. Tiredness seemed to settle on him like a shroud. Tiredness and resignation. 'Is that what they're saying, indeed,' he mused.

Hester stared at her uncle, thinking how old he'd

become. For a second their eyes met. Then she dropped her gaze to her plate.

'Of course it's worrying that circulation is down,' Will went on to Billy. 'But every business goes through these periodic dips. It's nothing to be unduly worried about.'

'Well, it's the first time *The Glaswegian* has had a so-called dip since you took over,' Billy replied slowly.

'Which just goes to show how high a standard I set.'

'No one is denying how good you were, Father.'

'*Were*?'

'Well that's the question. Are you still?'

'We'll see,' mused Uncle Will. 'We'll see.'

They were on their pudding when Christine said suddenly, 'Why doesn't Billy take Hester to the school dance? That would solve her problem for her.'

Hester was well aware that this was yet another jibe, the inference being that she had to resort to her cousin as an escort because she couldn't get anyone else.

Billy looked startled at the suggestion.

'Sounds like a very practical way out to me,' said Aunt Sybil. 'Hester gets her escort and Billy gets to meet the Maybank girls. Who knows what could come of that?'

Put that way, the notion appealed to Billy. During the past eighteen months he'd come out of his shell where girls were concerned, and now had a string of girlfriends behind him. Nor was he currently going out with anyone special.

'What do you think, Hester?' he asked.

Aunt Sybil was right, it was an ideal solution. She smiled across at Christine to let her know the jibe had back-fired. 'Thank you for the idea, cuz. I think it's a topping one.'

Christine scowled. No matter how hard she tried she never seemed to get the upper hand of Hester.

'I'm willing if you are,' Hester said, grinning.

'You're on,' Billy beamed back.

'Huh!' sniffed Christine.

*　　*　　*

Hester and Billy sat smoking side by side in the back of the car as it sped on its way to Maybank and the Christmas dance. It was a cold, crisp night, the stars above in the black velvet sky shining like polished diamonds.

'It won't be long now till you leave school,' Billy said.

'I can hardly wait.'

'Are you still adamant about working full-time for *The Glaswegian*?'

Hester smiled at Billy in the darkness. Why was he always so amazed at the attraction the newspaper business held for her? You'd have thought he'd have accepted it by now. And that she wasn't going to change her mind.

She'd learned a great deal in the two-and-three-quarter years since she'd first started working her holidays at the paper. But there was still a tremendous amount to be learned, and how she was looking forward to doing so!

'Adamant as ever,' she confirmed.

'You'll be the first female reporter in Scotland yet,' Billy said.

'I fully intend to be.'

'If Father allows it.'

'Oh, he will,' Hester replied, conviction in her voice. Her hold over him was too strong for him not to.

'You sound very sure of yourself?'

She smiled again, but didn't reply.

'Well, if he's promised you and reneges I'll give you the opportunity when I sit in that chair. You have my word on it.'

'You're very sweet, Billy.'

'Sweet be blowed. You'd do the job well. And if your appointment was a controversial issue, then so what? It could only be good for business.'

Hester laughed. Trust Billy to think of it like that.

Tam drew the car up outside Maybank's front gates and got out. He helped Billy first from the car. Then Hester.

'May I say something Miss Hester?' he asked.

'Of course, Tam. What is it?'

His eyes shone with admiration. 'You look extremely smart, Miss. Extremely.'

She squeezed his arm. 'Thank you, Tam. I appreciate that.'

Billy wasn't overly keen on Tam's familiarity with Hester, and had spoken to her about it only recently, but she'd dismissed his complaint saying she regarded Tam as a friend as well as an Oliphant employee. Besides, Tam never overstepped the mark. He was very careful about that.

'Ten-thirty on the dot, Ritchie,' instructed Billy.

Tam inclined his head. 'Right you are, Mister Billy.' But to Hester he threw a conspiratorial wink.

The first person Hester spied was Christine hanging on to the arm of Graeme Souter. Christine and Graeme had come in his car, an old heavy-bodied tourer he was very proud of.

Christine saw Hester and Billy and waved. Hester waved back. 'She looks like the cat who's just swallowed the cream,' she whispered to Billy, who laughed.

'I hope they don't come over. I find Specky such a twit,' Billy moaned.

'Then let's dance.'

He took her in his arms and they moved off. He was a good dancer, she thought. Light on his feet with a sense of natural rhythm. Not like some of the lads she'd danced with in the past. There were an awful lot of clog clumpers about.

As they danced Hester glanced around. All the chums were present. And with men. It would have been disastrous for her to have come on her own.

Patti Forbes was with an officer in the army, a handsome chap with long moustaches and a bright shiny face.

Elspeth Simpson-Ogilvie's escort was shorter than her, and seemed to laugh a lot. Hester guessed him to be a bank or insurance clerk. Elspeth was notoriously secretive about her men friends, rarely giving away who or what they were.

Moyra McNaughton's chap was called Bill, or Sir

William Gow to give him his full title. He and Moyra were madly in love and planned to get married soon after she left school. Many of the girls already referred to her as Lady Gow.

Hester didn't know who Violet Cochrane was with. Someone drummed up especially for the occasion as Violet didn't have a regular boyfriend.

Violet glanced across at Hester and smiled in recognition. Hester smiled back. Violet then mouthed something but Hester couldn't make out what it was.

'What do you think of the Maybank talent?' Hester asked Billy.

'Some of it's rather succulent,' he teased.

She screwed up her nose at him. 'You make us sound like slabs of beef hanging in a butcher's shop!'

He gestured sideways with his head at a girl called Helen Baird who was the school fatty. In traditional comic pairing, Helen was with a very thin, weedy lad.

'There goes a good few pounds of best sirloin trotting past on the hoof,' he said.

'You're horrid,' Hester replied. Then they both giggled. 'Idiot!' she hissed.

Coming off the floor, they made for the tables at the far end of the hall where bowls of non-alcoholic punch had been set up.

'Hester! You look absolutely gorgeous.'

Hester turned to find Violet and her escort coming up behind her. 'Thank you. You look quite stunning yourself,' she replied.

Billy had stopped so that the four of them were now standing in a group.

'Roderick Eardley, I'd like you to meet Hester Dark,' Violet said.

'Pleased to meet you, Hester,' Roderick bowed formally.

'And this is Billy Oliphant,' Hester said, completing the introductions.

Billy said how delighted he was to meet Violet and then shook hands with Roderick.

They moved on to the punch bowls. Hester didn't fail to note that Violet's eyes were more often on Billy than on her partner's.

'Your cousin!' said Violet when this had been explained. 'Of course, I should have realized. Oliphant. Christine's brother.' Adding impishly, 'You and she don't look alike.'

'No,' replied Billy. 'I take after my father.'

Violet smiled warmly at Billy, drinking him in.

'I think I'd like to dance again,' Hester said. A trifle annoyed, albeit she couldn't think why. There was absolutely no reason why Violet shouldn't make up to Billy. Except that it was rather rude as Violet was already with someone who, like Hester, must be aware of what was happening.

Violet suddenly rounded on Roderick. 'Hester's half American, you know, Roderick.'

'Really?'

'Roderick's absolutely potty on America and anything to do with it.'

'Land of the future!' smiled Roderick.

'He's going there in the New Year.'

'Just for a visit. Must say I'm looking forward to it,' Roderick said enthusiastically.

'I've never been there myself. I was born in England.'

'Was it your mother or father who was American?' Roderick asked.

'My father. He came from Boston.'

'Ah!' said Roderick.

'Listen,' said Violet, as though the idea had just struck her and it wasn't what she'd been angling at since having set eyes on Billy. 'As you two have so much in common, why don't you have a dance together? That's if Billy doesn't mind putting up with me?'

Clever, Hester thought. Very clever.

'I don't mind at all. In fact I'd love to have a dance with you,' Billy replied.

Roderick beamed and held out his arm for Hester.

'I'll be going to Boston while I'm over there,' he said.

'Really?'

As she and Roderick danced she saw that several other girls were staring at Billy in open admiration. For the first time Hester saw him not just as her cousin but as a man in his own right. And an extremely handsome one he was, too.

Reluctantly she brought her attention back to Roderick who was babbling on non-stop about America and the wonders to be found there.

Bore, she thought.

'Oh hell!' exclaimed Hester as her bra strap went. She was in the process of changing having just been to a gym class. 'Anyone got a safety pin?'

Pockets and purses were searched, but a safety pin couldn't be found.

There was nothing else for Hester to do but shrug herself out of the bra and put it in her case.

'Here,' said Moyra NcNaughton who was standing beside Hester. 'You've got brown nipples.'

'So she has,' exclaimed Fanny Williams, peering at Hester's breasts.

Hester blushed. It was true, her nipples were an unmistakable brown colour as opposed to the pink they'd once been. It was the first time her classmates had ever seen her breasts exposed.

'I thought that only happened when you had a baby?' Pattie Forbes queried.

All eyes turned on Hester.

'I was told it happens when you become pregnant,' Fanny said.

Hester took her time about buttoning her shirt. 'I don't know about that but mine have always been this colour,' she said.

One of the girls giggled and turned away. Hester ignored her and went on dressing.

'Are you sure?' Elspeth Simpson–Ogilvie asked, her eyes full of gleeful suspicion.

Hester was about to retort when Violet piped in. 'You girls know nothing.'

'What do you mean, Violet?' Moyra McNaughton asked.

Violet assumed a knowing air. 'You forget that Hester's half American.'

The girls looked baffled. 'What's that got to do with it?' Elspeth demanded.

'Red Indians not only have brown skins but brown nipples as well,' she declared.

The girls all gawped.

'Are you saying Hester's father was a Red Indian?' Patti Forbes asked.

'No, of course not. But he was an American, and from a very *old* American family. It's well known that the old American families all have some Red Indian blood in them on account of the fact many of the original settlers intermarried with the Indians.'

'I never knew that,' said Moyra slowly.

'Well, you do now,' snapped Violet. Then, most convincingly, 'So if Hester's got brown nipples it's because she's inherited them from some far off Red Indian ancestor.'

There was a pause, broken at last by Fanny Williams, eyes like saucers, saying, 'Gosh!'

'Ready Hester?' said Violet.

'Ready.' And side by side they left the changing room.

They managed to control themselves till they were well away from the others. Then with a great shriek of laughter Violet collapsed into Hester's arms. 'They'd believe anything as long as you told it to them with a straight face,' she gasped.

'Red Indian!' Hester hooted.

Holding one another they roared and roared.

When their mirth had subsided somewhat Hester said, 'Thank you, Violet. I appreciate it.'

Violet squeezed Hester's hand. 'You'd have done the same thing for me.' And having said that took a deep breath and changed the subject. 'I was wondering if you'd like to spend the weekend at my home? I've already mentioned it to my mother who said she'd be delighted to have you stay.'

'I'd love to. Providing Aunt Sybil doesn't object, which I can't see her doing.'

Violet grinned. 'We'll enjoy ourselves, I promise you.'

'Gin and It. Quite *the* drink wouldn't you say?' Violet said handing Hester a glass.

The two girls were in Violet's bedroom having supposedly retired for the night.

Hester tasted the contents of her glass. 'Hmmh! Lovely,' she enthused.

'I often have a little drink by myself at the weekends. It makes me feel quite wicked,' Violet smiled.

Hester offered Violet a cigarette which Violet accepted.

On her second attempt Violet blew a perfect smoke ring. '*Très* sophisticated,' she said, but couldn't keep up what she considered to be a sophisticated, languorous expression.

Hester was wearing a negligé that Violet had insisted she borrow. It was ankle length, cream coloured and made of the finest shantung silk. A complete contrast to the cotton nighties she normally wore.

'Who was he?' Violet asked.

Hester frowned. 'Who was who?'

'The man responsible for your brown nipples.'

Hester looked into her drink and didn't reply.

Violet gave a soft feline smile. 'Will I let you into a secret?' she said.

Hester glanced up.

Violet laid down her glass and cigarette. Reaching

inside her negligé she hefted out a large, well-rounded breast. 'Snap!' she said.

Hester stared at the brown nipple, then up into Violet's face.

'I had to sell off a piece of jewellery that had come down to me from my grandmother, pretending at home here that I'd lost it. I went to a woman in Maryhill whom I was assured might be expensive but knew what she was doing. It cost me ten pounds, and was worth every penny. That was just over a year ago.'

Hester said nothing. Sadness had suddenly descended over the pair of them as they sat there in the darkness huddled in front of a blazing fire.

Violet's eyes were moist when she went on. 'The boy gave me the old heave-ho, as though I'd become some sort of fallen woman. I never did quite understand that. It was he who got me pregnant.' She smiled cynically. 'They pester and pester till they get you on your back, and then afterwards they don't want to know because you gave in to them.'

'I didn't go to an abortionist,' Hester said slowly. 'I came off a horse and that was that.' She paused, then added quietly. 'I was damaged inside by the fall. I'll never conceive again.'

'Oh what rotten luck!' Violet whispered.

Hester still had nightmares about losing the baby. And the fact that she would never have any more. One of the recurring nightmares was that of a long line of happy, gurgling babies stretching endlessly into the distance. They were all holding out their hands, entreating her to pick them up. But whenever she tried to, they dissolved in her grasp like so much smoke. Only to re-form almost instantly further away from her.

'What happened to the father?' Violet asked.

Hester came out of her reverie. 'I stopped seeing him after that.'

'Would he have married you?'

'He was already married.'

'I see,' said Violet, not seeing at all.

Violet took Hester's glass and refilled it. She said suddenly. 'I want you to keep that negligé. It suits you.'

'I couldn't possibly. . . .'

Violet cut Hester's protest off short. 'Yes you can, and you will! I've got lots. My mother is the same size as I am and tires of her clothes quickly.'

Hester stroked the silk, enjoying its touch. 'Thank you,' she said.

Violet smiled. 'We fallen women have to stick together, eh?'

Hester laughed. 'Indeed we have.'

'I liked your cousin Billy,' Violet said simply, if abruptly.

'I know. That's why you asked me here.'

'I'm glad I did. We're two of a kind, you and I. And I don't just mean us having been pregnant either. We have, how shall I put it? Common qualities.'

That was true Hester thought. They were a lot alike. Both in make up and temperament.

'Did Billy mention me afterwards?' Violet asked.

'There was a reference in the car going home. I got the impression he was taken with you.'

'Ah!' said Violet, her eyes lighting up. 'I was hoping you'd say that.'

Hester stared into the fire, watching the flames flicker and dance over the coals.

'Will you help me?' Violet asked.

'How can I do that?'

'Tell me all about him. His likes, dislikes, that sort of thing. Then you could arrange to have me at your home for the weekend.'

Hester sipped her drink. The gin was having an effect on her now, making her feel a little lightheaded. Why not? she said to herself. And wondered why she was so reluctant.

'He's mad keen on the theatre,' Hester said slowly. 'And a Russian writer called Chekhov in particular.'

Violet listened intently, her mind absorbing the information Hester fed her the way blotting paper does ink.

'You're extremely fortunate to have such an excellent cook. Ours is absolutely dreadful. But then, as my mother says, you just can't get good servants since the war,' said Violet.

The family had just risen from dinner and were now on their way through to the drawing room. Violet was talking to Aunt Sybil, who was nodding agreement.

'The war changed all sorts of things,' Sybil replied. 'And not all of them for the better, either.'

'Exactly what my mother says,' Violet smiled, at the same time managing to turn round and catch Billy's eye.

Once inside the drawing room Violet indicated a new gramophone that the Oliphants had recently bought. 'I see you like music,' she said. 'I absolutely adore it myself.'

'Popular music I take it?' inquired Sybil.

'No. Classical. Wagner is my favourite.'

'Really!' exclaimed Billy. 'He's *my* favourite, too.'

'The Ring Cycle?'

'Rather!'

Violet clapped her hands. 'How marvellous!' she said.

Like a lamb to the slaughter Hester thought.

Violet and Billy talked avidly about music for a while, and then their conversation turned to the theatre.

Hester's gaze flicked across to Will who was lost in deep dark thoughts of his own. Her relationship with him wasn't as strained now as it had been at the beginning, but it was still strained none the less. The undercurrent of what had been, and what he would still like to be, was always there. Particularly on the rare occasions when they were alone together. But he'd never once come to her bedroom since she'd forbidden him to. Nor had he so much as touched her.

112

'Isn't that incredible Hester?'

She roused herself from her dream. It was Billy who'd addressed her.

'Sorry, Billy. I was day-dreaming.'

'Violet loves Anton Chekhov. She's read all his works.'

'*Incredible*,' she agreed.

'The sadness is I've only read his plays. I've never actually seen any,' Violet said.

Billy snapped his fingers. 'There's a production of "The Seagull" on next week. Why don't I take you to see it?'

'Would you!' Violet beamed as though surprised. 'That would be absolutely marvellous.'

'Consider that an arrangement,' Billy said.

'It would have to be Friday or Saturday night. I'm not allowed out at night during the week.'

'Then Friday or Saturday it shall be.'

'Imagine you two having so much in common,' said Sybil.

'Yes, imagine,' agreed Hester.

'Isn't she a beauty!' Billy exclaimed, his eyes shining with delight.

The car standing at the kerb was a pale beige Adler 'sportypen'. It was Billy's birthday present from his parents.

'She's a beauty all right, Mr Billy. You can take my word on that,' Tam Ritchie said admiringly.

Billy ran his hand over the gleaming bonnet. 'Just what I wanted,' he murmured.

'It has a long stroke four cylinder engine with the gearbox in unit,' Tam explained.

Christine sniffed. 'Not bad I suppose. But not nearly as nice as my Graeme's.'

'That's what I like about you. You're so gracious,' Hester said to her, smiling.

113

Billy laughed. 'Nothing she can say will spoil this for me.'

'I wasn't trying to spoil anything for you,' snapped Christine.

'Would you like to share the first ride with me?' Billy asked Hester.

'I'd love to.'

'Then get your hat and coat.'

'Won't be a minute,' Hester replied, and flew into the house.

Billy got into the car and ran his hands lovingly over the wooden steering wheel. Then he reached out to caress the hand brake protruding upwards from the running board.

'She's sweet as a nut. They make excellent machines the Germans. Have to give them that,' said Tam.

'Will you crank her for me?'

'My pleasure, Mr Billy.'

Tam twirled the starting handle once, twice, and then on the third revolution the engine roared into life.

Billy stared up at the window from where his mother and father were watching him. He waved to them and his mother waved back. He knew it was due to her urgings that he'd got the car. His father had been against it as sheer extravagance when there already was a car in the family, but his mother had known how desperately he wanted a car of his own and had seen he got it.

Hester came rushing from the house with Billy's over-coat slung across her arm. It was a bitter February day and they both needed to wrap up well against the elements.

Billy got out of the car and shrugged himself into his coat. Then he put on a scarf and cap which had been in its pockets.

While he was doing this, Tam Ritchie helped Hester into the passenger seat. 'Enjoy your drive, Miss,' he said.

'Ready?' Billy asked.

She nodded.

'Then here we go!'

Tam Ritchie and Christine, the latter not all that enthusiastically, waved to them from the kerb. Sybil waved from the window, but Will just stared.

'That's put her nose out of joint,' said Hester, shouting to be heard above the noise of the engine.

'You mean Christine?'

'I was getting tired of her, Graeme's car this, and Graeme's car that!'

Billy laughed. 'He'll turn pea green when he sees this. You just wait and see.'

Hester didn't like Specky Souter either. Both of them considered him not only a twit but something of a crawler. Perfectly suited to Christine, Hester had thought more than once. They made a pair.

Billy glanced at Hester and smiled. 'It's a truly fine car,' she smiled back.

Their eyes locked. And as they did his smile faded as something flowed between them. Something they both felt and were very much aware of.

Hester tore her gaze from Billy to stare at the houses flashing by. Houses she looked at but didn't see. There was a dryness in her throat and a quivering in her breasts. 'Where are we going?' she asked.

'Just round about. Unless you fancy somewhere in particular?'

Was it her imagination or did his voice have a huskiness to it that it hadn't previously? She was suddenly very aware of the closeness of his body.

'Anywhere will do,' she replied.

'Then we'll just drive round about.'

'Yes.'

The conversation had become stilted, as though each was having difficulty talking to the other. But that was ridiculous. They'd never had that problem before. So why should they suddenly now?

It was like an electric shock passing through her when he accidentally touched her leg.

'Sorry,' he mumbled.

115

'That's all right.'

'I didn't mean to.'

'I know that.'

They sat in silence for the remainder of the drive. Nor did they again look directly at one another.

Two weeks later at dinner, Sybil said to Billy, 'And when are we going to see Violet Cochrane again? Both your father and I thought she was ever such a nice girl. Didn't we, Will?'

Will grunted.

Billy shifted uncomfortably in his chair and looked faintly embarrassed. He cleared his throat and pushed some food round his plate.

'Violet and I aren't going out together any more,' he mumbled.

Aunt Sybil's face fell. 'Why not?'

'I suppose you quarrelled,' said Christine. 'That's one thing Graeme and I never do. We've never had a cross word.'

'We did *not* quarrel,' said Billy.

'Says you.'

'Christine, mind your tongue,' her father growled threateningly.

Christine sniffed.

'It just . . . well, petered out between us, that's all,' said Billy.

Aunt Sybil studied her son, her face set and sad. She'd taken a great shine to Violet.

'I don't really want to discuss it any further if you don't mind,' Billy said.

Hester looked up to find Billy glancing sideways at her. Emotions she daren't name surged within her. Was the same thing happening to him?

When she brought her attention back to her plate it was with the knowledge that she and Billy Oliphant were in love.

★　　★　　★

116

'I believe it's actually getting worse. If that's possible,' Hester said.

Billy cursed. 'It was a daft notion going to see Aunt Win at this time of year anyway,' he grumbled.

It was a Sunday, and early that morning he and Hester had set off to see his mother's elder sister, who lived in Perthshire at Bridge of Allan. The day had dawned a cold one, the air crisp and clear, and had remained that way till half an hour before when a snowstorm had suddenly begun.

'Whose bright idea was this anyway?' Billy said as snowflakes battered into them.

'Yours,' retorted Hester.

Billy grinned. 'Well it seemed a good one at the time.'

He drove slowly and cautiously, for although still late afternoon the blizzard had brought darkness with it, reducing visibility to only a few yards.

Despite the warm clothes she was swathed in Hester shivered. Her coat, hat and gloves were covered in snow. She and Billy looked like a couple of snowmen. 'Do you know where we are?'

'Somewhere between Auchenbowie and Dunipace. But just where exactly I couldn't say.'

The engine coughed, then coughed again. Its steady rumble became an ominous whine.

'Oh, not that as well!' groaned Billy.

'Serious do you think?'

'I really don't know, Hester.'

A few minutes later their worst fears were confirmed when the engine came to a sudden grinding halt.

'What now?' Hester asked.

'We hoof it.'

'In this?'

He turned to her. 'If you can suggest something better, now's the time.'

Billy was right. Walking was the only thing they could do. To remain in the open car would be suicide.

Billy got out and then, bent almost double against the

117

driving wind and snow, came round to Hester's side to help her. Arm in arm, they trudged forward and had only gone a dozen steps or so when, on turning round to look, Billy saw that the Adler was already lost to view.

Billy was only too well aware of how desperate their situation was. This was an extremely desolate stretch of road running through fairly wild, and not very densely populated, countryside.

'There must be a few farms or crofts around,' he shouted to Hester. 'Keep an eye open for their lights!'

She nodded that she'd heard. Around them the screeching wind was heightening.

An hour later they were still walking, but Hester was near collapse. Billy was supporting her, but even his greater strength was also almost exhausted.

His legs were leaden and each time he took a step it was harder than the last. Inside his clothes his body was numb. A numbness that was steadily seeping inward to also affect his mind.

Hester was gasping, the breath harsh in her throat. What a silly way to die, she kept thinking.

Like Billy, she'd been hoping the snow storm would cease as suddenly as it had started, but now she knew that wouldn't happen. It had settled in for the night.

Hester stumbled and would have fallen had Billy not been holding her. 'Must keep going,' he gasped.

'Yes,' she mumbled.

Billy wished he'd thought to bring some whisky or brandy with them in the car.

Suddenly he had to speak. Had to tell her what he'd been keeping inside in case this was the end for them. Stopping suddenly, he swung her around so that their faces were almost touching.

'I want you to know I love you,' he shouted. Close as they were he still had to shout to be heard.

She nodded. 'And I you.'

'Oh, Hester!' he said, and pulled her against him. Their

lips met, icy cold upon each other, but burning just the same.

The declaration of what they'd each known secretly for weeks gave them fresh heart. Arm-in-arm, they made their way forward with renewed determination.

A little further down the road Hester stopped. 'Listen!'

'I don't hear anything.'

Hester pointed off to the left. 'Over there. I heard someone laughing. I'm sure of it.'

They staggered to the side of the road and down into a small ditch. Then on their hands and knees, they crawled up the bank rising out of the ditch.

Billy got to the top first. Reaching down he grasped Hester's wrist and hauled her up beside him where they both collapsed against a hedge, beyond which the land sloped away and, off to the right, a number of bright lights pierced the darkness.

'Come on,' said Billy.

But the hedge was thick and intertwined and quite impenetrable. Again and again Billy tried to force his way through only to meet with repeated failure.

Finally Hester tugged his sleeve and shook her head. She indicated the hedge and then gestured ahead. 'Let's follow it!' she yelled.

Billy nodded and, taking her hand in his, plunged along the top of the bank.

On coming level with the lights, they could now make out the silhouette of a large building from which the lights were shining; the bank, and hedge, finished abruptly to fall away below them. On their bottoms they slid down to discover they were on a drive or path that led to the building.

Sobbing with relief they stumbled up the drive and were soon hammering on the building's large front door.

Ten minutes later Hester and Billy were sufficiently thawed out to have discovered they'd landed up at The Covenanters Inn where their hosts were a Mr and Mrs McPhail.

Mrs McPhail was a well-rounded, bustling woman who, having made sure they were on the way to recovery, hurried off to the kitchen to make them something to eat. While she was doing this Mr McPhail sat round the fire with Hester and Billy and heard their story.

'My, you were lucky,' he said shaking his head when Billy had finished recounting their tale. 'You couldn't have picked a worse part of the road to break down on. The farms and houses hereabouts are all set well back off the road, you see. And unless you knew where they were you'd never find them in weather like this.'

'It was fortunate for us Hester heard someone in the inn laughing,' Billy said.

McPhail stared from one to the other. 'Laughing?'

'A man's voice,' said Hester.

'I'm the only man in the inn at the moment. We've no guests. Wrong time of year. And . . . well, I certainly haven't laughed all night.'

'But you must have done!' exclaimed Hester.

'No lass. I can assure you.'

'Then who?'

McPhail shrugged. 'There's a lot more in Heaven and Earth than meets the eye. Someone, or something, must have been looking after you.'

Hester shivered, but not from the cold this time. 'That's ridiculous!'

McPhail smiled enigmatically. 'I'm a Highlander, lass. And we Highlanders have a very open mind about such matters.'

Hester lay in the darkness listening to the wind shrieking around the inn. Outside the snowstorm was still raging.

After their meal, Billy had telephoned home to explain what had happened, and to say they were both all right and that no one was to worry. He'd promised they'd be back in Glasgow just as soon as it was possible.

She snuggled down in the bed which had been heated with a warming pan. She was dressed in a thick cotton nightdress, several sizes too large, belonging to Mrs McPhail. She felt as though she was enveloped in a tent.

She thought of Billy and excitement raced through her. She loved him and he her. *Love*! It was such a marvellous feeling. It made her heart pound and her skin tingle. It also made her feel more gloriously alive than she'd felt in a long time.

There was a quiet tap on her door. Nothing had been said but she'd known he'd come. She'd seen it in his eyes.

Slipping from her bed she let him in, instantly aware of his nervousness and uncertainty.

Taking his hand she drew him to the bed. 'Get in, you'll freeze out there,' she urged.

He came under the bedclothes to lie by her side. He still hadn't spoken.

Putting her arms around him she held him close. With trembling fingers, she undid his shirt to stroke his bare flesh.

'Do you think it's wrong to love your cousin?' he whispered at last.

'I don't know. But I do know I meant what I told you back there on the road. Wrong or not I love you,' she said, holding him more tightly.'

'And *I* love you.'

'I thought you loved Violet Cochrane?' she teased.

'I never said that! I liked Violet, I'm not denying it, but I never felt for her what I feel for you.' He was silent for a little while, then went on. 'When I was out with Violet I found myself continually comparing her with you. And she was always coming off second best.'

'We're very alike in many ways.'

'I think that's why I was drawn to her in the first place. Without realizing it I was trying to find a substitute for you.'

He was holding her awkwardly, his body tense. He seemed to be getting more tense by the moment.

'Don't be afraid about anything,' she whispered. 'I'm not.'

'I want to make love to you,' he half-pleaded, half-sighed.

'And I want you to.'

His breath was hot on her cheek as he caressed her over the top of Mrs McPhail's voluminous nightdress.

'Wait a minute,' she whispered, and, sitting up, whipped the nightdress over her head and threw it away. 'Now your turn,' she said as she snuggled back down.

His shirt, vest and underpants went over the side of the bed. When he pressed his naked body against hers, she could feel the tightness of his muscles. The tenseness was a coil inside him that had somehow to be unwound – but without him realizing this wasn't the first time she'd been with a man.

'Just cuddle me for a moment,' she whispered as his hand fumbled at her.

'Oh, I want you, Hester,' he groaned.

'Billy?'

'Yes?'

She whispered in his ear. 'Don't rush at me, love. Help me to relax.'

'I didn't mean to . . .'

'No, no, it's me. I don't want to disappoint you after all.'

'You could never disappoint me, Hester.'

For a good ten minutes they lay touching, probing, getting to know each other's bodies. She leading him all the way, and he thinking he was doing the leading.

'Well that's your virginity gone,' he whispered when at last they were still.

She stroked his belly, then laid a gentle kiss on his chest. 'Yes,' she lied.

Hester sat at her dressing table brushing her hair and staring at herself in the mirror. The face that stared back was that of a woman in love. Her eyes sparkled, her skin glowed. She'd never before known such happiness. Gone were all the dark days of the past.

It was Easter, so Maybank had broken for the holidays and she was back working at *The Glaswegian*, the other great love of her life.

Half an hour earlier Will had received a telephone call from the paper and had immediately gone into town, saying it would probably be the small hours before he returned.

Shortly after that, Sybil and Christine had gone to bed.

Hester hummed as she brushed. Since their affair had started Billy had been coming to her room once, sometimes twice, a week. They hadn't thought it wise to risk more than that, and had picked the nights when Will had had that little bit extra.

She stopped brushing when the door opened and Billy entered. He smiled at her reflection in the mirror and she smiled back. He came to stand directly behind her, reaching under her arms to touch her breasts.

'Love you,' he said.

She closed her eyes and leaned her head against his chest. He opened her dressing gown to discover her nakedness. 'Hussy,' he hissed.

'Seducer,' she whispered.

The room was beautifully warm. He slipped her dressing gown over her shoulders and down her arms. Then he kissed first one shoulder, then the other.

Their lovemaking had come a long way since that first awkward night. They never tired of finding new ways of pleasing each other.

'I love you . . . I love you . . . I love you,' he whispered over and over again.

So engrossed were they that neither heard nor saw the door open. The first Hester was aware that she and Billy were no longer alone was when she looked up to find Will, red with rage, standing at the door.

'Oh, my God!' she breathed.

123

Billy was still miles away, his eyes closed.

'I knew . . . I just knew there was something going on between you two,' Will roared.

No sooner were these words spoken than Hester felt Billy begin to tremble. Roughly, he pushed her from him and turned to face his father, cringing under his fierce and accusing gaze.

Shocked, Hester grabbed for her dressing gown, with her eyes beseeching Billy to say something.

At last Billy found his voice. 'I thought you'd been called back to the paper,' he said weakly.

Will's eyes hadn't left Hester's body, but now he turned to his son. 'Precisely what I wanted you to think.'

'You. . .'

'I wanted to find out if my suspicions had any foundation. And they had. Oh, yes, they most certainly had.'

Hester found her voice at last. 'Put some clothes on, Billy,' she ordered, backing away from Will's angry leer.

'This isn't quite the way it looks,' Billy said, pulling his pants up.

'Oh?'

Billy glanced at Hester, then back to his father, his face bathed in sweat. 'We're in love with one another and want to get married.'

From being flushed, Will's face went completely ashen. 'Like hell you'll get married,' he snarled.

Fear froze Hester. No matter what happened, Billy mustn't discover that she'd once been his father's mistress.

'You'll not stop us,' Billy said quietly.

Will's eyes narrowed as he advanced on his son. His chest was heaving, his fists clenched.

He's going to hit Billy, thought Hester, dazed with panic.

'It's quite legal for first cousins to marry. I've made inquiries about that,' Billy said evenly, as though they were having a reasonable discussion.

'Oh, have you now?'

'We've talked it over and, providing nothing happens in the meantime to alter matters, we've decided to marry as soon as I graduate from university.'

'And what will you live on?'

Billy's eyes moved to Hester, then back to his father. 'What I'm paid from my job at the paper.'

Will smiled evilly. 'No you won't. Because I won't employ you.'

'You can't do that,' Billy whispered, his eyes wild with disbelief.

'But I can and I will. I assure you of that,' his father said pleasantly.

'The paper will be mine one day. . . .'

'Only if I say so,' Will reminded him.

Billy blinked. 'What does that mean?'

'Marry her and I'll disinherit you.'

There was a pause. Hester reached out and took Billy's hand in hers, her courage returning. 'We'll have one another, Billy. The paper's nothing compared to that.'

Stunned, he turned to her. 'But it's my inheritance,' he said in a strangled voice. 'I'm entitled to it.'

'I know that. But if we have to lose it to keep one another then lose it we will.'

'No,' Billy whispered.

Will's smile grew wilder.

Desperately she squeezed Billy's hand. 'I love you with all my heart and soul, Billy. I thought you loved me.'

'I do!' he cried, looking from one of them to the other.

'Then tell your father we don't need him or his paper. We'll get by somehow.'

Slowly, almost painfully, Billy shook his head. 'But I can't do that, Hester. I can't.'

'Why not?'

'I have no money of my own. We'd be penniless.'

'You'd find a job. We'd survive.'

'I don't want just to survive! I want what's due to me! What's *mine!*'

'But I'm yours!' she cried. 'You'll regret it all the rest of

125

your days, Billy. I swear to you, you will. Nothing, not even your inheritance, is worth that.'

'Father?' Billy pleaded, his body shivering, tears in his eyes.

'The day you marry her you leave my sight for ever.'

Hester stared at these strangers. In Billy's eyes were only weakness and fear. In Will's a twisted love and triumph.

'Forgive me, Hester,' Billy mumbled, and, turning from her, fled the room.

Will laughed. 'Aren't you going to threaten me that unless I change my mind you'll take your story to the other Glasgow papers?'

Hester felt sick. Sick with the weakness and the hatred. Sick of being used. Only minutes before she'd held the whole world in her hand. Now it was all gone.

'No,' she said softly. What would be the point? Billy had shown his true colours. Even though she still loved him she didn't want him any more; she would never respect him again.

'Because if you did,' he went on coolly, 'I'd say that you were trying to besmirch my name because I'd refused Billy permission to marry you.'

He moved towards her, smiling unkindly, and she hurriedly backed away. Was this the man she had loved? The man to whom she had given her heart and maidenhood? There was a terrible violence in him that frightened her.

'As for Mary and me, I'll deny that as well. Saying it was a complete figment of your embittered imagination and disturbed childhood.'

She felt she had to fight back here. 'Doctor McLeod and Mr Smellie could confirm I'd miscarried your baby,' she defended.

'No they can't. They could confirm you miscarried *a* baby. But they certainly couldn't say it was mine. In the light of your having an affair with Billy it would appear – and I would make sure it did – that I was the forgiving and protective father sorting matters out for his errant son and niece.'

'But that was two-and-a-half years ago!'

'Who's to say you weren't sleeping with Billy even then? Only Billy, and he'd keep his mouth shut if it meant his inheritance.'

Had she ever had any chance of winning against a man like this? A man who so loved power? 'You bastard!'

His laugh was low and rasping. 'And as for there being no smoke without fire, or some mud always sticking, just look at yourself as you are now. You're not a wee lassie any more.' Close to her now, he made to touch her. 'You're a damned big one. If anyone was inclined to believe you, which would be highly unlikely, you'd have lost all the sympathy you would have had before.'

She tried to dash for the door but he took a quick sideways step and blocked her. She then tried to slide around him, but he caught her by the shoulders and held her tightly.

'I've a lot more to say to you,' he said softly, but not gently. Thoughtfully, he stroked her hair, running a finger along her cheek. 'When I first suspected you and Billy I realized right away that it could work to my advantage. But him wanting to marry you! That was a surprise. And one which has given me the power to destroy completely your hold over me.'

Without warning, his hand snaked out to crack her across the face. With a cry she lost her balance, falling limply to the floor, her dressing gown falling open to expose her. Dazed, she stared up at him, afraid to move lest she provoked him more.

'From now on things are going to be the way they used to,' he said, his eyes not leaving her nakedness. 'Exactly as they used to be.' She was mesmerized by the mingled lust and violence in his eyes.

And then he was on her, his hands viciously kneading her flesh.

127

'Open yourself to me,' he commanded.

She did as she was bid.

After he'd gone, she sat on the edge of the bed with her head in her hands. This morning her life had been filled with joy, all the pain and loneliness and confusion behind her. And now. . . .

She couldn't continue staying here. Billy was lost to her. Nor did she want him any more, no matter what promises he might make. She dreaded even the thought of further attentions from Will.

She looked at her breasts which still bore the deep imprints of his hands. In the morning they would be black and blue.

But in the morning she would be gone.

She would worry about where she would live and how once she was safely away. Now all that concerned her was escape. She only had half a crown, which certainly wouldn't take her very far. She'd need a few pounds to get her started. Five at least. Ten would be better. But where to acquire a sum like that at this time of night?

A soft smile touched the corners of her mouth as the answer came to her.

Rising, she got dressed and packed a small case.

It was strange, she thought, but even before leaving it she was already thinking of the house, and the people who lived in it, as belonging to her past.

Below stairs she knocked quietly on Tam Ritchie's door. When there was no reply she opened it, thinking he might be asleep, but a flick of the light switch revealed the room to be empty. She knew then where he was to be found.

'Hello Tam,' she said.

He looked up from where he was sitting, a cigarette dangling from his lips and a small piece of engine in his hands. 'What are you doing up at this time of night?'

he asked, frowning when he noticed the case she was carrying.

'I'm running away.'

'Oh?'

'I, eh . . . I just can't live here any longer.'

'The Colonel is it?' Tam asked.

'How did you know that?' she asked quickly, wondering just what it was he did know.

He watched her thoughtfully, obviously judging how much to say. 'There's been tension between you two for a long long while now. There are times when the two of you are alone in the back of the car together that the atmosphere's so thick it could be cut with a knife.'

'We . . . we just don't get on any more,' she stammered, relieved that he seemed to believe her.

'A personality clash, eh?'

'Something like that.'

Tam pointed to her case. 'Are things so bad you've got to run off in the middle of the night, then? And where will you go?'

'I don't know, really. I thought I'd find a cheap hotel in town somewhere. Tomorrow I'll start looking around for a job and a room.'

He placed the piece of engine he'd been fiddling with on the workbench and wiped his hands on a rag, glancing at her out the corner of his eye, as though considering something.

'So why are you here?' he asked.

'I want to borrow some cash. As much as you can lend me. I promise I'll pay you back when I'm able.' She paused before adding softly, 'I've no one else to turn to, Tam.'

He grunted, still studying her, turning something over in his mind. 'There's no need for you to worry about digs,' he said at last.

'What do you mean?'

'There's a bed for you at my mother's house. There's only her and me left in the family, and I only sleep there on my nights off. I know she'll welcome the company.'

Hester stared at Tam, astounded by his unexpected offer.

'It's nothing grand, you'll appreciate. Just a working-class home, but you're welcome to it for as long as you like.'

Hester's eyes filled with tears. 'You're a real friend Tam,' she said. 'But if my uncle finds out that you helped me. . . .'

'And who's to tell him that?' smiled Tam, picking up Hester's case. 'I can't take the car out again, they'd be bound to hear. And the trams will be off. So it's Shank's pony I'm afraid,' he said.

'Shank's pony it is then,' she answered, linking her arm through his.

Ahead lay a brand new beginning.

PART TWO
The Lily-White Boys

Two, two, the lily-white boys,
Clothed all in green O,
One is one and all alone
And ever more shall be so.

From 'THE DILLY SONG' (Anon.)

6

Hester sat at her dressing table regarding her reflection in the mirror. She was twenty-three years old and lovely to anyone's eyes. Only her eyes betrayed her maturity and depth of experience.

It was Hogmanay night, 1927. Eight-and-a-half years since she'd first come to Glasgow as a lost wee lassie. It seemed at least a lifetime ago.

She smoked reflectively as she applied her make-up. She was going to a party thrown by some friends of hers in the motor trade. It was ages, thanks to a particularly heavy workload of late at the garage, since she'd been to a party. She was looking forward to this one.

When her make-up was finally completed to her satisfaction, she rose and crossed to a full length mirror to study herself. First of all from the left, then the right. Maybe she'd become too thin.

She ran her fingers through the brand-new hairstyle which she'd had done specially for the party. Gone were her long tresses. Her hair was now chopped off at the neck in a pageboy style.

She frowned, wondering if this new style might somehow detract from her authority at the garage by making her appear frivolous. Then her frown cleared. What utter nonsense, she thought. Authority came from within. Hairstyles, pageboy or otherwise, had nothing to do with it. The garage was hers, after all. She owned it. She was the boss. Her employees would jump when she cracked the whip, just as they'd always done. Aye, and customers too who tried to come it with her.

Half an hour later she was driving through the centre of Glasgow, headed for the south side. It was three hours still till the bells at midnight and the pavements were thronged with drunks in loud if unsteady good spirits.

She veered the car into the centre of the street to avoid a fight. One man had another on the ground and was sitting on his chest, banging the unfortunate's head again and again on the cobblestones.

Once past the fight Hester promptly forgot about it. That sort of scene was common any Friday or Saturday night. She'd seen it, or variations thereof, a hundred times before.

'Hester, I'm so glad you could make it!' Rachel Levi gushed when Hester arrived at the door. In her late forties, Rachel was fat and prone to gushing. Hester rather liked her.

The two women kissed each other on the cheek, then Hester was shepherded through to where the coats were being kept. 'I've got some nice single men coming tonight, maybe you'll take a fancy to one of them, eh?' Rachel said, winking slowly.

Hester laughed. Rachel thought it scandalous that at twenty-three she was still unwed, or not seriously attached. Truth was, since Billy she hadn't met anyone she'd even have jokingly considered marrying. There had been boyfriends, but all casual.

'You never give up do you!' Hester laughed. Rachel was always trying to fix her up with a man.

'A beautiful young woman like you shouldn't be alone in life. It's unnatural,' Rachel answered.

'So's a woman owning and running a business the size of mine. But I'm happy doing it.'

Rachel sighed, her pleasant face thoughtful. 'You know I envy you,' she confessed.

'Why?'

'You're so independent. So self-assured.'

'That all?'

Rachel's brown eyes took on a malicious glint. 'You break the rules and get away with it. You stand up to men and beat them at their own game.'

Hester whispered in a mock-confidential tone, 'I

think you're more than envious. I think you're down-right jealous.'

'True. Very true,' Rachel admitted, and gave a deep, rich, fruity laugh.

Together they went through to the party and for the next few hours Hester gave herself over to enjoying the festivities.

At five to twelve, Joe Levi, Rachel's husband and another garage owner, called everyone to order. He made a little speech wishing all present the very best for the New Year when it came. And now would they please have their glasses topped up as the New Year was almost upon them.

Clutching brimming glasses, those assembled waited for the church bells to ring out the arrival of 1928.

The first bell pealed in the distance. The room erupted. Backs were pummelled. Hands shaken. Kisses exchanged. Drinks swallowed. In a corner a small jazz group hired for the occasion struck up, and a number of couples immediately began to dance.

It was because Hester was standing by the door that she heard the knocking. She called Rachel over.

'That'll be the first foot. I've arranged for it to be someone who's tall, dark and handsome. A real smasher,' said Rachel.

A few seconds later the first foot came striding in waving a bottle of whisky in one hand, a tin of shortie in the other.

'A happy New Year tae ane an' a'!' cried John McCandlass.

Well well, thought Hester. Just look who it is!

The bottle of whisky, shortie and a lump of coal John produced were duly presented to Rachel, after which a huge dram was handed to him by Joe.

'A' the best a' the time!' John toasted. To a rousing cheer he drank off the dram in one hearty swallow.

Hester stared at John McCandlass, remembering when he'd briefly worked for her and Tam. It had

135

been about a year after Tam had opened the garage, and shortly after she'd become involved with it as bookkeeper.

She'd been appalled at what she'd found in those books. Tam's business in those early days had been in financial chaos mainly due to Tam giving unlimited credit. He'd been far too soft with his customers, many of whom had taken him for a ride.

Excellent mechanic that he was, it was equally abundantly clear that Tam was no businessman. Hester had told him in no uncertain terms that if things weren't changed the garage he had left the safety of the Oliphants' to start up, the garage which had been his dream for so many years, would quickly fold.

She'd tried collecting the outstanding bills herself, but with little success. Many of those who owed the garage had laughed in her face when she'd demanded payment, telling her to go away and raffle her doughnut.

But one of the debtors had been John McCandlass. She'd recognized him immediately from the newspapers. A hard-bitten, professional policeman, McCandlass had recently been booted out of the force amid a lot of noise and hysteria from the press for suspected corruption, though the case had never been prosecuted.

For all that, she'd liked McCandlass instantly. There was something honest and straightforward about him which, oddly enough considering his background, convinced her he was a man to be trusted. With none of the usual tears or threats, he'd explained why he'd been unable to pay his bill for repairs done on his car before he'd been ousted from the force. Now he had no job, and no car, either, since he'd had to sell it to keep himself going.

And then the idea had come to her. McCandlass was, after all, an ex-cop, a man who knew the ropes, knew how to handle people, and probably how to bully them as well. How, she asked him, would he like to work for the garage, on a strictly percentage basis, keeping twenty-five per cent of all the bad debts he collected on? It might not be quite the same as being an officer of the law, but it was, McCandlass knew, a lot better than nothing. They'd shaken on it right then, and he'd started work the next morning.

And an excellent job he'd made of it, too. By the time John McCandlass was done, there had been only two debts still outstanding – and those only because the money simply wasn't there to be got.

Once or twice in the intervening years, she had wondered what had happened to him. Of all the men who had come and gone in recent years, he was the one she remembered. The one she had always been strangely curious about. It had, in fact, surprised her at the time that he hadn't asked her out – he'd been interested, she was sure of that.

A hand tapped her on the shoulder, interrupting her thoughts. 'Are you for up?' asked the man, nodding towards the dancing couples.

'Are you asking?'

'I'm asking.'

'Then I'm for up.'

Laughing, she and the man joined the other dancing couples.

It was about quarter of an hour later when John McCandlass made his way over to where she was helping herself to another drink.

'Hello there. Remember me?' he asked.

The smile he gave her made something twist inside her. She smiled in return. 'They say bad pennies always turn up again. It must be true right enough,' Hester teased. She couldn't help noticing the expensive suit he was wearing, the silk shirt and gold cufflinks. 'You appear to be doing rather well for yourself,' she added, studying him appraisingly.

'Thanks to you.'

She raised an eyebrow. 'Thanks to me?'

'It was your idea I collect bad debts for Ritchie. Well,

when I left there I thought, why not collect bad debts for other people? It's a service that must be needed, and so it proved to be.'

'So you're a debt collector.'

McCandlass smiled, both shy and proud. 'I still do a bit, but I've moved on since then. Or, to put it another way, I've expanded the services I offer.'

Hester was intrigued, but was it what he said, or that smile?

'I'm now a private investigator. And I'm a pretty good one I might add. I've got the right background.'

'Modest with it, too, I see,' Hester jibed.

Unsure as to whether she was joking or not, he shuffled nervously. 'I never believed in hiding my light under a bushel. That always seemed downright daft to me.'

'And what sort of things do you investigate?' she asked, finding herself moving towards him.

'All sorts, really. Everything from theft to infidelity.'

It surprised her how glad she was to see him. 'I'm glad you're making a go of it,' she said, and meant it.

John took a small box of cigars from his pocket, removed one, then clipped and lit it.

Hester sniffed. The aroma of the cigar took her straight back to Julian Avenue, *The Glaswegian* and her uncle in the days when she thought she loved him.

'Can I have one of those?' she asked.

John stared at her in astonishment. 'What? A cigar?'

She nodded, as surprised at herself as he was.

'But women don't smoke cigars!'

'Oh? Is there a rule somewhere that says so?'

His face creased first with laughter and then suspicion. Maybe she was only trying to send him up. 'Are you serious?'

'Perfectly.'

He took another cigar which he clipped before handing it to her. The match he struck was still flaring when he held it to the end of the cigar. She jerked her head, and the cigar, out of the way.

'You should never do that!'

'Do what?' he asked, mystified.

She put on a mock-serious voice. 'A cigar should never be lit from a flaring match. It gives the smoke an acrid, sulphurous taste which completely ruins it.'

Again he stared at her in astonishment. 'You're extremely knowledgeable on the subject,' he said slowly.

'Not really. But I had an uncle who was.'

'And what you've picked up you know from him?' John asked, striking another match, this time waiting for the match to stop flaring before offering it to her.

'Almost everything I know,' she smiled, puffing the cigar alight.

Not bad, she thought, exhaling. If she persevered she could actually come to like it.

Several people had turned to stare at Hester, but she pretended to be oblivious of them.

John's eyes darted round the room. A natural extrovert, he was enjoying the fact Hester was attracting attention.

Rachel appeared as though from nowhere. 'How about that!' she said, staring at the cigar protruding from Hester's mouth.

Hester removed the cigar and then blew smoke in a thin stream past the side of Rachel's face. 'How about it,' she said, causing Rachel to laugh. Laughter which she and John joined in.

When Rachel moved on John said. 'Where's the boy-friend tonight? I don't see him around. Or is he your husband now?'

Hester frowned. 'Who are you talking about?'

Now it was his turn to be confused. 'Tam Ritchie. Him that owned the garage.'

'Tam was never my boyfriend. A close friend, yes, but never a boyfriend.'

'I was certain. . .' John broke off, then went on, 'sorry, I obviously read it wrongly. But the pair of you seemed so . . . together. Like a couple.'

'And what about you,' she asked quickly to cover her

139

sudden confusion. 'I take it you haven't got married in the meanwhile either?' Her heart was hammering madly. She was sure he must be able to hear it. 'No,' he said, suddenly serious. 'No, not me.'

They stared at one another for a few minutes, needing no words.

The jazz group concluded the number they'd been playing to enthusiastic applause, then broke into a romantic piece called 'Log In A Mist'.

'Like to dance?' asked John, his hand already reaching for her.

As they danced, electricity seemed almost to spark between them. A glance into his eyes told Hester he was as aware of it as she was. It also told her he wanted her very much.

'If you're not married then how about girlfriends? Surely there's someone special?' she inquired, trying to sound casual and failing.

He shook his head.

She turned her face away from his, not wanting him to see her relieved expression.

They danced three numbers in a row. Then she said she wanted to leave. As he helped her into her coat she watched him silently, that something twisting inside her again as he shrugged into his own.

Goodbyes were made. Rachel gave Hester a sly wink when John wasn't looking.

During the walk downstairs he slipped his hand into hers. Outside he said, 'How about a nightcap? I have whisky and gin at home.'

'Come to my place. I'd prefer that.'

He agreed. When she found out he had his car with him she said she'd lead the way in hers and he could follow on behind.

He whistled when he saw her machine, a Lancia V4 Lambda in pristine condition which she used as an advertisement for the garage.

'Do you know much about cars?' she asked.

'A little.'

She gestured at the Lancia, and in a tone of voice most women use when imparting a favourite recipe said, 'The engine is comprised of a monobloc aluminium casting with four cast iron cylinder liners set in narrow vee formation at twenty-two degrees. It has a three bearing crankshaft and the whole unit is notably short, compact and rigid.' She glanced at John who was goggling at her. 'Shall I go on?'

'Please do,' he replied drily.

'Bore and stroke are 75 x 120mm, which is 2120cc, and a single ohc operates the vertical overhead valves. Initial output is 49 bph at 2350 rpm. Although over 3000 rpm can be attained should it be desired.' She paused, then asked, 'What sort of engine has your car got?'

'It's *British* through and through,' John replied quickly.

Hester laughed, she liked that, she liked it a lot. On a sudden impulse she pulled his head down and kissed him. She liked that as well.

John followed close behind her all the way back through the town till they reached Ritchie's garage where he parked behind her while she got out and unlocked the front gates.

When she saw him staring at her in puzzlement she called out that he was to follow her into the garage courtyard, which he did. She then re-locked the gates.

'Home sweet home,' she said to him.

John was amazed. 'You mean you *live* here!'

'And have done for a long time now,' she replied, taking his hand again.

They went through the front office and into what had once been several storerooms beyond, but which she'd had converted into a luxurious, self-contained flat.

'Toilet's over there,' she said, pointing.

As she poured them both drinks she told John the story behind her coming to live there. She'd originally had digs

141

with Tam Ritchie's mother, Dot, but they'd never really got on very well.

She'd wanted a place of her own, but hadn't been able to afford one at first. Then, after coming to work for Tam, she had the idea of converting these storerooms which Tam had been only too happy to let her have rent free as it meant there would be somebody on the premises twenty-four hours a day.

She'd had the conversion done a bit at a time, each new bit of building taking place when she was able to afford it. The basics had taken two years from start to finish.

'It's very nice indeed,' John said admiringly.

'Glad you like it.'

He had a devil-may-care attitude about him that she found most attractive. He could have been a splendid pirate, she thought. All he needed was a cutlass and a bandana.

'Ritchie's business seems to have expanded quite a bit since I was last here,' said John, seating himself on the comfortable sofa.

As though unaware, she sat beside him. 'It isn't Tam's business any more, it's mine.'

She was full of surprises, he thought. It was just one after the other. 'You mean you own this garage?'

She nodded, her hand behind him on the sofa just touching his shoulder.

'What happened to Ritchie?'

Hester slowly swallowed some of her drink, her mind flying back over the years since she'd first come here to do Tam's books. He was a lovely man, Tam, and still her dear friend, but ambition wasn't in his make-up, and never would be.

'Tam and I came to an arrangement a while ago. As a result of that, he's opened another garage out in Springburn. It's a hole-in-the-wall, but it's a one-man business and that's what he really wanted all along. He's as happy as the proverbial pig in muck.' Hester might have been talking about Tam, but her eyes never left John's face.

142

'Did you fall out, then?'

Hester smiled, shaking her head. 'This garage just got too much for him. He said it gave him nightmares towards the end.'

'So now you own it.'

'Lock, stock and adjustable spanners.'

John helped himself to another drink. A woman owning a garage! He'd never heard the like before. And not just a woman, but one who looked like an angel.

'I knew nothing at all about cars when I first came here,' Hester continued, 'but I soon learned. When I began expanding I insisted on getting the very best mechanics, poaching them from other garages when necessary. That was a trick I learned from the same uncle who taught me about cigars. Always insist on the best in personnel and plant, it never fails to pay off.'

'How many mechanics do you employ now?' John asked.

'Twenty-six, plus four apprentices. A chap called Dan Black is head mechanic and in charge of the garage floor. He's my right hand.'

'But to begin with you were working for Ritchie?'

'To begin with. After a while, though, I became a partner. Now it's all mine.'

'And Ritchie's back where he started.'

'And where he always wanted to be. It was his decision entirely. He simply felt he couldn't cope with the pressure. Tam's a wonderful man but he's strictly a small-time operator.'

'Which clearly you're not,' smiled John, studying every inch of her.

Hester smoothed down the front of her dress, suddenly tired of talking about work. She hadn't invited him back to discuss cars. 'I'm going to have a bath. Are you staying the night?' she asked boldly.

'If you'd like me to.'

'I'd like,' she said gently, amazed by her own audacity.

'Then I'll stay.' He'd never known a woman who was

143

so direct. Many men might have found it offputting, but not him. He could also be direct when he wanted. 'If you're going to have a bath can I come and watch?' he asked, almost challenging her.

She gave him a lazy, feline smile, completely unrattled. 'Rather than watching, why not join me? It's a big tub.'

Reaching for his tie he started to undo it.

'Bring the bottle,' she directed, leading him from the room.

'Here we are,' said John, switching off the engine of the Lancia. He was taking her out for a meal, but hadn't told her where.

Hester stared in delight at the brass plate fixed to the building's front door: *Press Club*.

'How did you know?' she exclaimed, overcome with excitement.

John frowned. 'Know what?'

He hadn't known of course. She'd never mentioned *The Glaswegian* to him or her indestructible love of newspapers and their world. Bringing her here had been completely accidental.

'A journalist introduced me to the place last year and I took to it. The food's good and the prices are fair. That's a rare combination in Glasgow.'

'Well,' laughed Hester, regaining her composure, 'that's enough for me.'

The atmosphere of the club hit Hester at once. There could be no mistaking the newspaper people gathered here, or the feeling of excitement and energy they generated. It might have been her imagination, but it certainly seemed to her that the tang of printer's ink was in the air. Instantly she was back at *The Glaswegian*, lost in the deafening thunder of the presses and the unforgettable odours of paper, ink and hot metal. Hester nearly reeled, reacting like a drowning person suddenly pulled out of

144

the water into the sweet, clean air. How could she have lived so long without that old, familiar, and much-loved smell?

John had a marvellous sense of humour and soon had Hester laughing at his stories and anecdotes. The champagne sparkled and Hester glowed, enjoying herself more than she had in years. Despite her protestations, John insisted on ordering a second bottle of Krug. 'You'll get me tipsy,' she giggled, touching his foot beneath the table.

'Precisely what I had in mind,' he whispered, giving her a wicked leer.

But the ensuing laughter died in her mouth when she suddenly saw who was staring at her from the other side of the room.

'What's wrong with you? You look as though you've suddenly seen a ghost,' John asked in genuine alarm.

She tried to smile, but it didn't quite come off. 'In a way I have,' she replied softly.

'Someone you know?'

'My cousin, Billy. And a girl I used to go to school with.' Billy's companion was none other than Violet Cochrane.

'Which one is he?'

Hester explained the position of the table where Billy and Violet were sitting. Surreptitiously, John glanced across at them.

'Why, that's Billy Oliphant whose father owns *The Glaswegian*!'

'That's right.'

'And he's your cousin?'

'Yes.'

John gave a low whistle. 'Nothing like having connections in high places.'

Hester stared at Billy, who stared back at her, his expression one of sheer incredulity. Tearing her gaze away from him, she brought her attention back to John, her mind overtaken by memories.

145

A few minutes later a waiter handed Hester a folded note which she swiftly read. 'Billy wants to know if we'll join him for liqueurs?'

'Do you want to?'

Did she want to sit with the man who had so betrayed her? No, but she didn't see how she could avoid accepting. Besides, there was a part of her dying with curiosity despite her bitterness.

Her legs were a little unsteady as she rose from the table, and she felt curiously light, as though a half-decent puff of wind would blow her away.

Billy came to his feet as they approached, his eyes looking as though they were about to jump from their sockets. 'Hello,' he said, his voice quavering.

'It's been a long time, Billy,' Hester replied, her own voice amazingly controlled.

Billy nodded. 'A *long* time.'

He still loved her, it was there in his eyes.

'How's the paper?' she asked politely.

'Fine.'

Hester introduced the two men. 'And this is Violet Cochrane, an old school chum.'

'Actually it isn't Cochrane any more. It's Oliphant,' Violet corrected, fairly bursting with pride.

For a moment, Hester was stunned. But only for a moment. She recalled how keen Violet had been on Billy; the weekend invitation to Violet's home to tell Violet all about Billy's likes and dislikes; the way Violet had thrown herself at him. It seemed Violet had finally got her man.

'Congratulations, to both of you,' Hester said, despite her own hurt, sincere.

Billy's mouth twitched. 'Thank you,' he replied in a dry voice, waving the waiter over and ordering doubles all round.

'To celebrate the return of the prodigal cousin,' Billy smiled. His gaze never left Hester's face. What was he thinking? What was he remembering?

Her feelings towards him were a curious mixture of pleasure and pain. *She* certainly didn't love him any more, but a fondness did linger. He had meant so much to her, and betrayed her so badly.

She watched his gaze fall to her unringed finger, his expression softening in obvious relief.

'You ran away,' he said suddenly, as though they were alone.

She refused to meet his eyes. 'Yes.'

'We searched everywhere, you know. But you vanished without trace.'

'That was what I'd intended.'

'I wanted to go to the police but Father wouldn't allow it. He was afraid of . . . of. . . . He thought it would make you angrier.'

Did Billy really believe his father was thinking of her and not the possible scandal? He couldn't be that big a fool. But then, of course, it was clear that Billy still hadn't figured out the truth.

'In the end, we assumed you'd left Glasgow.'

She shook her head. 'No, no I didn't.' His eyes begged for information and silence. She could see that he wanted her forgiveness – and also that he didn't want her to say too much in front of Violet.

'Excuse me, I'm lost,' said John, smiling uneasily.

But Violet was oblivious to the tension. 'Hester used to live with Billy's family. One fine night she just upped and ran away from them. It was all very mysterious,' Violet explained.

'How are you, Violet?' Hester interrupted. 'You're looking very well.'

'I'm marvellous. Never better. A happy marriage does that to a girl,' Violet bubbled innocently.

Billy's eyes went to John, then back to Hester. There were obviously a dozen questions he was bursting to ask her.

Violet said, 'Maybank was in an uproar over your disappearance. All sorts of wild rumours flew about.'

147

'Like what?'

'One was you'd met and had run off with an Indian maharajah. A fabulously wealthy maharajah. . .'

Hester burst out laughing. 'How wonderful, a maharajah! Where on earth did that come from? Did we elope on an elephant?'

Violet giggled like a schoolgirl. 'Where does any rumour come from? Who knows?'

'There's nothing more fertile than the imagination of young girls cooped up in a place like Maybank,' Hester agreed, shaking her head.

'You don't know how good it is to see you again,' Billy said softly, the expression on his face a caress.

Hester turned, smiling, to John. 'I'm afraid you'll have to forgive us. We've a lot of catching up to do.'

'Don't mind me, I'm fascinated.' But it was impossible to read his thoughts.

Hester brought her attention back to Billy. 'How's Uncle Will? And Aunt Sybil?'

'Mother's fine, but I'm afraid that Father . . . well . . . it's been all downhill for him, I'm afraid. He'd started to decline before you left if you remember, but after you went he just got worse and worse. You'd hardly recognize him now.'

'I'm sorry to hear that,' Hester said softly, assailed by old emotions.

'He's still in charge of the paper, but he can't go on much longer. It really is too much for him only, of course, he won't admit it.'

'Then you take over.'

Billy smiled, a politician's smile. 'At the moment I'm news editor, which I enjoy, but frankly I can't wait to get into the old man's chair and really make some changes.'

'Oh yes, your inheritance.'

He dropped his eyes, his smile vanishing.

Violet caught the undercurrent and frowned, but only for a moment. After all, Hester and Billy had always been close, she reminded herself. No doubt what she was picking up was something to do with old family secrets. Yes, that must be it, she decided: family secrets from before her time.

'And Alan Beat, the best sub-editor in Scotland? How's he?'

'As bad-tempered as ever. He still asks if we've heard anything from or about you, like everyone else at the paper. You were always popular.'

'You used to work for *The Glaswegian*?' John asked in amazement.

But it was Billy who replied. 'She wanted to be the first female reporter in Scotland. Might have done it, too, if she hadn't run off.'

'Well, well,' mused John, regarding Hester with new curiosity.

'Will you give Alan my regards? And the others who've asked after me,' Hester said to Billy.

'Certainly. But why not pop in and see them yourself?'

A thousand times she'd thought of doing just that. And a thousand times she'd stopped herself. When a wound had partially healed you didn't go and rip it open again. Only she could see now that the wound had never even begun to heal, that had been wishful thinking.

The Glaswegian. Even just saying the words to herself filled her with a warm glow; and a terrible yearning.

Hester shook her head adamantly.

'Why not?'

'You know what I feel for the newspaper business, Billy. To go back there would hurt too much. Explain that to Alan. He'll understand.'

'You still hanker after it, do you?'

Her eyes took on a faraway look. 'As your father once put it, I've inherited the family bug.'

'I could have a word with Father, I'm sure we could find a job for you.'

It was almost a temptation. But the past had better be left where it was. 'No,' she said quietly.

'There still isn't a female reporter in Scotland, Hester.

149

That honour could yet be yours. You have the capability. You know that as well as I do.'

It was a mistake coming into the Press Club, she realized that now. She should have told John to take her somewhere else. Talking to Billy like this, here in this atmosphere; it was as though she'd never been away.

'I already have a job thank you,' she replied.

'Oh, do you?' cried Violet gaily. 'What do you do?'

'I own a garage.'

Billy stared at her as though she'd said she robbed banks. 'You what?'

'I own a garage. Ritchie's. Perhaps you've heard of us?'

'Isn't that the one that specializes in foreign makes?' Billy asked. 'But that's a fairly large concern.'

'Thanks to our specializing. It was doing that that transformed us from being a pokey little shop into something different. It was your Adler that gave me the idea.'

'My Adler!'

'Remember how it broke down once and you had to get Tam to fix it because nobody could do it locally? It was thinking about that that made me realize there was no provision made for foreign cars in Glasgow. So we became the garage that specialized in repairing foreign cars, and after that there was no stopping us. It was like a snowball running downhill.'

'Hold on a minute. First of all you say you own this garage. Then you talk about *us*. Who're us?' Billy asked.

'Tam Ritchie, your father's ex-chauffeur. He and I were partners until I bought him out.'

Billy looked as though he'd been pole-axed. 'Bugger me!' he said eventually.

'Billy!' Violet exclaimed.

'He left father's employment shortly after you ran away, but we never thought to link your departures,' Billy said.

Hester beckoned the wine waiter over. 'There was no link,' she said. 'Things just happened that way.'

150

But Billy was remembering the Adler he'd got as a birthday present, and the snowstorm on the way back from Aunt Win's. The night he'd slept with Hester for the first time.

'You'll have to come and see us sometime. We're living in Kelvinside,' Violet said to Hester when they were ready to go.

Billy fumbled in his wallet, then handed Hester his card with their address on it. She accepted it silently.

She had no intentions whatever of visiting them.

7

They had awoken early with the sun streaming in through the only partially curtained window and, as though still dreaming, had made love. They had been together for eight months now, and were not only lovers but the very best of friends. How had she got through all those lonely years without John's affection and warmth? Without his companionship and caring?

Normally he stayed with Hester at her place, but this morning they were at his.

'Tea?' John asked, sitting up at last, reluctant to let her go.

'Please,' she smiled.

She watched his hard, lean, well-built body as he got out of bed and slipped on a dressing gown. Then he was gone, through to the kitchen to put the kettle on.

His bedroom was a tip. Dirty clothing lay scattered about, and there were piles of junk in every corner. The bed linen needed changing and there was thick dust everywhere. The walls and ceiling, originally light yellow, were now the colour of old custard. There was a spider's web inside and around the light bowl.

When it came to housework, John was simply lazy. It

wasn't that he didn't know how to do things, but rather that he couldn't be bothered doing them.

Several times she'd been tempted to clean the place out herself, but had always thought better of it. After all, why should she? She was his lover, not his cleaning lady.

Hester lay on the rumpled bed, not bothering to cover herself. Although early September, it was unseasonably warm.

John returned with a tray full of tea things and poured her a cup. After he'd poured his own he lit two cigarettes and handed her one.

'Hester?' he began slowly, studying the smoke from his cigarette.

'Hmmh?'

He pulled a face. 'This is a bit embarrassing.'

She knew then what was coming next. 'How much?'

'Only till Friday. I have some money due me which I should be picking up then.'

'How much?' she asked again, the languorous mood of the morning broken.

'Five?'

His borrowing money from her was becoming something of a habit – as was the fact that he didn't always pay it back.

'Hand me my bag,' she sighed.

As he gave it to her he smiled boyishly. 'Ten would be better. It's only till Friday. Promise.'

She took two white fivers from her purse and held them up for him to take.

'You're an angel,' he said, kissing her lightly on the mouth at the same time as his fingers found the notes.

It wasn't the loans that she minded. Lord knew she earned more than enough for her own needs, but his being continually short was due to extravagance and nothing else.

The dressing gown he was wearing was a perfect example. It was cashmere and cost a fortune. And though

152

he looked undeniably handsome in it, an ordinary wool one would have done just as well.

But that was John, she thought fondly. When he had money he spent it like water. Strictly a today man, he rarely gave a thought to tomorrow.

He waved the fivers at her. 'I'll take you out to dinner tonight if you fancy it?'

Incorrigible, Hester thought, unable to resist a smile. Absolutely incorrigible.

For a moment or two Hester failed to recognize him so changed was he.

The last time she'd seen him, his auburn hair had dulled and started to turn grey in patches, but now it was snow white. The face was even more flushed with the drink than she remembered, etched with dozens of deep lines that ran like crazy tramlines in all directions. And his body, the body she could still recall so well, had lost all its power and grace. It was the body of a man who was old before his time. Old and broken; used up and defeated.

'Hello, Uncle Will,' she said, trying to hide her shock.

He stared at her, speechless, drinking her in.

'I expected you long before now,' she smiled, searching his eyes. It was seven months since that night when she and John had run into Billy and Violet at the Press Club.

'Do you mind if I sit?'

'Please,' she replied, indicating the chair she kept for customers.

'I would have come directly after Billy told me where to find you but . . . well, the truth is, lass, I took ill.' He smiled ruefully.

'Badly?' Though it was hardly a question. He looked like he'd come back from the dead.

'A heart attack.'

'I'm sorry,' she said. 'Truly sorry.'

He fumbled in his coat to produce a leather case from

which he extracted a cigar. It took her back, watching him clip and light it.

'I'm not supposed to,' he said, shrugging. 'But what the hell!'

'How long were you ill?' she asked, automatically passing him an ashtray.

'I've only been allowed out of the house for a month.'

'And the paper?'

He scowled at his cigar as though it were bitter. 'I had to stand down. Billy took over. Got his great wish at last. There was nothing else I could do.'

'So now Billy has his inheritance,' Hester said softly, a trace of bitterness in her voice.

'Aye, it's all his now. At least as far as the running's concerned. I'm still the owner, though. I'm not buried yet.'

'And how's he getting on?'

'Not too bad,' Will admitted grudgingly. 'But he'll never make a real newspaperman. He hasn't got the right heart.'

Hester kept a small drinks cupboard in the office which was useful in dealing with some of her customers. 'Would you like a dram?'

'I wouldn't mind. But only if you're having one.'

She poured them each a generous tot, liberally topping hers up with water.

'Here's to you, Hester,' he toasted, his eyes never leaving her face as though the answer to some important question was to be found there.

'Why did you run away like that?' he asked suddenly, desperately.

She put down her drink with a click. 'You know why.'

'I couldn't let you marry Billy, Hester. I couldn't have stood that. Not my own son.'

'You raped me that night . . . you treated me as though I was your whore.'

'I. . . .'

'There's no excuse possible. You *raped* me.'

154

'I loved you, Hester,' he whispered, head bowed, 'I still do.'

'I know,' she answered softly. 'I know you *call* it love.'

He held out his empty glass. Silently she took it and refilled it.

'You've no idea what it was like to find you gone the next day. It had been hard enough living in the same house as you without being able to come to your bed. But to possess you one last time. And then have you vanish.' He shook his head. 'I thought I was going to lose my mind. Every day I prayed for the strength to kill myself.'

She stared at him with both loathing and love. 'You should have prayed for the strength to behave like a decent human being,' she whispered, swallowing back the tears, trying to understand this man whose passion and selfishness had nearly ruined her life.

For several minutes they stared away from one another in painful silence, their thoughts overtaken by the mistakes and misunderstandings of the past.

Will was the first to break it. 'Billy told me all about you and Ritchie,' he said in a bluff, hearty voice. 'At least you had one friend in Julian Avenue.'

'Yes. One of the best I've ever had.'

Will grunted. 'It's a successful garage, from all accounts. You're to be congratulated.'

'Thank you.'

'And it's all yours, Billy says?'

'Tam's a great mechanic, but I'm afraid that he found me and my ideas too high-powered for him. He was happy just getting by. If it had been left up to him he would have gone bankrupt within a year or, at best, just managed to get by.'

'You've got Robert Dark's determination,' Will grinned admiringly. 'And there's a bit of me in you as well.'

They stared at one another, frankly and openly, aware of all the secrets that they shared.

'Do I still look like her?' she whispered at last.

'More than ever.'

With fingers trembling, Hester lit a cigarette. She hadn't thought of her mother for a long time. And yet she still missed her so. Still longed to hear her voice and to be comforted in her arms. During the long years since her mother's death, no female friend had appeared to replace her. Suddenly, Hester felt like a frightened child again.

She realized anew how lonely she'd been. Life for her, even amongst the luxury of Julian Avenue and Maybank, had been hard and unyielding. There had never been the comfort of a woman's touch and understanding.

'This man you're with now, what does he do?' Will broke in.

'I'm not *with* John. I go out with him. I'm what you might call his lady friend. He's a private investigator.'

Will's face suddenly became cold as winter, but he said nothing.

She took his glass and poured him another. 'I don't suppose there's any chance of me seeing you from time to time?' he asked at last, nervously fingering his glass.

She regarded him closely, turning it over in her mind. 'I don't think that's a good idea,' she said after a moment.

'Only for a meal. And perhaps the theatre?'

But it wouldn't stop there. She knew that. He might be old, but he was still Will Oliphant.

'No.'

'Please, Hester?'

'No. And I won't change my mind so don't ask again.' She turned away from him, her heart pounding, her mind on fire.

He seemed to sink in upon himself, to shrivel before her eyes, the fight all gone from him.

'I think it's time you went now. I have an awful lot to do,' she said, indicating the pile of paperwork on her desk.

He came to his feet, swaying slightly. 'It was good of you to give me as much time as you have. Thank you.'

She started to rise.

'No, no, I'll see myself out.'

She sat down again, watching him as he made for the door. It was hard to believe this was the same man who'd seduced her when she was only a girl. In ten years he'd aged thirty.

He opened the door, then turned. 'If there's one thing I regret . . .' He stopped, then continued, 'No, it's stronger than that. If there's been one thing on *my conscience* it's that you can't have children because of me. I know it's asking a lot, but can you find it in your heart to forgive me for that Hester?' She didn't reply right away. 'It would mean an awful lot to me.'

Carefully she stubbed out her cigarette. She couldn't forgive him, but he didn't have to know that. 'I forgive you,' she lied.

His eyes were moist and glistening. 'God go with you Hester,' he breathed, closing the door quietly behind him.

Children, she thought, after he'd gone. Children. She looked around at the pile of work on her desk, at the pictures on the walls and the handsome carpet under her feet, listening through the room's quiet to the sounds of the garage. She had more than most women ever even imagine. More than her own mother had had.

Children. Hester sat at her large and busy desk, in her attractive office, in her successful business, with her head in her hands, a look in her eyes of indescribable loss, and cried.

One afternoon, the following spring, Hester was in Sauchiehall Street at the Charing Cross end. She'd come into town on garage business and had taken the opportunity to do a little shopping of her own.

She was just returning to her car when she walked by a gallery she occasionally browsed through, and was actually past it when she realized what she'd seen in the window. Swiftly, she retraced her steps.

It was a good painting, she thought. A damn good one. Ian McAskill had caught her perfectly – almost brilliantly.

She smiled to herself, remembering her stint as a model at the Glasgow Art School, in the period between her running away from Julian Avenue and starting work for Tam.

Things had been desperate, with jobs not to be had for love nor money, especially for an unskilled girl. Stony broke, she'd needed to pay for her board and lodgings when, in a roundabout way, she'd heard that the Art School was looking for models. No experience or training necessary.

She'd applied in the morning, and started work that very afternoon. The pay hadn't been spectacular, but it had kept the wolf from the door and Tam's mother, her landlady, off her back.

To begin with she'd been embarrassed, undressing in front of so many people. But then she'd realized that the artists weren't interested in her sexually, and with that realization she'd begun to relax and had come to enjoy the work.

She remembered Ian McAskill quite clearly. At the time he'd been considered one of the school's most promising students.

She brought her attention back to his painting of her. She was sitting in a chair, legs slightly apart and a quizzical expression on her face. The mood of the painting centred on both her sexuality and her innocence, so that she seemed child and seductress at once.

There was a statement in the painting, but Hester couldn't decide precisely what. It was an impossible picture to forget. The price ticket said 75 guineas, and she knew she had to have it.

The bell tingled as she entered the shop and the man behind the counter looked up with a smile.

Hester said she was interested in the McAskill in the window.

'Excellent canvas by a very bright and rising young artist. A local lad who's making something of a name for himself in London,' the man said as he took the painting from the window.

He stood the painting on the counter so Hester could examine it more closely. 'It's called *Lady On A Chair*,' he said.

The fact McAskill had specified lady and not woman wasn't lost on Hester. She noticed the man was staring at her, frowning.

'Have you been in here before?' he asked.

'Once or twice' she replied sweetly.

He shook his head, trying to place her. 'Then we've met before?'

'No, I don't think so.'

'I'm sorry. I'm being very ill mannered. It's just that you seem so familiar.'

She wondered whether she should tell him why, but decided not to. 'I'll buy the painting,' she replied briskly.

'I'm sure it'll bring you great pleasure. And may I also say that if McAskill becomes as big as a lot of people think he might then this will prove to be a marvellous investment for you.'

She hadn't thought of that. Nor did it really matter. She wanted the picture for itself.

'I'm afraid I don't have that amount of cash on me. Nor do I have my cheque book. May I leave a deposit and call back later in the week to pay the balance and collect it?'

'That would be perfectly acceptable.'

When she left the shop a few minutes later the man was still staring after her, the puzzled frown again creasing his face.

She wondered if he'd have worked it out by the time she returned.

That evening after work she sat down to go through her personal bank statements. She could well afford the 75 guineas she'd be paying for the painting but she wanted to see in what sort of state it left her current account.

While doing this she also added up an additional column of figures she'd been keeping, and the total she arrived at caused her to look very thoughtful indeed.

By now John was more or less living with her, returning to his own house only occasionally.

A little later John breezed into the lounge, having let himself through the front gates with the key she'd given him, and kissed her on the cheek. 'I could murder a drink. How about you?' he asked. She shook her head. 'Not now. Maybe later.'

She watched him pour himself a large one, then help himself to a cigarette from the box she always kept beside the drinks.

Anger suddenly flared in her. He was taking advantage, playing her for a mug. The more she gave him, the more he took.

'I've just been working out how much you've borrowed from me so far,' she said quietly.

He blinked, looking at her in astonishment. 'What's that, love?'

'I've just been working out how much I've loaned you over the last few months.'

'You mean you wrote it all down?'

'Of course.'

He regarded her as thoughtfully as she was regarding him. 'Well come on, tell me,' he said.

'Four hundred and ten pounds.'

He whistled, clearly surprised. 'I'd no idea it was that much!'

It was his extravagance she resented most.

'You'll get it all back, love. I swear. It's been marvellous of you to help me through this bad patch when there's been so little work around. Well, you know what it's been like. The situation's been dreadful.'

Which was true, she reminded herself. It wasn't as though he was lazy or trying to avoid work. He was out

160

every day trying to drum up business. But there simply was none.

'Is that a new suit?' she asked suddenly.

'Aye it is. Do you like it?'

Her anger, just beginning to settle, increased. That was typical of him. 'Don't you think it's a bit thick, buying a new suit in the circumstances?' she snapped.

'It's not an expensive suit, Hester. I bought it from the thirty bob tailors.'

'It's still a new suit which you hardly need. You have three other perfectly good ones.'

'I liked the material,' he smiled, fingering it lovingly. 'Don't you think it looks good on me?'

'That's not the point, John,' she replied irritably. 'You're living way outside your income. Can't you understand that?'

His face clouded. 'Oh well, if you grudge lending me a couple of bob to get by on!'

'I hardly call four hundred and ten pounds a few bob!' she retorted, her voice rising.

'I didn't realize I was into you that much, Hester, honest. But you'll get it all back. You have my word on that.'

Hester sighed. 'You're so irresponsible about money.'

'In what way?'

'In every way! When you have some it runs through your hands like water.'

A teasing smile flickered across his face. 'If when you say I'm extravagant you mean I like the better things in life, then I have to plead guilty. I always have done. Which is why I was, and still am, so drawn to you,' he said, leaning over her tenderly.

Hester laid down her pen. 'Don't try and flannel me. . . .'

'I'm not!' he defended. 'I meant what I said. And what's more you know it.'

She felt herself melting.

'Anyway,' he went on, 'my financial problems should

161

be about over. I've just landed myself a right good job today.'

Thank God, she thought. That's more like it. 'What's the case?'

'A chap having trouble with thieves at his factory. He's had the police in a number of times but they can't find out who the culprits are. The plan is for me to work there under cover and get them that way. From the inside.'

'And the fee?'

He smiled, obviously pleased with himself. 'Last year he lost a little over fifteen thousand pounds worth of goods. He's agreed to pay me ten per cent of what I save him in the coming year. So, assuming I nab the thieves, instead of losing fifteen thousand he would be down to say a thousand, or even less, per year. He'll always lose something. No matter how hard you try to stop it there's always some petty pilfering going on.'

'So your fee would be ten per cent of fourteen thousand?'

'Or whatever amount I save him. I think that's pretty good. Don't you?' he said, kissing the top of her head.

'It's not bad. But, of course, it all depends on you catching the thieves.'

He was clearly pleased to be employed again. 'I'll catch them all right. Don't you worry about that.'

The prospect of him happily working again meant as much as the money. 'When do you start?' she asked.

'Monday. My cover is going to be that of a packer. My client thinks that's the department where a lot of his stuff is going astray.'

'Then I wish you all the best of luck,' she said. 'You will be careful?'

'Of course. There's nothing to it. Just you wait and see. And Hester, I am sorry for having borrowed so much off you. I do feel a bit of a heel. But I will pay it all back. You have my solemn oath on that.'

What more could she ask? He was so appealing and genuine that her anger and resentment completely evaporated. 'All right, I believe you. I never thought you wouldn't, given the opportunity.'

His reply was to place his hand on her breast, his mouth against her neck.

'What about dinner?' she asked.

He smiled, winking. 'We'll have dinner after.'

She came to her feet and into his arms, kissing him fervently. 'Bed,' she whispered huskily.

After they'd made love he asked if now that his prospects were looking a lot brighter could he borrow another tenner just to be getting on with?

Hester laughed. And agreed.

She called back to the art shop that Friday. The proprietor, who still hadn't realized why she was so familiar, started to wrap it for her. While he was doing so the shop door opened and another customer entered.

She was startled when a few moments later a voice at her elbow said, 'Excuse me, but didn't I meet you once at Mrs Rosenbloom's? You were a customer of hers.'

She turned to find herself staring at an extremely handsome and urbane man who, because of the impression he'd made on her during that long-ago meeting, she recalled instantly.

'You gave me a lift to *The Glaswegian*,' she laughed.

He acknowledged this with a slight nod of this head. 'Rory McNeill. . . .'

'The Right Honourable something or other,' she interrupted.

He gave her a dazzling smile. 'Viscount Kilmichael, actually.'

'And I'm Hester Dark.'

They shook hands.

'May I call you Hester?'

'If you like.'

'And you'll call me Rory.'

'If *you* like.'

They both laughed.

'Here you are, Miss Dark. Thank you for your custom.' The owner handed her the wrapped painting.

'That's rather large for you to carry. Do you have a car?' asked Rory, like the gentleman he was.

She was about to answer that she did have a car, but on a sudden capricious impulse, changed her mind. 'I thought I'd get a taxi.'

'In that case, may I offer my services once again?'

'That's extremely kind of you. It would be a big help,' she smiled.

She'd send one of the mechanics to pick up the Lancia later she thought as she watched and listened to Rory conducting his business with the man behind the counter. When that was concluded, they made their way out into Sauchiehall Street, Rory carrying her painting for her.

Watching him load the painting into the boot of his car, she couldn't help wondering what he'd say if he could see what was behind the brown paper wrapping.

'I had intended having a spot of tea right about now. Would you care to join me?' he said, startling her from her thoughts.

She pretended hesitation.

'It would make my afternoon,' he coaxed.

'All right then,' she said. 'If it'll make your afternoon.'

He hooked his arm in hers.

Forward, she thought.

'Ah!' said Hester as a three-tiered rack of *petit fours* and cakes was placed in front of them.

'You approve?'

'Most decidedly.'

'Haven't got a sweet tooth myself,' Rory said. 'I wonder why it is that women all seem to? Must be a chemical thing in their make up.'

Hester chose a gorgeous chocolate cake with a cherry

164

on top. 'If women have a penchant for sweet things wouldn't you agree that most men seem to have a craving for alcohol? No doubt a chemical thing in *their* make up.'

Rory laughed. '*Touché*!'

'I really am surprised you remembered me. I was in my school clothes that time we met,' Hester said, laughing.

'And very attractive you were in them, too.'

Smooth she thought, very definitely smooth. And God was he handsome! All that and a title, too.

Hester had a second cup of tea, then started in on her third cake. 'I'm making a pig of myself but these really are delicious,' she giggled. He made her feel like a girl again.

'I take it that you're one of those fortunate women who can eat as much as they like without having a weight problem?' he teased.

She nodded, her mouth filled with cake.

'You're very lucky.'

Strange conversation she thought. She wasn't used to men discussing such things as weight problems and penchants for sweet things. It was nice she decided. Nice and refreshing. Glasgow men usually had very little to say to a woman.

'Another?' he asked, when she'd demolished the third.

'That would be sheer gluttony. I think I'll have a cigarette instead.'

Instantly his cigarette case was in his hand, a heavy silver one with his initials inscribed in a corner.

They smoked for a few seconds in silence. Hester felt amazingly at ease in his presence, as though they had always been friends. 'Tell me, what do you do?' she asked finally.

He gave her a lazy smile. 'I'm one of the privileged few. I don't do a damn thing. I'm what's called a gentleman of leisure.'

She shook her head.

'You disapprove of doing nothing?'

'Not exactly, but isn't it boring? A man should have something to occupy his mind. I believe everyone needs that.'

'Oh, but I have plenty to think about.'

'Such as?' she asked.

'I ride a great deal. I have a large house that needs running. . .'

She cut in, laughing, 'Don't tell me you actually run it yourself?'

'No,' he said slowly, 'I have servants who do that. But someone has to keep an eye on them. I'm sure you'll appreciate that.'

She smiled, thinking that rather amusing. 'You don't have a wife to do that for you then I take it?' she said.

'Alas, no.'

'And yet I distinctly recall Mrs Rosenbloom saying you were a great one for the ladies?'

He coughed. 'I have known a great many absolutely marvellous women,' he admitted, 'but in the final analysis none of them was right for me.'

'I see.'

'And you, are you married?'

'No,' she smiled.

'Now that does surprise me.'

'Why so?'

'I would have thought a beautiful woman like yourself would have been snapped up long before now.'

'I'm only twenty-four,' she replied. 'Hardly over the hill yet.'

'Dear me, was I rude? I certainly didn't mean to be.'

'I was nearly married. But in the end it simply didn't work out.'

'Brokenhearted?'

'Not in the least.'

'Good.'

After he'd paid the bill, they went outside and made their way back to his car.

'Where to?' he asked, once they were both inside. She gave him the address of the garage.

His car was a magnificent Rolls Royce Phantom I in yellow and black. It purred away from the kerb, the engine so quiet you had to strain to hear it.

'Have you ever driven a Silver Ghost?' she asked.

'Yes I have, actually.'

'And do you prefer the Phantom I?'

He gave her an amused, sideways look. 'Do you know something about cars then?' he smiled.

'A little.'

'Yes, I do prefer the Phantom. I find it easier to handle.'

It was her first time in a Phantom, and she liked the experience. 'Do you find the longer stroke makes a difference?' she asked.

He blinked, lost. 'Longer stroke?'

'Why, yes. The Phantom's stroke is 108 x 140mm which gives 7668cc.'

'Really?'

She was teasing him deliberately. Since meeting him he'd seemed so in control of himself and the situation that she couldn't resist the temptation to upset his composure. She'd been absolutely certain he'd know very little, if anything at all, about his car, or cars in general. He wasn't the type.

'Interesting wheel brakes on this model, don't you think?' she asked.

His reply was a non-committal grunt.

Hester smiled inwardly. Over tea he'd built up a picture of the type of woman he'd thought her to be; a picture she was now deliberately tearing apart.

'Surely you know they're Hispano-Suiza type mechanical servo four-wheel brakes?'

There was a fairly lengthy pause during which she made it obvious she was waiting for a reply. Finally he said, grudgingly, 'No, I wasn't aware of that.'

At least he wasn't pretending to know what he didn't. She gave him full credit for that.

'And I believe the machine gets 105bhp,' she said blandly.

She could tell he was dying to ask her what bhp was, but couldn't bring himself to do it.

They drove the rest of the way in silence, Rory completely thrown by her knowledge of cars and the internal combustion engine.

He raised both eyebrows when they pulled up in front of the garage.

'I work here,' she said.

He stared at her in wonder. 'You're not going to tell me you're some sort of female mechanic?'

She laughed. 'No, nothing like that. I own this place.'

He nodded. Then a twinkle appeared in his eye as he realized she'd been teasing him.

'Thank you for the tea,' she said, as he came round to the door and helped her out. 'I thoroughly enjoyed it.'

He took her painting from the boot and brought it round to where she was standing. 'I'll take this in for you,' he said.

'No need for that,' she replied, catching the attention of one of the mechanics. She turned again to Rory. 'Goodbye then,' she said, extending her hand for him to shake.

Her taking the initiative threw him again. She'd guessed correctly that he was used to being the one who led.

As she made her way into the garage she was aware of his eyes boring into her back. She couldn't help but wonder just how rich he actually was.

'Well?' she asked as John came through the door. He'd just completed his first day working under cover at the factory.

'I've settled into the job all right. No problem there,' he replied.

She poured him a drink and handed it to him. He looked tired. 'Any ideas yet?' she inquired.

He shook his head. 'Too early for that. They're all just faces to me so far. It'll take me a few days to get everyone sorted out. After that it's very much a case of keeping my eyes and ears open and seeing what's what.'

'Still confident that you'll catch them?'

'I'll do that all right. That fourteen hundred pounds, or whatever it comes out as, is already as good as in the bank.'

She decided to have a drink herself and crossed to pour one. When she turned to talk to him again she discovered he'd slipped off to sleep.

She went through to the kitchen to put the meal on.

Through the glass-panelled front of her office she watched the Phantom drive into the garage. It was the week following her tea with Rory. She'd been expecting him back. She'd even dreamt of him once or twice, confused, restless dreams that left her hot and bewildered.

She dropped her eyes to her desk and immersed herself in some paperwork. Let him come all the way to her. She had no intention of going out and greeting him.

'Come in!' she called when there was a knock on the door.

She waited till he stood in front of her before looking up. 'Oh, hello!' she said, feigning surprise.

'How are you?'

'Fine. And yourself?'

'Never better.'

He was just that tiny bit nervous. Which certainly pleased her. She gestured him to a chair.

'To what do I owe the pleasure?' she asked.

He coughed, clearing his throat. 'The old girl needs a service. You seemed to know so much about her when we were chatting the other day, I thought I'd bring her to you.'

That car needed a service about as much as she did a third leg she told herself.

'We specialize in foreign cars only,' she explained. 'A Rolls Royce is hardly that.'

'I'm sorry, I didn't realize,' he stumbled, clearly crestfallen.

She smiled at him. And waited, saying nothing.

He started to rise. 'It seems I've wasted your time . . .'

Before he could finish she interrupted. 'But in your case, and because it's a Rolls, a car for which I have enormous respect, we'll happily accommodate you.'

His face lit up immediately. 'That's splendid!'

'Shall we get all your details then?' she said, producing an invoice pad with a flourish.

'Address?'

He gave it to her.

'Telephone number?'

He gave her that also.

'And it's a service.'

'Yes, please,' he replied, his tone suggesting something else.'

Service, indeed, she thought. And smiled inwardly.

'Why can't I come in?' Rory asked. They were in his Rolls, parked just along from the garage, having just returned from dinner together.

'Because I've got work to do, which I won't get done if you're there,' Hester lied.

Rory drew her to him, and she came not unwillingly.

His mouth tasted of salt. This close, she could smell the faint tang of expensive cologne.

He kissed very differently to John. There was more subtlety in Rory's kiss, a delicacy in the way he used his tongue, in the way he held her in his arms.

'You're so beautiful,' he murmured. 'So very beautiful.'

Then his lips were again on her mouth. Caressing. Touching. Asking questions.

170

She pulled herself away. This was ridiculous. 'Rory, please, this is silly.'

He caressed her hair. Then her neck. 'I'm mad about you. You realize that, don't you?' he breathed.

She was attracted to him. Very attracted. And perhaps had been since the day she met him at Mrs Rosenbloom's. But there was John. John with whom she had known the first true joy of her adult love.

'I shouldn't have gone out with you tonight. It was a mistake,' she said, overwhelmed with guilt.

He stiffened, but didn't move away.

She hurried on. 'It's not that I don't like you. I do. Tremendously. It's just that . . . well, the truth is that there's someone else.'

He took her hands in his. 'This other person, do you love him?'

That was the question she found so difficult to answer. She certainly didn't love John the way she'd once loved Billy, with all that innocence and eager passion. Her feelings for John were more sober and quiet; more mature. Whether that constituted love or not she couldn't really say.

Love was such a small word to encompass so much, she thought. Instead of one word there should be a dozen or more to convey all the various shades of meaning.

'You don't love him, then?' persisted Rory, not letting go her hand.

'I don't know. But I am extremely fond of him.'

'Why did you see me tonight then, Hester?'

That was difficult to answer as well. One part of her had been only too aware that she was being disloyal to John. And yet, knowing this, she'd still gone ahead and manoeuvred Rory into asking her out.

For that was precisely what she'd done. Starting from the moment she'd bumped into him in the art shop and accepted his invitation to tea.

'What I mustn't do is go out with you again,' she said firmly, dodging his question.

The hands gripping hers tightened. They were stronger than they looked.

'I want to see you again, Hester. And I will.'

'Do you always get what you want?'

'No. But I *nearly* always do.'

There was something exciting about him. And different. Oh, yes, he had a title and was rich, but that wasn't it. It was the man himself. She knew she'd have been drawn to him no matter what his station or financial position.

Suddenly she realized just how confused she really was. On the one hand there was John whom she cared about and wanted. She was clear about that. Their relationship was a good one and would be even better once the niggle caused by his money problems had been cleared up.

But, on the other hand, here was Rory. Fresh, new and exciting. A man like none she had ever known before.

'I must get in,' she said.

'Can I see you again, Hester?'

She should tell him no. Cut whatever was starting to develop between them right here and now. Make a clean break of it.

'I'll phone you in a couple of days,' she whispered.

It wasn't particularly cold as she walked the short distance to the garage, but she started to shiver almost from the inside out.

John glanced up from his paper as she came into the lounge.

'How was your day?' she smiled.

'Excellent. I made real progress.'

'Drink while you tell me about it?'

'I'll pour them,' he said, rising.

She could see he was bursting with his news. Feeling guilty, she resolved to be the most attentive of audiences.

'I've found out how it's being done,' he announced, when they were both seated with glasses in their hands.

She opened her eyes wide. 'How?'

172

'Simple really. In fact hellishly so. There's a chap works alongside me called Joey McKay. A wee, dark-haired fellow, quiet sort, not very friendly. Anyway, that's neither here nor there. What is important is that he lives in a tenement adjoining the factory. You can actually come out of his kitchen window onto the factory roof. See the possibilities?'

'I'm beginning to.'

'I put two and two together when I discovered there's a small skylight right at the back of the factory which is just big enough for a small man to get through. And Joey McKay is certainly small.'

'Is he doing all the thieving on his own then?' she asked.

John shook his head. 'There are at least six of them involved. There has to be that for them to move the stuff and cover one another while they're doing so. McKay and three others I'm certain of. The remainder I still haven't worked out. But I will. And soon.'

'You're very clever,' she said admiringly, flushed with affection.

He beamed at her, pleased with himself. 'Come and sit on my lap,' he said.

She snuggled up against his shoulder.

'You know you're the best thing that's ever happened to me,' he said in a quiet voice.

Her guilt cut into her like a knife. She closed her eyes as he spoke again.

'I'll succeed, Hester. Not just in this job but generally. I'll make something of myself. And make you proud of me. I swear it.'

A tear trickled from her eye. She brushed it away with a finger. She felt so rotten, she would have done anything to start the night again.

John went on. 'I know I'm a bit daft at times, but don't ever leave me because of it, will you? Oh, love, you've come to mean just about everything to me.'

He'd never spoken to her like this before. For the first time he'd completely opened up.

'I won't leave you,' she whispered.

'I've never mentioned marriage up to now. But I want you to think seriously about it.'

'Are you proposing?'

'Not quite yet. I won't do that till I've paid back the money I owe you and got myself a few quid in the bank. But I will be, Hester. Unless you want to tell me right here and now to forget any such idea?'

She was choked with emotion, and could hardly speak. 'Let's go to bed,' she managed to whisper.

'Aye. Let's do that.'

Her eyes were moist and glistening with tears as they made their way through to the bedroom.

'No, Rory, I'm sorry. But I definitely can't,' she said into the telephone.

'But why?'

'I've thought it over and it would be completely wrong of me to see you again. I'd be leading you on which just isn't fair.'

'Maybe I don't mind being led on.'

Hester sighed. 'You're not making this easy for either of us,' she said.

'I don't intend to.'

'Listen, Rory, I take all the blame for what's happened. . . .'

'Nothing has – yet.'

She puffed on her cigarette, desperately trying to think of the right words to get herself out of this. She was determined to end things between them here and now.

'Can't we just be friends?'

'Certainly. Let's meet and talk about it,' he laughed.

God, but he was persistent. Under different circumstances she would have found that most flattering.

'Has this boyfriend of yours found out about us, then?' Rory asked.

'No, he hasn't.'

'Then why the change of heart? I thought we got on splendidly the other night.'

'We did.'

'So what's the problem?'

She sighed again. 'I've told you. I already have a chap and it would be disloyal of me to see someone else. Now I have to go. I have a garage to run.'

'What about your word?' he said quickly.

'What word?'

'You gave me your word you'd go out with me again.'

'I did nothing of the sort!'

'You may not have exactly said it. But you did imply it.'

This was impossible, she thought. It seemed the only way she was going to get rid of him was to vanish.

'One last meeting. Please?' he pleaded.

'No, Rory. And that's final.'

'Then I'll come round to the garage this evening and speak with you there,' he threatened.

'No!' she exclaimed in panic.

'Well, then?' he chuckled.

For once the boot was on the other foot. He was throwing her off balance. Through the glass-panelled front of her office she could see Dan Black making his way towards her.

'I really do have to go,' she said.

'Do we meet or do I bang on your gates?'

She gave in. The last thing in the world she wanted was him meeting John. She named a time and place.

Rory said he'd be there, then hung up before she could change her mind.

She was smiling and feeling decidedly mellow as she headed the Lancia in the direction of the garage. Lunch had been excellent. The claret, nectar. The conversation, on Rory's part anyway, extremely witty and amusing.

He is marvellous to be with, she thought. Funny,

serious, highly intelligent, irreverant, charming, thoughtful. In fact all the things a woman looks for in a man. And so rarely finds.

She giggled suddenly remembering the tag line of a joke he'd told her. The joke had been disgustingly filthy and yet somehow he'd got away with it without being offensive or even crude.

She was humming when a little later she turned the Lancia into the garage forecourt. The humming died abruptly when she saw Dan Black deep in discussion with a uniformed policeman.

Both Dan and the policeman glanced in her direction when she drove the Lancia to where she normally parked. Immediately they started to hurry in her direction.

Dan opened the door and helped her from the car. 'What's the trouble, Dan?' she asked as the door banged shut behind her.

'It's John McCandlass,' Dan blurted out. 'He's had an accident.'

'Oh, my God, he's not. . . !'

'No,' Dan interrupted, shaking his head. 'But he's in a bad way.'

'And asking for you,' the policeman added.

Hester took a deep breath. 'Take me to him,' she commanded. 'Take me right away.'

8

Sister Reid was a tall, no-nonsense type of woman somewhere between forty and fifty. Her face was grey and tired, dominated by eyes that had seen just about every facet of human suffering there is – and forgotten none of it.

'Mr McCandlass has been repeating your name

endlessly ever since he was brought in,' she said. 'You and he are very close I take it?'

Hester attempted a smile which disintegrated into a sort of wavering grimace. 'You could say we're unofficially engaged.'

'I see.'

'And what eh . . . what exactly is the extent of his injuries?'

'Both legs have been broken, and an arm. There's also some internal damage. The degree of which we're not sure of yet,' Sister Reid replied grimly.

What a catalogue, Hester thought. Poor John. 'How did it happen?' she asked.

'According to what we've been told a heavy wooden crate fell on him. He's lucky he wasn't instantly killed.'

Hester put a hand to her mouth. Her stomach was churning with nausea and she also felt lightheaded.

'Would you like to sit here for a moment before going on down to see him?' Sister Reid asked kindly.

Hester shook her head.

'I'll have a cup of tea brought to you.'

'Thank you. That would be most welcome.'

'If you'll follow me then.'

Curious eyes were turned on Hester the moment she entered the ward. There was one small cot square on in the centre aisle. A young boy of about four or five smiled at her as she passed.

There were three beds in the ward surrounded by screens. John's was one of them

'Oh my God!' she exclaimed softly when she saw him.

Both legs were in plaster as was his left arm. From his pelvis to his chest, he was swathed in bandages.

'Hester. . . .' he mumbled. 'Hester . . . Hester . . . Hester. . . .'

There was a chair by his bed, where she now sat. Reaching out she clasped his right hand. 'I'm here, John. I'm here.'

'Hester . . . Hester. . . .'

177

She squeezed the hand, gently stroking his face.

'I'm here, John. I've come to be with you,' she said.

Suddenly he stopped his endless repetition of her name. The faintest of smiles settled on his lips.

'Good,' said Sister Reid, nodding. 'He's recognized your voice. That's what we were hoping for.'

Hester wanted to take off her coat, but couldn't bring herself to let go of his hand.

'The doctor thought that you being here might bring him round all the sooner. It sometimes works with loved ones,' Sister Reid said.

Hester turned her head away. She didn't want the Sister to see she was crying.

'I'll get that cup of tea,' Sister Reid said tactfully. And left Hester alone with the semi-conscious John.

'Miss Dark? Miss Dark?'

Hester exclaimed and came awake to discover Sister Reid shaking her by the shoulder. 'I'm sorry, I dozed off,' she apologized.

The Sister laid a cup of coffee and a plateful of sandwiches on John's bedside table. 'I want you to have these and then go home,' she said.

'But. . . .'

'No buts about it, Miss Dark,' Sister Reid interrupted. 'We asked you to come in. Now we're telling you to go home and get some proper rest. You have been at Mr McCandlass's bedside for thirty-six hours, after all.'

Hester nodded. She was bone tired and desperately craved a bath, a hairwash and her own bed.

'If you're sure there's nothing else I can do?'

'Your being here has made him a lot easier in himself. He'll come round when he's ready, it seems. And not before.'

Hester rose and stretched her aching back. She felt a wreck and was certain she looked one as well. 'Will you telephone me at home if there's any change? Or if he becomes distressed at my leaving?'

'You have my word on that.'

On the way back up the ward Hester, noticing an empty space, asked what had happened to the little boy in the cot.

'Wee Bobby Love,' Sister Reid said, the vaguest trace of pain in her voice. 'We lost him during the night.'

Hester remembered some minor commotion during the early hours, but she hadn't looked out from behind John's screens to see what was going on.

'You mean he's dead?'

'Yes,' Sister replied, giving a thin, rueful smile.

Suddenly, Hester felt like crying again.

She took off her coat and hung it up. She was about to go into the bathroom and run the bath when she remembered the fire hadn't been on so there wouldn't be any hot water.

She briefly thought of making the fire but decided she didn't have the energy. She would sleep first, then bathe.

She poured herself a large whisky, sinking into a chair in front of the long-dead fire.

She could still smell the hospital. Its stink seemed to have permeated her clothes and hair. It was a strange smell; sinister and foreboding. Chloroform mingled with the acrid odour of human fear.

She'd tried to talk to one of the doctors about John's internal injuries, but he had refused to speculate, saying they wouldn't know what was what until a series of tests had been carried out and analysed. These tests, he'd said, couldn't be done until after John had regained consciousness.

She was still thinking about John and the hospital when sleep abruptly descended on her. A profound sleep enjoyed by only the totally exhausted.

She was brought awake by the insistent ringing of the telephone. A glance at first the clock, then outside, told her it was the following morning. She'd slept right through.

'Miss Dark?'

'Speaking.'

'Sister Reid here. Mr McCandlass regained consciousness half an hour ago. The doctors are with him now. After that the police want to speak to him. If you come in about an hour he should be free by then.'

'The police? What have they got to do with this?'

There was a pause, then Sister Reid said, hesitatingly, 'Well . . . I did hear it said that perhaps Mr McCandlass's accident wasn't one. That the crate was pushed. At least that's what Mr Rice and the officers seem to think.'

'Mr Rice?'

'I believe he owns the factory where Mr McCandlass works.'

'I see.'

'You'll come in an hour then?'

'I'll be there, Sister. And thank you for telephoning me. I do appreciate it.'

Hester hung up, then stared off blankly into space. It had never entered her mind that someone had tried to kill John. And they'd come within a whisker of doing so, too.

The thieves at the factory had found out that John was on to them. That was the obvious explanation.

She shook her head. John hadn't been nearly as clever as he'd thought.

The screens were still round John's bed and he had a visitor, a short, tubby man with a bald head, presumably Mr Rice.

'The police have gone, I'm told,' she said to John after kissing him hello.

'Aye. Not long since.' He was pale and drawn, but obviously happy to see her.

'A terrible business,' said Mr Rice.

'And nearly a fatal one,' commented Hester.

'I've given the police the names of Joey McKay and the others I'm certain are involved in the thieving. They're on their way now to pick them up,' John said, clinging on to Hester's hand.

'You're sure the crate was pushed?' Hester asked.

'Oh, it was that all right,' Rice replied quickly. 'No doubt about it. The way those crates are stacked it's impossible for one to fall unaided.'

'Did you hear or see anything?' Hester asked.

John shook his head. 'One moment I was walking along. The next I was in this bed with doctors and nurses fussing round me.'

'You've not to worry about the money side of things, John. I'll see you right,' Rice said.

'If I'd known I was going to end up like this I'd have charged you more than ten per cent,' John joked.

Rice looked thoughtful, then said, 'I think that's fair comment. I'll up the percentage to twelve-and-a-half. How's that?'

'Music to my ears,' John answered, grinning despite his obvious pain.

'Right. I'm sure you two want to be on your own for a while. So I'll be away.' Rice made his goodbyes to Hester, then, with a final salute to John, disappeared through a gap in the screens.

'An extra two and a half per cent!' John exclaimed jubilantly.

'Those thieves must have really had the wind up to attempt murder,' Hester said.

John's expression became grim. 'It was bloody careless of me to let them discover I was on to them. A bad mistake on my part.'

'We all make those.'

He shook his head in self-condemnation. 'Bad lads,

181

yes, but murderers? I just didn't figure them for that at all. Another mistake,' he said bitterly.

In answer, she kissed his hand.

He changed the subject. 'Sister told me that you stayed by my bedside for thirty-six hours when I was unconscious. Thank you, Hester.

'You needed me. So I came,' she said simply. She took his right hand and squeezed it. 'From now on you'll have to concentrate on getting better. That's the important thing.'

'I'll be out of here before you know it,' he bluffed, putting on a brave smile.

She knew then that he was desperately worried about his undiagnosed internal injuries. 'Of course you will.'

'Kiss me, Hester.'

His lips were cold and almost lifeless. His breath was tainted from the medication he'd been given.

The screens parted and a nurse entered carrying a kidney-shaped dish covered with a cloth. 'You'll have to go now, I'm afraid,' she ordered Hester.

'Can I come back later?'

'If you mean outside the regular visiting hours you'll have to speak to Sister about that.'

'I'll see what she says,' Hester said to John. 'Hopefully she'll make an exception. At least for today.'

'I'd like you to be here. Or around. It would help,' he replied in a small voice.

The nurse removed the cloth from the dish to reveal a very large metal syringe filled with a colourless fluid.

Hester gulped when she saw the size of the syringe. It looked more appropriate for an elephant than a human being.

'I'll just have that word with Sister,' Hester said. And fled.

Hester poured herself a large glass of the Dutch gin, Jonge Genever, that she'd developed a taste for of late. It had been an extremely busy day, and then there had been John to go and visit after the garage shut. She'd been to see him every single day of the two-and-a-half weeks since he'd been in hospital.

She was thinking with dismay about the bother of having to cook herself something to eat when the telephone rang.

'Hester, it's Rory McNeill. How are you?'

She was pleased to hear from him but pretended otherwise. 'Do you never give up?' she asked.

He chuckled. 'That's how we aristos get to the top in the first place. Try, try and try again.'

'Well, you're certainly very trying,' she jibed.

'Now I know you don't mean that!'

He had such a nice, warm voice, as though it were filtered through velvet. 'To what do I owe the honour? I thought I'd made it clear I wasn't going out with you again,' she said.

'Ah! But that was before I discovered *the surprise*.'

She frowned. 'What surprise?'

'The one I've got for you when you come to my home for dinner.'

She was intrigued. Just as she knew she was meant to be. A surprise? And very mysterious sounding. Whatever could it be?

'I told you I've already got a boyfriend,' she said.

'I'm advocating dinner, Hester. Nothing else.'

She was tempted. Particularly as she was bored silly having stayed in alone every night since John had been injured.

'Will there be other guests?' she asked hopefully.

'I can have a chum of mine and his girlfriend along if that'll make you feel safer.'

That settled it. She needed a break she told herself. And she did so enjoy Rory's company.

'When did you have in mind?' she asked.

'The sooner the better. How about tomorrow night? Could you manage that?'

'Let me think now,' she mused, making him hang on as though she was consulting her diary. 'Yes, that will be all right. What time?'

'Eightish for pre-dinner drinks?'

'I'll see you then,' she said.

'I'm looking forward to it,' he replied. And was chuckling when he hung up.

What on earth could this *surprise* be, Hester wondered.

A footman answered her ring. 'This way if you please.'

If the house was impressive from the outside then it was even more so inside. The decor was tasteful and expensive, showing not only money but knowledge and background. Money alone could have bought the house, but not its furnishings.

Her wrap was taken from her and she was shown through to a drawing room where she found Rory standing before a roaring fire, sipping champagne.

'Welcome to my home. Be it ever so humble,' he said as she entered the room.

'Humble indeed!' she smiled.

He set down his champagne glass, took her hand and kissed it gently. 'You look ravishing,' he said. 'And I can't tell you how pleased I am that you've come.'

'The others haven't arrived yet then?' she asked, glancing around the empty room.

Rory pulled a face. 'Bad news there, I'm afraid.'

She raised a sceptical eyebrow.

'Peter, that's my chum, rang twenty minutes ago to say he's suddenly come down with the most dreadful, and dreary, tonsilitis. He's devastated that he can't meet you and sends his apologies. Naturally the girl he was bringing wouldn't come on her own.'

'Naturally,' said Hester.

'I didn't arrange it this way, I promise.'

'But now it's happened you're not complaining?'

He gave her a soft smile, 'No, not too much.'

'Where's the surprise then?'

He wagged a finger. 'Patience is a virtue. Not till after dinner,' he said.

He poured a glass of Dom Perignon and handed it to her, then took up his own glass and clinked it against hers.

'What's the toast?' she asked.

'To absent friends.'

She frowned, thinking he was getting at John, but quickly realized he was referring to his friend Peter. 'To absent friends,' she echoed.

Hester thought the meal disappointing: the gravy was cold; the vegetables overcooked; the custard a thick, gooey mess which, had she been in a restaurant, she would have sent back immediately.

'Port?' he asked when the meal was concluded.

'Please. And a cigar if you have one.'

He stared at her, completely taken aback.

'Any objections?'

'No. It's just . . . a . . . little unusual, that's all.'

'I don't smoke them regularly. Just from time to time when the mood takes me. And it's taken me now.'

'Then a cigar you will have!' he declared, ringing for the butler.

When their cigars were lit, Rory having decided to join her, Hester said, 'Now, what about that surprise?'

He gave a secretive, pleased-with-himself smile. 'For that we have to go into my study. Bring your drink.'

The study wasn't at all what she would have expected. She'd have thought to see lots of wood, leather, that sort of thing. Instead it had a distinctive feminine air about it.

'What do you think?' Rory said, indicating a painting hanging over the fireplace.

It was a McAskill – an unmistakable one. The pose was different to the painting she had at home. Here she was standing sideways, her head twisted around so that she appeared to be staring straight out from the painting. There was a sad, reflective, almost tragic expression on her face.

'Spitting image wouldn't you say?'

She turned from the painting to him. 'You think so?'

'Oh, definitely! Of course, I wouldn't know the more intimate details, but that face is you to a T.'

Hester sipped some port, then puffed on her cigar. 'Where did you buy it?' she asked, though she already knew the answer.

'That gallery where we first bumped into one another.'

'Interesting.' She turned her attention back to the painting. She actually preferred it to her own.

'I wonder who she is?' Rory said.

Hester had refrained from committing herself. Wondering if he'd realized it actually *was* her. Now she knew he hadn't.

Should she tell him, or let him go on thinking that the woman who'd posed for the painting was her *doppelgänger*?

'I take it you bought this painting because she looks so much like me?'

'That's correct.'

'I'm flattered.'

'It doesn't . . . offend you in any way? I was slightly worried about that.'

'Not in the least.'

'I just had to buy it once I'd seen it.'

'An expensive whim for a moment's amusement,' she replied.

'There was more to it than that, Hester,' he said, his voice wavering just the tiniest fraction.

She decided then that she was going to tell him she was the painting's subject. But not yet. 'One surprise deserves another. When can you come and have dinner with me?' she asked.

He feigned outrageous amusement; so much so that he caused Hester to laugh.

'You mean . . . I'm actually invited to the inner sanctum? The holy of holies?'

'Well, I wouldn't exactly call it that. But yes, you are,' she laughed, liking him even more than she had before.

'Tomorrow night?'

She had meant to deal with some pressing paperwork tomorrow night, but she could put it off till the following evening. The only real trouble was getting a meal prepared *and* visiting John. She smiled inwardly as the answer came to her.

'Tomorrow night,' she agreed.

She looked more lovely than he'd ever seen her; more lovely and more relaxed. 'Welcome to *my* humble abode,' Hester said, ushering him in grandly.

Rory stared about him, taking everything in, especially her.

Hester pulled a bottle of Dom Perignon from an ice bucket and handed it to him. She'd bought a case especially that morning.

'Will you do the honours?' she asked.

He removed the cork expertly, and quietly, then filled two fluted glasses almost to the brim. Seeing her at home, he now realized, was different from seeing her anywhere else. She was so completely Hester.

When their glasses were empty she told him to refill them, then sit at the table. When she re-entered the room she was carrying two plates, a newspaper-wrapped bundle on each.

Rory frowned as his plate was laid before him.

'*Bon appétit,*' Hester smiled and sitting across from him immediately began unwrapping her bundle.

Rory started to laugh. A laugh that became a full-blooded roar. 'You really are the absolute limit!' he finally spluttered.

Although the table was set with cutlery, Hester was using her fingers. 'I hope you like fish and chips,' she

187

grinned mischievously, popping a piece of batter into her mouth.

'I adore them,' he said graciously. 'Especially with champagne.'

For the next few minutes they ate in silence.

Rory noisily sucked his fingers when he was through. 'First class,' he announced.

'I thought it would be a change from your usual fare.'

He refilled their glasses. 'The newspaper makes all the difference.'

Hester nodded her agreement. 'Now, how about some pudding?'

'Oh, yes, please.'

She placed his dirty plate on top of hers, scrunched the papers into a ball, and disappeared from the room.

When she returned she was holding a very large ice cream cone in either hand.

'I hope you like raspberry on top,' she said, handing him his.

'Some prefer to have it without, but I'm not one of them,' he winked.

'Port and cigars after this. Then the surprise,' she said, her mouth rimmed in ice cream and syrup.

'You mean the meal wasn't it?'

'Oh no, there's something more,' she replied, smiling mysteriously.

A little later, when the port had been poured and the cigars lit, she told him to follow her. At the door to her bedroom she paused.

'Just because I'm taking you into my bedroom doesn't mean I'm inviting anything untoward. Is that clear?'

'Crystal.'

Inside she flicked on the light, moving to the foot of the bed.

'Snap!' she said, pointing to the painting hanging over the headboard.

Rory blinked. Hester moved to stand beside him. 'Same subject. Same painter. Different pose,' Hester said.

'How? I mean . . . Hester, I don't understand.'

'It's me,' Hester said quietly. 'Did you really not know?'

Rory was thunderstruck. 'You?'

'Me,' she nodded. 'In the flesh.'

He looked from the painting to her, and then back again to the painting. 'Good Lord!' he exclaimed. 'I can't believe it!'

'Do you wish to leave now?' she asked.

'Why should I?'

'I thought you might be embarrassed, dining with a notorious artist's model.'

Rory laid his port down on the bedside table. 'Do you have any whisky?' he asked weakly. 'I think I need something stronger.'

She led him back to the other room and poured them both a stiff one.

'Tell me about it,' he said, studying her with new interest.

Hester gave him a carefully edited version of her running away from Maybank and Julian Avenue, and then having to find a job to pay for her keep. 'The Art School was all I could find at the time,' she explained. 'I had no training or skills, you see. Maybank didn't educate us for work, heaven knows.'

'Fascinating.' Rory shook his head in wonder. 'But how did you progress from that to owning a garage?'

She explained about her friendship with Tam, and how she'd started off doing Tam's books, and how gradually one thing had led to another.

Rory listened to her story in amazement, asking the occasional question when he wanted some point or other expanded on.

He had never known a woman like this before. She was one in a million, that was certain. More resourceful and independent than he would have supposed.

'I've thoroughly enjoyed last night and tonight,' he said, when it was time for him to go.

189

She helped him on with his coat. 'I have too.'

Suddenly his lips were on hers and his tongue inside her mouth, searching passionately. He clasped her close, running his hands up and down her back.

She pushed him away. 'Enough Rory,' she ordered breathlessly.

'I've never been attracted to any woman as I am to you,' he whispered huskily, almost pleading.

She tried to bring back the lightness of the evening. 'I'll bet you say that to all the ladies.'

'No, I don't. That was the first time.'

She believed him. She couldn't not.

'The parents are having a do on Saturday. Will you come with me? Please?'

Her first impulse was to refuse him. But he was such fun to be with. And what could be the harm?

'Please, Hester?'

'I don't know,' she hedged, reminding herself of what the harm might be.

'They'd love to meet you. I know they would.'

'I . . . .'

He could see her hesitation. 'Good. That's settled then. I'll pick you up here at half-past seven,' he stated firmly.

Before she could say anything further he was gone, vanishing round the bend in the stairs.

'Two hundred pounds in advance,' John said, his eyes shining. 'I thought that was very decent of Mr Rice.'

'It was the right thing for him to do in the circumstances,' Hester replied. 'After all, you can hardly earn when you're laid up here.'

'I still think it was decent of him. And it gives me the chance to pay back some of that money I owe you.'

'What you owe me can wait for the moment.'

'No, no! I insist. It would make me feel better.'

She laid her hand on his. He was very pale, his cheeks

190

still sunken. He didn't look at all well. No matter what the doctors claimed.

'There's no need. But if it'll make you feel better then I'll accept a little something on account. Twenty-five, say.'

'Twenty-five be damned!' he roared. 'I'm giving you a hundred.'

Typical John, she thought. Always the big gesture.

'Say you do give me a hundred. Will the hundred that's left be enough for you to get by on till you're fit to work again?'

'Och, more than enough.'

'Are you sure? What about your rent and things like that? Not to mention your day-to-day expenses: cigarettes, drink, food.'

He grinned, disarmingly. 'Well, if my money runs out I can always borrow the hundred back again, can't I?'

Incorrigible, she thought. Absolutely incorrigible. 'Of course you can,' she smiled ruefully. 'Of course you can.'

'The doctor had a long talk with me this morning,' he said after a silence, his tone changing completely.

'What did he say?'

'It seems my liver has been badly damaged. He thinks that they should operate.' He dropped his eyes but not so quickly that she didn't see the fear there.

'When?'

'Next week sometime. Possibly Thursday or Friday.'

She was at a loss for words. What could she say? 'Is it a big operation?'

'The doctor said he wouldn't know for sure until he opened me up. It might not be as bad as he fears.'

She could well understand John's alarm. She would have been terrified herself. 'Is there any . . . any danger?' she asked in a voice just above a whisper.

'The doctor says not. I'm healthy otherwise, after all. There shouldn't be any complications.'

Was he lying so she wouldn't worry? She would ask the sister on her way out. She wanted to know the truth – not what John would say to spare her.

'I miss you awfully,' John said softly.

Gently, she stroked his hand. 'I miss you too.'

'I'll have to go,' Hester said as a nurse announced that the visiting hour was at an end. 'Promise me you'll rest, love. That's the best thing for you.' She rose from the bedside chair, bending again to kiss him on the mouth. Suddenly, all she could think of was how much she missed him: the feel, and touch and scent of him.

'See you tomorrow,' he said, reluctant to let her go.

But the next day was the Saturday of Rory's parents' party. It was impossible for her to visit John *and* go.

'Oh, love. Do you mind if I miss just this once? I'm behind at the garage and I just must have an evening all to myself to get it sorted out,' she lied.

He tried to hide his disappointment. 'I understand. You mustn't neglect the business because of me.'

'Till Sunday, then.'

'Aye. Till Sunday,' he echoed, finally letting go of her hand.

At the doorway of the ward, Hester turned to wave goodbye, but he was not looking her way.

Rory's parents lived just outside the small Renfrewshire village of Ranfurly, and the drive was a pleasant one.

It was a beautiful summer's night, stirred by a warm, gentle breeze. The blood-red sun hung low in the sky, casting a primeval light on the heathered countryside.

Hester's thoughts kept returning to John. Sister had assured her that though there was a certain element of danger in the forthcoming operation, there was nothing to be unduly worried about. John was a strong, healthy man, Sister had reassured her. There was every reason to believe he would take the operation in his stride.

'Penny for them?' Rory asked.

'I was just thinking that I should get out of Glasgow more.'

'You work too hard. At least I think so.'

'Work doesn't bother me. I enjoy it.'

'That's obvious,' he smiled.

'You should try it sometime. It might do you the world of good,' she jibed.

'Are you offering me a position?' he asked eagerly.

She caught the double entendre, as he'd intended her to. 'No,' she said firmly, but couldn't help smiling.

'Pity. I think we'd make a good team. In fact, I'm certain of it.'

'Are you now?'

'Oh, yes,' he replied softly, reaching out to lay his hand lightly on her thigh.

Hester removed his hand and put it back on the wheel. 'We don't want an accident do we?'

He smiled. 'I'm glad you came tonight. I've been thinking virtually non-stop about seeing you again since that night at your place.'

'I'm flattered. But it's all rather futile isn't it?'

'You mean because you already have a boyfriend?'

'Yes.'

'Perhaps. Perhaps not,' he replied smoothly.

It would never occur to Rory that he wouldn't get his own way.

At the lodge gates they stopped while the gates were opened for them. The road leading to the house was narrow and full of twists and turns. On either side of it were mature fir trees, dark and foreboding, stretching away into Stygian blackness. Then, abruptly, they were out from behind the screen of trees and into the open again. Hester was momentarily stunned when she saw the size and grandeur of the house looming in the middle distance.

'It doesn't have a name. The folk in the village and round about just refer to it as The Big House,' Rory said.

And appropriate that description is, too, Hester thought. It looked more like a palace than a house.

'The family seat,' Rory explained. 'And has been since 1497 when it was built. The family was temporarily

193

displaced after Culloden, because we'd mistakenly fought on the losing side, but the next generation did some political manoeuvring which returned to us our possessions. And the two generations after that got us back on our financial feet by a series of brilliant overseas investments. To this day we still own large tracts of Canadian lumber, an Australian sheep station and the biggest money-maker of all – a Colombian emerald mine.'

Hester stared at the house, blazing with light from what seemed to be a hundred windows.

'I think you'd better tell me about your mother and father before I meet them,' Hester said, suddenly feeling very uncomfortable and unsure of herself. She'd been expecting something special, but nothing quite like this. A Colombian emerald mine indeed!

'Father and Mother are the Earl and Countess of Strathmere.'

'And how do I address them?'

'You call them Lord and Lady. It's that simple.'

'And this party, what sort of party is it going to be?'

'Well,' said Rory, untypically flustered, 'it isn't a party exactly. It's more of a ball.'

'What?' Hester turned to him in disbelief. Before leaving her home she'd asked him if she was dressed appropriately, and he had assured her that she looked absolutely splendid. A vision, he had said, entranced by the contrast between the deep crimson of her new dress and the coal black of her hair.

'A ball. The parents always have one at this time of year.'

Hester was torn between fury and panic. 'You might have warned me. I'd have dressed differently had I known.'

'I did tell you. You look absolutely splendid. If I'd thought your apparel was the least bit inappropriate I would have said. I'm not that insensitive, for God's sake.'

'Still, you should have told me,' she pouted.

He parked in front of the house alongside another Rolls. Every car there was an expensive one.

She took his arm walking up the short flight of steps leading to the front door which was flanked by two footmen.

The assembly was a glittering one, the men dignified and handsome in their evening dress, the women fairly alight with jewels.

The ball room was huge, illuminated by row upon row of sparkling crystal chandeliers. Its floor was inlaid marble, its walls and ceiling cream and gold.

'There you are, Rory. We were beginning to think you weren't going to make it!' The man who spoke was undoubtedly Rory's father, the resemblance was so unmistakable.

Rory turned with a smile. 'I always like to arrive late. You know that, Father. It's part of my style.'

The earl was the same height as Rory, but his hair was silver and he had a healthy outdoor complexion. His eyes, like his son's, were warm and kind.

'Allow me to introduce you,' Rory said to him. 'Father, this is Miss Hester Dark. Hester, this is my father, the Earl of Strathmere.'

Hester took an immediate liking to the earl. But not to the countess, who suddenly appeared beside him.

'Have you known my son long?' she asked, giving Hester a long, appraising look and clearly not being satisfied. 'He's never mentioned you.'

This one is a proper bitch, Hester thought. The countess would make even Aunt Sybil seem giving and kind.

'We were first introduced years ago when I was still at school,' Hester replied, evenly. There, let's see what the old cow makes of that.

'And which school was that?'

'Why, Maybank, of course,' smiled Hester sweetly.

'Maybank!' the countess exclaimed, taken aback. 'Then there's someone here you'll know.'

Hester's heart sank, fearing the worst. 'And who is that?'

'Miss McSween, who used to be headmistress there. She retired recently, of course.'

Oh Christ, thought Hester with a hopeless sigh.

'Hector, see if you can find Miss McSween and bring her over,' the countess commanded her husband.

'I think I know where she is,' replied the earl, obviously used to this sort of treatment, and strode away.

Rory handed Hester a glass of champagne from the footman's tray. A drink was just what she needed.

Miss McSween! Of all the rotten luck! She dreaded to think what Miss McSween was going to say to her – yet alone about her.

Miss McSween didn't look a day older than Hester remembered her. The white hair, despite the occasion, was still tied back in a bun, the eyes still flinty and hard; the skin still thick and leathery.

'Well, well,' said Miss McSween on joining them.

It suddenly dawned on Hester that she wasn't scared of Miss McSween any more. She was a full grown woman now, not a child, and well able to look after herself.

'Good evening, Miss McSween,' she said politely.

'So it is you, Dark,' said Miss McSween, exactly as though they were still at Maybank.

'*Miss* Dark,' Hester corrected.

'You do remember Miss Dark then?' the countess asked with some surprise.

'Oh, indeed I do! Miss Dark was the only girl ever to run away from Maybank. It caused quite a sensation at the time.'

The countess looked as though she'd been struck.

'And not only from school, but from her aunt and uncle as well. It was quite a scandal, I assure you. Imagine, after all the Oliphants had done for her, taking her in and caring for her when her parents died.' Miss McSween looked as though the shock might still kill her.

Hester could still recall the thrashing she'd had from

Miss McSween. And how much the headmistress had enjoyed it. Just as she was enjoying herself now.

'There were personal reasons for my behaviour,' Hester said quietly. 'And I have absolutely no intention of disclosing them.'

'I'm sure you had your reasons, gel,' the earl suddenly piped up. The women both threw him looks like daggers.

'Where did you go, Dark?' Miss McSween persisted.

'*Miss* Dark,' Hester corrected again.

'*Miss* Dark, then.'

Hester sipped her champagne. 'I never left Glasgow. I took lodgings and found myself a job,' she said, at last.

'Good for you, gel!' exclaimed the earl.

The countess shot him a reproving glance which he completely ignored.

'A job,' Miss McSween disapprovingly. 'Surely you mean a career?'

'I went to work in a garage. Call it what you will.'

The countess looked shocked. 'A garage!'

'Well, I'm blowed,' said the earl.

Miss McSween's eyebrows arched in distaste. 'And you a Maybank girl,' she hissed.

'I don't see that it's common to earn your way,' replied Hester. 'And, furthermore, I now own the garage. And a thriving business I've made of it, too, thank you very much.'

'Jolly good for you, gel!' exclaimed the earl, receiving another reproving look from his wife.

Hester thought Rory was being exceptionally quiet during this exchange, but a glance at his face told her that he considered her entirely capable of standing up for herself. She rather liked him for that.

'I think a woman owning a garage is an absolutely splendid thing,' boomed the earl. 'After all, if they could drive trams and buses during the war why shouldn't they own garages? Female emancipation and all that.'

'Hector!' exclaimed the countess, shocked.

'How many people do you employ, gel?'

'Thirty-five, including myself.'

The earl's eyes twinkled. 'There's nothing common about that. Enterprising's the word more like. And now I'm going to ask you for a dance, Miss Dark?'

'It would be my pleasure, My Lord.' Then added, just a trifly coyly, 'And you may call me Hester.'

Miss McSween's expression was thunderous.

As Hester moved off on the earl's arm she glanced back at Rory who gave her a wink.

'Thank you for a marvellous evening. I thoroughly enjoyed myself,' Hester said to Rory at the garage gates in the frail dawn light.

'Aren't you going to invite me in for a nightcap?'

She considered him with mock-seriousness. 'Only if you promise to behave.'

He licked the tip of his finger and traced the sign of the cross over his heart. 'Word of honour.'

'All right, then.'

She was tired, but happy. Today was Sunday so she could sleep as long as she liked, then have a nice hot bath and laze till it was time to go and see John.

As she poured a whisky for Rory and Jonge Genever for herself, she thought about the ball and the people she'd met there. Rich people, fabulously so many of them, enjoying their pleasures and privileges to the full. That life attracted her immensely.

'You were a big hit. Especially with the old boy. But then you know that,' Rory said, as she handed him his glass.

Her choice of dress had turned out to be inspired. If she'd known it was to be a ball, and in that sort of company, she would have chosen something less dramatic and more formal. As it was she'd stood out, but acceptably so.

'Tell me, will you be earl when your father dies?' she asked.

198

Rory nodded.

Which meant that the estate and its mansion, not to mention the Colombian emerald mine and the other lucrative sources of income, would all belong to him – and whoever he married.

'Were you impressed by tonight?' Rory asked.

'Should I have been?'

'You tell me.'

She smiled. 'I met some very nice people. Also some horrors. . . .'

'Amongst which we can count Miss McSween,' laughed Rory.'

'Amongst which she was most *definitely* counted,' Hester affirmed. Then added, after a short pause, 'I had a good time. What else would you like me to say?'

He gave her a searching look, but didn't go on.

'What are you doing a week today?' he asked suddenly.

'Why? What do you have in mind?'

'You mentioned earlier that you wanted to get out of Glasgow more often. Well, why don't we do just that? I'll pick you up here and we'll drive wherever the fancy takes us.'

It would be good to get away from everything – even for only a day. 'We could have a picnic!'

'Jolly good idea! I'll provide the hamper and the wine. Is it agreed?'

'All right, but I'll have to be back here by early evening.'

'The boyfriend?' asked Rory, a humourless smile on his lips.

Hester nodded, wondering how much she should say. She hadn't told Rory about John being in hospital. Not only was it none of his business, but it seemed to her unfair to John to tell Rory all about him and him nothing about Rory.

Rory laid his glass aside, then came to his feet, 'Shall we say ten o'clock? That way we can make a real day of it.'

'I'll be ready and waiting.'

At the gates she stopped to give him a sisterly kiss goodnight, but he took her in his arms, holding her as though she were some rare and precious item he was afraid of damaging.

He kissed her long and deeply. Then he kissed her again.

'Till next Sunday,' she murmured, pulling away.

He bent suddenly, kissing her on the neck. There was something extraordinarily intimate about that kiss.

A shiver ran through her. At that moment it would have been the easiest thing in the world to take Rory through to her bed and lose herself and all worries and fears of the past weeks in his arms.

But there was John.

'Till next Sunday then,' Rory said, turning away.

She remained standing there watching him as he walked to his car.

A copy of *The Glaswegian* lay spread before Hester. She was gazing at it fondly, her mind filled with memories, wondering what might have been if Billy had never happened. Perhaps she really would have gone on to become Scotland's first female reporter.

How she missed working for *The Glaswegian*. The hustle, the bustle, the smell, the thunder of the presses. Being without it was almost like being without an arm or a leg.

No, she thought grimly, it was even worse than losing an arm or leg. It went deeper than that.

She stared round her office. The garage was a huge success, entirely through her own efforts, and yet it meant almost nothing. She'd have sacrificed the garage gladly to have been able to walk into *The Glaswegian* and take up again where she'd left off.

'Damn!' she muttered angrily, gathering up *The Glaswegian* and screwing it into a ball. 'Damn! Damn! Damn!'

As the paper thudded into her wastepaper bin the telephone rang.

'Yes?' she snapped.

'May I speak to Miss Dark, please?' a woman's voice asked.

'Speaking.'

'This is Theatre Staff Nurse Lancaster at the Southern General Hospital. . . .'

Hester's heart skipped a beat. John had been scheduled to have the operation sometime that day, but had insisted that she stay away.

'I'm ringing about Mr McCandlass.'

'How is he?'

'You'll be pleased to know that the operation was a success. He's still under anaesthetic, but he should be coming round fairly soon.'

Hester gave a sigh of relief. She'd barely slept at all the previous night and had been edgy and restless for days. Despite the assurances she'd had, she'd been worried and anxious that something might go wrong.

'May I see him tonight?'

'Yes, I'm sure you can. But for a little while only.'

'I understand.'

'Goodbye, then.'

'Goodbye. And thank you for taking the trouble to ring me.'

When she again focused her attention on her work, she felt as though a great weight had been lifted from her shoulders.

Promptly at ten the following Sunday morning, Rory appeared at her door, dressed very sportingly in a blazer and flannels.

She asked him where his boater was and he said that he thought that would be going too far, even for him.

Once in the Phantom, Rory suggested that he just point the car and let it take them where it would.

Soon the ugly grey sprawl that was Glasgow was left behind as they headed north west towards the Clyde coast. The day was warm and sunny, with only the occasional cloud floating in the enormous blue sky.

'I hope you didn't forget the hamper?' Hester said as they turned northwards at Dumbarton.

'Everything's arranged,' Rory smiled in reply.

He was a handsome man she admitted to herself. In fact almost beautiful. She would possibly have preferred it if he had been a little more rugged looking like John.

Hester looked up as the car flashed past a sign which announced they were headed in the direction of Loch Lomond. Another sign further along the road said they were about to enter Balloch. Rory turned left to head up the west bank of the loch. The loch itself, when it came into view, was calm and enticing, making Hester wish that she'd thought to bring a swim-suit with her.

'How about here?' suggested Rory, pulling the Phantom off the road.

They stopped on some grassy ground beside a clump of trees, the water of the loch lapping at the shore less than a dozen feet away.

'Absolutely perfect,' declared Hester. After the city, it was paradise.

They got out of the car and strolled to the water's edge to stare out over the loch. Hester could see a castle on the far bank and off to the left, a number of islands, some covered with trees, rising up out of the loch.

'Listen, what's that?'

Rory cupped a hand to his ear. 'Sounds like music to me.'

Music it was. Romantic and haunting – and it was coming from somewhere close by.

'Champagne, Miss Dark?' asked a cultured voice behind her. She started in fright, and turned around to discover Rory's man, Harkness, smiling at her for all the world as though he were in the drawing room back home. He held two glasses in one hand, a bottle of unopened champagne in the other.

Hester stared over Harkness's shoulder in amazement to where, from the clump of trees, three gypsy musicians magically appeared.

'I thought this was supposed to be some sort of mystery tour?' Hester said to Rory, her eyes bright with excitement and delight.

'It was a mystery to you, wasn't it?' replied Rory in feigned innocence, deliberately popping the champagne.

Hester laughed as the champagne bubbled into her glass. 'This is just marvellous,' she said, bubbling herself.

'I'm glad you approve.'

'If you don't mind, I'll get on with things now,' Harkness said, and giving them a little bow, he disappeared round the trees.

What next, wondered Hester. To Rory she said, 'You've been to this spot before I take it?'

'Only with Harkness. We did what I believe is called a recce yesterday.'

Hester watched Harkness set up a folding table. Over that he threw a snow-white cloth. On the cloth he laid a vase containing a dozen red roses.

'You're the first woman I've ever brought here if that's what's flitting through your mind?' said Rory, eyeing her sideways.

Which was precisely what had been flitting through her mind. 'After we'd been to the ball at your parents you asked me if I'd been impressed. Well, I am now. I've never been so impressed in my life.'

The cold meal Harkness laid out was magnificent. There was galantine of duck with liver paté stuffing, two whole lobsters and a beautiful fresh salad. And after that, succulent strawberries topped with thick cream. There was also a variety of cheeses including white and blue stilton.

They ate slowly, enjoying their food, their surroundings, the music, the conversation – and each other.

By the end of the meal they were on their third bottle of champagne. And Hester was feeling the best she had felt in her life. This was, indeed, the way to live.

'Can I sketch you?' Rory asked suddenly.

'If you like.'

'Against a background of the loch I think.'

She rose, feeling deliciously sensual, and wandered back to the lochside. Behind her the gypsy trio continued to play, the music now almost wistful and moody.

There are certain days in one's life – though very few – which always remain in one's memory as a time of complete happiness and perfection. Hester knew this would be one such day for her.

'Standing or sitting?' Hester asked when Rory appeared beside her, armed with sketchbook and pencils.

'Sitting. With the water behind you.'

Harkness brought over one of the chairs for Rory while Hester seated herself on a grassy tussock. The wind played warmly against her skin, the sun seemed almost to kiss her. How long had it been since she'd last felt so alive? And had she ever been so pampered or made to feel so special?

Covertly, she glanced at Rory, already immersed in his sketching. Not only was he handsome, but worldly and mature as well. Although fourteen years older than she, she found that an advantage. It gave him the wisdom and strength of character she'd always sought but never found.

Of course, there was also his immense family wealth. Rory was a fabulous, once-in-a-lifetime catch, that no one could deny.

The question she still hadn't resolved within herself, and on which she now pondered, was how serious was he about her? Because if he was deadly serious, and if she could encourage him, then marriage could be the outcome.

The breath caught in her throat at the prospect. Viscountess Kilmichael, future Countess of Strathmere. A member of the ruling class, and stinking rich to boot.

Was such a thing possible, she asked herself. A warm glow filled her that had nothing to do with either the champagne, the food or Rory's company. The image of herself at fourteen, as she had been when she came to Glasgow, came back to her.

Rory sketched for a good hour-and-a-half during which he asked her to change position several times. Finally he looked up and smiled. The furrow of concentration that had divided his brow disappeared. 'Enough for now,' he announced with a laugh.

Hester rose and stretched. 'Can I see?'

'If you like. But remember, I'm only an amateur who does it for the enjoyment.'

There were three different sketches. Hester studied each in turn. Two of them were very plausible indeed.

'Not bad,' she said. 'You're better than you think.'

Rory looked like the proverbial dog with two tails. 'That's very kind of you to say so.'

'Not at all, it's true. You definitely have talent. But tell me, why have you made me so slim?' she asked, leaning against him as they studied the drawings.

'You are slim.'

'But not as slim as you've made me. Why, in this sketch here, I look positively boyish.'

He took the sketch in question and stared at it for a moment. 'Let's just call it artistic licence shall we?'

'Can I keep one of these?' she asked.

'I'd be honoured. Take your pick.'

She would have it framed and hung in her bedroom as a memory of today, she decided.

Harkness was gone, having packed up everything during the sketching session and reloaded it into the van, hired especially for the day, which had been waiting beyond the clump of trees. The gypsy trio was also gone.

'Would you like a stroll before heading back?' he asked.

She nodded.

They put the sketches and sketching items on the back seat of the Phantom. Then Rory presented her with a rose. 'A perfect flower for a perfect girl,' he said almost solemnly.

'Thank you.' Without even thinking, she pressed the rose to her breast.

Hand-in-hand, they walked along the lochside, gloriously happy and content, as though caught in a magical moment.

John was sitting up in bed and staring vacantly into space. It was the Wednesday night after Hester's trip to Loch Lomond with Rory and her confusion over the two men was worse than ever.

Hester could see right away that he was depressed. 'Hello, love,' she said, kissing him on the cheek.

He smiled at her. Pleasure at seeing her momentarily replacing the worry in his eyes.

'How are you tonight?'

He pulled a face. 'A little bit down.'

'Why's that?'

'The doctor's sending me to a hospital out in the country, called Garnhill. It's a place for long-term patients. It seems they need the bed here.'

'I see,' said Hester, her heart suddenly skipping a beat.

'They think the country air will help my recuperation. I'm still going to need a fair bit of convalescence to get over everything.'

'And just where is this Garnhill?'

'Stirlingshire. A wee bit north of Denny.'

'And when do you go?'

'Next Monday morning.' His voice was slightly strained.

She understood the reason now for his depression. Garnhill was too far away for her to visit him nightly as she had been doing.

'I'll come every Sunday – without fail,' she assured him.

206

He gave her a resigned smile. 'According to the doc I'll be there between three and six months. But it's more likely to be nearer six than three.'

'That's not so long!' she said cheerily, trying to lighten his mood. 'It'll fly by before you know it.'

'I can only hope so,' he said glumly.

'The main thing is to get you well and fit again, John. Nothing else matters.'

'Oh, but it does, Hester. You matter. You're more important than anything else to me.'

A lump came into her throat so that she could barely speak. 'Thank you,' she whispered.

'I love you,' he said. 'I love you so.'

Tears filled her eyes. She turned aside, fussing with the things on the table, so he wouldn't see.

'I think about you all day long. And every night, you're in my dreams.'

'I think about you too, John. All the time.' How she wished it could be that simple again.

'It's going to be dreadful only seeing you once a week.'

'I know, dear, but it's just till you're better.'

'This is only a temporary setback, Hester, you wait and see. I'll be a success yet. I promise you. I'll make up for everything.'

'I know you will.'

'Do you like children?' he asked suddenly, getting excited.

'Yes,' she admitted reluctantly, 'of course I like children.'

'We'll have lots then. A whole houseful of them. Six for you and six for me.'

'A whole houseful,' she agreed, almost choking on the bitterness of the lie.

She rummaged in her handbag for her hanky. All the old hurts stirred to join the new ones. Love? She still didn't know whether she loved John or not, but one thing she did know: she didn't want to hurt him as she had been hurt by others.

When she'd dried her eyes she stared into his, flinching

inwardly at the trust she saw there. If only things were black and white! But of course, they never were. If life had taught her nothing else it had taught her that.

9

Hester liked Rory's friend, Peter Elliot, thinking him enormous fun. He was a tall man, the same age as Rory, but he was completely bald on top, with just a fringe of hair left over the ears and at the back of his head. There was an unusual softness about him, as though his flesh contained more fluid than was normal, and he had quite a distinct paunch. But he was marvellous at telling blue jokes.

Hester was roaring with laughter as she and Rory tottered through from Peter's dining room where they'd just finished dinner. Moments earlier Peter had delivered the tag line of the evening's bluest story yet.

Behind Hester and Rory came Peter and his girlfriend, Antonia Bowie, known to everyone as Tony.

This was Hester's first meeting with Peter and Tony, but she'd taken to them instantly – as they had to her.

Both men were extremely mellow. A great deal of wine had been consumed before and during dinner, and Hester was none too sober herself. Neither she nor Tony, however, were swaying as badly as the men as they walked across the room.

'My God, but Cambridge was marvellous!' exclaimed Peter, collapsing onto a sofa with Tony. 'How I miss the old place.'

'I'll bet you were a right couple of rakes when you were there,' Hester teased.

'My dear,' winked Peter, 'you'll never know the half of it.'

'Cambridge and beloved Magdalen College,' Rory

sighed. 'It nearly broke my heart when it was time to leave.'

'How many times were we sick on beer?' asked Peter, as though actually eager to know.

'Without number,' Rory smiled back.

'The University Arms,' said Peter. 'The starting off point for many a drunken debauchery.'

'Tell us more about that,' coaxed Tony.

'The pub or the debaucheries?'

'The *debaucheries* of course!'

Peter laughed and kissed Tony wetly on the lips. 'It would shock you to hear, my love,' he teased.

'Peter is exaggerating. Which, you no doubt must realize by now, he is somewhat prone to do,' Rory intervened, laughing. 'What he calls debaucheries were no more than a couple of undergraduates, namely he and myself, letting off steam.'

'I'm disappointed,' frowned Tony. 'I was dying to hear some juicy tales.'

'Were you two friends all the way through University?' asked Hester.

'Longer than that,' Rory replied, with a fond look at Peter.

'We were in the same class together at Kelvinside Academy,' Peter chipped in. 'Bosom pals years before Cambridge and Magdalen hove in sight.'

Rory pretended to flourish a sword. 'They used to call us the two musketeers.'

Peter lurched to his feet. 'I think all this calls for another drink. Now who's for what?'

'We used to be very grand at Cambridge,' Rory continued, making his voice sound even more posh than usual. 'We both wore spats for a while.'

Hester giggled.

Rory pretended to glare at her. 'And we each carried a cane. Went nowhere without them.'

'I can just picture the pair of you,' Hester said, giggling some more.

'Mine was ebony with a silver ring round the knob,' Rory said rather loftily.

'And Peter's?' asked Tony.

'An ordinary cane. But topped very tastefully in gold,' Peter replied, adding, 'I must have a look for it sometime. I haven't seen it in ages.'

'And then there was the Pitt Club,' grinned Rory.

'Ah! The Pitt Club!' Peter breathed, his eyes lighting up.

'And what went on there?' Hester demanded.

Rory winked at her. 'Not what you're thinking. It was men only. But a great fun place all the same. Eh, Peter?'

'What did you graduate with?' Hester asked. 'I take it you did graduate?'

'I did indeed. With a Lower Second.' Rory replied. 'Is that good?'

'It's not bad at all. But he would have done a great deal better if he'd applied himself properly,' interjected Peter.

'He has the brains, you see. Bright lad, our Rory.'

'And what did you get?' Tony asked him.

'A Third, I'm afraid. Which was pretty reasonable really. I just don't have the grey matter Rory has.'

'Pity it's wasted,' Hester said, suddenly serious.

Rory turned to her in surprise. 'How do you mean?'

'You know precisely what I mean. You should do something with your life rather than merely frittering it away playing the gentleman.'

'I don't play at being the gentleman. I *am* one,' retorted Rory.

'Semantics,' Hester snorted. 'It doesn't change the point. Wouldn't you like to feel you were doing something worthwhile in life?'

Rory took a swallow from his drink. 'I think we should change the subject.'

'You work for a living, don't you Peter?' Hester asked.

'Banking. And bloody tedious it is too.'

'Do you really mean that? Or are you just saying that because you feel it's expected?'

210

Peter pursed his lips, giving his face a babyish look. 'I suppose . . . well, I suppose when we get down to the nitty-gritty I don't mind it half so much as I make out. In fact, sometimes it's jolly absorbing. Not too often, though,' he added, winking.

'I'm too old to start something now,' Rory defended. 'Even if I wanted to.'

'I don't believe you're too old at all,' said Hester.

Anger sparked in Rory's eyes. Suddenly the atmosphere in the room wasn't happy and carefree any more.

Peter looked on in concern. Tony bit her lip.

Hester was well aware she should drop it, but something inside her kept driving her on.

'Is there nothing you've ever wanted to do? Nothing at all?' she persisted.

Rory's reply was to snarl something incomprehensible and stalk from the room.

'Oh dear!' said Peter from behind his drink.

'Sorry if I've put a dampener on things,' Hester apologized.

'Will he be all right?' Tony asked in some concern.

Peter topped up his glass, at the same time saying, 'He'll be fine. Just give him a few minutes to get hold of himself.'

Hester glanced nervously towards the other room. 'I seem to have touched a raw nerve.'

Peter gave her a lazy smile. 'More raw than you realize. You see, Rory desperately wanted to be a doctor, or a surgeon, to be more precise. That's been an ambition of his nearly as long as I've known him. And we do go way back.'

Hester frowned. 'So what happened?'

'His mother happened. She strictly forbade it. Big scene, threats and tears. The works.'

'But why?'

'She didn't think it fitting. Future earl and all that.'

'And Rory bowed to her wishes?'

Peter nodded. 'Damn shame, though, Rory would

211

have been first class at medicine. I'm convinced of that.'

'I hope you don't mind me saying this, but I did think the countess a proper bitch when I met her. I must have been right,' Hester said.

'Couldn't agree more,' Peter replied. 'A full-blown dragon lady that one.'

'Poor Rory,' said Tony.

'What did he read then?' Hester asked, curious.

'Same as myself. Classics.'

The conversation ceased abruptly when the door opened and Rory entered the room.

'Heard the one about the one-legged sailor and the randy parrot?' he asked.

Hester didn't fail to note the pain still deep in his eyes as he told the joke.

Hester stared in satisfaction at the letter before her. It had arrived with the morning's post and all day she'd been taking it out to have another look at it.

The letter was from the editor of *The Scotsman*, an Edinburgh paper, saying he was extremely impressed with the article she'd submitted on the subject of the foreign motor car in Scotland. Not only was he prepared to publish the article but would be interested in publishing a monthly column from her on the same subject, if the idea appealed to her.

If it appealed to her! That was the understatement of the year.

With the letter had come a cheque for eight guineas, which would be her monthly fee for the column. *The Scotsman* was a fine newspaper, with a wide readership.

A smile creased Hester's face as she re-read the address on the letter: Mr H. Dark. She'd signed her article simply H. Dark, and *The Scotsman*'s editor had assumed she was a man, as she'd intended him to.

It was a small deception. But one that had worked.

Her own monthly column! Excitement surged in her at the very thought.

'*Mr* Dark indeed!' she laughed.

Her laugh turned to a frown when the bell connected to the garage gates rang. A glance at her watch told her it was ten past eleven. Who on earth could be calling at this time of night?

She was astonished on opening the gates to find an obviously nervous Billy Oliphant standing there. She couldn't have been more surprised if he had been the king himself.

'Hello, Hester,' he said softly.

'Come in,' she replied, gesturing him into the yard.

'I'm not interrupting, am I?'

'No.'

'You're sure?'

'I asked you in, didn't I?'

'I was just passing and I thought . . . well, I thought I'd stop by and see how you were,' he told her as they went through the front office.

There was more to this than that, she thought, but decided to let him tell her in his own time.

'Drink, tea or coffee?' she asked when they reached her lounge.

'Whisky, please. If you have it.'

She poured him a generous measure, and a weaker one for herself.

'So this is your home. On the way here I was wondering what it would be like.'

'I thought you just happened to be passing?' she asked sweetly, her eyes not moving from his face.

That disconcerted him. For a second his face went completely blank, then he recovered himself. 'In a manner of speaking,' he said.

Hester sat, nodding him to a chair opposite.

'I was out for a drive and got thinking about you. Then I realized I wasn't all that far away from here. But I must

213

say I wasn't aware of just how late it was when I had the bright notion to come visiting,' he said lamely.

Liar, she thought. He'd known full well what time it was.

'Everything all right at home?' she asked politely.

'Fine! Fine. Couldn't be better. Violet's expecting.'

A pang of jealousy shot through Hester. 'Congratulations!' She smiled trying to hide her surprise. 'When is she due?'

'November the fifth.' He smiled suddenly. 'If the baby arrives on the day I'm going to call him Guy.'

'And what makes you so sure it's going to be a boy?' she laughed.

He shrugged. 'No reason really. It's just a feeling.'

'I hope you won't be too disappointed if it's not.'

'No. At least I don't think I will. What really matters is that it's born healthy with all its bits and pieces in the right place.'

Imagine, Violet pregnant, thought Hester. Mind you, Violet hadn't been exactly quick off the mark in that respect.

'It's marvellous seeing you again. Just like old times,' Billy went on, a faint sheen of perspiration appearing on his forehead.

'Not quite,' Hester replied evenly.

'No, I suppose not,' he admitted reluctantly.

'You're looking well.'

'And you.'

'How's Violet getting on with the pregnancy?' she asked. 'Everything going as it should?'

Billy cleared his throat. 'She's had something of a hard time, actually,' he replied nervously.

'In what way?'

'She had a bit of trouble early on. Nothing serious, but she had to rest up in bed for a couple of months. She's fine now, just has to take things very easy.'

'I'm sorry to hear that,' said Hester, sympathetically.

They talked for a few more minutes, then Hester,

unable to resist, asked sweetly. 'And how's your inheritance?'

He jerked, as though she'd slapped him. 'The paper's fine. Never better,' he replied in a low voice.

'And sitting in your father's chair, being number one, how does that feel?'

He lit a cigarette with hands that had suddenly begun to tremble. 'You know about that?'

'Uncle Will came and saw me some time back. He told me then.'

With effort, he recovered himself. 'I thoroughly enjoy running the paper. We make more money than we ever did in his day.' It almost sounded like a speech. 'I take great pleasure from that, I can assure you.'

'And the staff, Alan Beat and the rest, how are they?'

'All right, I suppose.'

'You *suppose*! Don't you know?' she asked, unable to hide her shock.

He glanced away.

'Your father would have known,' she reminded him.

'My father and I are two very different people and we run *The Glaswegian* in completely different ways. And what's more, I happen to believe that my way is the better one.'

She doubted that very much indeed. But instead of pursuing the topic rose to her feet and excused herself for a few minutes.

Billy's eyes followed her all the way to the door. There was clearly more on his mind than he was saying.

Hester returned to find the lounge empty. Frowning she went in search of Billy. He was in her bedroom, staring hungrily at the McAskill above her bed.

'What are you doing in here?' she demanded angrily.

He replied without taking his eyes from the painting. 'I was curious and thought I'd have a look around. I didn't think you'd mind.'

'Well I do,' she said tartly.

Still without moving his eyes from the painting, he

215

went round the side of the bed to stand as close to the picture as he could get without actually climbing onto the bed.

'Violet and I fight all the time. It's terrible,' he said hollowly, not daring to face her.

'I'm sorry to hear that.'

'I made a mistake marrying her. She's never really understood me. She's never known what I needed.'

'I don't think you should be telling me this,' Hester said.

He shuddered. 'Since you ran away there hasn't been a day gone by that I haven't thought of you. Wanted you. You were the most wonderful thing that ever happened to me.'

He turned to face her and it startled Hester to see that tears were streaming from his eyes. The anguish he was in was genuine, she knew, but also self-centred.

'We were children,' Hester said simply, moving to leave the room.

'No!' he cried. 'Don't demean it!'

'I'm not, Billy. But these things must be put into perspective. What happened between us was years ago. We're not the same people any more.'

'But I still love you! Just as much. More so!' He came at her, grabbing her and pulling her tightly to him. He was a man half out of his mind. Or still a boy. 'We can start again and it can be just like it was,' he pleaded. 'Just like it was.'

She pulled away from him with all her strength. 'That's impossible, Billy, you're behaving like a fool. You're married and your wife is expecting your child.'

'I don't care about either of them. Only you!' His voice was almost a scream.

Hester was appalled. How could he say such things? How could he delude himself so much? Had he ever cared for anyone but himself?

She tried to leave, but he swung her back against him and the next second his lips were hot and urgent upon her own.

She beat at his chest and shoulders with her fists, every inch of her recoiling from his hateful touch.

'I don't love you any more!' she screamed, wrenching her lips free from his.

He stared at her, stunned and shaken. 'I don't believe you,' he said slowly. 'I don't believe you.'

'It's true. Are you so selfish that you can't see that?'

'It can't be. You must still love me the way I still love you.'

Slowly she backed away. 'You disgust me,' she said quietly.

Something erupted inside him, and the next second his open hand exploded against her cheek.

Screaming, Hester stumbled backwards where her heel caught on a rug and she fell sprawling on the bed.

In a flash her mind was back in Julian Avenue the night she'd run away. What had happened then wasn't going to happen now. Quickly, she rolled onto her side and started to come to her feet.

She screamed again as his hand grasped her hair and viciously tugged it. Then he was on top of her, trying to pin her to the bed. She could sense, rather than hear or feel, him fumbling with his trouser buttons.

'You're only saying you don't still love me. I know you do,' he said thickly, his eyes crazed, his breathing heavy.

Her mistake had been letting him into the garage in the first place. But how could she have possibly known this would happen? Desperately, she pushed and shoved him, but he was too heavy for her to budge, and too strong with his madness.

'All these years. In bed with Violet. I've pretended it was you I was making love to,' he gasped.

'Don't, Billy! Billy, don't!' But he seemed not to hear.

One of her shoes flew across the room to bang against the wall. He pulled wildly at her clothes. Still she continued struggling frantically, praying for a miracle.

'Just like it used to be,' he whispered.

217

She tried to claw his face, but he caught her hand and twisted it. She cried out in agony. Her other shoe clattered to the floor.

'Oh, the nights I've dreamt of this!' he ranted as, with a cry of exultation, he tried to force his way inside her.

Hester threw her arms out, groping for a weapon. Anything to stop this insanity. Her hand closed over a large nail file that in the struggle had been knocked off the bedside table onto the bed itself.

He thrust himself inside her, filling her, powerfully. As he moved above her, her hand stabbed down at his tightened buttock.

Billy howled with pain as the nail file sank into his flesh. He threw his head back, his back arching, his eyes bulging. His huge erection died instantly. He leapt from the bed, dancing in pain, the blood pouring from his wound. The nail file, still stuck in his flesh, waggled up and down.

Hester rolled off the other side of the bed, half-mad herself now with fury and humiliation. To be treated like this by someone she had loved so much. By a man for whom she would have sacrificed anything! If there had been any shred of innocence or trust left in her it was dead now.

He grasped hold of the nail file and jerked it free, throwing it against a wall.

'Bastard!' she screamed. 'You blind, bloody bastard. Get out of my house!'

Billy continued to dance on the spot. 'I'm wounded, Hester,' he sobbed, 'I'll bleed to death.' He screwed his head round to stare down at his blood-covered hand. 'Oh, my God!' he gasped, swooning.

'I'll get a bandage,' she said, unable to leave him as he was, much as she wanted to see him suffer.

When she returned she was carrying not only a bandage, but a bottle of iodine and some cotton wool as well. 'Lie on the bed,' she commanded, not worrying about the covers which were already blood-stained.

It was difficult to judge how deep the wound was, but she thought the nail file must have penetrated an inch or two. 'You'll have to go to the hospital and get a couple of stitches in this,' she said.

She wiped away some of the excess blood, then liberally applied the iodine. Wishing she had some tape, she plonked a thick wad of cotton wool over the wound, and told him to stand again. In that position she wound the bandage round and round his bottom, finally fixing it off with a safely pin.

'That'll hold for a little while, but it needs medical attention.'

Gingerly he pulled up his trousers, neither looking at her nor speaking.

'Go straight to hospital now,' she instructed. 'And don't ever come here again.'

'It really is true, then? You have stopped loving me?'

'A long time ago.'

'Is there no hope at all for us getting back together?'

'Like this?' she asked. 'Is this your idea of love?'

'Then what's left of my life isn't worth . . .' he snapped his fingers, 'isn't worth that!'

'You've got your wife and a child on the way,' said Hester from very far away. 'And, of course, you've got your inheritance.'

He stared at her, eyes full of bitterness and a new-born hate.

'Goodbye, Billy,' she said, as he hobbled through the gate. It was like watching a part of herself disappearing for ever.

Hester had never seen John look so worried. His brow was creased like corrugated iron as he stared blankly off into space.

'Surely it can't be that bad?' she said, having stood at his bedside for several seconds without him realizing she was there.

219

He blinked, then brought his attention to bear on her, his face immediately lighting up with pleasure. 'It's you, love! It's great to see you!' he smiled warmly.

She kissed him, laying the presents of fruit and juice she'd brought him on top of his bedside cabinet. Having glanced round to make sure none of the nurses were watching her, she then slipped several packets of cigarettes inside the cabinet. They seemed a small sin for a man who had gone through so much.

'So what's this problem?' she asked, sitting on the solitary chair provided.

He looked at her as though he had forgotten how to speak. 'It's Mr Rice,' he said at last. 'He's dead.'

'Dead!'

'The week before last. Fell down in the street with a heart attack.'

Hester made a soundless whistle. 'How did you find out?'

'He was supposed to come and see me early on last week, but never showed. When I didn't hear from him I thought I'd better write him a letter to make sure everything was all right. The reply came in this morning's post from his wife. The funeral was a week last Thursday.'

'And you're worried about the money he owes you?'

'Precisely.'

'Didn't you have anything in writing?'

John shook his head.

'Buggeration!' she exclaimed softly.

'It was a gentleman's agreement. We shook hands on it. That was all.'

'And what about his wife? Doesn't she know anything about your arrangement?'

'She doesn't refer to it in the letter she sent me,' he replied.

'Can I see it?'

He extracted the letter from a cubbyhole in the cabinet and handed it to Hester, anxiously gnawing his lower lip while she read it.

'What do you think I should do?' he asked when she'd finished.

'Would you like me to go and see her? After all, she must know about Joey McKay and the thieving that was going on at the factory. With a bit of luck, her husband referred to your part in bringing them to boot. And with a bit more luck he mentioned the deal he made with you.'

'It would be a big relief to me if you'd pay her a visit, Hester.' He smiled ruefully, indicating his plastered legs and arm. 'I'd go myself, but. . . .'

'I'll call on her tomorrow or the day after. You can rely on that.' It was probably just as well that she went, she thought, John wasn't much of a business man.

He reached out with his good arm to clasp her hand in his. 'You're the only person I've ever met in my life that I've ever been able to rely on,' he said.

On hearing that Hester flushed. John thought she'd blushed because of the compliment he'd just paid her but in reality it was because the words had filled her with a burning shame.

Through the Phantom's windscreen Hester stared at the long, grey Glasgow street stretching before her. The slums had always been wretched places, but recently they had become even worse. Everywhere she looked there were men lounging on street corners – sullen men with long faces and dulled, glazed eyes.

The unemployed had always gathered on the street corners. But in living memory their numbers had never been as great as they were now. For the working man a job, any job, was a prize to be treasured. Something to cling onto at any price.

The recession was eating the country alive, Hester thought. Only those with great wealth tucked away were at all safe.

She, with her up-market, specialized trade, had been lucky so far, but now even Ritchie's was beginning to feel the pinch. For the first time she was going to have to contract rather than expand. Business had dropped off so much in the past few months that she was going to have to give four of her mechanics their cards at the end of the following week.

'Cheer up! You're awfully morose,' Rory said gaily. He then proceeded to chatter on about Commander Byrd's forthcoming attempt to fly over the South Pole, a subject which had captured his interest and imagination.

Hester listened with only half an ear, smiling or nodding occasionally when she felt it was required.

Things were bad. And going to get worse. She was convinced of that. And the thought sent a chill wind blowing up her spine. She could still remember the sight of those orphans when she was a girl.

Who knew what tomorrow might bring? It wasn't totally inconceivable that she, like many other garages, would go to the wall. Unlikely perhaps, but not completely impossible.

The Viscountess Kilmichael, and future Countess of Strathmere, would never have to worry about ending up flat broke, she thought. On the contrary, the viscountess would be rolling in it, just like her husband and in-laws. She looked over at Rory. Was she becoming mercenary, she wondered? She who had always stood on her own two feet? But she did care about him. And the opportunity would never come again.

An hour later found Hester and Rory out in the countryside on horses galloping into the wind. The horses, of course, were from his own stable. They'd been here on a number of previous occasions, and thoroughly enjoyed themselves each time.

Hester raised her head against the whipping wind. Ahead of her Rory was galloping flat out. She knew she hadn't a hope of catching him, but she found the ride tremendously exhilarating none the less. The breath rasped in her nostrils, and her cheeks burned with a combination of wind and excitement.

222

About a mile further on she slowed the horse down to a canter, and then a walk. She'd had enough galloping for the time being.

A small clump of trees hove into view. On reaching them she dismounted and tied the reins to a low hanging branch. She then sat on the ground with her back to one of the trees and closed her eyes.

'Are you all right?' Rory asked, suddenly appearing on his horse from behind the trees.

'Fine. I just wanted a breather.'

'Jolly good idea,' he said, quickly dismounting to sit beside her.

She opened her eyes when his arm went around her neck. Then his lips were on hers. She stiffened slightly as his hand slipped under her coat to touch a breast. It was the first time he'd tried to be intimate with her since that night in the Rolls.

Instead of giving herself to the moment, she tore her mouth from his. 'Can I ask you something?' she said.

He looked surprised, but not annoyed. 'Anything you like.'

'Tell me about wanting to be a surgeon.'

A grim expression settled on his face. 'Who told you about that?' he demanded, settling back against the tree inches from her.

'Peter.'

'Then he damn well shouldn't have! It's an entirely personal matter.'

And, without moving, he retreated from her, staring moodily over at where his horse was cropping grass.

Hester lit two cigarettes and passed him one. She then lay back against the tree beside him waiting for him to say something.

'Sorry. I shouldn't have snapped your head off like that,' he apologized after a while.

'I understand, you know.'

He turned to stare at her, a quizzical expression on his face. 'Do you?'

223

'Yes. There are things I've badly wanted and never got.'

He turned back to staring at his horse, blowing a stream of smoke into the wind which quickly whirled it away. 'I still feel sick inside when I think of it.'

'Your mother forbade you, Peter said.'

He nodded.

'Why didn't you defy her? After all, what could she do to you?'

He smiled wryly. 'You've met my mother. She's what's called a dominating woman. Too strong for me, I'm afraid.'

'I find that hard to believe, Rory.'

'It's true. She crushed me when I was a child. I've never been able to stand up to her since.'

'And your father?'

'Oh, he does from time to time. But there's absolute hell to pay when it happens.'

'I like him.'

'And her?'

Hester puffed on her cigarette. And didn't reply. 'Are you serious about me?' she asked suddenly.

The question caught him unawares. 'Why?'

'You keep asking me out, and I keep going. Despite the fact that I already have a boyfriend. I'd like to know just what's what, Rory.'

He threw his cigarette away, then took her in his arms and laid her flat on the ground. 'The truth?' he asked.

'The truth.'

'I'm absolutely dotty about you. Besotted. Completely over the moon.' He kissed her again, fumbling with the buttons of her blouse.

But she'd made up her mind as to just how far she was prepared to let him go. His tongue moved inside her mouth as he eased her bra over her breasts, then fell upon them like a hungry infant.

When his hand moved down along her body she pushed it away. 'No, Rory. No.'

'Please, Hester.'

'No!' she repeated, sitting up and pulling her clothes together again.

'I desperately want you.'

'I know that.'

'Then why not?'

'Is that what you really think of me? Someone to be had out in the open under a tree?'

'No, of course it's not!'

She buttoned her blouse concentrating on what her hands were doing and not on the look in his eyes.

'I told you I was crazy about you,' he said, hurt in his voice.

She gave him a cynical smile. 'Is that a euphemism for randy?'

'You know better than that.'

'Do I?'

He came to her and took her in his arms. 'I'm sorry. I shouldn't have done that. You're quite right. It wasn't respectful.'

'Don't you ever go against your mother's wishes?'

He blinked. 'Why?'

'Because I don't think I'd like to be with a man who's browbeaten by a woman. Mother or otherwise.'

He blushed.

'From what little you've told me I suspect not becoming a surgeon is the worst mistake you've ever made. We get so few chances of happiness. Careerwise, love or whatever. It's a tragedy to throw one away.'

'I've regretted it ever since. But then that's obvious,' he said ruefully.

She touched his cheek. 'Be your own man, Rory. Anything else isn't worthy of you.'

'You really are marvellous,' he said.

She'd sown the seeds she'd planned to. From now on she'd nurture them carefully.

* * *

Mr Ruthven, of Munro, Son and Ruthven, was a grave middle-aged man with pebble glasses and dandruff. He was Mrs Rice's solicitor whom Hester was now seeing having been referred to him by Mrs Rice earlier on in the week.

'It really is unfortunate for Mr McCandlass that Mrs Rice knows nothing about an oral agreement between him and her late husband. But Mr Rice wasn't in the habit of taking her into his confidence about business matters.'

Just John's luck, thought Hester. 'You do accept the fact that he did unmask the thieves?'

Ruthven made a pyramid with his hands, and somehow managed to look even graver. He might have been the Archangel Gabriel announcing Armageddon.

'The facts as I understand them are this,' he said. 'Mr McCandlass is a private investigator.'

'Correct.'

'But at the time of his accident he was working for Mr Rice as a factory hand.'

'Working under cover,' Hester corrected firmly.

'With due respect, Miss Dark, we have only his word for that. There's absolutely nothing in writing.'

'Why else would a private investigator be working in a factory?'

Ruthven gave a humourless smile. 'Perhaps his investigating wasn't paying as well as it should have and he took the job to make ends meet?'

'That's ridiculous!' Hester said, eyes sparking.

'It isn't at all, Miss Dark. It's perfectly feasible.'

Hester sat grim-faced. 'Are you saying that Mr McCandlass is trying to defraud Mrs Rice?'

'That's putting it a bit harshly, Miss Dark. Let's just say that it could be possible, just possible mind you, that a man in Mr McCandlass's position might be trying to turn the tragic demise of Mr Rice to his own advantage. After all, we have absolutely no evidence whatsoever that such an agreement existed except for Mr McCandlass's word that it did.'

'What about the two hundred pounds that Mr Rice has already paid to Mr McCandlass? How do you explain that if Mr McCandlass was only working for Rice as a mere factory hand?'

Ruthven again treated Hester to his humourless smile, spreading his delicate, well cared for hands wide before him.

'Let's put it another way. If we accept that Mr McCandlass was working for my deceased client in his role of private investigator, then what evidence is there that the two hundred pounds wasn't the total fee agreed on? In itself it is a substantial sum, as I'm sure you'll agree.'

'It was on account. Not the total sum,' Hester said patiently.

'So you and Mr McCandlass say. But again, and do please pardon me for suggesting this, but as a solicitor I have to consider all possible facets, this might just be Mr McCandlass trying to turn the situation to his own advantage.'

'Mr McCandlass is an honourable man,' Hester said stiffly. 'As was your Mr Rice. If he were here today he'd be appalled to think you were trying to go back on the agreement he made with Mr McCandlass.'

'But he's not here and that's the nub of the matter,' Ruthven replied.

'The nub of the matter is that money is owed Mr McCandlass. Money you are trying to wriggle out of paying.'

'That's not true.'

'It is from where I'm sitting.'

Ruthven sighed. 'My job is to protect my client. Which is precisely what I'm doing.'

'What you're doing is going back on a deal he made.'

'A deal you and Mr McCandlass say he made. Where's your proof? Show me some and I'll happily honour the deal!'

'There is no proof. It was a gentleman's agreement.'

'Which has no legality whatever.'

'Mr McCandlass and I appreciated that fact before I came to see you. We can't take this further. We know that. But despite the fact it has no legal standing, the agreement existed. And we hoped Mrs Rice would honour it.'

Ruthven sat back in his chair and regarded Hester thoughtfully. 'You're asking for a further fourteen-hundred and fifty pounds, Miss Dark. That's a small fortune.'

This was John's new estimate of his fee, computed at twelve-and-a-half per cent, rather than the original ten.

'Small compared to what Mrs Rice will have saved at the end of the year now that the thieves are behind bars. Thanks entirely to Mr McCandlass. Who came within inches of being killed. And who is still in hospital recovering from a serious operation on his liver which was badly damaged when the crate fell on him. And let's not forget the two broken legs and broken arm he also sustained.' She paused for effect. 'In my opinion, Mr McCandlass more than earned every penny that's owed him. A sentiment I know Mr Rice agreed with.'

'Hmmh!' said Ruthven.

Hester went on, her tone now soft. 'As we've already agreed, Mr McCandlass can't prove that money is owed him, but it is. You have his word and mine on that. And I think you'd be shaming Mr Rice's memory if it isn't paid.'

Ruthven drew in a deep breath through his nose, then slowly exhaled it.

'I shall speak with Mrs Rice and discuss the matter with her. But before I do, I'll go through all Mr Rice's papers in case there's anything there which could corroborate Mr McCandlass's claim. When I've done both these things, I'll come back to Mr McCandlass.'

'Contact me instead, if you don't mind. He's given me full powers to act on his behalf.'

'It'll be about a fortnight I should say.'

'Fine,' replied Hester, rising.

She gave Ruthven her business card before leaving.

The audience applauded warmly as the curtain on the first act of Oscar Wilde's 'Lady Windermere's Fan' rang down.

'Jolly good!' enthused the Earl of Strathmere, who was sitting behind Hester and the countess and next to Rory in their private box.

Rory came to his feet and his father did likewise. 'Time for a cigarette and a stretch of the legs,' Rory said.

Hester was about to rise also, but the countess put a restraining hand on her arm. 'Stay and have a chat with me. It'll give us a chance to get to know one another better,' she said, smiling.

'If you like,' Hester smiled back, curious as to what this was all about.

'We're avid theatre-goers,' said the countess once she and Hester were alone. 'What about you, my dear?'

'I'm afraid I only go occasionally. But when I do I invariably enjoy it.'

'Have you seen any Wilde before?'

'No, this is my first,' Hester replied.

'Such a witty man. And never more so than when dealing with society, but then that's a subject you must know very little about.' The last was a definite statement not a question.

'If you're saying I don't belong to the upper class, then you're quite right,' Hester replied coolly.

The countess nodded, obviously pleased that she'd made her point.

'But then I've always considered good manners more important than class or position,' Hester went on smoothly.

The countess scowled. 'I hope you don't have any designs on Rory, my dear. You're quite unsuitable you know. For a permanent relationship anyway,' the countess said, her smile no more than a sneer.

The gloves were off now, Hester thought. They were down to the nitty-gritty.

The countess went on. 'It's always been my dearest wish, and the earl's, that Rory would marry Lord Lyon's daughter, Elisabeth. She's a delightful girl. She and Rory have known each other since they were children.'

'If that's so she must be a bit long in the tooth now. And still unwed? She can't be all that delightful.' Hester smiled sweetly.

'Elisabeth has great charm,' the countess said coldly. 'And although she and Rory were childhood friends, she is considerably younger than he.'

'And what does Rory think about this proposed match?'

'He appreciates how much it would please his father and me.'

'In other words, he isn't interested.'

'Not at all!' the countess snapped, becoming rather flushed.

'Then why hasn't he married her before now?'

The countess cleared her throat, her eyes sparking with anger. 'A young man should sow his wild oats before entering into marriage. Which is precisely what Rory has been doing up until now.'

'Then if I'm only that, one of his wild oats, why is it worry you so much? Or do you have this little chat with all the so-called unsuitable women he goes out with?'

'No, I don't,' replied the countess. 'You're the first.'

'I'm flattered.'

'I've seen the way he looks at you. You're different.'

'He certainly seems to think so.'

The countess leant forward and rapped Hester's wrist with a stiffened finger. 'Different or not, forget any ambitions you have in his direction for they'll come to nothing. I promise you that.'

'I think Rory's old enough to decide his own future, don't you?' Hester replied.'

'He'll do as I say. Oh, he might fight me, but in the end he'll do as I want.'

The countess was a formidable lady. There was no denying that. But Hester thought she had her measure.

'We'll see my lady,' she purred. 'We'll see.'

Hester sipped champagne and stared across the table at Rory who was tucking into a plate of veal and spaghetti.

'It seems we're going to have to stop seeing one another,' she said.

Rory's fork stopped halfway to his mouth. 'I beg your pardon?'

'It seems we're going to have to stop seeing one another,' she repeated.

Carefully he laid his fork down. Then wiped his mouth with a napkin. 'The boyfriend?'

'No. Your mother.'

He frowned. 'I don't understand.'

'That little chat we had after the first act tonight. It was to warn me off. She says I'm unsuitable and that you're to marry Elisabeth.'

Rory laughed. 'I wouldn't marry Elisabeth Stirling if she was the last woman on earth. She has bow legs and acne. And must be one of the most stupid women ever born.'

'I didn't think you were interested, somehow.'

'The old girl's been after me for years to marry Elisabeth. But she hasn't mentioned it of late. I thought she'd finally given up on the idea.'

'Apparently not,' said Hester. 'But tell me, why is she so keen on this match?'

'Elisabeth is the Lord Lyon's daughter and only child. Our marriage would unite the two houses. Much to the benefit of any issue Elisabeth and I might have. It's what's called a good match.'

'I see.'

He curled a finger around one of hers. 'You were only teasing about us not seeing one another more, weren't you?'

'That depends.'

'On what?'

'On whether or not you jump when your mother cracks the whip. She's the one who says we're not to see each another again. Not me.'

'Damn her!'

'She says you might fight her, but in the end you'll do as she says.'

'Did she now?' he asked, an odd expression in his eyes.

'Her exact words.'

Using his free hand, Rory poured them both more champagne. His face was set in a thundercloud of anger. His lower lip trembled.

'It's you wanting to be a surgeon all over again isn't it?' said Hester softly. Adding even more softly, 'Which you've regretted ever since.'

'She'd no right to say that to you.'

'I don't think your mother worries too much about the rights and wrongs of things. Only what *she* wants. And what suits her.'

'Well this time she's not going to get her own way!' Rory said defiantly.

'You say that now. But will it still be the case after she gets to work on you?'

'You think I'm weak don't you?' he said suddenly.

She smiled, gently twisting the finger in hers. 'It's not that I think you're weak. But rather that I think your mother is particularly strong. I believe you *can* stand up to her. You have it in you. What you have to do is find the motivation to do so.'

'And you're it?'

'Only you can answer that question.'

'I'd do anything for you,' Rory whispered. 'I think I'd even defy the Devil himself.'

Hester raised his entwined finger to her lips and kissed it. 'Knowing your mother, it might be exactly what you are doing,' she smiled.

★　　★　　★

'What I'm about to tell you is in the strictest confidence. Is that clear?' Ruthven asked.

Hester nodded. She was back at the solicitor's at his request.

'Financially, the late Mr Rice's factory is not in good standing. In fact, for the last couple of years it's been losing money hand over fist.'

'Because of the thieves?'

'They were a contributory factor, there's no denying that. If the thieving had never taken place it's possible the factory might just have survived, but that's merely conjecture. It's really impossible to say.'

'Might have survived? Are you telling me the factory is about to fold?' Hester asked, her heart sinking. Was John never to be lucky?

'A victim of the times, I'm afraid,' Ruthven confirmed.

Hester sucked in a deep breath. Poor John, he was a born loser. A lovely man and one she was desperately fond of, but a born loser the less.

Ruthven went on. 'Mr Rice knew this, of course, but he deluded himself. He sincerely believed that he could save the firm. The whole thing was an enormous worry to him. A great burden that he carried daily on his shoulders. And which I personally think probably killed him in the end.'

'And Mrs Rice knew nothing about the factory's predicament?'

'No,' Ruthven replied. 'It was a complete surprise to her. The truth only emerged when I, acting on her behalf, had a look at the company books. That was when the whole sorry mess came to light.'

'I take it you're trying to tell me that Mr McCandlass isn't going to get any more money?'

'Not quite. I've talked the matter over at length with Mrs Rice, having first of all made inquiries about Mr McCandlass's character and business reputation. You'll be happy to know people all speak well of him.'

There was a glint in Ruthven's eye which told Hester those inquiries had been extensive and revealing. 'You found out he was booted out of the police force for suspected corruption?' she asked quietly.

'Taking back-handers, I believe. Yes. I was told about that. But since that unfortunate incident he appears to have kept to the straight and narrow.'

'So you believe his story that he was working for Mr Rice in his investigatory capacity?'

Ruthven sat further back in his chair, his eyes gleaming behind his pebble glasses. 'Fourteen hundred and fifty pounds, calculated at twelve and a half per cent, was Mr McCandlass's estimated figure I believe?'

'Correct,' replied Hester.

'Well, we're prepared to make an offer. But one which is nowhere near that amount, I'm afraid.'

'How much?'

'He's already been paid two hundred pounds.'

'On account,' Hester confirmed.

Ruthven leant forward to open one of his desk drawers, and extracted a wad of fivers which he laid before him.

'Another two hundred. And not a penny more. Take it or leave it.'

It was a mere seventh of what John had hoped for. But it was considerably better than nothing.

Ruthven went on. 'Mrs Rice can't really afford even this, but feels, because of the injuries Mr McCandlass received and the fact that he'll be laid up for some time to come, that she has to give him something. Two hundred pounds is her absolute limit.'

Better than a kick in the teeth, Hester thought. But John was going to be so disappointed.

'He accepts,' she said. It was the only realistic thing to to. Crossing to Ruthven's desk, she scooped up the wad of fivers.

'I'll need a signed receipt,' Ruthven said.

Hester wrote her name with a flourish.

★   ★   ★

Hester smiled in the darkness. She was in bed, but her mind was too restless for sleep.

Her plan not to have intercourse with Rory was working perfectly. The more she denied him the more he wanted her. Tonight he'd been almost beside himself.

As far as she was concerned the hook had been baited. The fish caught. What she was in the process of now doing was reeling the fish ashore.

But she mustn't congratulate herself on being successful too soon she warned herself. A lot of fish have escaped only inches from the bank. Until in the net and on dry land all could yet be lost. And at any moment.

Suddenly she went cold. Was there any chance that she was making the same mistake Will had made all those years ago when he'd thrown over her mother to marry Sybil? Was history repeating itself? No, she told herself. The difference between her situation now and her uncle's was that he had given up love for money. Whereas if she did love John it was no more than she felt for Rory. She couldn't stay with him out of pity – that would be even worse.

In her heart, she believed that she would never fall in love again. She didn't think that could happen more than once in a lifetime. Not the real thing. There was not enough left of her heart for that.

Three nights later found Rory and Hester at her place wrestling before a roaring fire. He was flushed with both drink and desire.

He pinned her to the carpet, lying on top of her, holding her arms out to the side.

'I must have you.'

'No.'

'But, Hester, why not?'

'Because I just won't and that's that!'

He pulled one of her hands against him. 'Feel me,' he whispered.

She pulled her hand away again.

'If you won't let me make love to you properly then there are other ways,' he pleaded.

'No!'

'Oh, for Christ's sake!' he yelled. Releasing her, he came to his feet, trembling and glaring down at her.

Being furious suited him, she thought. It gave him a wildness and power not usually there.

'What have I got to do?' he pleaded.

Hester didn't reply, continuing to hold his gaze.

He stomped across to the champagne and pulled the bottle from the silver bucket, spilling some onto the carpet as he refilled his glass.

Pulling herself together, she brought herself to a sitting position.

'This boyfriend of yours,' Rory said.

'What about him?'

'You're still seeing him?'

'From time to time, yes.'

'I think the time has come for you to choose. You can't continue seeing both of us.'

'Why not?'

'Because . . . because it's driving me bloody insane with jealousy, that's why!'

'He wants to marry me,' she said softly.

With an oath Rory threw his glass into the fire. It exploded into orange flame.

'I thought you'd want to know.'

'Damn and blast you!' he roared. Then his arms were around her, his head against her breast. 'Marry *me*,' he pleaded in a strangled voice. 'Please, Hester. Marry me.'

A thrill ran through her. 'I thought you'd never ask,' she whispered.

His mouth fastened onto hers, and she seemed to melt in his arms. All the passion she'd been denying all these long weeks welled up inside her. All the love and longing, she had kept hidden inside her surged to the surface. Oh, how she wanted him. How she wanted him now!

236

With all her resolve, she tore herself away from him and stood by the fire. She was breathless and her skin was flushed.

'I take it you accept then?' Rory said, his chest heaving.

'Can I have some more champagne please?'

Rory poured her a brimming glass. 'Well?'

Hester sipped, trying to regain her self-possession. 'Ask me again. Tomorrow. When you've had time to cool down and think this over. It would be wrong for either of us to make a decision like this in the heat of passion. There must be no regrets. Understand?'

'I love you Hester,' he whispered.

It was the first time he'd ever said that. She believed him.

'I love you too.' Was it really a lie?

He hung his head for a moment. 'I never told you before. I was afraid the feeling was all one way.'

She came to his side and touched his face.

'I think I'll die if I don't have you soon,' he said.

She smiled. 'You won't die. This is Glasgow, not Paris or Venice. Men here are made of sterner stuff.'

'Are you sure you won't give me an answer tonight?'

'Tomorrow, love. Ask me again tomorrow. After we've both had time to sleep on it. And now I think you should go. I need a bath after rolling around the floor with you.'

But when he was gone, the doubts returned. Could Rory, even with her backing, stand up to his mother as he'd said he would?

She poured herself the rest of the champagne.

Only time would tell.

Hester was pleased with her second column in *The Scotsman*. Even she could see that it was better than the first. She stared for the millionth time at her by-line. H. Dark, and for the millionth time a thrill ran through her.

If she had one regret it was that the column was only monthly. Still, she told herself, better a small contribution than none at all. At least she was working in the news-paper business – even if at something of a distance.

She folded *The Scotsman* and laid it aside, then picked up that morning's copy of *The Glaswegian*. She'd already read it over breakfast and been angered by it. More than angered – affronted.

The Glaswegian was not the paper it had been when Will Oliphant had been in charge. The standards set by Billy were nowhere near as high as his father's had been.

She glanced up as the Phantom drove into the garage, waving when she saw Rory look up at the window.

She watched as he parked the car and entered the building. Then, slightly flushed, he joined her in the office. He's already had a drink or two, she thought, going towards him for a kiss.

'I've slept on it and I still want to marry you,' he said in one breath, before he'd even passed the doorway.

Hester took a deep breath. She'd been almost certain he'd repeat his proposal. Nevertheless, the hours of wait-ing had been anxious ones.

'Then I accept,' she replied, in a voice as solemn as his own.

Rory gave a delighted whoop and swept her into his arms. As he kissed her an embarrassed Hester saw a number of grinning mechanics staring at them through the office's glass-panelled front.

Releasing Hester, Rory delved in his pocket to produce a jeweller's box which he pressed into her hand. His eyes shone as he waited for her to open it. He seemed as excited as a kid at Christmas.

The diamond ring was so huge it momentarily took Hester's breath away. 'My God!' she whispered.

'Like it?'

'Like it? It's magnificent!'

'Try it on. It's probably too big. I didn't know your size, but we can soon get that readjusted.'

'Oh Rory!' Hester whispered when the ring was sparkling on her finger.

238

'Do I get another kiss?'

'Thank you, love,' she smiled, her eyes alight with joy and happy tears.

'This calls for a drink I think,' he shouted and immediately dashed from the office.

Through the glass-panelled front, Hester watched him open the boot of the Phantom, gesturing one of the mechanics over to lift out what was inside. As the mechanic carried the crate of champagne to the office, Rory called out to all the other workers to come and have some bubbly. An invitation they accepted without any second bidding.

'I'm afraid it's not chilled,' apologized Rory, bouncing a cork off the ceiling. 'But you can't have everything.'

Dan Black led the men in their congratulations. 'It's right happy we are for you both,' he said, pumping Rory's hand.

There were only two glasses available, so tea cups where used.

'Come in! Come in!' shouted Rory above the din when a bemused customer appeared at the doorway. 'The more the merrier!'

'A toast,' called Dan Black. Gradually the room fell silent.

When he had everyone's attention, Dan went on with great solemnity. 'To the boss. May she and Viscount Kilmichael be as happy together as we've been working for her. God bless you both!'

The men drank in unison, then clapped and cheered.

'Speech!' Dan shouted. 'Speech!'

The cry was taken up. 'Speech! Speech!'

Hester held up her hand for silence. When she had it she said, 'When we are married I obviously won't be able to run the garage the way I have been. But I promise you this: whatever happens, the garage will remain open and in business. You have my word on that.'

A cheer went up. Followed by three rousing choruses of hip, hip, hurrah.

When that had died down Hester said, 'Now I think you should all get back to work. There's still a lot to be done today.'

Smiling and joking, the mechanics filed out.

Rory was beside himself with joy and didn't notice the worried look on Hester's face. 'There are a lot of plans to be made. Like when the wedding's going to be. But first there's the newspaper announcement to be made.'

'Leave that till Monday will you?' She was staring out of the window, new tears in her eyes.

He frowned. 'Why?'

She'd never told him that John was in hospital, but she had to now.

'I want to be the one to break the news to him,' she said when she had finished. 'I don't want him reading it in the paper first.'

Rory nodded, an arm around her shoulder. 'Fair enough.'

With a great effort, she pulled herself together. She'd made her decision, it was for the best all round. 'And, talking of breaking the news, when do you plan to tell your mother?'

Rory poured himself another glass of champagne which he swallowed in one long swallow.

'No time like the present,' he grinned, reaching for the telephone. 'Mind if I use this?'

'Help yourself.'

She sat behind her desk and stared at her ring. It was the most beautiful one she'd ever seen.

She looked up as Rory started speaking, smiling encouragingly when he winked at her.

'Hester and I have just got engaged,' he was saying into the telephone.

There was a long pause. Then he carefully replaced the receiver.

'What did she say?' Hester asked.

His smile was strained. 'She didn't. She hung up.'

Now for the storm, Hester thought.

Hester sat in the Lancia, staring at the ugly monstrosity that was Garnhill. The drive from Glasgow had been a terrible one, largely thanks to very bad patches of fog which at times had reduced visibility almost to zero. If she could have turned back, she would have, but she'd had to get through. The announcement of the engagement was to be in tomorrow's *Glasgow Herald* and *The Times*.

She felt sick inside. Dreading the ordeal to come, she lit a cigarette, putting off seeing John a little bit longer.

At that moment she hated herself; more than she had ever hated anyone in her life.

He was sitting up in bed reading a book. She was almost at his bedside when she realized that his injured arm was out of plaster.

When he saw her he gave her a grin and, lifting the arm that had been broken, waggled his fingers at her.

'Congratulations,' she said, kissing him on the cheek.

'Hey! Don't I get a proper one?' he demanded, tapping his lips.

'Got the plaster off two days ago,' he said as she sat down beside him. 'And the left leg will be having its plaster off in the middle of next week.'

'And the right leg?'

John pulled a face. 'Some time yet, I'm afraid. Week after next, hopefully, but not before.'

Hester laid some things she'd brought him on the bedside cabinet, slipping the usual number of packets of cigarettes inside the cabinet.

'Smashing!' John whispered, conspiratorially. 'You are a winner.'

'How are you feeling in yourself?' she asked.

'A lot better. And getting more so every day.' He held the arm that had been broken out in front of him. 'Having

241

the plaster off this makes all the difference. I feel I'm well on the road to recovery now. The only big worry is . . . well, the money I'm owed. Is there any news yet?'

It was several weeks since her final meeting with Ruthven. She'd wanted to hold off telling John as long as possible, hoping that she would be able to sort something out. With Rory's proposal she knew what she would do.

She would give John what really amounted to a consolation prize. Although he would never realize that.

'I've finally had a decision from Ruthven,' she said.

Expectation mingled with apprehension filled John's face. 'Well?'

'You've got your money. They found your estimated figure reasonable and offered to pay the fourteen hundred and fifty pounds then and there. Needless to say, I accepted on your behalf and the money went into your bank on Friday.'

'Oh, my God, that's bloody marvellous!' he exclaimed, the tension evaporating from his face, and sank back on his pillows.

The money *was* in John's bank but twelve hundred and fifty pounds of it had come from her. It was the least she could do in the circumstances. It was all she could do.

'Fourteen hundred and fifty smackers. Absolutely fantastic,' he breathed, for the first time in weeks looking like his old self.

She rubbed her hands together. Her flesh was cold and clammy.

'What do you say to us getting married as soon as I get out?' he asked.

Suddenly she was numb all over, in mind, in body, and in heart. Self-loathing filled her; self-loathing, blame and pity for John.

'I can't marry you, John' she whispered. 'I'm marrying someone else.' She could barely hear her own trembling voice for the pounding of her heart.

John smiled. 'Pull the other one! It isn't April the first, you know.'

'It's true, John,' she nearly sobbed. 'I'm sorry, but it's true.'

His smile widened. 'Will you come off it, Hester? I'm serious.'

Tears welled in her eyes, running slowly down her cheeks.

'Hester?'

'There'll be an announcement in tomorrow's papers. His name's Rory McNeil. Viscount Kilmichael.'

John's smile faded. In its place was an expression of stunned disbelief. 'You're serious,' he said slowly.

She nodded.

He opened his mouth, but no sounds came out.

'I'm sorry,' she whispered, 'Truly I am.'

He stared at her, his eyes reflecting pain and hurt. 'How long has this been going on?' he asked.

'I first met him years ago. But it's only recently. . . .'

'How long?'

She bit her lip. All she wanted to do was rise and flee from the ward, the hospital, and John.

'Since you've been laid up.'

'Are you sleeping with him?'

'That is not the point.'

He reached over to grab her arm. 'I want to know. It's important to me.'

She shook her head, unable to meet his eyes.

'Swear to me?'

'I haven't slept with him yet. I swear.'

John sighed, releasing her arm. 'And do you love him, Hester? Do you really love him? Does he love you? Does he love you as much as I do?'

'We've had some good times together, John. I'll never forget them.'

'I thought I meant something to you. I really thought I did.'

'You do.'

He smiled cynically. 'But not enough. This viscount whatever, he obviously means an awful lot more.' His voice suddenly turned vicious. 'All this time since I came into hospital you've been letting me make a fool of myself. Planning marriage, children. Telling you I loved you. And all the while you've been going out with someone else. Did the pair of you get a good laugh at my expense?'

'Don't be stupid! No one's been laughing at you.'

'So you say. But how can I believe anything you tell me now?'

There was no reply.

'I think you'd better go. And don't come back. I never want to see you again. Ever.'

'John . . .'

'Please, Hester. Just go.'

She drew in a deep breath, almost staggering to her feet. She would have liked to kiss him on the cheek in farewell. To touch him one more time, but knew she daren't.

'Goodbye,' she whispered. 'Good luck.'

'I haven't forgotten that I still owe you money. Now that I have what was due to me from Rice I'll send it on to you.'

'There's no need for that.'

'Oh, yes there is. A man has his pride.'

She used her hanky to wipe her eyes before turning to face the centre of the ward. She walked to the doors looking neither left nor right.

She didn't look back.

The clock chimed eight, slowly and sonorously. 'They'll be here any time now,' Rory said.

'You look like you could use a drink,' Hester said. 'I know I could.'

'Good idea,' he replied. 'Whisky?'

Rory's parents were coming for dinner, at the countess's suggestion. Both he and Hester were prepared for the worst.

She stared at Rory who was obviously nervous and apprehensive. 'Will you be all right?'

'I'll be fine. I promise you.'

She smiled encouragement. 'I love you,' she said. 'Just remember that.'

From off in the distance came the faint sound of the doorbell ringing. 'That's them,' said Rory, and swallowed off his drink.

A few minutes later Harkness showed them into the room. The moment Hester saw the expression in the countess's eye she knew her worst fears were justified: she was about to do her best to break the engagement.

'How are you, my dear? You're looking quite fabulous!' the earl said to Hester, pecking her on the cheek. 'Congratulations! I think my boy's picked himself an absolute winner.'

His sentiments were obviously genuine. The earl did like her. She at least had him on her side.

Rory kissed his mother who remarked that she thought he appeared a little tired. Then she sat down without having acknowledged Hester's presence or having offered her congratulations on their engagement.

'Drink?' asked Rory, trying to sound cheerful.

'Can't wait to be a grandfather,' remarked the earl, oblivious to the atmosphere in the room. 'You're going to give Rory lots of boys I hope.'

Hester's heart sank, but she smiled bravely.

The earl's eyes shone. 'An heir to carry on the family name. Just the ticket!'

Rory handed his mother a sherry and his father a large malt. When all four of them had glasses in their hands the earl raised his in a toast. 'To the happy couple!' he said.

The countess raised her glass to her lips, but didn't drink. Only her husband seemed not to notice.

They made small talk for a few minutes, without the countess joining in. Then the earl said to Hester, 'Damndest thing. Saw an article in *The Scotsman* recently about foreign cars. Written by a chap named H. Dark. Not anything to do with you, perchance?'

'I wrote the article,' replied Hester proudly.

'Good for you. And a fine piece it was, too. Thoroughly enjoyed it.'

'Hester's family have a long history in the newspaper line. Her uncle owns *The Glaswegian*,' Rory said.

'He's retired now. My cousin Billy has taken over,' Hester explained.

'And tell me do you still do nude modelling?' asked the countess sweetly. Just like that, straight out of the blue.

'Eh!' the earl exclaimed, nearly spilling his drink.

'Did I forget to mention it to you, Hector? Miss Dark was a nude model at one time. Isn't that right, Miss Dark?'

Hester glanced at Rory who'd gone ashen. 'Yes. That's correct, My Lady,' she replied levelly.

'Goodness gracious!' said the earl. 'Nude? With all your clothes off what? In the buff?'

'Completely starkers,' Hester smiled.

The earl was visibly shaken. He swallowed his malt, then quickly held out his glass for more. 'I'll have another if you don't mind, Rory. Why ever did you do a thing like that?' he asked Hester while Rory was filling his glass.

'Money. Pure and simple,' Hester replied.

'At the art school I believe,' the countess went on.

'For mixed classes: men *and* women,' Hester added.

The earl looked both bemused and confused.

'Too stunned to speak?' the countess asked Rory.

'Not at all.'

'Then what have you got to say about all this? Surely now you realize this preposterous engagement can't be allowed to continue?'

Rory glanced at Hester, then back to his mother. 'I won't be a minute,' he said and left the room.

'As a matter of interest, how did you find out?' Hester asked.

The countess smirked, but didn't reply.

Cow, Hester thought. She would have loved to have had something on her.

She smiled inwardly when Rory reappeared carrying his McAskill.

'You're not telling me anything I don't already know,' he said to his mother, holding up the painting so that she and his father could see it.

'Goodness gracious,' muttered the earl, colouring slightly.

'Little better than being a common prostitute,' sniffed the countess, pretending to avert her eyes in righteous horror.

'I don't agree at all,' said Rory simply. 'Like now, jobs were extremely difficult to come by when Hester did this. I rather admire her guts for taking it on.'

'Hmmh!'

'That's a good point,' the earl remarked, thoughtfully for him. 'You were very hard up at the time I take it?'

'*Very*,' Hester replied.

'Well, a person's got to eat. And that's a fact,' the earl said.

Rory stared defiantly at his mother who glared back at him.

'You're making a mistake,' the countess said.

'I don't think so.'

'I forbid this marriage. She's far beneath you.'

'I won't be browbeaten by you, mother. Not now or ever again.'

The countess's lips became a thin, bloodless slash. 'You'll do as I say, Rory.'

'No,' he said firmly. 'I'll do as I like.'

'She'll disgrace the family.'

'I'm the one who's marrying her, not the family. Anyway, it's sheer bunk to say she'll be a disgrace. As well you know.'

The countess laid her now empty glass on the floor, then rose, drawing herself up to her full commanding height.

247

Rory's face was set hard, but there was a sheen of perspiration on his forehead as he gazed steadfastly back into the blazing eyes locked on his.

The battle of wills lasted only a few seconds, but it seemed more like a lifetime. When the countess finally relaxed fractionally, Rory knew he'd won.

'Come, Hector,' she snapped. 'We'll dine elsewhere.'

'Just a moment.' There was approval in his gaze when he turned back to Rory. 'Despite what I've learned tonight, I want you to know that I still think Hester to be a fine, fine woman. And one who'll do you proud.'

'But Hector . . .' the countess began, only to trail off and bite her lip when she saw her husband's expression.

'Thank you, My Lord,' Hester said quietly.

His reply was a warm smile. Then he turned again to Rory. 'With a wife to keep, and children hopefully in the not too distant future, you'll need more than your present allowance. Therefore the day after the marriage I'll instruct the necessary papers to be drawn up transferring fifty per cent of the family holdings into your name.'

'What!' the countess looked as though she might have a stroke.

'Fifty per cent,' repeated the earl.

'Thank you, Father. On behalf of both of us.'

The countess knew there was no arguing with the earl. He'd committed himself to something he deemed important and would never go back on his word. Nothing she could say or do would make him change his mind. Giving a snort of disapproval, she swept from the room.

The earl took Hester's hand, raised it to his lips, and kissed it gently. 'Lots of grandsons now, mind,' he said, adding mischievously. 'And I think the painting is a dashed excellent one. Makes me wish I was twenty years younger, I can tell you.'

'Father!' Rory exclaimed, pretending to be outraged.

The earl gave Hester a wink. Still chuckling, he started after his wife.

Hester took a deep breath, and poured two large drinks, handing Rory one when he'd returned from seeing them off.

'I'd be lying if I tried to make out that that was easy,' Rory said. His heart was still hammering, but he felt marvellous.

Hester gazed at Rory, understanding, instinctively, how great a battle that had been for him – and how great a victory. He had always been a fine man, and now he was a brave one, as well.

'Why don't we just forget the meal and have a snack after?' she smiled, taking his arm in hers.

'After what?'

She led him to his bedroom.

'Hester! Hester Dark!' a broad Scots' voice cried. Seconds later her hand was being pumped vigorously.

She'd just locked the door of the Lancia outside the house in Julian Avenue. It was the first time she'd been back since running away. She had never really thought she'd see it again.

Her face broke into a smile when she realized who it was. 'It's good to see you again, Alan,' she said.

If anything, Alan was craggier than ever, his thick bushy eyebrows falling over his eyes in a tangled cascade. 'Well I never!' he beamed.

Hester gestured towards the house. 'You've been in to see Uncle, I take it?'

'Aye. I see himself every few weeks or so and we have a good crack together. Does us both the world of good.'

'And also keeps him up to date with what's going on at *The Glaswegian*.'

Alan winked. 'There were never any flies on you, lassie. And I can see you haven't changed. Aye, well I have to admit what's been happening at the paper usually gets mentioned. But only by the by, you understand.'

249

'Oh, of course!' Hester replied, winking back, causing them both to laugh.

'What made you run away like you did, lass?' Alan asked, suddenly very sober.

'It's an awfully long story, Alan. And very personal.'

'Then I won't pry. Your uncle told me he saw you, and passed on your regards. He also said you were now connected with a garage?'

'I own one.'

'So you *are* the H. Dark who writes for *The Scotsman*?'

'I am, indeed,' Hester admitted. 'The editor thinks I'm a man.'

'It's good copy, lass. But then I always said you had talent. You know, I've always hoped you'd return to *The Glaswegian* one day. There isn't a female reporter in Scotland yet so it could still be you.'

She shook her head. 'I'm getting married, Alan. I'm to be the Viscountess Kilmichael.'

'Well, well,' he replied slowly. 'Congratulations, Hester. I hope you'll both be happy.'

'Thank you.'

'Viscountess, eh?' he mused, rubbing his chin. 'Which means, I take it, that you'll be in constant contact with the aristocracy?'

'I presume that'll be the case,' she replied, wondering what he was driving at.

'Just a thought, mind you, but after you're married and settled down, why don't you approach Billy about writing a society column for *The Glaswegian*? It's hardly our usual fare, but I have a feeling if handled the right way it could prove popular with the readers. Something on a monthly basis like your automobile column with *The Scotsman*, maybe.'

Hester liked the idea immediately, but it would be impossible to work for Billy now. Not after what had happened.

'I'll think about it, Alan,' she replied. 'It might not be a bad idea.'

They talked for a short while longer. After he'd gone, promising to keep in touch, she rang the once-familiar doorbell, her hands perspiring, her heart pounding, her mind overwhelmed by memories.

'This is a most pleasant surprise!' Will exclaimed as Hester was ushered into the drawing room.

Hester paused just inside the door. Her gaze travelled from Will to Sybil who was sitting on the sofa, the look on her face hardly a welcoming one.

'Return of the prodigal,' said Christine who was also present. Her look wasn't particularly friendly either.

'And to what do we owe this honour?' Aunt Sybil asked icily.

Hester came straight to the point. 'I'm getting married soon, and I've come to ask you all to the wedding. I was hoping Uncle Will would give me away.' She smiled sweetly at her aunt. 'It should be *the* Glasgow wedding of the year.'

It was Rory's idea that the Oliphants should attend the wedding. He thought it would go some way towards appeasing his mother. To begin with Hester had resisted this suggestion, but had finally decided that this was, perhaps, the time to make peace with the past.

'We read the announcement in the papers,' Sybil replied, stiffly. 'You've certainly come up in the world.'

'It's quite a contrast to owning a garage,' Christine said snidely.

Hester noticed Christine was wearing a wedding ring. 'I see you've got married, too, Christine,' she said, hoping to distract her.

'To Graeme Souter. Remember him?'

'I remember him,' Hester smiled, but couldn't resist the temptation to tease her just a little. 'His people had a biscuit business, didn't they? A *small* one wasn't it?'

Christine flushed. 'Not that small.'

'Naturally, Graeme's invited as well,' Hester said. 'And Billy and Violet of course. Has Violet had the baby yet? Was it a boy?'

251

Will's face fell. 'You obviously haven't heard, Hester. The baby died at birth two days ago. It was a girl.'

'I am sorry,' murmured Hester, genuinely distressed. 'Poor Violet and Billy.'

'They've taken it extremely hard,' Sybil said, as though it might have been Hester's fault.

Hester glanced across at her cousin. 'And what about you? Have you any family of your own yet?'

'Not so far,' Christine replied softly. 'But we're hoping.'

Hester left a little later, after it was agreed that the Oliphants would come to the wedding, and that Will Oliphant would give her away. It was too much of a temptation for either Sybil or Christine to turn down, no matter what they felt about Hester. Will had seemed pleased to have effected a truce at last.

Hester stood on the steps of the house on Julian Avenue as the door shut behind her, feeling that, at last, those chapters of her life were finally closed.

Hester's marriage to Rory McNeil, Viscount Kilmichael, took place in Glasgow Cathedral on November 30th, 1929.

Months back, Hester had prophesied to Rory that things would get worse economically before they got better. Over in America she was being proved right.

On the Saturday of their wedding Wall Street crashed.

10

He'd changed in the three-and-a-half years since she'd last seen him. The old pirate's swagger had gone. The vitality and power he'd always exuded were gone as well and he moved stiffly. A legacy of the broken bones he'd suffered and, perhaps, the broken heart.

He stood now, staring down at her. The hint of his old

expression hovering on his lips. His eyes were smiling, but behind them there was sadness.

'Hello John,' she said, surprised at how unsettling it was to see him again.

'Hello, Hester. Or do you prefer "My Lady"?'

'I prefer Hester, actually,' she answered softly, gesturing him to a seat across the table from her.

'Coffee or a drink?'

'Coffee, please.'

She nodded, beckoning the waiter.

'Living with the toffs certainly isn't doing you any harm,' John said when the waiter had gone. 'You look great.'

'You look good yourself.' She couldn't take her eyes from him. 'It really is good to see you.'

He smiled at the white lie. He knew he wasn't the man he used to be.

'How's the private investigating business?' she asked, feeling slightly embarrassed.

'Not bad at all. Oddly enough, the Rice episode gave me something of a reputation. When I got out of Garnhill and back into harness I found I was much in demand. A silver lining you might say.'

'I'm pleased for you,' she replied. 'You certainly deserve it.'

'I must admit, Hester, I was surprised to get your telephone call.'

'I noticed that you've moved.'

He grinned. 'A place in the West End. I've been there a while now.'

'Very nice, too,' she said admiringly.

Their eyes met, and held. 'You're not the only one who likes to get on, you know,' he replied, the old sardonic smile returning.

Hester looked away.

The coffee arrived, breaking the moment of tension.

'You mentioned some problem on the phone,' John said while she poured.

She nodded. 'I need a private investigator. I immediately thought of you.'

'Does that mean I'm the only one you know?' he teased.

'True,' she smiled back. 'But there's more to it than just that. I need someone who's not only good but discreet. Someone I can trust.'

He gave her a quizzical, searching look. 'So what's the job?'

Hester coloured slightly. 'It's . . . it's my husband, Rory. I think he's seeing someone else.'

John sipped his coffee, his gaze never leaving her face.

She went on slowly. 'I might well be wrong. I'm hoping I am, of course, but I have a feeling. . . .' Her words trailed off into nothing.

John extracted a box of cigars from his pocket. 'I had these at home. I thought you might want one.'

Hester glanced round the lounge of The Ivanhoe Hotel. If she were to light up in here every eye in the place would be on her. Which was the last thing she wanted or needed.

'Not for the moment, thank you,' she replied. 'I'm flattered you remembered.'

'Are you?'

She spooned sugar into her cup, stirring it slowly. 'Will you take the job?'

'Of course.'

'Thank you,' she smiled. 'I feel better already.'

He leaned forward in his chair bringing himself close to her. 'What makes you suspect Rory is being unfaithful?'

She winced at hearing the word out loud. 'Nothing in particular. Just a lot of little things that add up, or seem to add up.'

'Such as?'

She glanced sideways at him. 'I don't find this easy to say. Especially to you.'

'I appreciate your difficulty. And, of course, you don't

254

have to tell me anything if you don't want to – but it would help.'

Hester said slowly, speaking with effort. 'Well, I suppose the main thing is the obvious one. About a year ago he stopped being as attentive to me in bed as he had been.'

'And did this happen suddenly or gradually?'

She paused to reflect. 'You know I can't quite remember so I suppose it must have been gradual. But there was one specific day when I suddenly realized that where we used to make love four or five times a week it was now down to one or two. And some weeks not at all.

'And is that how it still is?'

Hester dropped her gaze. 'No. Now, it's about once a fortnight. If that.'

John nodded, biting his lip. 'What other things have made you suspicious?'

'A look in his eye I sometimes see. A look of love which has nothing to do with me. And, oh, lots of other things. No lipstick on his collar, or anything. Just feelings.'

'Such as?'

'Dowsing himself with talcum powder before he goes out in the evenings, staring vacantly into space, just not being as close to me in spirit as he used to be.'

'Have you no hard evidence of any sort? No obvious lies about where he's been? No scent or perfume that isn't yours? No letters or telephone calls that might be suspicious?

'No, nothing.'

'So there's very little to go on, really. Except that he isn't making love to you as often as he was?'

'Yes.'

'Have you considered the possibility that there's no one else and that you're just imagining there is? Maybe it all means nothing, Hester. Maybe he's just cooled down.'

She glanced at him to see if that had been intended to hurt, but his expression was one of concern.

'I have, John. I've thought of all those things.'

255

'And you still think there's someone else?'

'Let me put it this way,' she said. 'If there is then that's one problem I'm faced with. And if there isn't then that's another. But I want to know which one it is so I can try and deal with it.'

'Fair enough. When do you want me to start?'

'As soon as you can.'

He thought for a few seconds. 'Well, I'm on something at the moment, but I can have it wrapped up by the weekend. How about next Monday morning?'

'That would be fine.'

'If there is someone else do you think he's only seeing her through the day? Or at night? Or both?'

Hester shrugged. 'I really couldn't say. Often Rory doesn't get in till fairly late. And, of course, he doesn't work during the day so his time's his own then.'

John looked thoughtful. 'In that case, I really should take on some help. That way we can keep a twenty-four-hour watch on him.'

'I think that would be best. I want this settled as soon as possible.'

'I'll contact you when I've got something, one way or the other. Is that satisfactory?'

'Quite.'

'Then leave it to me.' John rose, extending his hand. 'A pleasure seeing you again, My Lady.'

She watched him weave his way past the tables, and until he'd disappeared out into the street.

Hester stared down at the open magazine on her lap but her thoughts were elsewhere. With a shake of the head, she focused her attention on Rory who was sitting across the fireplace from her, immersed in a book.

'God, how I wish I had more to do with my life. It's so boring doing nothing all day long,' she said.

Rory grunted and glanced up at her. 'What was that, Hess?'

She repeated what she'd said.

'I'd hardly call looking after this house nothing. There are menus to plan, servants to organize, a dozen things or more to occupy your mind. And then you have your column in *The Scotsman*, as well, and the other one in the *Herald*. A pretty full itinerary, I'd say.'

Hester's column in the *Glasgow Herald* was the society one Alan Beat had suggested that day outside the house in Julian Avenue. She'd thought about it for a while, then gone to Will to ask his advice – and use his connections.

Will had appreciated why she couldn't, and wouldn't, work for Billy, and told her to leave it with him. Within the week he'd organized the column with the *Herald*, Glasgow's most prestigious newspaper.

The society column came out monthly, and had been a big success. Her by-line for it was Viscountess Kilmichael, but for *The Scotsman* she was still H. Dark.

Hester wrinkled her nose. 'An hour in the morning takes care of the house. And as for my columns, two afternoons every month is all they require. Which leaves me an awful lot of time on my hands.'

She thought about the garage, but with a sinking feeling. She could always resume the running of that again, if she wanted to, but the truth was that she'd completely lost interest in it. Besides Dan Black, whom she'd put at the helm shortly after her marriage, was doing a splendid job. It would only be a mistake on her part to rock that particular boat in any way.

No, the garage was definitely out. Dan Black would stay in charge, and she would remain contented to take the profits that came her way every week, and leave it at that.

Of course, what she really wanted to do was become a reporter, Scotland's first woman reporter, but that dream was more impossible now than ever before. Writing a society column was one thing, being a reporter another. Not even Will's influence could help her acquire such a position.

'I'll get it!' Rory said when the telephone rang.

Hester watched him narrowly as he picked up the receiver, barely breathing lest she miss a word. It was Monday night. John had begun his surveillance that morning.

'Oh, hello, Peter! How are you?' Rory said, perhaps a little loudly.

Peter, she wondered? He'd seen Peter only that afternoon. Or so he'd claimed.

'I think a game of squash would be a champion idea!' Rory enthused. Then, turning to Hester, 'Do you mind?'

She shook her head.

'Right, it's on. I'll meet you there,' Rory said into the phone, and hung up.

Had it really been Peter Elliot? She had no way of knowing. The telephone was too far away for her even to hear whether the voice had been male or female.

'A game of squash is precisely what I feel like right now,' Rory said heartily, crossing to Hester and pecking her on the cheek.

'Enjoy yourself, then,' she smiled up at him. 'And don't worry about hurrying back. I'll have an early night.'

'Righto!' Rory said cheerfully, and fairly bounced from the room.

Was it John or the person he'd taken on to help him who'd be waiting outside, Hester wondered? Whichever, they'd be following Rory to the squash courts. Or any other rendezvous.

She was pouring herself a liberal measure of Dutch gin when the outside door banged shut. She smiled grimly.

Blonde or brunette she wondered. Or was it a redhead? And what would she be like?

It was a blustery April day. The wind had a cutting edge to it as it swept in off the Atlantic, the sky overhead was grey and leaden, the sea angry and as grey as the sky.

Hester stared off to the right where she could just see the small town of Seamill, which they'd come through on their way here.

'You're looking very thoughtful,' Peter said.

She turned to him. He was sitting beside her on the Black Watch tartan blanket spread on the pebble beach.

'Not really. Just a little cold that's all.'

He twisted the top off a flask and poured out some coffee which he handed to her. 'That'll warm the cockles,' he said.

Hester smiled at Peter. She liked him. He was very easy to get on with, and had a great natural sense of fun.

She sipped the black coffee which smelled strongly of the whisky that had been mixed into it. 'Lovely.'

Peter lit cigarettes and passed her one. 'There's Rory now,' he said indicating further down the beach to where Rory had just come into sight having been off on his own for a ramble.

They watched Rory make his way to a large finger of stone that stood by the water's edge pointing skywards. On reaching the stone, Rory leaned against it and stared out to sea.

'I've enjoyed this run down to the coast,' Peter said. 'It was a good idea of yours.'

'Well, anything to get out of the house. I feel trapped in there at times.'

'That bad, eh?'

'That bad,' she confirmed, giving him a brief smile.

She laid her head back and, closing her eyes, sucked in a deep lungful of tangy air. As a result of the Atlantic wind, her cheeks were ruddy with colour.

'Why did you never marry?' she asked suddenly, opening one eye to stare at him.

'What makes you ask that?' he asked lightly, but regarding her thoughtfully.

'I was wondering about it on the way down here. I would have thought some enterprising female would have snapped you up long before now.'

'There have been a few who have certainly tried,' he grinned.

'Such as Tony Bowie?' Tony had been Peter's girl-friend at the time she'd first met him, but for some reason they'd stopped seeing one another.

Peter nodded.

'I liked her. I thought you made a good couple.'

He picked up a pebble and threw it into the sea. 'I liked her too. But not enough to propose marriage. Anyway, I'm too set in my ways for that sort of thing. Too much the confirmed bachelor.'

'Rory managed to cope. I'm sure you're no more set in your ways than he was.'

Peter glanced across to where Rory was still standing at the finger of stone staring into the endless distance. 'I don't have the great need for an heir that he has,' he said quietly.

What a strange remark, Hester thought. Insulting too, if taken the wrong way. But what was the right way to take it?

Hester watched John weaving his way through the tables and chairs of The Ivanhoe's lounge as he made his way towards her. It was a fortnight to the day since her last meeting with him here.

She was tight inside. Nervous. Prepared for the worst. Her left thigh was trembling.

'Hello,' he said, sitting down across from her.

'Coffee?' she asked. 'A drink?'

He shook his head.

She'd been hoping he'd ask for a drink so she'd have an excuse to have one herself. Now she'd have to make do with the pot of tea standing before her.

'Let me have it then,' she said.

John sat back in his chair. His face was composed, but his eyes were guarded from within. 'There's absolutely nothing to let you have,' he said.

Her eyebrows shot up. She stared at him, waiting.

'He's definitely not seeing another woman, Hester.'

'You're positive?'

'Absolutely. We've followed him everywhere. I probably know more about his movements than he knows himself. There's no other woman.'

There was a pause. 'Then it's simply that he's gone off me,' Hester said slowly.

John's lips thinned as he stared at her.

'Well, at least I now know where I stand.'

For a brief second pity showed in John's eyes, then it was gone. 'I'll be off then,' he said, already starting to rise.

'Wait, John. What about your fee?'

He smiled at her mockingly. 'This one's on the house.'

'Don't be daft! You've a living to earn. I've taken up two weeks of your time, not to mention the help you took on.'

He shook his head. 'This one's on me. That's the way I want it.'

'I can easily afford it, John. Money's the least of my problems.'

'Yes, I know that,' he said gently. 'So let's just say this is a gesture. For old times.'

She stared up at his now completely impassive face. 'Then thank you,' she said softly. 'Thank you very much.'

He nodded, obviously eager to be gone.

She was about to say goodbye, but he'd already turned and started to weave his way back through the tables and chairs.

She beckoned the waiter over and ordered a drink anyway, to blazes with what anybody thought. She was in no mood for convention now.

Part of her was greatly relieved that Rory wasn't having an affair. But another part was deeply hurt that the fault seemed to lie with her. Another woman was one thing. She could cope with that, but if he simply didn't love her any more, what could she do?

Where had she gone wrong? It was a question she was to agonize over for many days and nights to come.

It was early afternoon, not long after lunch. The earl had appeared out of the blue to pay them a visit.

The chat so far had been of this and that; about nothing in particular. But Hester sensed it was leading up to something.

'No news yet, my dear?' asked the earl, smiling expectantly at Hester.

She frowned. 'What sort of news?'

'Additions to the family. My first grandson.'

The old pain and guilt stabbed through her when she saw how eager he was. What a fraud she was. There would never, could never, be the grandson he so desperately craved.

Rory shifted uneasily in his chair.

'There's nothing wrong in that department, I hope?' his father asked reluctantly.

'No, no!' Hester replied quickly. 'Just a case of nature taking its course. Eh, Rory?'

'Quite so,' he replied, refusing to look her straight in the eye.

'You've been married a while now. . . .'

'Only three-and-a-half years. Hardly any time at all!' Hester tried making a joke of it. 'Give us a chance, will you!'

He smiled ruefully. 'It's just that . . . well, I am getting on, you'll appreciate. And tempus does fugit.'

'We do realize how important this is for you, Father,' Rory said softly.

He was such a marvellous old man, Hester thought. She would have done anything to provide the heir he wanted to continue his family line.

'Would you be upset if I suggested something?' he asked, looking embarrassed. 'Merely for my own peace of mind.'

'What is it?' asked Hester.

He cleared his throat nervously. 'I'm sure nothing *is* wrong. But just to be on the safe side, why don't you both visit a doctor?'

'You mean have ourselves checked out?' Rory snorted. 'Honestly Father! What a vulgar idea!'

Alarm fluttered in Hester. Going to a doctor was the last thing she wanted.

'I agree with Rory,' she said. 'And, anyway, it's early days yet. Lots of couples go far longer than we have before something happens. I honestly think worrying about it is the very last thing we should be doing. Worry can *create* problems where there were none before.'

'Hmmh!' murmured the earl.

'So let's have no more talk of doctors and the like,' Hester smiled.

And quickly changed the subject.

Perhaps a little while apart would stimulate matters between them again, she decided a few days later, glancing sideways at Rory who was sitting with a glass of whisky in his hand, staring vacantly off into space. The more she thought about it, the more the idea appealed to her.

'Rory dear?'

He brought himself out of his reverie to glance across at her.

'I was just thinking,' she said. 'Would you mind if I went down to London for a week?'

'London!' he exclaimed. 'Why there?'

'Well, for a start I've never been, and I would like to see it, at least once. Then there are the shops I've heard so much about: Harrods, Liberty's, Fortnum and Mason. I've wanted to have a good traipse round those for as long as I can remember.'

'Then I don't see why you shouldn't go,' he replied. 'Would you like me to come with you?'

She smiled fondly. 'You know you hate shops. If I

want to enjoy myself in them it's best I go alone. Thank you for offering though, I appreciate it.'

'When do you plan to be off?'

She considered. 'How about Monday morning? I'll travel back the following Sunday.'

'Fine,' he replied.

'And for not minding my going, I'll bring you back a special present.'

'Done!' he replied happily, and toasted her with his glass.

Late the following Saturday night Hester was on her way home in a taxi from the Central Station. Having been told by the receptionist at her London hotel that there was always a certain amount of delay travelling by rail on a Sunday – apparently that was when all the repair work was carried out – she'd decided to return home twenty-four hours early.

Hester was in a happy, joyous mood. She'd had an absolutely splendid time. She'd gone on a real spending spree; most of her purchases were being sent up by parcel post.

One item she had brought with her was Rory's special present, which she'd purchased in Harrods. She'd noticed some time ago that his shaving brush was almost worn out, so she'd bought him a new one. It was a splendid brush made of badger bristles with an ivory handle inlaid with a silver crest on which she'd had his name inscribed. She knew he'd be pleased with it.

On arriving at the house, she saw that the lights were out. Everyone, it appeared, had gone to bed early. Rather than ring the bell and rouse the servants, she opened the door herself and instructed the taxi driver to bring her cases into the hall.

After paying the driver, she quietly made her way up the stairs to the master bedroom.

She paused inside the bedroom door to listen to the

sound of Rory's snoring. It was a sound she'd missed in the week she'd been away.

Her heart jumped within her when, eyes finally accustomed to the dark, she realized that there were two figures in the bed.

The soft smile she'd been wearing died.

He *was* having an affair after all! And he even brought the bitch into *her* bed. Reaching out, she snapped on the light.

Rory and Peter, naked from the waist up, lay in each other's arms. On the bedside table stood an empty champagne bottle and two glasses.

Hester stood rooted to the spot, struck speechless by the sight confronting her. This was the last thing she'd expected.

Suddenly everything clicked into place. A hot sickness rose inside her. For a few terrible moments she thought she might faint or be ill.

Her husband was a homosexual!

The world spun. She had to lean against the wall to steady herself.

Anger boiled into a blind fury. She'd been right all along. Rory had been in love with someone else. Only not with another woman as she'd naturally imagined. But with his best and lifelong friend.

Scarcely knowing what she was doing, she ran to the chest of drawers where the ice bucket, now filled with melted water, stood. Uttering a sob, she snatched up the bucket and threw its contents over the two sleeping men.

Rory yelled. Peter spluttered. Then they both ducked behind their arms as a storm of missiles was hurled at them. Hairbrushes, combs, perfume bottles. Anything, and everything, Hester could lay her hands on she threw at them. Even a wooden chair which splintered against the back wall.

'Hess! Hess!' Rory called out.

But she wasn't listening. She ran from the room, rushing blindly downstairs and banging the outside door behind her as she fled into the night, her body racked with sobs.

Her car was still at the kerb and its keys were in her pocket. It was the work of seconds to get inside and start the engine. With a roar and the screech of tyres, the car shot off down the street.

She could hardly see for the tears flooding her eyes. She gave great gulping sob after sob as she drove automatically, with no destination in mind.

The picture of what she'd seen would be imprinted in her mind till the day she died. Even in her dreams she would see them, the looks on their sleeping faces, the familiarity of their embrace.

A queer.

The word burned in her brain. Revulsion swept through her.

Things became hazy after that. She drove on and on, with no thought of where she was going or what she would do once she got there. Where could she go?

It wasn't until she was driving through the West End that she suddenly thought of John. She would go to him. He would help and comfort her.

Not knowing his address by heart, she had to stop at a phone box and look it up in the book. She was only a few streets away from where he lived.

The iron gate fronting the close squeaked as she opened it. The close itself was newly whitewashed, lighted by a flickering gas lamp.

She found his nameplate on the third landing. She tugged at the bell-pull, then rapped the heavy oak door.

When there was no reply, she again tugged the bell-pull and rapped the door. A few seconds later, she heard noises from within.

'Who's there?' demanded a woman's voice.

For a moment, Hester was at a loss. 'It's Hester McNeill. I want to speak to John,' she replied at last.

The door was opened cautiously to reveal a pretty red-haired woman. 'I'm afraid my husband's out,' she said.

Husband! John had never mentioned being married. Then she realized she'd never asked him anything about himself during their two meetings in The Ivanhoe. What arrogance, she thought. It had never entered her mind that John would be married, or even seriously involved. For some completely ludicrous reason, she'd presumed he'd be living on his own. Fool, she chided herself. Had she thought he could never replace her?

The woman smiled kindly 'We've met before, actually. At Garnhill. I was a nurse there.'

Hester returned the smile. 'I remember now,' she lied. She had no recollection whatsoever of the face before her.

'Can I get John to ring you when he comes in?'

'No, I needed him now. But as he isn't available I'll find someone else,' she said. Another lie. But it neatly extracted her from her predicament.

'I'll tell him you called, shall I?'

'Sorry to have woken you,' Hester said. Then with a nod of her head she turned and made her way back down the stairs.

Once back in the car she started driving aimlessly again, criss-crossing Glasgow from north to south, then east to west. Dawn was beginning to glow on the horizon when it suddenly came to her that John must have known about Rory and Peter.

What had his exact words been? 'He's definitely not seeing another *woman*, Hester' and 'There is no other *woman* involved'.

Both times he'd been quite specific about that. It was the only thing he had been specific about.

How must John have felt to discover that the man she'd thrown him over for was not a man at all? It said a lot for him that he'd witheld the truth from her, instead of rubbing her nose in it the way he might have done.

Suddenly she was thankful John hadn't been at home. She doubted she'd ever be able to face him again, especially because of his sensitivity.

'Oh God!' she whispered, and making a fist with her

right hand, she beat the steering wheel again and again and again.

When she got home a little later she found Rory dressed and waiting for her. His face was cream-coloured, his eyes strangely calm.

'Drink?' he asked.

She nodded, wordlessly.

'I suppose we'd better talk about last night,' he said, when he was sitting facing her.

The whisky was raw and pungent. It burned away the vile taste that had lingered at the back of her throat. 'What do the servants know?' she asked.

'They don't. With the exception of Harkness. I told him about Peter when he first came into my employ a little over ten years ago.'

She looked Rory straight in the eye, though it took all the strength she had. 'Are there others?'

Rory held her gaze. 'No. Peter's the only one there's ever been,' he replied softly.

She could tell that was the truth. Something inside her eased a little. 'You and Peter. . . . Since Cambridge, then, I take it?'

'Before. Kelvinside Academy,' Rory answered quietly.

'As long as that.'

'Yes.'

She sipped her whisky, though more for something to do than because she was enjoying it.

During her aimless driving, she'd remembered something Peter had said when the three of them had gone down the coast together. He'd said he didn't have the great need for an heir that Rory had.

'Did you marry me just to have children?' she asked in a flat, empty voice.

'No, Hester. There was a lot more to it than that.'

'I find that difficult to believe.'

He said, patiently, tenderly. 'Let me try to explain. Will you listen?'

268

She nodded, sitting further back in her chair.

'Peter and I became lovers during our second year at the Academy. Right from the word go we'd been very drawn to one another. Bosom pals. That sort of thing. And somehow it just sort of developed from there.'

She stared at him, frozen. Surely this was a terrible nightmare from which she'd waken any second now.

But it was no nightmare. It was the horrible reality.

Rory went on gently. 'Peter set his cap at Cambridge when he knew that was where I wanted to go and to our great delight we both got places. So we stayed together and our relationship deepened.'

'But when I first met you I was told you had a reputation as a ladies' man!'

Rory smiled softly. 'Peter and I both took out a number of women, during Cambridge and after. But none of them ever meant anything to us, they were there simply as a blind.'

'But surely you and Peter slept with some of these women?'

Rory shook his head. 'Peter, never, though I did once or twice.'

'You mean Peter and Tony Bowie. . . ?'

'No.'

Hester couldn't hide her surprise. How true that you never really knew about people! 'What I still can't understand is why you married me if it wasn't merely for the purpose of producing an heir?'

Rory cleared his throat, then drank some whisky.

'For years the old boy had been going on at me to get married. He was forever reminding me that it was my duty to see that the family name was carried on. So, eventually, and very reluctantly, I decided to fulfil that duty.'

He paused, memories flooding his face. 'Peter and I discussed the matter at length. We decided that we'd go on seeing one another, but break off sexual relations. If either of us were to marry, then we'd have a proper shot at making it work. So, having agreed that between us, we started looking.'

'Which was when you met up again with me?'

'Not quite. Two years had passed before I bumped into you in the gallery. Two years of sheer hell. We'd both met and taken women out a lot, but neither of us found any one we even considered going to bed with.' Suddenly Rory stopped. 'Does this upset you?' he asked.

Her silence was reply enough.

'We were about to give it up as a bad job and get together again, when suddenly I met you, and something happened. Because you were different, I was genuinely attracted to you. You were the first woman who'd ever had that effect on me. You have to believe that.'

'I do believe you, Rory. I suppose I should be flattered.'

'I don't know about that,' Rory laughed sadly. 'But I knew if I was ever to get married and make it work it would have to be to you.'

'But why *me*?'

'I can't explain why you. You had – you have – a quality with which I empathize. You also have the same sort of easiness about you, at least to me, that Peter has. I feel relaxed in your company. You're the second-best friend I've ever had.'

'But did you actually fancy me?'

'Yes,' he said, and laughed softly. 'That must sound like the worst sort of backhanded compliment. But I did. I still do.'

'My boyish figure?'

'I'm sure that was part of it,' he replied honestly. 'But only part. I fell in love with you, Hess. Only the second time it's ever happened to me.'

'If you still love me, why did you resume your affair with Peter?' she asked, more bewildered than curious.

He shrugged. 'We didn't plan to. But Peter had become so wretched. Our separation had worked for me: I had you. But it hadn't for him. He was all alone.'

'But surely if he keeps on looking he'll find someone? There must be some woman somewhere who'll attract him?'

'Peter doesn't think so. We both believe I was extraordinarily lucky in finding you. A chance in a million. Odds like that don't come up twice.'

'And you resumed with Peter because he was so wretched?'

Rory nodded.

Hester sighed. What a complicated situation this was turning out to be.

'And having gone back to Peter you're now off me?'

Rory pulled a face. 'I honestly didn't realize how I'd been drifting away from you lately. Neglecting you. Taking you for granted. It's only since you ran out last night that I've understood how badly I've been treating you.'

'I think I'll have another drink,' she said, her mind a jumble of confused thoughts and feelings. She needed time to sift through all she'd been told and all that had happened. Time to consider and digest it all.

Inwardly, she smiled as the full irony of it hit her. Rory had originally gone looking for a woman capable of giving him an heir, and ended up, in love if he was to be believed, with one who could never do so.

'Do your parents know about you and Peter?' she asked.

'Good Lord, no! It would kill the old boy if he ever found out. He's pretty tolerant in his way – but there are things he could never accept.'

'And your mother?'

'It wouldn't kill her, but it would shake her up quite a bit. I think I can safely say she'd never be the same again.'

Hester was suddenly tired. She had no strength left to think, yet alone talk. In less than twenty-four hours, her world had turned completely upside down.

She rose, smoothing down the front of her dress. 'I must get some sleep, Rory. I'll have a bed made up in one of the spare rooms.'

'Then what, Hester?'

'Then I don't know. I'll go away for a few more days. There's a great deal I've got to think about.'

She was halfway to the door when he said, 'I'm sorry Hess.'

She turned to look at him. 'I am, too.'

She took a suite in one of the better hotels in the centre of town. It was from there that she telephoned Julian Avenue three days later.

An hour after she'd made the call Will arrived. 'I came right away,' he said, flushed and out of breath.

She showed him to a chair and poured them both a stiff drink.

'You look terrible,' he said.

'I haven't been sleeping well for the past few nights.'

'It shows.'

She couldn't help but laugh. 'You're great for a girl's ego,' she said.

'What's wrong Hester? And how can I help?' he asked softly.

'I rang you because you're the only one I can speak to about this,' she said, holding on to her drink as though it were a life raft.

He took out a cigar, clipped and lit it, his gaze never leaving her face.

'I'm afraid it's . . . it's very embarrassing.'

'After all that's happened, Hester, there's nothing you and I can't say to one another. There's no need for embarrassment. Tell me what's bothering you.'

She took a deep breath, staring down at her hands. 'It's Rory. I've just discovered that he's been a homosexual since he was at school.' Having managed to speak those words out loud, she immediately burst into a flood of tears.

Instantly, Will was out of his chair and by her side. Taking her in his arms he held her tightly against his chest.

272

The dam of pain and hurt had broken. The tears flowed in torrents while she sobbed.

'There, there, lass,' Will mumbled, helplessly patting her on the back.

Only after a long while did the flood become a trickle and the sobbing cease.

'Tell me about it,' Will said, when she was finally calm. Together they sat on a sofa, one of her hands in his, as Hester told him about her London trip, and what she'd found on her return. She also told him almost word for word the subsequent conversation she'd had with Rory.

'Well,' he said when she was finally finished. 'Well.'

'What am I to do?' she asked, her eyes huge and wet. Will got to his feet and poured them both another drink. 'Do you love him?' he asked at last.

She wiped at the tears still in her eyes. 'I'm not in love with him, if that's what you mean. But I am genuinely fond of him.'

Will sipped his whisky, his brow creased in thought. 'May I ask what your reasons were for marrying him?'

'He's an intelligent, good-looking man who I thought was in love with me. He has position, money, charm. Everything a girl could dream of. And he made me happy. Being with him made me forget how lonely I had been.'

'And does he love you?'

'He says he does. But he also loves Peter.'

'Then you have to ask yourself two questions. Number one: do you want to hold on to Rory? Despite what's happened, he's still the man who so attracted you in the first place.'

'And the second question?'

'Are you willing for him to continue his relationship with this Peter?'

'No!' she exclaimed. 'That I won't have. I won't share him with someone else, man or woman.'

'Does that mean you would stay on with him, provided he gave up Peter?'

273

Hester's mind was whirling. Did she or didn't she? Could she ever forgive him or ever forget? What chance would they have now?

She shrugged her shoulders.

'Then you must take time to examine your feelings and motives thoroughly. There is time, Hester. You needn't be in a hurry.'

'And what about Rory? He might not want us to continue together?'

'What do you think?'

She shook her head. 'I really don't know. What I do know is that both he and his father are desperate for the family line to go on.'

Will's eyes grew dark. 'Which means, I take it, that they don't know that you can't have children?'

'Yes,' she whispered, avoiding his gaze.

'Is that fair, Hester?'

'Is life fair?' she sobbed, fresh tears welling up. 'Was it fair of you to seduce me when I was only a child? Was any of it fair? Who the hell are you to talk of fair?'

'Indeed,' he sighed. 'Who am I to talk.'

'Oh!' she wept, burying her face in her hands. 'Don't think I don't feel guilty about it. But it was never really intentional. I didn't realize until it was too late just how much it might mean to him. I only wanted to be happy. Is that so big a crime?' She turned her red and hunted eyes to him. 'Do you think that's such a crime?'

'What I think is that you've changed a lot since you left Julian Avenue,' he answered softly. 'And maybe I am the one to blame.'

Hester had arrived home just before dinner, which had been eaten mainly in silence. It was exactly one week to the night since she'd discovered Rory and Peter in bed together.

She and Rory were now facing one another across the

274

fire. They both looked up when there was a discreet knock on the door.

Harkness entered. 'Will there be anything else tonight, My Lord?'

'No, Harkness. We'll look after ourselves now, thank you.'

Harkness inclined his head, then left the room, closing the door quietly behind him.

'We can talk now,' Rory said.

Hester allowed a few moments to elapse before saying, 'The main question to be answered is whether we go on together or get a divorce.'

'I want us to go on,' Rory replied instantly.

'Are you absolutely certain about that?'

'Yes,' he answered. 'And you? How do you feel?'

She stared ahead of her at the dancing flames. Finally she said, slowly, hesitatingly, 'If we do continue, there would have to be certain conditions, Rory.'

'Which are?'

'First that you sever all connections with Peter, once and for all. I won't share you with anyone else. It's either Peter or me. You have to make a choice.'

Rory took a deep breath, running his hands through his hair. 'I was expecting you to say that,' he replied miserably.

'One or the other. You can't have both.'

Rory bowed his head. 'If I gave you my word that Peter and I would only have a platonic friendship from now on. . . .'

'No!' Hester said sharply. 'It wouldn't stay that way. You know it wouldn't. You sever all connections. I won't budge from that.'

His eyes remained fixed on the carpet. His left hand trembled slightly.

'Well?'

Rory gave the slightest of nods.

'If you agree, then look at me and say so.'

The eyes reluctantly brought to bear on hers were

filled with anguish. 'I must see him one last time to finish it between us. That's the least I can do after all these years.'

'One last time then,' Hester replied more gently, her own heart pounding.

She allowed another silence to grow between them, then said, 'The second condition is that we sleep apart for a while. I need time before I let you near me again.'

'All right,' he whispered.

'And the last thing is that you get rid of that bed, the one that was ours. I want it out of this house first thing tomorrow morning.'

'I understand,' he said. 'I'll see to it myself.'

One night two months later Hester was on her way upstairs when suddenly everything seemed to dissolve before her eyes, and she felt herself falling.

It was one of the maids who found her, trying to crawl along the corridor. Within seconds, Rory was by her side, cradling her in his arms. He felt her burning forehead. 'Get a doctor,' he snapped to Harkness who immediately set off at a run.

Lifting Hester, he carried her through to her bedroom, where he insisted on tending to her himself. Carefully, and very gently, he stripped her and got her into her nightdress. Then he put several extra blankets on the bed, making sure they were tucked up to her chin.

She smiled at him weakly. 'It came on so suddenly,' she whispered. 'One moment I was fine. The next it was as though the world had caved in.'

He patted her reassuringly. 'Harkness is fetching a doctor. We shouldn't have long to wait.'

It pleased her he'd said *we* and not you. 'I feel like I'm on fire,' she whispered.

Instantly, he was on his feet and crossing to the sink. He soaked a hand-towel in cold water and used it to wipe and cool her face.

'Very tired,' she mumbled.

'Then sleep.'

'Should wait for the doctor.'

'Sleep till he comes.'

Hester heard that last as though from a long way away. She tried to answer, but it was beyond her. She floated off into space. In her mind she was riding a fluffy white cloud that was bearing her up to the stars.

Hester came to with a start. Her mouth was tacky. Her head throbbing. Rory was sitting by the bedside smiling at her.

'Has the doctor been yet?' she asked.

'Hours ago. You've got a bad dose of flu.'

'Is that all? I thought it must be the plague at least.'

They both laughed at that, and the laughter was good between them.

'The doctor gave you an injection. He's left some tablets. He said you were to take two when you woke up.'

She tried to struggle onto her elbows, but found she didn't have the strength. Rory helped her, catching her under the arms and drawing her gently up the bed. He put a shawl round her shoulders. Then went to the sink for a glass of water.

The tablets were relatively small, but felt huge in her mouth. Like gobstoppers, she thought, her mind going back to those far-off days in Bristol when her father used to buy them for her as a Saturday treat. She smiled to herself at the memory.

'Anything you'd like?' Rory asked.

She started to shake her head, but quickly stopped because it hurt too much.

'Then get some more sleep. That's the best thing for you.'

'Yes,' she whispered, feeling dreadfully tired again.

Rory removed the shawl and helped her slip back down the bed into a sleeping position. He then placed a fresh glass of water within easy reach.

'If you need anything during the night just call out. I'll hear,' he said.

'Goodnight,' she whispered.

'Goodnight, love,' he replied.

She was well enough to get up, she decided. She'd been in bed for six days now, and the last two days she'd definitely been on the mend.

'Come in!' she called out when there was a knock on her door.

Rory breezed in carrying her breakfast tray. 'How are you today?' he asked brightly.

She told him her decision. He agreed that she was looking a great deal better.

'I still feel a wee bit weak, mind you,' she said. 'But once I'm up and about that'll soon pass.' She reached out to touch his wrist. 'I want to thank you for how kind you've been. I appreciate it.'

'It wasn't a chore, I can assure you,' he replied softly.

The look in his eyes told her he wanted her. And, in truth, she knew she wanted him. It had been a long two months.

There was a strange newness about her, as if she'd been born a second time out of the fever that had wracked her mind and body. Perhaps it was the perfect time for a fresh beginning.

'If you want to, you can lock the door,' she suggested.

A little later they lay together, his head against her breasts. She stroked the thick hair at the nape of his neck. 'I'll have my bits and pieces moved back into our bedroom,' she whispered. 'What do you think?'

In answer, he looked up at her and smiled.

Smiling in return, she pulled him back to her breasts.

Rory laid down his knife and fork. Then wiped his mouth with a napkin. He and Hester were in the middle of dinner.

'I know we agreed to sever all connections but none the less I had a telephone call from Peter today while you were out at work,' he announced.

Hester glanced up. It was now five months since Rory and Peter had made the break. She gave Rory her full attention, waiting for him to go on.

'He's off to Ottawa in a fortnight. His bank had a post open there which he applied for and got. He say he's looking forward to it. He rather likes the idea of Canada.'

'I think he's wise going away. Best thing for him,' Hester replied, unable to hide her relief.

'The reason for his phone call was not only to tell me he was going abroad. He wanted to know if I'd see him off. I'd like to Hess. What do you say?'

What could she say? If Peter was going away for good, she could hardly forbid them their goodbyes. It would be both childish and cruel. 'Is he leaving from the Clyde?' she asked at last.

'Yes. Mavisbank Quay.'

'Then you'd better be there to say goodbye. You've been friends a long time, after all. And take him a present. Something really nice. He'll appreciate that.'

'Good idea.' He eyed her uneasily then asked, reluctantly, 'Would you like to come?'

She smiled, touched by his dilemma. 'I think it best you see him off on your own, don't you? You know I've always liked Peter, Rory. In spite of everything.'

'You are welcome,' he said, completely unconvincingly.

'I'm sure, but it's best you go alone.' Hester leaned over and laid her hand on his. 'You go,' she said gently. 'And wish him bon voyage from both of us.'

Darkness was falling when Rory got back. He found Hester waiting for him, a bottle of champagne cooling in the ice bucket by her side.

'I thought we'd share it,' she said, rising to kiss him.

'Smashing!' he replied jauntily. His smile seemed oddly fixed.

'How did it go?' she asked as he poured, watching him with concern.

'Fine. Quite an occasion, actually. There was a band and bunting and streamers.'

'And not a dry eye in the house?'

'Something like that,' he smiled.

They talked for a little while, as though it were an ordinary night, then Rory announced he was going to have a bath. He gave her a spontaneous kiss on the cheek before he left the room.

Hester finished off what remained of the champagne, then followed him upstairs.

Outside their bedroom door she paused. The door was ajar and through it she could see Rory sitting on the edge of the bed with his head in his hands. He was so still he might have been a statue.

She opened her mouth to speak, but changed her mind.

Turning she tiptoed back the way she'd come.

One night the following winter, Hester was motoring along Argyle Street. There had been a snowfall earlier and the streets were slushy and dangerous. Because of this, she was driving with extra care and attention, not letting her mind wander for a second from the road.

If she hadn't been so intent, she might have missed the figure crossing the street in front of her with several others on the pedestrian crossing.

Peter Elliot! There was no mistaking him.

Shock followed by anger filled her as she watched that so familiar figure hurry off into the night.

She came to her senses again when there was a hoot behind her. Putting the car into gear she moved forward, and after a few yards Peter was lost to sight. He might never have been there at all.

What was he doing back in Glasgow? she asked herself? And how long was it since he'd returned? But, more important, did Rory know?

He must, she thought. Peter was bound to have got word to him, contacted him even. So why hadn't he mentioned it to her?

The hands gripping the steering wheel tightened till their knuckles glowed white in the dark. There was only one reason why Rory would want to keep Peter's return secret. To let her go on believing that Peter was on the other side of the world: they had started seeing one another again.

She took a deep breath, deciding that the first thing to do was to find out if Peter was home for a visit or for good. If it was only for a visit her best policy might be to do and say nothing.

But if it was for good, then something would have to be done.

Rory had gone home to visit his parents, giving Hester the opportunity she needed. She rang Tony Bowie.

'Tony, it's Hester McNeill. How are you?'

'This is a surprise!' Tony exclaimed. 'I'm very well, thank you. And how's yourself?'

They made small talk for a few minutes, then Hester said, 'Listen, I'm hatching something of a conspiracy to do with Rory and I was wondering if you would help me?'

'If I can,' Tony replied, without hesitation.

Hester smiled to herself. She'd never known any female who would turn down the chance of being in on a conspiracy.

'Marvellous,' she said. 'Tell me, did you know Peter Elliot went off to Canada?'

'Yes, I did. We had an evening out together shortly before he left. And a most pleasant one it was, too.'

'Well, he's home again. I saw him in the street only yesterday.'

'Are you sure it was him?' asked Tony.

'It was him all right, there was no mistake about that. Now the thing is this. I need to know if he's back for a short time or for good. If it is only for a short time then I'll postpone the little item I've got cooked up for Rory as he won't want to go away while Peter's in town. But if Peter's home to stay a postponement isn't necessary. They can get together again afterwards. I would telephone Peter myself, but I'd have to explain everything to him and that's the last thing I want. Those two never could keep a secret from one another.'

'So you want *me* to telephone him?'

'Right. Would you do that? You could say it was you who saw him in the street.'

'I'll be happy to help you out.' She then continued, thoughtfully, 'You know I never did understand what went wrong between Peter and me. I was convinced we'd end up married like you and Rory.'

If only you knew, Hester thought. If only you knew!

'I'll ring you back once I've spoken with him,' Tony assured her.

'If you manage to get hold of him today, telephone me after nine this evening. Rory will be out then. Otherwise, I'll come back to you. And thanks, Tony. I'm most obliged.'

They said their goodbyes.

It had been a fairly convincing performance, Hester thought. A bit vague and woolly perhaps, but that made it ring all the more true somehow.

Hester drank some claret and stared at Rory across the table. Several times during dinner she'd considered casually mentioning Peter's name to see what response it evoked, but on each occasion had decided against it. Peter's name hadn't come up between them for months. If she mentioned it now, no matter how casually, it might make Rory suspicious.

A sudden doubt assailed her. Could it possibly be that she'd jumped to the wrong conclusion and that Peter and Rory hadn't been in touch? Was she creating problems where none existed? But no. It was one thing for them to be in the same town and not see one another, but for one to go so far abroad, then return without informing the other — that she just couldn't believe.

If Rory knew Peter was back in Glasgow, why hadn't he said so to her? Because he was seeing Peter again. That *had* to be the answer. Every instinct she possessed told her so.

Rory glanced across to catch her eye.

She smiled. 'Excellent claret,' she said.

'Hester? It's Tony. He *is* back for good. Returned three-and-a-half weeks ago.'

'Did he say why?' Hester asked.

'There's been some sort of "palace revolution" at the bank, his words not mine, and in the ensuing re-shuffle he was invited to return to Glasgow. Apparently it was a big promotion which, naturally enough, pleased him greatly. He was delighted to hear from me and asked me out next week. We're going to a dinner dance.'

Hester's stomach was churning. She'd been praying he was only home on holiday. 'Did he mention where he was staying?'

'With some friends at the moment,' Tony replied. 'He's bought a house out in Queen's Park, but he's having it completely redecorated before moving in. It's one of those old properties facing the park itself.'

'Well, that answers my question. Thank you very much, Tony. I'm in your debt.'

'Not at all. Any time, Hester. And listen, why don't we get together sometime? Just the two of us? We could have a few drinks and a natter?'

'I'd like that. I'm a bit tied up at the moment. I'll contact you in about a fortnight's time and we'll arrange something then?'

'I'll look forward to hearing from you.'

'Enjoy your night out with Peter. And we'll keep these

two telephone conversations to ourselves, all right?'

'Mum's the word,' said Tony, laughing softly.

'I'll be in touch, then.' After she'd hung up, she lit a cigarette, striking the match viciously against the box's abrasive side. 'Damn it!' she swore. 'Damn it!' She blinked back the tears.

Before confronting Rory she'd have to have proof that he was seeing Peter again. She'd already decided how she was going to get that proof.

She picked up the telephone again and rang Dan Black. When he came on the line she said, 'Dan, it's Hester. I want you to buy a car for me. And I want to take possession as soon as possible.'

'Certainly,' he replied. 'What did you have in mind?'

'Something nondescript and domestic. Four or five years old, perhaps. The sort of car you wouldn't look at twice. Can you do that for me?'

'No problem at all. I can nip up to the Car Market tomorrow morning and have it in the garage by the afternoon. Would you like it serviced before you use it?'

'No, that's not important. I'll drop by the garage late afternoon and pick it up.'

'It'll be ready and waiting for you.'

'Thanks, Dan. I'll see you then.'

She hung up, smiling grimly to herself.

A tail, was how John McCandlass had once described what she had in mind.

Four evenings later, at the conclusion of dinner, Rory said he had the notion to drop into his club for a few drinks and a game of billiards.

'Then off you go,' smiled Hester encouragingly.

'You don't mind?'

'Not in the least. I have a bit of research to do for my next column anyway.'

He kissed her on the cheek. 'I'll be careful not to wake you should you be asleep when I get back.'

Her smile never wavered till the door closed behind him. Then it vanished instantly, replaced by a look of both anguish and fear.

She waited till she heard the outside door slam shut, then hurried as quickly as she could to the rear of the house.

She opened the French windows and slipped outside, closing them behind her. She ran across the garden to the gate which let her out onto a side street where the Riley Dan had purchased for her stood waiting.

She'd left a coat in the car which she now hastily threw on against the bitter night. Seconds later she was turning left to follow the Phantom's rear lights ahead of her.

She didn't have to worry about the servants wondering where she'd got to. They'd assume she was pottering around somewhere; it was rare for them to go upstairs after dinner unless specifically asked to do so.

This was the fifth time she'd followed Rory. The other four times he had gone precisely where he'd said.

She kept a good distance between herself and the Phantom as Rory drove down Sauchiehall Street, finally turning into Buchanan Street.

Her heart sank. It looked like this was going to be yet another wasted trip. Buchanan Street was where his club was situated.

He could be meeting Peter in the club of course. That was a possibility she hadn't considered before, so she decided to hang around for a while after he'd gone inside in case he came out again with Peter in tow. But instead of stopping at the club, the Phantom kept on, heading south.

They crossed the Glasgow Bridge, which brought them into the filth and squalor of the Gorbals. Here the Phantom stood out like a diamond in a pile of rocks. People stopped to stare at it as it passed, but none of them gave the Riley a second glance. Hundreds of such cars were to be seen making their way through these blighted streets every day, headed for the more affluent suburbs further out on the south side.

When they reached Pollokshaws Road, Hester knew for certain what Rory's destination was. Less than half a mile further on was Queen's Park.

As the dark patch that was the park itself came into view, it started to snow again: large flakes that were soon swirling densely.

Hester sat hunched over the wheel, peering through the blurred windscreen. The wipers swished rhythmically.

When the Phantom drew up to the kerb, Hester overtook it to turn into the first side street she came to. Stepping out into slush, she hurried back the way she'd come.

The house the Phantom was parked outside was tall and imposing. Only one light showed at the very top.

She mounted the front steps to see if there was a nameplate, but there wasn't. Leaning over a railing she peered into a curtainless window to see a bare room in the middle of being decorated. Strewn about were a pair of ladders, several pots of paint, and floor covers. She knew then this was the right house.

She tried the door, but it was locked. What should she do next?

The sensible thing was to go home and confront Rory when he got back. After all, he could hardly deny he was seeing Peter again when with her own eyes she'd seen his car outside Peter's house.

She was actually heading back to the Riley when she decided to have a look round the rear of the house to see if she could gain entrance there. She discovered a narrow alleyway running off the main street itself and behind the row of houses amongst which Peter's was numbered. She counted off the houses till she came to Peter's, but was disappointed to discover that the back gate was closed. Then she saw a metal dustbin outside the gate of the next house along and, lifting it as best she could brought it back to stand it beside Peter's gate.

The wall into which the gate was built was a fraction over six feet high. Once up on the dustbin it was not too difficult to scramble over and she dropped down into a jungle of weeds.

The back of the house was in total darkness. Only the light spilling over from the adjoining houses enabled her to pick her way forward.

Her heart was thumping in her chest as she mounted a short flight of steps to the back door. Putting her hand on the heavy metal handle she turned it. The door swung open.

The smell of fresh paint mingled with turps was strong in her nostrils as she stepped inside.

Her hand groped and found a light switch, but when she flicked it nothing happened. Cautiously, she inched her way along the pitch-black cavern that was the hallway. Once through the hallway it became easier to see because of the street lights outside which gleamed through the curtainless windows.

She found and tried another switch. When that one also failed to work she concluded that the power must still be turned off. Thinking about the light she'd seen at the top of the house, she started up the stairs.

On the second landing she stumbled, her foot catching in a floor cover that had been left bunched up. She threw out her hands to catch hold of the bannister, saving herself from tumbling over and falling back down the stairs again.

Her heart was thundering now, her skin cold and prickly. She strained her ears in the direction of upstairs, but all she heard was a brooding silence.

She continued slowly, barely breathing, on her way. The higher she climbed the stronger grew the stink of paint and turps.

There were four flights of stairs. On reaching the top she paused to catch her breath.

Several doors led off. Through one she could see a

chink of light at the bottom. Tiptoeing to this one she pressed an ear against it, but she still couldn't hear anything.

Her hand was shaking as she took hold of the door handle. Silently it turned and the door opened.

The first thing she saw was a candle burning on top of a chest of drawers. Then she saw another. This one on a marble-topped washstand.

There were five candles in all, each casting eerie, flickering shadows on the newly painted ceiling and walls. Painters' paraphernalia lay strewn everywhere. In one corner of the room there was a double bed partially masked by a Chinese screen with red flying dragons painted on it. From behind the screen came the soft sound of heavy breathing, and the unmistakable sounds of lovemaking.

Hester bit her lip. Should she call out? Should she retreat? Very slowly, she started walking towards the screen. Her mouth was dry, her brain on fire, her heart racing. Like a person in a trance she took one step, then another, incapable of stopping herself. Until she came to the very end of the screen and could see what lay behind it.

Peter and Rory naked and passionately embraced. Peter and Rory, their heads together, their bodies almost one. Peter and Rory, oblivious to everything but each other.

She stared, sickened but mesmerized as though only by forcing herself to witness this could she ever really believe it. Ever give up all hope.

At that moment Rory turned his head to discover her, eyes large and full of horror and tears, standing only a few feet away.

'Oh Hess!' he whispered, immediately starting to disentangle himself.

'No!' cried Peter, grabbing hold of Rory and trying to restrain him.

Uttering a cry, Hester whirled and blundered for the door, her hand to her mouth, blinded by tears.

She never even felt herself bang against the table on which one of the candles stood. The next second, the candle was rolling on the floor, coming to rest against one of the many floor and furniture covers scattered about.

Rory threw Peter from him, dashing after Hester.

Peter fell backwards onto the bed, but as he did, one of his legs hooked around one of Rory's and, with a yell, Rory went crashing to the floor.

Hester heard a 'whoof', followed instantly by the urgent crackle of flames. Before her horrified gaze, a line of fire shot across the room.

Peter was bent over Rory, slapping him on the cheek. 'He's out cold!' he shouted to Hester. Already the flames were licking hungrily at the ceiling.

'Help me!' Peter shouted, struggling to get Rory into a sitting position. Rory moaned and his head fell sideways. He moaned again when Peter started tugging him to his feet. Already gasping, Hester ran to Peter's aid. Between them they manoeuvred Rory upright.

'Do you think you can manage him on your own?' Peter demanded in a choked voice.

'I don't know,' she gasped. 'He's awfully heavy.'

Peter took one of Rory's arms and put it round Hester's neck. She then grasped hold of the arm, slipping her own free one around Rory's waist. Coughing and gasping, she staggered for the door, dragging Rory along with her.

'Bloody place isn't insured yet!' Peter yelled, grabbing one of the covers and using it to beat some of the flames. 'I'll lose everything!' he cried, hysteria mounting in his voice.

At the door, Hester paused to look back. Peter was frantically whacking the flames and actually seemed to be succeeding in extinguishing some of them.

Hester choked as more smoke engulfed her. Beside her, Rory started to show some signs of coming round.

She stumbled through the door onto the landing

beyond, then with Rory's sweat-slicked body clutched against her, she started down the first flight of stairs.

On the second flight they nearly fell, but somehow she managed to keep the semi-conscious Rory and herself upright.

'Wha. . . what happened?' Rory mumbled as they reached the ground floor. His eyes were now open and gazing blankly about him.

'We've got to ring the fire brigade. The house is blazing,' she choked. Her words came out so quickly they almost tripped over one another.

'Blazing? What do you mean blazing?' he demanded, leaning against a wall and running a hand over his face.

'One of the candles got knocked over and started a fire. Peter's trying to put it out.'

Rory frowned, shaking his head. 'Fire? Peter? What are you talking about?'

'He's up there now trying to put it out,' she screamed. 'We've got to get him help, Rory. Can't you understand?'

They were in the kitchen. Rory staggered across to the sink and turned on the tap, sticking his head underneath the water.

'Tell me all that again slowly,' he commanded.

Hester repeated herself, while he stared at her in disbelief.

'Christ Almighty!' he exclaimed when finally he understood. Running back to the bottom of the first flight of stairs, he shouted at the top of his voice. 'Peter! Peter! Come down here you silly bastard!'

When there was no reply he grabbed Hester. 'Run next door and dial the fire brigade. I'm going back up there.'

'No!' she pleaded, grabbing hold of him fearfully.

'I can't just leave Peter on his own, Hess. He needs my help!'

There was something in his voice which told her he

wouldn't be dissuaded. 'For God's sake, be careful,' she begged. 'Please.'

He gave her a quick peck on the cheek, then dashed back up the stairs, shouting, 'I'm coming Peter! I'm coming!'

Once outside Hester glanced up at the house. What she saw chilled her. Smoke was billowing from windows that had already blown out from the heat, their now empty sockets glowing cherry-red. Like entranceways into the very depths of hell itself, she thought. The entire top floor of the house was a raging inferno.

She was about to resume hurrying next door when there was a sound of shattering wood, followed by a dull crashing noise. In a great shower of sparks the roof caved in.

She knew then that she'd never see Rory alive again.

The Procurator Fiscal was a tall, slim man with deeply etched skin that looked like parchment. He had a thick, bulbous nose and eyes that were cold and fishlike. His name was Bonney.

He tapped the police report he held in his hand, staring hard, but not unkindly, at Hester. 'Is there anything in your statement you'd like to alter, My Lady?' he asked.

Hester held his gaze. 'No,' she replied evenly, the vaguest hint of a smile on her lips.

Bonney took out a pipe and filled it slowly. 'The Devil's weed. A terrible thing,' he said.

'Do you mind if I smoke?'

'Not at all!' he exclaimed, and came round the desk to light her cigarette.

'Now let me get this straight,' Bonney said. 'You and your husband were visiting Mr Peter Elliot, an old school chum of his, in Mr Elliot's new house which was in the process of being redecorated and consequently filled with inflammables?'

'Correct,' Hester nodded.

'You're not quite sure how, but a candle got knocked over and it was that which started the fire. A fire which spread rapidly, and ferociously, because of the many combustibles in the room?'

Hester nodded again, trying not to be hypnotized by those eyes boring into hers.

'Your husband helped you downstairs to safety, then returned to assist Mr Elliot who was trying to put out the blaze. You were to run next door and telephone the fire brigade?'

Hester nodded again.

'Hmmh!' said Bonney, scratching his head.

Hester knocked ash into a white metal ashtray. She was like a coiled spring inside. The police had accepted her story. Why was this man doubting it? For he was; his manner told her so.

Bonney sat facing Hester but stared off into space somewhere over her left shoulder. 'There's just one small item that doesn't seem to tie in with what you've told me, My Lady,' he said.

'And what's that?'

He cleared his throat. 'The police experts have now established that neither of the two bodies recovered from the fire were wearing clothes. How do you account for that?'

'Your experts are wrong,' Hester said firmly.

The cold eyes settled on hers. 'No, My Lady. They're not.'

Hester dropped her gaze. She'd been desperately trying to save Rory's name. She'd felt she owed him that. What point was there in the whole sorry mess coming to light now?

'It happened just the way I said,' Hester insisted.

Bonney sighed, took his pipe from his mouth, and squinted at it. 'I'll have the truth, My Lady. Either here or in open court. It's entirely up to you.'

'Are you calling me a liar?'

His face became expressionless. 'What I'm saying is

that the evidence conflicts with your story. And the two have to be reconciled. Now I'll ask you again, My Lady. Is there anything in your statement you'd like to alter?'

She'd done her best, she thought. But Bonney had her backed into a corner and the only way out was to tell him what had really happened. Better here than in an open court.

Hester nodded. Bonney sat back in his chair to puff on his pipe, his eyes never leaving her all the time she spoke.

When Hester finally stopped, he grunted, and opening the file still in front of him jotted down a few notes. It was more or less as he'd known. He'd had to have the truth from Hester to make sure there had been no foul play involved.

'I think this matter need go no further,' he said quietly. 'It would only cause great distress to the families involved. A verdict of accidental death will be recorded.'

'Does that mean it won't come up in court?' Hester asked hurriedly.

'That's right,' Bonney said gently. 'No one apart from myself, and you of course, will know the true events of that tragic night.'

Relief welled through Hester. Rory would keep his good name after all.

'Thank you,' she whispered. 'Thank you very much.'

'I'll have the bodies released for burial,' Bonney replied.

Her gratitude showed plainly on her face as he escorted her from the room.

PART THREE
Her Baby

11

The marmalade toast stopped halfway to Hester's mouth as an article on page three of that morning's *Glaswegian* caught her attention. Frowning, she returned the toast to her plate and read the article through. Then she read it through again, this time more slowly.

The Clarion, another city daily, would shortly be closing. No specific reasons were given, but it was clearly inferred that over the years *The Clarion*'s readership had deserted it for Glasgow's leading daily, *The Glaswegian*.

Snide, that last bit, Hester thought as she laid the paper down and lit a cigarette. Hooking an arm over the back of the high wooden chair she was sitting on she stared thoughtfully at the article.

The Clarion was closing. But what exactly did that mean? Had it already been sold, either as a newspaper or for its premises to be turned into something else? Or could it still be bought?

If it was up for sale, she was interested. Most definitely so.

As far as Hester could remember, this was the first Glasgow newspaper – daily, evening or Sunday – to come on the market in years. It could be a unique opportunity for someone. And why shouldn't that someone be her?

She would certainly have no trouble raising the capital required to buy it. Rory's death had made her an extremely wealthy woman in her own right, if an extremely lonely and haunted woman as well. If she could buy *The Clarion* it would give her a new lease of life.

She decided that the first thing to do was to find out about the paper itself.

★   ★   ★

'Come away in, lassie,' Alan Beat said, gesturing her inside. 'It's grand to see you.'

'And it's grand to see *you*,' she enthused, pecking him on the cheek, and causing him to colour a little.

He closed the door, then led her down a long hallway. The room she followed him into was very large and high ceilinged.

Up until that moment she hadn't known whether Alan was married or not. Now it was plain, from the untidy mess of the place, that he wasn't. She smiled inwardly on seeing some laundry peeping out from underneath a sofa. She couldn't help wondering how long that had been there.

The room was dominated by a window through which she could see several ships' funnels, towered over by cranes and derricks. Behind these the Clyde glittered greyly.

'I was terribly sorry to hear about your man,' said Alan. 'It must've been a terrible blow.'

'Yes, it was,' she replied softly.

This was the first time she and Alan had met since Rory's death seven months previously.

Alan shook his head. 'What a tragedy. I remember subbing the story myself. Burned to death like that. An awful end.' He looked at her suddenly. 'Am I being insensitive?' he asked.

'No, it's all right. It bothered me for a while afterwards to speak of it, but not now.'

'That's the spirit, lass. And speaking of spirits, will you take a dram?'

'A wee one, please. And a lot of water. I'm driving.'

After they'd toasted one another, Hester said, 'Tell me about *The Glaswegian*. How's it getting on?' It was always the first thing she asked Alan when they met.

He gave her a sour look. 'Och, it's doing good business all right. But it lacks the oomph it used to have. You read it from the front page to the back and when you put it down nothing has stuck in your memory. That wasn't the way it used to be when your uncle was in the hot chair. Then there was always at least one story would keep you thinking afterwards. He made sure of that.'

'Oh, Billy!' Hester sighed, pulling a wry face.

'That cousin of yours is just not a newspaperman,' Alan went on. 'Being a bloody accountant is more his style. For that's all he thinks about. Pounds, shillings and pence. Which is not the way to run a newspaper.'

It might have been Will himself speaking. Even years ago he'd often levelled the same charges at Billy, much to Billy's fury.

As always, it was disappointing for her to hear this sort of thing from Alan. She loved *The Glaswegian* and always would. But in another way, it might well be good news, and to her ultimate advantage.

'But enough of *The Glaswegian* for the moment,' Alan said. Then, raising a bushy eyebrow, asked, 'You mentioned on the telephone that I could help you about something?'

'Will you tell me everything you know about *The Clarion*?'

Alan poured himself another dram, and offered her one, which she refused.

'*The Clarion*, eh?' he mused. He gave her a strange look, then said slowly; 'It's owned by a group of businessmen who bought it just after the war from a chap called Sandy Ross. A newspaperman of the old school like your uncle. It was a great paper before the war. And would no doubt have continued being one if it hadn't been for the war itself.'

'What happened?'

'Ross had three sons. All of them worked at *The Clarion*. Well, at the outbreak of the war, all three joined up. And a little over a year later they were all killed on the same day.'

'How awful!' Hester exclaimed.

'It broke the old man's heart. He was never the same after that. He lost all interest in *The Clarion* and it rapidly declined. After the war he sold it to this group of businessmen who thought they could make a go of it. Only they didn't. During the last few years *The Clarion*'s been losing money hand over fist.'

'What about its plant and staff? Any idea what they're like?'

'The plant's fairly old, but well maintained I believe,' Alan said. 'So it should be good for a number of years yet if the paper was to continue. As for the staff, well I wouldn't exactly rate them very highly. Some decent men amongst them mind, but for the main part second and even third raters.'

'I see,' murmured Hester.

'Now can I ask you a question?'

She smiled, knowing what was coming. 'If you like.'

'Why do you want to know about *The Clarion*?'

'Because I'm contemplating buying it,' she said simply.

Alan stared at her, and whistled. He then poured himself more whisky. This time Hester accepted when he offered her another tot.

'What about your columns in the *Herald* and *The Scotsman*?' he asked.

'I've enjoyed doing them. And I've learned a tremendous amount. But they're not enough to satisfy me. Whereas this, if it came off. . . .' She paused for a few seconds, her eyes far away. 'A newspaper of my own. That really would be something. Better even than being the first ever woman reporter in Scotland.'

Alan laughed suddenly. 'You'd certainly put Billy's nose out of joint if you did buy it. And that's for sure.'

'What's your opinion, Alan? Do you think *The Clarion* could be made viable again?'

'Oh, aye. It's possible all right. But it would have to be at the expense of *The Glaswegian*. You appreciate that don't you?'

Hester nodded.

'You'd have more or less completely to change the

staff, and re-think the paper itself. But if you could do that and come up with the right answers then you could well be on to a winner.' He gave a huge smile. 'Christ, it's exciting just thinking about it!'

'Tell me, Alan. Are there others at *The Glaswegian* just as discontented about the situation there as you are?'

'There are indeed,' he replied, a twinkle in his eye. He could see the way Hester's mind was running.

Hester sipped her whisky. What Alan Beat had told her had given her much food for thought.

Mr Ruthven's eyes glinted behind his thick pebble glasses as Hester entered his office. 'It's good to see you again, My Lady,' he said. 'Will you have some coffee?'

'No, thank you,' Hester replied, sitting.

'And what can I do for you?'

'I was most impressed by the way you handled that Rice business,' Hester said.

Ruthven acknowledged this compliment by inclining his head ever so slightly.

'Now will you handle something for me?'

Ruthven's face broke into a smile. 'I'd be honoured.'

'It has to be in the strictest confidence. I don't even want the people you're to approach to know you're representing me. Which is one of the reasons I've come to you instead of using the family solicitors. I don't want anything traced back.'

'I understand,' said Ruthven smoothly.

'*The Clarion* is closing down. What I want you to do is to find out if it's for sale, and, if so, what the price is. While you're doing this you can also find out everything you can about the paper. Anything you think might be of interest to a potential buyer. If other bids are to be made, or have already been made, I want you to discover first of all who's made them, then either what they're to be or are. Do you think you can do all that for me?'

'Is there any haste?'

'I don't know. So let's say the sooner the better. Because if there are other bids in then I don't want the matter settled without me having had the opportunity to make a counter offer.'

'Then I'll get onto it right away,' Ruthven smiled.

On leaving Ruthven's office she drove the Phantom out into the country. Parking it at the side of the road beside a small hill, she then climbed to the top of the rise.

The view afforded her from this vantage point was an excellent one. Off in the distance was Glasgow, a crouching grey beast topped, as it nearly always was, by a haze of industrial and domestic smoke. And there was the Clyde, the city's main artery, black today as it flowed quietly and ominously down to the sea.

The air around Hester, in complete contrast to Glasgow, was sweet and filled with summer smells. She sucked in a deep lungful appreciatively.

Suddenly she was assailed by doubt about the wisdom of what she was considering. True, she'd run a garage successfully, but that was small beer beside a newspaper. Certainly beside the sort and size of newspaper she envisaged.

Her mind went back to the first days of her taking over at the garage. What had she learned then that she could apply here, she asked herself. Providing she managed to buy *The Clarion*, that was.

Something Will had once said came back to her: know your market and only use the very best.

That was precisely what had worked for her at Ritchie's. Tam had been a mechanic *par excellence*, and every mechanic they'd subsequently engaged had been one as good. That, coupled with their specialized market, was why the garage had succeeded.

Which was the lesson she had to apply now. She had to back herself with the very best staff. People with true talent, energy, knowledge and ideas. The best that not only Glasgow, but all Scotland had to offer.

With a team like that behind her – together with her common sense and natural organizational and administrative ability – she knew she could make a success of the new *Clarion*.

The New Clarion, she thought. Now that had a nice, strong sound to it. It sounded like success.

One evening several days later, Hester was standing on a chair in her main reception room re-hanging several of the sketches Rory had done of her that day on Loch Lomondside.

Hester straightened the last one, then stepped down and back to admire them. They'd been in a spare bedroom where she'd only seen them occasionally, but that afternoon she'd decided they would be better in here. They reminded her of the many good times she and Rory had shared. Despite everything, she missed him still.

There was a discreet tap on the door and Harkness entered. He had surprised her by choosing to stay on with Hester after Rory's death.

'A Mr Ruthven to see you, My Lady,' he announced.

Hester glanced at her wristwatch. Ruthven was bang on time. She gestured Harkness to replace the chair. After which she said, 'Show Mr Ruthven in.'

'Would you care for a drink?' she asked, when Ruthven entered the room.

'A small whisky please.'

She indicated he should sit, which she did as well.

Hester waited till Harkness had gone. 'So what have you got to tell me?' she asked eagerly.

'*The Clarion* is up for sale,' Ruthven replied.

Hester breathed a sigh of relief. Since instructing Ruthven, she'd been constantly worried that the paper, or its premises for conversion into something else, had already been sold.

'What's the asking price?'

Ruthven mentioned a sum which was less than she'd been expecting.

'Hmmh!' she said, thoughtfully sipping her drink.

'There have been no bidders to date,' Ruthven added.

Hester's eyes glowed when she heard that. 'Excellent!'

Ruthven then went on to trot out a stream of facts about *The Clarion* and its present staff and premises, all of which Hester listened to intently.

'You've done well,' she said, when he'd finally stopped.

She sat further back in her chair and closed her eyes for a few seconds. It was a trick she'd learned at the garage when she wanted to concentrate fully with others present, or when there was a great deal of din going on.

Make a bid now or wait? If no other bidders emerged it would leave her with the whiphand.

Finally she opened her eyes to fix Ruthven with a level stare. 'Wait ten days. And if there are no other bids in that time, then make an offer one quarter less than their asking price. In the meantime, keep your ear well to the ground. If another bidder does appear I want to know of it, and the name of the bidder, immediately. Is that clear Mr Ruthven?'

'Quite, My Lady,' he replied.

After Ruthven had gone Hester poured herself another small one, smiling to herself and raising her glass in the empty room 'To *The New Clarion*', she toasted out loud.

For their next meeting, Alan Beat came to her, having been invited to dine.

The meal was a delight. Alan was an excellent, if somewhat couthy, conversationalist, with a never-ending stream of anecdotes about newspapers and the people who worked in them.

She waited till the coffee was poured before getting down to business.

'About *The Clarion*,' she said. 'My first question to

you is: will you come and work for me if I succeed in acquiring it?'

Alan smiled. 'Let me ask you a question, lass. Why do *you* think I should?'

She regarded him steadily. He was a key figure in her plans. 'Because I intend printing the sort of newspaper my uncle once did. I'm going to make *The New Clarion* bigger and better than *The Glaswegian* ever was. I'm going to make it the top Scottish daily.'

Alan's eyes shone as he listened to her. 'And, by God lassie, I believe you'll do it, too. You've got your uncle's feel for the business, and his fire.'

'So will you work for me?' she asked.

'Aye, Hester. You can count me in. I wouldn't miss this experience for the world.'

Hester rose and came round the table to where he was sitting. She extended her hand. 'We'll shake on it,' she said.

Alan pumped her hand warmly, grinning back at her.

Hester sat down again. 'How do you feel about being editor-in-chief?' she went on.

Alan blinked, obviously taken completely by surprise.

Hester lit a cigarette and sat back waiting for a reply.

'Alan Beat, Editor-In-Chief,' he said slowly. 'It has a fine ring about it wouldn't you say?'

'I would. That's why I proposed it.'

He sipped some claret, then carefully wiped his mouth with his napkin. 'It's a helluva compliment, and I have to thank you for it, lassie, but I'm afraid the answer has to be no.'

It was Hester's turn to be surprised. 'Why?' she exclaimed.

'Do you remember your uncle calling me the best sub-editor in all Scotland?'

'I remember it well. It was the day I first met you.'

'Well, he was right. I am the best sub-editor. A fact I take great pride in. But to be editor-in-charge of a desk, yet alone editor-in-chief, that's beyond me. I'll tell you here and now I'd be out of my depth. And that's the truth.'

Hester allowed a few seconds to tick by before asking, 'This isn't a display of false modesty is it?'

Alan shook his head.

Hester was bitterly disappointed. She'd hoped to solve what would be one of her greatest problems by appointing Alan to that crucial post.

'There's a young fellow working at *The Evening Citizen*,' Alan went on. 'Name of Stuart Coltart. He's already editor of their news desk, and destined for big things. Speaking off the top of my head, I think he might well be the right man for you.'

'Stuart Coltart,' Hester mused.

'I've met him. Personable chap. And sharp as a razor. He's certainly worth considering.'

'Right,' said Hester, 'Put him at the very top of a list I want you to draw up. A list of what you consider to be the cream of Scottish talent. The ideal team for the ideal newspaper. And don't concern yourself about availability. That'll be my worry.'

Alan nodded. 'Now, what about me if I'm not going to be editor-in-chief?'

'In charge of the subs' table as you are now for *The Glaswegian*?'

'Done!' he said, and making a fist banged the table in front of him.

At least she had him and his vast knowledge and experience, so vital in these early stages. Even if it was not in the job she'd wanted him for.

'The next step is actually to buy the paper itself,' she said.

'I'll drink to that!'

'And so will I!' Hester laughed.

And they did. A number of times.

Hester paced up and down. A glance at her wristwatch told her it was just past eleven o'clock. She'd been pacing since nine, the hour of Ruthven's meeting with the owners of *The Clarion*.

She paused to swallow some tea, but didn't really taste it. 'Come on! Come on!' she muttered to the telephone standing silently in the corner.

She resumed pacing, hands clasped behind her back. Up and down. Up and down. Willing the telephone to ring.

Forty-five minutes later it did. She immediately snatched it up.

'It's Ruthven, My Lady,' he said in a quiet voice.

'Well?' she demanded.

'Another offer has been made.'

'Damnation!' she bit her lip. 'How much?'

'The asking price.'

Waiting the ten days to try and pick *The Clarion* up more cheaply had been a gamble. Unfortunately, it hadn't come off.

'I found out who's making the bid, as you asked. I think the name might interest you,' Ruthven went on.

'Who is it then?'

'A Mr William Oliphant.'

Breath hissed from between Hester's teeth. What was Will doing trying to buy another newspaper at his age? And then the penny dropped. 'Is that Mr William Junior, Billy Oliphant?' she asked.

'So I understand.'

But why would Billy want *The Clarion*? Ruthven, though, had the answer. 'It seems he's interested in turning it into a Sunday paper,' he explained. 'A sister, or companion, paper to *The Glaswegian*.'

Clever idea, thought Hester. 'How keen is he on purchasing?'

'Fairly so according to my sources.'

'Hold on a minute till I think.' Hester laid the telephone down, lighting a cigarette while she thought. She wanted this newspaper. She'd set her heart on it, and she was damned if she was going to be thwarted now – not by Billy of all people. He already had *The Glaswegian* – his *inheritance* she thought wryly – let him be content with that.

She went over several new figures in her mind, settling on one which increased her offer considerably, but not too much.

Picking up the telephone, she told Ruthven what the new figure was. She then added he was to somehow put the rumour about that his client intended selling off the plant, and turning the premises into a warehouse.

After she'd hung up she grinned suddenly. Billy after *The Clarion* as well! If she'd been determined to have it before, then she was unstoppable now.

It was twenty-five past four when Ruthven rang back. Hester ground out her umpteenth cigarette of the day before lifting the telephone. Her heart was thudding.

'Oliphant has upped his bid again,' Ruthven said, quoting the new figure.

Hester considered. 'He still doesn't know it's me he's bidding against?' she asked.

'No, My Lady,' Ruthven replied quickly, sounding a trifle shocked, hurt even, that Hester thought he might have let that information slip out.

Hester had a pad and pencil ready by the telephone. She wrote down Billy's new bid, and stared at it for several seconds. Then wrote down what her next one would be, and stared at that for several seconds as well.

'Very good, My Lady,' Ruthven said when she told him. 'I'll see that's put before those concerned right away. I doubt if I'll be able to come back to you tonight, though. It'll be sometime tomorrow morning at the earliest I should imagine.'

'I'll arrange to be in all day,' she replied, adding, perhaps unnecessarily, 'and Ruthven, this is very important to me.'

'I appreciate that, My Lady,' he said, and hung up.

★　　★　　★

Early afternoon four days later found Hester sitting glowering at her knitting. 'Bugger!' she swore as she dropped yet another stitch. Not normally clumsy, she felt as though her fingers were all thumbs.

The reason for her knitting was to try and soothe her nerves which were stretched to snapping point. It wasn't succeeding in the slightest.

Ruthven had been on the telephone again that morning to say that Billy had upped his offer for the fifth time. She had immediately made a counter offer.

Billy was being extremely persistent about this, and she could understand why. The idea of a Sunday sister to *The Glaswegian* was an excellent one, and it might be years before another paper came onto the market.

He could start one from scratch, of course, but she thought that was probably financially beyond him right now. It made more sense to pick up *The Clarion* for a quarter the price it would cost to start one up.

The question was, how much capital did Billy have available? And if the bidding went beyond that, was he prepared to raise money on *The Glaswegian*? She doubted that very much. As for capital, although a relatively wealthy family, a great deal of the Oliphant money had been sunk back every year into *The Glaswegian*, a long-term policy of Will's which she could only hope Billy had continued.

She almost leapt out of her seat when the telephone rang.

'*The Clarion*'s yours as of three minutes ago,' Ruthven said without preamble.

Hester wanted to let out a great whoop of joy, but managed to restrain herself.

'My Lady?'

'I'm still here, Ruthven. Just catching my breath, that's all.'

She put her hand to her heaving breast. 'When do I take possession?'

'The beginning of the month?'

309

'Excellent.' That was three weeks away; sufficient time for her to get organized.

'When are the papers to be signed?'

'Later on in the week after they've been drawn up. Will you be signing them yourself?'

'No. For the time being, I wish to continue keeping my identity a secret. You'll be signing them on my behalf. You've done well, Ruthven. I'm very pleased. Now come and see me tomorrow. I'll have fresh instructions for you then.'

'Very good, My Lady. And if I may say so, congratulations!'

'Thank you, Ruthven. Thank you very much. Till tomorrow.' She hung up.

And *then* she whooped.

Stuart Coltart was small, even by Glasgow standards, with a puckish face and prominent ears. His accent was Edinburgh, Morningside.

Hester was wearing a dark, tailored business suit which she'd thought appropriate for the occasion. She shook Coltart by the hand and asked him to take a seat.

He did so, regarding her so quizzically that she felt like some rare specimen under a microscope.

She'd decided a neutral place was best for these interviews, of which Coltart was the first, and had therefore taken on a suite at the Central Hotel.

'Would you like some tea or coffee?' she asked.

Coltart shook his head.

She was nervous. And he wasn't making it any easier for her. Smiling she sat and lit a cigarette.

She talked non-stop for five minutes, outlining her plans and aspirations for the new paper she'd be producing, and ending up by saying that he'd come highly recommended for the position of editor-in-chief. Was he interested?

Still wearing that same quizzical look he'd regarded

her with since entering the suite, he studied her silently for a few seconds. 'I'm very flattered,' he said slowly. 'And I must say the idea of being in at the beginning of a new paper, especially in such a powerful position, is an enticing one. I am tempted. I won't deny it. . . .' He trailed off.

'If I have my way, you'll be heading the best team in Scotland. You have my word on that,' Hester said.

'So it's wholesale poaching, eh?'

There was something nasty about Coltart, Hester decided. She could sense it lurking under the surface. 'Poaching goes on all the time. Wasn't that how *The Citizen* got you for the job you're in now?' Hester replied.

Coltart grinned. 'You've done your homework, I see.'

'I wouldn't be offering you the job I am if I hadn't,' Hester retorted coolly. She had the definite feeling this man was mocking her.

Her first interview and it was all going wrong. She knew then that she'd handled the interview incorrectly. The offer of a job shouldn't have come at the beginning, but at the end, when she knew whether or not the candidate was the sort of person she wanted working for her. It wasn't enough to have the right credentials, the personality of the candidate was also of prime importance. In such a crucial post, it was especially important it didn't clash with hers. It was a mistake she wouldn't make again.

'I thank you for considering me, but I'm afraid I must decline,' Coltart said.

Relief surged through her. Thank God for that! It saved her the embarrassment of having to withdraw the offer.

'As a matter of interest, do you mind telling me why?'

His answer surprised her. 'I couldn't work for a woman,' he stated baldly. 'Not under any circumstances.'

'Why ever not?'

He shrugged. 'To be quite truthful, I think a woman's place is in the home. That's what they know and what they understand. And that's where they should stay.'

'Does that mean you think women are inferior?' she asked.

He didn't reply to that.

Now she knew the reason behind that quizzical smile. From the moment he'd entered the suite, the bastard had been patronizing her.

'If you feel that way, then why did you agree to come and see me?' she asked.

'Let's just say I was curious,' he replied.

'Indeed!' she said icily.

At the door he said, 'I wish you well with your venture.'

'But you don't think it'll succeed with a woman at the helm?'

'No. I don't,' he replied honestly.

She would have liked to have slapped him. Instead she said, 'Time will tell Mr Coltart. Time will tell. In the meantime, I would remind you that you were asked here today in strictest confidence. I hope you won't betray that trust.'

'It's been a pleasure meeting you, Viscountess Kilmichael,' he replied.

'And an education meeting you,' she said.

He laughed.

For the briefest of moments she thought he was going to make some sort of pass at her. She *would* slap him if he did, she promised herself, but he didn't.

Arrogant pig, she thought as he swaggered down the hall. Closing the door she turned to lean against it.

What a start to her recruitment drive!

A few minutes later Ruthven arrived. If he noticed she was still white with anger he didn't mention it.

'What about *The Clarion* staff?' he asked. 'They're getting restless wanting to know who the new owner is and what their fates are to be?'

'Fire them,' Hester replied.

Ruthven blinked behind his pebble glasses. 'All of them?'

312

'The lot. Give them a fortnight's severence pay and whatever holiday money they're due.'

Ruthven fiddled with the briefcase on his lap. 'I presume you know what you're doing?'

Hester fixed him with a flinty stare. Thinking of Coltart made her wonder if Ruthven would have asked her that had she been a man.

'I do, Mr Ruthven,' she replied emphatically. '*I do.*'

Hester had good reason to be well pleased with herself. She'd now interviewed all of the people on Alan Beat's list and seventy-five per cent of them had agreed to join the new paper.

Many of the new staff would be coming to Glasgow from all over Scotland, but the solid nucleus would be coming from one paper in particular: *The Glaswegian*.

Today was Wednesday. On Friday all her people would be handing in their notice. Then hell would break loose when the extent of her poaching became realized.

She glanced across at Alan who was sitting by her fireside sipping whisky. 'What do you think of me holding a press conference on Monday and revealing myself as the owner of the new paper?' she asked.

Alan stared into his drink – blend, not malt, malt being, in his opinion, glorified mouthwash patronized by the would-be sophisticates. 'I would prefer we had an editor-in-chief first,' he replied.

Hester's mouth twisted in a frown. That was by far her biggest remaining worry, and one she was going to have to resolve fairly quickly.

'Pity about Coltart,' Alan went on. 'He had all the right qualifications.'

'The man's an arrogant pig. And a misogynist to boot, I shouldn't wonder!'

Alan chuckled. 'Naw, naw, Hester! You know better

than that. From what you've told me, despite his relative youthfulness, he's just an old-fashioned man. There are plenty of them to be found in Glasgow and that's a fact.'

'But not you, Alan?'

He replied, eyes twinkling, 'Let's just say I realize there are exceptions to every rule.'

Hester laughed. Alan had great charm when he wanted to. 'Getting back to the editor-in-chief,' she said. 'I think we're going to have to go down south for our man. Which I didn't want to do. I really wanted a Scotsman for the post. And ideally a Glaswegian. Someone already attuned to the pulse and feel of the city.'

Alan twisted one of his bushy eyebrows into a curly spike, his face set in a frown of concentration. 'It's a sod right enough. I've racked and racked my brains. I did briefly consider a chap called Alex Henderson who works for D. C. Thompson in Dundee. But, good man that he is, in the final analysis he lacks that certain something, that wee bit extra.'

'Pity,' said Hester, shaking her head.

Alan swallowed a mouthful of whisky. 'Of course, what we need is someone like the Colonel. Now he would have been perfect.'

Hester stared at Alan. 'Say that again?'

'Your uncle. He would have been perfect.'

It was a thought. Jesus, was it a thought! Will Oliphant as editor-in-chief. If his health was up to it she wouldn't find a better one.

But would he even entertain the idea? He still owned *The Glaswegian*, after all, and even the command post of editor-in-chief would be a come-down for someone who'd been in his position for so many years.

Well, one thing was certain. It wouldn't do any harm to speak to him about it. None at all.

'Pour yourself another dram. A big one. You might just have earned it.' Hester said to Alan, and, thinking that if she was going to get in touch then there was no time like the present, she rose and made for the telephone.

He'll never agree to it, Alan thought, staring after Hester's receding back. Having realized what she intended doing.

But then, Alan didn't know the Colonel was in love with Hester.

'Fat bum! Fat bum!' the parrot cried, glaring at Hester through beady black eyes.

'I have nothing of the sort,' she hissed in reply, smiling at the same time.

'Fat bum! Fat bum!' the parrot repeated, then slowly winked.

Hester laughed, and moved on to the next cage which contained Australian galahs. She was in Calderpark Zoo, having arranged to meet Will here.

He came into view a few minutes later, exactly on time. She'd been early.

'Shall we stroll?' she asked.

'Nothing I'd like better. Am I allowed to take your arm?'

She extended a crooked elbow and he slipped his hand round inside it. 'You smell marvellous,' he said.

'Uncle!'

'Sorry,' he mumbled. 'I meant you smell terrible.'

She had to laugh. 'You're incorrigible,' she said, thinking that was a word she'd always associated in the past with John.

Will winked. Just the way the parrot had done. 'I hope so. For when I stop being that it'll be time to put me six feet under.' He halted suddenly. 'I hope you don't find that offensive? Rory and all. . . .'

'No, I'm not so thin-skinned.'

They resumed strolling. Athough it was still August,

315

there was a nip in the air. Portents of a harsh winter to come, Hester thought.

'Now, what is all this about? And why the great secrecy?' Will asked, at last.

'First of all, tell me how your health is. Have you fully recovered from your heart attack?'

'How do I look to you?'

'Like you drink too much. But then you've looked that way for years now,' she replied.

'Guilty I'm afraid.'

'You shouldn't you know. Not so much anyway,' she chided softly.

He smiled and glanced up at the sky. 'Drink can make life easier to bear. And that's all I'm going to say on the subject.'

Age had mellowed him considerably she thought. The man by her side was a far cry from the martinet of her youth. She liked him far more now than she ever had then.

'But your heart itself, how's that?' she asked.

'Fine. And has been for ages now. I might not look it, but I'm actually in pretty good nick. Far more so than I was when I was at *The Glaswegian*.'

This was precisely what she'd been hoping to hear. *Praying* to hear.

He went on. 'I suppose the sustained pressure over several decades just got too much for me. The heart attack was nature's way of forcing me to take a complete rest.'

There was silence between them for a few seconds after that. Then she said, 'Have you heard *The Clarion* has been sold?'

'So I believe. And to a mystery buyer. Billy tried to get hold of it but was outbid. Did you know that?'

'Yes,' she smiled. 'It was me who outbid him.'

Will swung round on her, his face filled with surprise. 'You!'

'Me. I now own *The Clarion*. And I'm shortly going to

start printing a brand new daily. One that will be in direct competition with *The Glaswegian*.'

Will threw back his head and laughed, a deep leonine roar that caused several people close by to turn and stare. 'Well, I'll be damned!' he exclaimed.

'He doesn't know it was me yet. But he will on Monday when I announce it at the press conference I'm holding,' Hester said.

Will's eyes were shining in admiration as he stared at her 'Good for you, girl. I wish you all the best with it.'

'You can do more than that. You can come and work for me. That's if you think you're up to it,' she replied.

He put a finger to his ear and waggled it up and down. 'I don't think I heard that correctly?' he said.

'I want you to be my editor-in-chief.'

'But I *can't*. I still own *The Glaswegian*. To work on another paper, especially one in direct competition, would be a conflict of interests.'

She'd already anticipated this argument. 'Since you've now regained your health: why haven't you taken over as number one at *The Glaswegian* again then?'

He pulled a face. 'It was part of the agreement when I stepped down in favour of Billy. Once out I stayed out. I gave my word on it.'

'But you would like to get back to work?'

'Of course I bloody well would! Only I can't!' he exploded.

He may have mellowed but there was still a lot of fire left in him yet she thought. Fire she wanted to harness to her own cause.

'You could if you didn't own *The Glaswegian*,' she said.

'What exactly are you trying to say?' he asked slowly.

'*If* you didn't own *The Glaswegian* would you come and be my editor-in-chief? Alan Beat and I both agree you're the perfect man for the job.'

'Alan Beat!' Will exclaimed. 'You've got him?'

'And about a third of *The Glaswegian* staff. Something

else Billy doesn't know about yet. Alan and I have put together the best newspaper team in all Scotland. All we need now is the best editor-in-chief.'

'You said *if* I didn't own *The Glaswegian*? You don't want to buy that as well do you?' he asked a little acidly.

'I'd hardly have poached so many of their staff if I did. No, what I had in mind was that you signed it over to Billy. It becomes his anyway when you die. So why not give it to him now? Which would leave you free to have a little fun out of life by working for me. That way there's no more conflicting interests you see.' She paused for breath, then added shrewdly, 'My paper will be in direct competition with *The Glaswegian*. So it'll be you against Billy. Or *us* against him. I thought that might appeal to your sense of fun.'

He gave her a wolfish grin. 'You know damn well it does.'

'A paper with oomph! Like *The Glaswegian* used to be. That's what I want. Now what do you say?'

He took a deep breath, and then another. 'I should talk it over with Sybil first before I give you a reply.'

'Fine. If you think that necessary,' Hester said slowly.

'It's the fact it's you I'd be working for.'

'She never found out about us, did she?' Hester asked in sudden alarm.

'No. But I suspect that you running off the way you did made her suspicious that I was somehow involved. I'm sure it's never even entered her head that we had a physical relationship, but because you're so much like your mother she's always been uneasy about you. More so I think after you ran off.' He turned on Hester seriously; 'I'll come back to you as soon as I can, Hester. But by discussing it with her first I know I'll be averting any possible future trouble from that direction. Trouble for *me* that is. Not you.'

'Then so be it,' Hester replied.

★　　★　　★

318

Early the following morning Will arrived on Hester's doorstep. 'When do I start?' he asked as soon as he walked into the room.

'Sybil didn't object then?'

'She wasn't exactly enthusiastic, but she didn't put her foot down,' Will replied. 'So my answer to you, young lady, is yes, I will be your editor-in-chief.'

Relief flooded through her. The biggest remaining obstacle was now overcome. 'There are two conditions though,' she said.

'And what are they?' he smiled.

'This is purely a business arrangement. Ever lay a hand on me, or even attempt to do so, and that's you out.'

He stared at her, hard. 'I can see you mean that,' he said slowly.

'I do.'

'And the second condition?'

She shook her head. 'I can't really make it a condition. So I'll make it a request. Will you try and cut down on your drinking? For me?'

He turned away so that she couldn't see his face which was strangely contorted. 'All right, Hester, I'll *try*,' he replied. Then so softly it was almost a whisper, 'For

'The gentlemen of the press,' Harkness announced as a gaggle of journalists burst into Hester's main reception room where a table with drinks and snacks had been set up.

Hester smiled at the journalists. 'Thank you for coming. If you'd like to help yourself to refreshments, I'll tell you why I've asked you here today.'

They swarmed round the table, pouring huge whiskies and gins. Hester grinned to herself when she saw Harkness raise an eyebrow imperiously skywards.

What she was about to say wouldn't be news to a number of those present. She had interviewed them in the Central Hotel and most of them had agreed to join her

319

new paper. As had been the agreement, they would have all simultaneously handed in their notice three days ago on Friday.

Friday night, Alan had telephoned her to say there had been absolute uproar at *The Glaswegian* with so many notices being handed in at once.

She waited a few minutes to allow them time to down more than one drink. Alcohol never disappears more quickly than when journalists are getting it for free. Then she asked for their attention.

When she had it she said, 'As you all know, the old *Clarion* was bought over. I would like to take this opportunity to announce that I am the new owner.'

As she'd anticipated that caused a buzz of interest among those not in the know.

'But we heard it was going to be turned into a warehouse?' a fresh-faced man called out.

'I heard that myself,' Hester replied, keeping a straight face. 'But I'm afraid it was only a rumour. And one that certainly had no substance to it.'

'But all *The Clarion* men were sacked!' the same man said.

'A new broom and all that,' Hester replied. 'I thought it best in the circumstances.'

She'd had the rumour put out that *The Clarion* premises were to be turned into a warehouse for two reasons: one, it would make it easier to get rid of the staff; and two, Billy having heard it, as he was bound to, he would eventually call a halt to his bidding at a lower figure than if he had known that *The Clarion* was to be transformed into a brand new paper in direct competition with *The Glaswegian*. In both instances the rumour had paid off, saving Hester a great deal of aggravation and money.

She held up a hand and the buzz quietened. 'The name of the new paper is to be *The Scottish Daily News*,' she said, a name she'd finally decided on only hours previously.

'And will you be running the whole kit and caboodle?'

a journalist from the Edinburgh *Scotsman* asked.

'I'm owner and therefore the paper will broadly follow my dictates and policies. But these will be interpreted and put into operation by my editor-in-chief.'

'Who is?' the man from *The Scotsman* asked quickly.

She smiled. 'I'm afraid I'm not at liberty to tell you that at the moment. What I will say, however, is that a name will be announced within the next few days. And that it will be a Scottish one as well as a familiar one.'

'When do you start publication?' a man from *The Evening Times* asked.

'A date hasn't been finalized yet, but it'll be as soon as possible I can assure you.'

The questions came thick and fast after that. Hester answered most of them, and deftly turned aside those she couldn't.

When the questions began to flag she decided that was enough. 'So much for talking. How about another drink?' she said, moving towards the drinks table.

Instantly the room was filled with hubbub as virtually every journalist present moved along with her.

She caught the eye of a chap called Hedderwick who'd be joining the news desk. He gave her a smile and a slight nod of the head.

Her press conference had been a success.

Half an hour later the telephone rang. Harkness answered it. 'Mr Billy Oliphant,' he announced.

Hester glanced at her wristwatch in surprise. The journalist from *The Glaswegian* could only just have got back. He must have gone straight to Billy to report orally why she'd called a press conference.

Hester accepted the telephone. 'Hello, Billy? It's nice to hear from you,' she said pleasantly.

'It was *you* bidding against me!' he shouted.

'That's right,' she replied sweetly.

'And you who's poached God knows how many of my staff!'

'Right again.'

'What the hell are you playing at?' he screamed.

'I'm not playing at anything,' she said levelly. 'I'm starting up a new newspaper. And as for the staff you've lost you can replace them easily enough.'

'How?' came the bitter reply.

'From the staff of the old *Clarion*. I re-hired a dozen or so of them, but the rest are out of work. I'm sure they'd jump at the chance of joining *The Glaswegian*.'

From the sounds Billy made she was sure he was going to have a seizure.

'Is Violet well?' she asked.

'To hell with bloody Violet! What sort of paper is this *Scottish News* going to be?'

'*Scottish Daily News*,' she corrected. 'And I think you should wait and see.'

'All right. If that's the way you want it!' he choked. And smashed the telephone down.

If he was that furious now she wondered what he'd be like when he discovered his father was going to be her editor-in-chief.

Grinning, she went back to what she'd been doing.

At about midday on Wednesday, Will arrived at her house. There was a spring in his step and his face wasn't quite as flushed as usual. For the first time in a long time he had a clean sense of purpose about him.

'That's everything signed, sealed and delivered. Billy now officially owns *The Glaswegian*. And good luck to him. For he's going to need it.'

'Did you tell him you're joining me?'

'Nope. He can find out about that the same time as everyone else.'

'Which will be tomorrow, then,' Hester said. 'I'll arrange for a press release to be made this afternoon.'

Will rubbed his hands together, his eyes shining with excitement and enthusiasm. 'By the way, I like the name you chose: *The Scottish Daily News*. It has substance and market appeal. The right combination. What I do think we should have, though, is a logo like the *Express*'s knight.'

'Good idea,' Hester said quickly. 'Any suggestions?'

'What about a thistle? It's distinctive and completely Scottish.'

A thistle? She conjured up the image in her mind – and liked what she saw. 'A thistle it is then,' she decided.

Will smiled, pleased that his first suggestion had been accepted.

He hefted his bulging briefcase and waved it in front of her. 'Although I haven't been in touch with you these last few days, I haven't exactly been idle. I've jotted down all sorts of things which I'd like you to consider.'

'Then let's get started,' Hester agreed eagerly.

He threw his briefcase on the sofa where it bounced. 'Before we begin I'm absolutely parched,' he said, raising an enquiring eyebrow.

Hester stared him straight in the eye. 'What would you like?' she asked quietly.

His face suddenly blossomed into a huge, teasing smile. 'I could murder a cup of tea,' he said.

Hester laughed. Then laughed again. He'd completely taken her in.

'I'll ring for Harkness,' she said.

At 8 a.m. on the first day of the new month Hester, Will and Alan Beat met up in front of what had been *The Clarion* premises and were now those of *The Scottish Daily News*.

The building was an old one, with a run-down appearance, but there was something about it which appealed to Hester. Staring up at it she suddenly thought of an old dog, shaggy and shambling and wise in the ways of the world. The sort of dog who would completely steal your heart away.

'Shall we go in?' asked Alan.

Will gestured that Hester should be first. She entered the building with the same feeling she would have had going into church.

'Good morning, My Lady,' said a middle-aged man who'd been waiting inside. This was Mr Millar, one of the old *Clarion* employees re-hired by Hester.

Hester smiled, returning his greeting.

'Would you like me to show you up to the management offices?' Millar volunteered.

'Please,' Hester replied.

That sweet yet tangy smell of printer's ink permeated the place, as though the entire building had at one point been immersed in it.

Hester sucked in lungful after lungful, and shivered. Her skin prickled with excitement.

Will took her hand and squeezed it affectionately. He knew exactly how she felt. 'And it's all yours as from a minute past midnight,' he said.

It seemed to Hester that her entire life had somehow been leading up to this moment. As though everything she'd done and experienced had been in preparation for the adventure on which she was now about to embark.

Behind her she could hear voices. Although the staff hadn't been called till nine it seemed some of them had decided to arrive early. It was a good sign.

After looking around her office, which delighted her by reminding her of Will's at *The Glaswegian*, the three of them went on a tour of the premises, starting at the very top and working their way down.

Everything for the production of a newspaper was there, just as the staff of *The Clarion* had left it.

In the basement they stopped to stare at the huge presses, silent for the present, but soon to come roaring to life again.

'Let's go back upstairs now,' Hester said. 'The staff should all be here and I want to have a word with them.'

'I'll get them together in the cafeteria. You can speak to them there,' Alan said, and immediately hurried off.

Hester and Will made their way slowly to the cafeteria in order to give the others time to get there before them. They arrived to find an excited, jabbering throng, all looking expectant and many just a little nervous.

Friendly smiles were flashed at Hester as she made her way through to get to the front. Alan suggested she address the gathering from atop a table, and helped her climb up on a chair.

'Welcome to *The Scottish Daily News*,' Hester began. 'For those of you who haven't already heard me say this, it's my intention that *The Scottish Daily News* will be *the* Glasgow daily. Not only the biggest but the best. Today is a historic one. For today sees the start of a *great* newspaper. Of that I'm totally and utterly convinced.'

She had to stop while a cheer ran round the cafeteria. She waited for it to die down before continuing.

'And why am I convinced it's going to be a great paper? Well I'll tell you. You yourselves actually being here convince me. Because all of you, from the highest to the humblest, represent the very best, the cream, of the Scottish newspaper industry. Together you make a team, the like and quality of which Scotland has never seen before. And leading you is a person of outstanding ability. The man who created *The Glaswegian*, and who is now going to be instrumental in creating an even better newspaper: Mr William Oliphant!'

Thunderous applause broke out. Will, looking rather sheepish for once, acknowledged it with a wave of his hand.

Hester went on. 'Today we get settled in and get to know one another. Tomorrow we produce the first dummy, of which there will be at least one every working day till zero hour.'

She paused, allowing a smile to creep across her face, knowing they were all on tenterhooks, anticipating what she was going to say next.

'The first issue of *The Scottish Daily News* goes on the streets three weeks today,' she said.

It was a date she and Will had decided on together. Deeming it not too short. Nor too long. But just right.

'For she's a jolly good fellow!' someone sang out at the back.

And the whole place erupted with laughter. No one laughed louder than Hester herself.

Hester pored over the first dummy. Not bad, she thought, though there was room for a great deal of improvement.

She pushed the paper away from her and sat back in her chair, lighting a cigarette and thinking hard.

She was missing something. Something important. But what? It had starting niggling at her the previous night, and had continued to do so all that day.

She tried clearing her mind, thinking of acres and acres of nothing, hoping that whatever was worrying her would suddenly reveal itself.

But it didn't.

Sighing she went back over the dummy and seconds later was making a series of notes. These points and suggestions she intended bringing up with Will.

She'd just got home and had sat down when, out of the blue, it came to her. Advertising! That was what had been bothering her! Not the advertising the paper would carry, that department was already set up, but advertising the paper itself.

None of the Glasgow papers now in existence really did anything about self advertising, which seemed to her a state of affairs she could exploit to her advantage.

What was needed was for the name of *The Scottish Daily News* to be on every pair of lips even before the paper itself appeared.

The trick would be to get people to try the new paper. If she could get them to do that, then she was more than halfway to keeping them as customers. She was *that* sure of the product she was about to put on the market.

The Americans had the right idea, she thought. And because hard-line selling was so novel over here, it was bound to have a great deal of impact.

She decided an advertising agency was what was needed. She would tell them what she wanted, and they would create it using their professional expertise and knowledge.

She wondered if there were any advertising agencies in either Glasgow or Edinburgh. There were bound to be in London, but she preferred something local.

She'd make enquiries first thing in the morning and see what she could come up with.

Will sat across from Hester watching her closely while she read the latest dummy. 'What do you think?' he asked when she finally looked up.

She scratched her cheek while formulating her thoughts. There was no doubt the dummy in front of her was the best produced so far, but it was still lacking something.

Part of the problem was that Will was trying to re-create *The Glaswegian*, which was wrong. Their paper had to be different – and better.

'We need more emphasis on the female angle,' Hester said slowly. 'A full page twice a week.'

Will snorted. 'That's daft! It's men who buy newspapers.'

'True enough. But they take them home where the women read them as well.'

'But they're not actually *buying* them!' he said emphatically.

Hester sighed. Sometimes men could be so dense where women were concerned.

'Half the population are women. Correct?' she asked.

Will's eyes suddenly grew cautious. He'd learned to be careful when arguing with Hester. She had the awful habit of being right more often than not. He nodded.

'Therefore, it's safe to assume that half our readers will be women?'

'More or less, I suppose,' he admitted grudgingly.

'And why shouldn't women be catered for as well as men? Men have their sports pages and features, which is fair enough. But what about the poor women? What's in the newspaper that's specifically for them?'

'They have their own magazines and that sort of thing,' Will replied. 'D. C. Thompson do an excellent line of those.'

'But I'm not talking about magazines. I'm talking about newspapers.'

'But you don't cater for someone who doesn't buy what you're selling!' he said doggedly.

Hester smiled. So wise, so naive.

'And who tells the man what to buy?' she asked softly.

Will blinked, and sat back in his chair. He then did something he rarely did. He chomped on the end of his cigar.

Hester said patiently, 'Let's say I'm Mrs Average Woman. My husband's been bringing home *The Glaswegian*, or another daily, for years. Then I happen to read *The Scottish Daily News*. And lo and behold! It's got things in it for me which the others haven't. So the next day, or day after, or whenever I think of it, I say to my husband as he's going out to his work, "Get a *Scottish Daily News* today, Jimmy. I much prefer it." Which the man will then do. Because when it comes to buying things nine times out of ten the husband will buy what his wife tells him. For peace and quiet if nothing else.'

Will coughed. 'I hadn't looked at it quite that way before,' he conceded.

'And neither has any other newspaper in this city. Which is why we're going to be different. The other thing that's struck me is that I feel we should have a comic strip. They're always good value. And very popular.'

Will took the cigar from his mouth, the end of which was now ruined, and stabbed it at Hester. 'I was about to

328

suggest that myself. I'll see someone gets onto the syndicate who deals with these things tomorrow morning.'

'No,' said Hester. 'Not the syndicate. Get me someone local. The strip's to be set in Glasgow. And reflect the Glasgow situation.'

'It's very short notice for someone completely new,' Will said, cautiously.

'There's bound to be a dozen people capable of doing such a strip, any one of whom would jump at the chance. Contact the Art School. They're certain to be able to make some recommendations. Mr Garston is the person to speak to. Providing he's still there, that is. He'll be only too happy to help.'

Will raised an enquiring eyebrow. 'Sounds like you've had previous dealings with the Art School?'

Hester smiled enigmatically. 'You could say in a round about way it was instrumental in bringing Rory and me together. So without it, you could equally say, there would be no *Scottish Daily News*.'

'Well, well, well,' Will replied, waiting expectantly.

But Hester refused to be drawn further. Instead she said, 'There's a researcher called Sally Petrie who came to us from *Saltire Monthly*. I've decided that she's going to make the big break through and become Scotland's first woman reporter. Tell her she's going to write a bi-weekly women's page for us. She'll have her own by-line and picture at the top of the page. Our female readership will like that last bit, and identify with it. You can also tell her I want a specimen page in three days time.'

'And what if she can't deliver the goods?' Will asked cautiously. 'After all, if she's been a researcher she's got no experience writing copy.'

'If she's no good then she goes back to researching and I look around for someone else,' Hester replied. Adding testily, 'Even if it gets down to me doing it myself there's going to be a women's page written by a woman.'

'Nothing like being determined,' Will muttered under his breath.

Sudden doubt assailed her. 'Am I making a pig's ear of it all?' she asked quietly.

'You're doing just fine. We're all, and I include myself, very impressed,' Will replied, equally quietly. 'I'll speak to this Sally Petrie right away. After that I'll get the comic strip organized.'

After he'd gone, Hester took a very deep breath.

She then re-read the dummy lying in front of her to see if there were any more new ideas or suggestions she could come up with.

Hester was dog-tired. She'd been ten hours at the paper that day, and couldn't wait to get home to a hot bath, food and bed. In that order.

When she saw the billboard loom out of the twilight, she smiled and her tiredness momentarily vanished. She drew the Phantom into the kerb so she could stare her fill.

'*The Scottish Daily News* Is Coming' proclaimed the poster in enormous print. Then below it, in far smaller print so that you actually had to stop to read it: 'Glasgow Will Never Be The Same Again'.

It was a damn fine ad, she thought. She'd liked it when she'd read the copy and seen the mock-up. She liked the real thing even better.

On the top right-hand side of the poster was the thistle logo, giving it that finishing touch. Modern, but Scottish. Forward looking, yet traditional. Exciting, while at the same time secure. The poster suggested all these qualities.

During the remainder of her drive home Hester saw four more billboards carrying her ad. A smaller version would also be on the trams and underground.

The Scottish Daily News was coming indeed. And it was Hester's profound hope that Scotland *would* never be the same again.

*   *   *

Sally Petrie had come up trumps. Her specimen page was excellent, exactly what Hester had wanted. 'First class,' she said to Will who, just a little reluctantly, agreed with her.

The paper was almost there now, Hester felt. But not quite. There were still one or two things which needed reconsidering and altering.

'More pictures,' she said suddenly. 'That would make all the difference. I can see it clearly now. What we want is more visual impact of the sort that pictures provide. News and sport in particular. There's too much copy at the moment. Splendid as it is, it makes for a visually boring page. Pictures grab initial attention. Once you've got that, reading the story will automatically follow.'

'It'll be expensive,' Will cautioned.

'That's the short-term viewpoint. The long-term one is that it'll more than pay for itself through increased sales.'

'We'll have to get some more photographers to cover the extra load,' Will countered again.

'Then hire them.'

At the door Will muttered, just loud enough for Hester to hear 'Visual impact! I'll have to remember that.' Then added in a very broad Glasgow accent, 'Really grand executive expression, so it is.'

'Piss off!' laughed Hester.

Hester was walking her domain as she liked to do at least once a day. Typewriters were clattering. Telephones ringing. The hum of purposeful activity was everywhere.

Below her feet the presses rumbled into life, turning out the latest dummy. Not long now till the real thing, she thought. A shiver of anticipation ran through her.

The boy approaching her had a pinched face, sallow complexion and remarkable cowlick. He almost typified the ragged urchins with which Glasgow's working class areas teemed.

'Excuse me, your Viscountesship, but Mr Beat said I was to give you this,' the lad mumbled, thrusting some copy into Hester's hand.

A journalist close by sniggered, causing the boy to blush beetroot red.

'Well, I wasn't sure what to call you!' the lad said defiantly. Glaring at the journalist, he turned to hurry off.

'No, wait!' called Hester.

Reluctantly, the boy paused, as though caught doing something wrong, then turned back to face her.

'What's your name?' she asked.

'Bobby Timpson.'

'And you're a copy boy, I take it?'

'Aye. That's right,' he admitted grudgingly.

'Your first job?'

He nodded warily.

She was aware, as was Bobby, that a number of those around were listening to their conversation. 'I'm normally addressed as Viscountess or My Lady,' she said. 'But you know, now I come to think about it, perhaps it's a bit formal for a newspaper office. Don't you agree?'

Bobby didn't reply, but it was obvious he did.

Hester went on. 'So I'll tell you what. From now on call me Mrs McNeill. In fact, I think everyone should call me that. Will you pass the word around?'

'Right you are, then, Mrs McNeill,' Bobby grinned.

'Run along then,' she said, only just stopping herself at the last moment from patting him on the head, which most certainly would have mortified him.

She waited till the boy was out of earshot before turning on the journalist who'd sniggered. 'Shame on you!' she admonished.

This time, much to the amusement of his colleagues, it was he who blushed beetroot red.

The next morning Hester was in the newspaper library when two journalists from the news desk entered.

Masked as she was by some large filing cabinets, they were unaware of her presence.

One was a small Neanderthal-looking man called McFadyen. The other's name was Hislop. Both had come from *The Glaswegian*.

Hester couldn't help but overhear their conversation, which quickly had her full attention.

'I saw old man Oliphant in the canteen yesterday,' McFadyen said. 'Sitting there having his dinner he was. Just like one of the lads.'

'That a fact!' said Hislop.

'He had the haggis same as I did.'

'Oh, what was that like? I quite fancied it but in the end plumped for the pork chop.'

'It was very good. I can recommend it,' McFadyen replied.

'Eating in the canteen eh?' said Hislop. 'Christ, could you imagine his son Billy doing the likes of that? Now there's a right stuck up prune if ever there was one.'

'Not a patch on his father. You know, all the time I was at *The Glaswegian* I don't think I spoke to him once. And I'm sure if I'd asked him my name he wouldn't have known it.'

'Old man Oliphant called me Ronnie a couple of days back,' Hislop said. 'That impressed me I can tell you.'

'I think if the lads at *The Glaswegian* had known he was going to be editor-in-chief they'd have deserted Billy *en masse*,' McFadyen chuckled.

'Cold as a witch's tit that Billy,' Hislop said. 'And patronizing to boot.'

'It's the old man who's got the style. No doubt about it.'

Still chatting, the two journalists left the library, the door clicking closed behind them.

Eating in the canteen with all the others. Now why hadn't she thought of that?

She'd been having sandwiches in her office at lunch-time, working straight through without taking a proper break. Admirable in many ways, but a mistake in others as she could now clearly see.

McFadyen was right. Will Oliphant did have style.

Or, as she would have put it: a very shrewd head on his shoulders.

At lunchtime the next day, or dinnertime as it was officially called, Hester walked into the canteen joining on the end of the snake-like queue.

Eyes flicked in her direction, and a few heads turned. She shuffled forward pretending not to notice.

She asked for egg salad and juice, refused pudding, and took some mousetrap with biscuits. Holding her tray before her, she looked around for a place to sit. Spying Alan Beat, she was just about to cross and join him when she saw the copy boy, Bobby Timpson, at a table on his own.

'Mind if I sit here?' Hester asked.

Bobby looked up, gaping dumbly. 'No . . . no. The seat's free,' he stuttered.

She smiled at him as she sat. 'What's the food like?' she asked. 'It's my first time here. I've been too busy up until now.'

'It's not bad,' Bobby mumbled. Then with a sudden grin. 'But not as good as my Ma's scoff.'

'I'm sure it's not,' Hester grinned.

That broke the ice.

Bobby groped in his pocket, then placed something in front of her. 'I got that coming to work this morning. I think it's great,' he said.

It was what the advertising agency called a handout. About half the size of an ordinary leaflet and glossy, it was a smaller version of the poster which was now to be seen all over Glasgow.

'*The Scottish Daily News is* coming. And soon!' Hester read.

'My Da said he saw that as an advert in the pictures when he went the other night,' Bobby said, eyes wide with wonder.

'That's right,' Hester replied. 'An interval ad has been placed in all the cinemas that could take it.'

'Jings!' said Bobby.

'Did your Dad think it a good ad?' Hester asked.

'Oh, aye. But then he would. Me working for the paper and that.'

Hester laughed. 'Well let's hope the great Glasgow public think it's a good ad as well.'

'People are talking about the paper,' Bobby said quickly.

'Are they indeed?'

'I've heard it mentioned lots of times.'

Hester smiled into her salad. She'd been desperately wondering if her advertising idea had been working out as well as she'd hoped.

Now she knew.

It was an experience unlike any she'd ever undergone before. The feeling was unreal, almost hallucinatory. She was sure if she'd stuck a knife into her flesh she wouldn't have felt a thing.

She listened to the rumble of the presses, and it was as though the sound came from a million miles away.

'Come in!' she called out when there was a knock on the door.

Will entered to stand for a second staring just at her. His eyes were bright and feverish, and his chest was pumping in and out as though he'd been running.

Slowly he crossed to stand in front of her. 'The first ever edition of *The Scottish Daily News*,' he said, and laid it on her desk.

Hester's mouth was sand-dry and her hands trembling when she picked it up.

'You want my honest opinion?' Will asked.

She nodded, not trusting herself to speak.

'I think it's an absolute cracker. You've an awful lot to be proud of this day.'

Reaching into a drawer she pulled out a bottle of

whisky and two glasses. She poured fairly large ones.

'No water, I'm afraid,' she whispered, almost unable to speak.

'As you know, I've stopped drinking when working, but today's an exception,' Will grinned. He held his glass aloft in a toast. 'To *The Scottish Daily News*. Long may it prosper!'

'Amen!' toasted Hester. 'And to all those who've believed.' Her eyes were glistening when she added softly, 'I could never have done it without you, Will.'

He nodded. 'True enough. But I was only a helping hand like everyone else downstairs. A more important one, perhaps, but a helping hand none the less. Whereas you, Hester, you were the brains, the creativity, behind what's been born today. *The Scottish Daily News* is your baby. Make no mistake about that.'

Will put his now empty glass on Hester's desk, then silently strode from the room, closing the door quietly behind him. He knew she wanted to be alone now.

She glanced down at the paper, running one hand caressingly over it.

Her baby.

The tears that fell were like soft, warm rain.

12

The afternoon of March 14th 1935 found Hester poring over the next day's main feature. *The Scottish Daily News* had now been in existence for six months.

The article was a political one, spelling out the deep and dire trouble Ramsay MacDonald and his government were currently wallowing in.

Finally Hester pushed the copy aside. An election had to be just round the corner, she told herself – one she doubted MacDonald would win.

Oh, he'd take Scotland all right, that was certain. But Baldwin would carry the nation as a whole.

Her reverie was interrupted by a tap on her office door. 'Come in!' she called out.

Will entered, his face wreathed in smiles. 'I've got the latest Glaswegian figures,' he said, waving a sheet of paper in front of him.

'Bad, eh?'

'Disastrous,' he smiled. 'If I was Billy right now I'd be having nightmares.'

Hester accepted the sheet of paper and silently studied the figures it contained. These figures came weekly to Will, courtesy of an old friend of his working in *The Glaswegian*'s circulation department.

Hester pursed her lips and gave a low whistle.

'This is the fourteenth straight week we've outsold *The Glaswegian* and the gulf is widening,' Will said gleefully.

Hester made a rapid mental calculation. 'We're now selling a third more than they are.'

Will grinned and nodded. 'It's no flash in the pan, lass. Billy's really getting his nose ground in it.'

'But we've got to keep our impetus going,' she warned. 'We mustn't get complacent.'

Will laughed. 'I can't see that happening. At least not while you're sitting in that chair.'

'Does that mean you think I'm driving everyone too hard?' she asked quickly.

'No. But I *do* think you're driving yourself too hard.'

'I'm all right,' she said wearily.

'You're nothing of the sort. You're tired if not completely exhausted. What you need is some sort of break. If only a wee one.'

'You're not going to suggest a holiday I hope?' she asked in alarm.

'I would if I thought you'd go. But you wouldn't even entertain the idea would you?'

She shook her head.

337

'I knew that. And you know how I knew? Because I remember what it was like when I was sitting in that seat over at *The Glaswegian*. Mind you, in the end I had to have holidays and the like. I'd have fallen over otherwise. But it'll be a while yet before you relent and give in to common sense. So, as you won't take a holiday how about indulging in the next best thing and coming out to dinner with me tonight?'

'Will!' she said, sharply.

'No, no. Don't misunderstand my meaning, Hester. I just think a night out would do you the world of good. And I think we've both deserved it after all! Now what do you say?'

'No ulterior motive?'

'Word of honour!' he replied, crossing his heart.

'It would be nice,' she said quietly. 'I haven't been out in the evening since buying the paper.'

'That's it, then!' he exclaimed. 'I'm treating us both. Slap up meal! Best bottle of wine on the card! I'll go and ring Sybil now and tell her I won't be in till late. And I'll pick you up here after work, young woman.'

'I'm already looking forward to it,' Hester smiled.

'So am I, lass. So am I.'

Hester had insisted Will come home with her while she washed and changed. If she was going out she wanted to do it properly, and not be grubby and still in her working clothes.

Will relaxed with a whisky while Hester was upstairs. For a while he stood staring at the drawings Rory had done of Hester that long ago day at Lochlomondside. When he returned to his chair there was a sad, almost mournful expression on his face. An expression which vanished instantly when Hester appeared, ready to go.

'Hungry?' he asked, after telling her how gorgeous she looked.

'I could eat a horse,' she laughed.

'I'll try and do better than that for you,' he grinned.

Hester gave a happy cry of surprise when they parked outside the Press Club.

'Well, where else would I take you to celebrate the last few months?' Will asked in mock-horror.

'It's perfect,' Hester smiled. 'Just perfect.'

On the pavement Will offered her his arm, and laughing and joking, they made their way inside.

The *maître d'* told them they'd have to wait about ten minutes for a table. Will suggested that they wait at the bar.

When Hester saw Billy slumped over a drink she couldn't believe her eyes. She'd only been to the Press Club twice in her life, and on both occasions she'd run into him. Either it was an incredible coincidence, or he used the place an awful lot.

Suddenly she had the suspicion that she was being manipulated. If Billy did come here a great deal, then Will probably knew about it. Had he intended them to run into Billy?

Her suspicion deepened when she glanced into Will's face to see that his eyes were glinting mischievously, and that there wasn't even a hint of surprise to be seen there.

'Well, well. If it isn't my son and heir,' he said in a barbed voice.

Billy looked up, his gaze going from his father to Hester, then back again.

'Hello Billy,' said Hester, hiding her discomfort.

Billy grunted.

'Mind if we sit beside you?' Will asked.

Billy raised an eyebrow, but shook his head.

Hester said she'd have a small whisky. Will ordered her a large one as it was a celebration. What would Billy have?

'I'm fine,' Billy replied tightly.

Hester was at a loss to know what to say. She was acutely uncomfortable and ill at ease in Billy's company.

But Will wasn't. He was bluff and jovial, full of

bonhomie. 'How's Violet?' he asked. 'I haven't seen her in ages.'

Billy glanced at Hester. That was the question she'd asked him last time they'd spoken on the telephone. Just before he'd hung up on her.

'She's pregnant again,' Billy replied morosely.

'That's marvellous!' Hester exclaimed. 'I'm so pleased for the pair of you.'

Billy gave her a black look.

'How far along?' Will demanded.

'Four months.'

'So it's quite definite then?'

'Yes.'

'Then that certainly calls for a drink. And this time you won't refuse,' Will declared, doing everything but slapping his son on the back.

Hester could tell Billy was as uncomfortable and embarrassed as she was. She guessed that the only thing keeping him at the bar with them was his pride. He wouldn't want to look as though he was running away.

'And what's the celebration that brings you here?' Billy asked.

Will turned to stare at him, smiling, but didn't reply.

'Nothing special,' said Hester hastily.

Billy nodded slowly. A muscle in his left cheek jerked uncontrollably. It couldn't have been more clear what the celebration was for had it been spelled out in capital letters.

'The baby! May its life be a long and happy one!' Will toasted, raising his glass in salute.

'The baby!' Hester echoed.

Tight-lipped, and exuding ice-cold anger, Billy drank his down in one gulp.

'Here's hoping it's a boy. There's nothing like having a son and heir,' said Will.

Billy and his father stared at one another, the atmosphere between them thick with hatred.

Billy opened his mouth to say something, but at that moment the *maître d'* appeared beside them.

'Your table's ready now, Mr Oliphant,' he said to Will.

Thank God for that, Hester thought. Another few seconds and things might have got really nasty.

'Please give Violet my regards,' she said, rising.

'I'll do that,' Billy answered in a tight whisper.

'And mine. And your mother's,' Will said.

For a moment their eyes met again, then, with an infuriating smile, Will turned away to grasp Hester's arm.

It wasn't what had been said, but what had been left unsaid, Hester thought as she and Will made their way to their table.

She could feel Billy's gaze boring into her back. It made her want to hide.

'Hester, do you have a minute?' Will asked, popping his head round her office door.

'Of course.'

He ushered McFadyen in ahead of him. 'You know Mike, don't you?'

McFadyen was one of the two journalists Hester had overheard talking in the newspaper library. 'I should do. I interviewed him.'

Will smiled. 'Sorry, I forgot that for the moment.'

'Problem?' Hester asked.

Will gestured McFadyen to a chair. 'Not a problem. But something you should know about. Tell her what you told me, Mike.'

McFadyen cleared his throat. 'I had a telephone call last night from Billy Oliphant. He wanted me to go back to *The Glaswegian* and offered me more than I'm getting here.'

'Did he now indeed!' said Hester softly.

'And I'm not the only one. A number of ex-*Glaswegian* lads have had a call as well,' McFadyen added.

'What did you and the others say?'

McFadyen shrugged. 'Money isn't everything. We like it here, and we didn't over there. There's no reason to think things would change if we went back.'

Hester took a deep breath as the fluttering in her stomach subsided.

'I . . . I mean *we* thought the management should know,' McFadyen added.

Hester glanced over at Will who was grinning like the Cheshire cat. Then she brought her attention back to McFadyen.

'Will you give the others a message from me?' she asked.

'Certainly.'

'Tell them if I had any lingering doubts about the quality of this newspaper and the staff who work for it then they've just blown them out of the window.' She paused for a second. 'Thank you. Thank them.'

McFadyen rose. 'Well, I'd better get back. There's lots to do.'

'I'll stay here,' Will said.

Once McFadyen had left he rounded on Hester. 'What do you think?' he demanded.

'I'm very touched by their loyalty.'

'Aye, well, they know when they're onto a good thing.'

'Trying to re-poach his people. I should have foreseen that.'

'Now you know he's trying it on what are you going to do about it?' Will demanded.

'I don't see that there is anything I can do.'

'Oh, but there is. You leave it to me.' Thrusting himself out of his chair and crossing rapidly to Hester's desk, he picked up the telephone.

When Hester realized he was getting in touch with Billy personally, she tried to get him to ring off, but he'd have none of that. Covering the telephone mouthpiece, he hissed that he knew what he was doing.

'Ah, Billy!' he said when he was through to *The Glaswegian*.

Hester sank back in her seat, chewing one end of a pencil. She just knew this was a mistake.

The dialogue that followed was short, sharp and nasty. Hester winced as Will viciously tore Billy to shreds.

Finally, with a last scathing comment, Will hung up. He turned to Hester, his face alight with satisfaction.

'He won't try that again in a hurry,' Will said happily.

'I don't think you should've done that. It wasn't the way to go about it.'

'You're wrong. Billy's always been one who needs smacking down hard. And the harder, the better.'

Hester sighed. It could be Will was right. But she doubted it.

The telephone rang and Hester answered it. 'Fine, I'll tell him,' she said. 'You're needed to make a quick decision down on the floor.'

'On my way!' he cried gaily, and hurried from the office.

As the paper was doing so well she decided to up all the pay packets a little the week after next. She didn't want any second thoughts by the former Glaswegian staff on the offer Billy had made them.

Will breezed into Hester's office waving a paper in front of him. It contained the latest Glaswegian circulation figures.

'And yet another punch to the solar plexus leaves our opponent reeling!' he announced.

Hester accepted the paper and laid it in front of her.

'It's a massacre,' Will said, fairly dancing with joy.

Hester pursed her lips and slid the paper away from her. It was the nineteenth straight week *The Scottish Daily News* had outsold *The Glaswegian*.

'If this continues, bearing in mind that virtually every one we add to our circulation is one away from theirs,

343

we'll be outselling them by fifty per cent within the next month,' Will smiled.

Hester stared up at him pensively. 'I almost feel sorry for Billy. He must be at his wits' end,' she said.

'Nonsense!' Will exclaimed. 'He's only getting his come-uppance.'

'I think you're being a bit harsh.'

'He always contended his way of running a newspaper was better than mine. Now we know the truth of the matter.'

'But as you've pointed out in the past, Will, this paper is my creation. With enormous help from you and the others, of course, but, in your own words, it is *my* baby.'

'Which I'm the first to agree with, Hester. So let me rephrase what I said. The success of *The Scottish Daily News* is the triumph of old-fashioned gut journalism over Billy's cold, clinical, accountant's approach. You and I are the same. Newspapers run in our blood. The only things that run in Billy's are columns of figures and balance sheets.' Will chuckled. 'Only those figures and balance sheets can't look too good of late. In fact they must look downright disastrous!'

Hester lit a cigarette. Below her the presses rumbled, sweet music to her ears. And a sound she never tired listening to.

At first the runaway success of *The Scottish Daily News* – almost completely at the expense of *The Glaswegian* – had thrilled her. During the last few weeks, however, with their success continuing unabated and *The Glaswegian*'s circulation slipping lower and lower, she'd begun to feel both pity and compassion for Billy.

As if reading what was in her mind, Will said, 'If the tables were turned he'd have no compunction about putting the boot into you. I hope you realize that?'

'Do you think *The Glaswegian* will eventually fold?' she asked seriously.

A look of sadness settled on Will's face. 'I hope it won't

come to that. But certainly its strutting days are over. Billy will eventually, if he's any sense that is, have to change the format, and it'll end up in the third league, where *The Clarion* was before it finally went under.'

'But if *The Clarion* had to pack up, then surely *The Glaswegian* will suffer the same fate?'

Will's lips twisted upwards in a cynical smile. '*The Glaswegian* is privately owned and that'll make all the difference. A private owner will take a lot more financial punishment than a group of businessmen who are just in it for the profit.'

'Isn't Billy just in it for that?'

The cynical smile hardened to become almost a grimace. 'That,' said Will, 'will be Billy's final test.'

A heavy, brooding silence reigned between them for a few moments. Then Hester said, 'I want your opinion on an idea I've had for a special weekly feature aimed at the entire family.'

Soon they were both caught up discussing the viability of Hester's new proposal.

A pang of envy knifed through Hester as she watched Violet enter The Ivanhoe's lounge. Violet's swollen belly caused her to lumber, the way pregnant women do.

Hester pulled out the chair beside her, and Violet sank into it gratefully. 'I'm only six months, but it feels like the entire nine,' she puffed. 'God knows what I'll be like when I do reach that stage. An overweight elephant, most like.'

'How has it been affecting you otherwise?'

'I've only just stopped being sick in the mornings. Now it's varicose veins. The left leg's bad in particular, but the doctor says he's pretty certain they'll disappear after the baby's born. I'm praying he's right.'

'Tea, coffee or a drink?'

'Tea, please. I'd love a gin but have sworn off all alcohol for the time being.'

'Then we'll both have tea,' Hester replied, summoning a hovering waiter.

'It's good of you to see me like this at such short notice,' Violet said after the order had been placed. 'But it wasn't till yesterday morning that Billy told me he intended going along to The King's tonight to watch a touring version of Chekhov's "Uncle Vanya". I was supposed to go with him, but in the end I cried off saying I wasn't feeling well enough. An excuse to allow me to meet up with you.'

'So he's still keen on Chekhov,' Hester smiled.

'That's never changed. Although it's not that often he gets to see one. Funnily enough, this is the same touring company that brought "The Seagull" up years ago. That first time he and I went out together.'

'I remember,' Hester said.

'A long time ago now,' Violet mused, shaking her head almost sadly.

They reminisced for a few minutes until the tea arrived. Hester poured.

'Now what's all this about?' she asked, handing Violet a cup.

Violet sat back in her chair. Her eyes were filled with pain, and anger. 'You didn't mind me telephoning?'

'Of course not. You said you needed my help. If I can give it to you I will. Only I hope it's not about *The Glaswegian* and *The Scottish Daily News*?'

Violet smiled thinly. 'It is. And it isn't. But it's really about Billy's father and what he's been doing over the past few weeks.'

Hester frowned. 'What's he been up to then?'

'He's been visiting us. Regularly.'

That took Hester completely by surprise. Will had mentioned nothing about this. 'Visiting you?'

'The pretext is the baby. It'll be his first grandchild, after all. So he's started coming to inquire after my health and play the concerned father-in-law.'

'I'm surprised Billy lets him into the house after what

346

Will said to him on the telephone a little while back.'

'I didn't know about that,' Violet said, new concern in her eyes.

'He tore a strip off Billy. Very nastily, too, I thought.'

Violet shrugged. 'Well, he lets him in. Probably too flabbergasted to do otherwise. But it's driving him insane every time his father calls.'

'Why?'

'First of all, and I'm only telling you this because I care so much for him and am trying to help him, his nerves have been very, very bad since this business started about *The Scottish Daily News*. In fact, if I'm being totally honest, it goes deeper than nerves. I think all the pressure is affecting his mental health. I've never known depression like it. From morning to night he walks around completely lost to it. You only have to say the slightest wrong thing for him to fly right off the handle.'

'I'm sorry,' said Hester, and meant it. 'So are you telling me that Will is coming over to your place and needling Billy?'

'Not at all. Nothing about either newspaper is ever mentioned. it might be better if it was.'

'So what's the problem?'

'The Colonel's grinning.'

'His *grinning*!' Hester exclaimed.

'Sounds stupid, I know. But it's really getting through to Billy. His father just sits there and grins at him.'

Not stupid at all, Hester thought. She could just imagine it. For Billy each grin must be like a whiplash, reminding him how much he was failing and his father winning. The old cock was crowing over the young rooster.

'What do you want me to do?'

'Can you get him to stop visiting us? I don't want to be seen to interfere personally. Billy might interpret that the wrong way. He's unbelievably touchy about anything concerning his father.'

Hester nodded. It seemed a reasonable request. 'Leave

it to me. I'll get him to tell me about these visits and then take it from there.'

Violet reached across to clasp Hester's hand. 'I'm really obliged.'

'Don't mention it,' Hester replied warmly. 'I'm sure you'd do the same for me.'

Hester poured more tea for the pair of them. 'I take it you haven't had any problems with this pregnancy?'

Violet grasped the side of her chair. 'Touch wood! Not so far. Everything on that front has been as right as rain.'

'And I'm sure it'll continue to be so,' Hester agreed quickly. 'But tell me, how are things between you and Billy generally?'

'What have you heard?' Violet asked, instantly on edge.

'Nothing,' Hester lied.

'But you know our marriage hasn't exactly been the happiest of ones?'

'I guessed something of the sort.'

Violet went on. 'We've certainly had our ups and downs. For a long time we fought like cat and dog. But recently the fighting hasn't been quite so bad. I think the basic problem is that he simply doesn't love me. . . .'

'Oh, surely that isn't true!' Hester protested.

Violet gave a rueful, fatalistic smile. 'I love him. But. . . .' She trailed off, and shrugged. There was a few seconds pause before she added, 'I've often suspected there was someone before me. Someone he still hankers after. I asked him point-blank about it once but he denied it. Said it was all in my imagination.'

Hester went cold.

'Do you know if there was anyone?' Violet asked.

Hester shook her head. 'Not to my knowledge,' she lied.

'Well, perhaps I am wrong,' Violet said. 'But something in here tells me I'm not,' she added, tapping her heart.

Hester busied herself lighting a cigarette. She didn't

want to look Violet in the eyes until she'd got herself under control.

They left The Ivanhoe together and Hester escorted Violet to her car, waving her off cheerfully.

Grinning, she thought as she returned to the Phantom which was parked close by.

She was surprised Billy hadn't punched his father. The fact that he hadn't must be indicative of the state he was in.

'Do you fancy a drink after work?' she asked. 'I'd like to have a chat with you about the sports pages. Nothing immediately important. Just some long-range innovations.'

'I'd like that fine, lass,' Will replied.

'It's a date then,' Hester said, pretending to re-immerse herself in what she was doing.

She looked up after he'd gone. Her plan was to get him halfway sozzled and then winkle the story of his visits to Billy and Violet out of him. Once he'd told her, the rest would be easy. When she wanted to, she could still wind him around her little finger.

Hester was relaxing with a Dutch gin and a last cigarette before going to bed when the doorbell rang. Who on earth could it be at this hour, she wondered, coming to her feet.

'Violet!' she exclaimed in surprise on opening the door.

Violet's face was scrubbed clean of make-up and her clothes looked as though they'd literally been thrown on. Her eyes – wide, inquisitive and a little fearful – flickered over Hester's shoulder to take in the hallway beyond.

'Is he here?' Violet asked in a whisper.

'Who?'

'Billy.'

349

Hester shook her head. 'Should he be?'

Violet bit her lip.

'Don't just stand there, come in,' Hester commanded, firmly closing the door behind Violet. 'Now what's all this about?'

It was less than a fortnight since Hester had last seen Violet at The Ivanhoe Hotel. It was the day following that meeting that she'd had the drink with Will after work and extracted his promise to stop visiting Violet and Billy.

'I was sure Billy would be here,' Violet said nervously.

Hester ushered the agitated Violet into the house.

'I've never seen him like that before,' Violet was saying, nearly hysterical. 'He was like a zombie. Eyes starting from his head, walking stiffly. When he left the house it sent shivers racing up and down my spine just to look at him.'

'Did his father call round again?'

'No, nothing like that. It was what I said. About you. That caused Billy to go the way he did. That's why I thought he'd come here.'

Hester said patiently. 'Start at the beginning Violet and explain it from there. Otherwise I won't be able to make any sense of this.'

'Sorry,' Violet mumbled, her body trembling.

Hester sat facing her. Waiting.

Violet nervously flicked some hair out of her face. 'It was a stupid thing for me to say, I suppose. But it just sort of slipped out. I never do think completely clearly in moments like those.'

'Moments like *what*, Violet?' Hester asked, slightly irritated. 'You haven't started at the beginning. Or if you have, you're not making much sense so far.'

'Sorry,' Violet repeated, moving restlessly in her chair. 'Billy and I were in bed. We'd . . . we'd just made love. I was . . . well, I was in that sort of rosy mood you get in. I wasn't thinking too clearly.'

Hester patted her hand. 'I understand, Violet.'

'We were both lying there, when he began chuntering

350

on about *The Scottish Daily News* again. Something he's been doing almost non-stop since it began. Anyway, this time he was on about you as opposed to his father. He said it was a great pity your husband had never made you pregnant because if you'd had a child to worry about you'd never have got round to buying *The Clarion*.'

'So what did you say?'

'I said there was no chance of you ever having a child. Because you couldn't. It was merely a passing remark but he seized on it and wouldn't let go. He made me tell him how I knew such a thing and I was forced to tell him.'

Hester's heart sank. She nodded numbly. 'What else did he ask you?'

Violet took a deep breath. 'Billy wanted to know who the father was. I couldn't tell him that, but what I could tell him was that you lost the baby because of a fall from a horse. And that as a result of your fall you'd never again be able to conceive. I also said, from something you once let slip, that I was pretty certain the father had been with you when you'd come off the horse. And that the father was already married.'

Without realizing it, Violet had handed Billy the answer on a plate, Hester thought. For the pieces of information Violet had given him added up to one man, and one man alone. His *own* father.

'What did Billy do then?' Hester asked, beginning to be worried.

'He got out of bed and started to dress. I asked him where he was going at that time of night but he wouldn't answer me. He was absolutely frightening to look at. Like a mad thing. And then he left the house without uttering another word.'

Hester came to her feet, but Violet kept talking. 'You and he were always like brother and sister rather than cousins. So I presumed he'd come over here to have it out with you about your childhood pregnancy. The way a brother might who feels he's been let down in some way. Since it was my big mouth which caused the damage, I thought the least I could do was follow him to try and mediate as best I could. Only it seems I was wrong about him coming here.'

After all these years, it must have been mind-shattering for Billy to find out his father had beat him again, Hester thought. That she'd been his father's mistress before his. God alone knew what thoughts were running through his brain. And this on top of the war between the papers.

'We have to hurry,' Hester said.

'You mean you know where he's gone?'

'Yes. Now let's go.'

When they arrived in Julian Avenue it was to find an ambulance and police car outside the Oliphant's house.

Violet started and sat up straight when she saw them. 'Oh Jesus!' she whispered in a strangled voice.

Hester parked the Phantom and got out. She then ran round to the other side to help Violet who was much slower and more awkward because of her pregnancy. Arm-in-arm they headed for the house.

Some neighbours and passers-by had gathered to stare with ghoulish curiosity. A policeman was standing at the open door. Every window in the house was blazing with light.

Violet started to sob. 'Something awful has happened. I can feel it.' She held on tightly to Hester's hand.

The policeman stopped them at the door, and Hester immediately launched into an explanation of who they were. She was in the middle of this when a voice from inside the hallway shouted out.

'Make way there! Move aside!'

The voice belonged to one of the two ambulancemen, carrying a stretcher between them. On the stretcher was a figure covered by a blanket.

'Billy! Billy!' Violet moaned, staring in horrible fasci-nation at the stretcher. Then with a heart-stopping scream, she threw herself forward to rip the blanket halfway down the stretcher.

Hester stared in horror at what was revealed. Will. He was mutilated about the face and chest. There was a large puncture in his throat and several more dotted about the front of his shirt. The other injuries consisted of slashes. Incredibly, and despite the blood and damage, it was clear that he was grinning.

Violet recoiled. Her hands going to her mouth in horror. Hester wrapped her arms about her.

The policeman hurried forward to whip the blanket back into place.

Violet started to shake. Within seconds her entire body was heaving.

The policeman turned to them, but before he could speak there was a sudden noise in the hallway, followed almost instantly by the appearence of three men. The one in the middle was Billy. His clothes were splashed with blood. He was handcuffed to the men escorting him.

Billy's face was stony and completely white. His eyes were dull, the pupils no more than pinpricks.

Struggling free of Hester, Violet threw herself at him, sobbing wildly and piteously.

But it wasn't his wife that Billy looked at. It was Hester.

For a few moments their eyes locked. For Hester it was like looking through the gates of hell.

Billy spat viciously, tears coursing down his cheeks. Very slowly he shook his head.

'Let's go,' said one of the detectives quietly.

Violet started to wail. 'You can't take him! He's my husband! He's my husband! You can't take him!' Then, pleading, 'Please? Please?'

The policeman took Violet by the shoulders, trying to pull her off Billy, but she hung on as though for dear life. The two detectives pulled Billy in the direction of their car. Violet and the policeman were dragged along with them.

Suddenly Violet gave a great shriek and collapsed on the pavement. The policeman fell on top of her.

Seizing the opportunity the detectives bundled Billy into the car, and seconds later it roared into life, speeding off down the road.

The policeman twisted himself into a kneeling position, intending to help Violet back onto her feet. Hester ran forward to help.

Violet started to writhe. Her legs jerking this way and that. A dull moaning coming from somewhere deep in her throat.

Hester was about to speak when she noticed the blood stain on the front of Violet's dress. A stain that was widening rapidly.

The policeman had also seen the stain by this time. 'There's a doctor inside,' he said. Then looking over to those gawping on, he called out that he needed some help. Immediately a young man hurried across.

'Easy, Violet, easy!' Hester whispered as the policeman and young man lifted her.

Violet's eyes were open and staring, beads of sweat on her forehead. Her legs had stopped jerking, but every few seconds one of them gave an involuntary twitch.

Hester led the way to the lounge where Violet was placed on the sofa. When the young man stood back his arms from his wrists to his elbows were covered with blood.

'The doctor's upstairs with the lady of the house,' the policeman said.

Aunt Sybil! Hester had completely forgotten about her. Of course she would have been at home and probably with Will when Billy arrived.

Hester dashed upstairs to Sybil's bedroom, tapping on the door before entering.

She found the doctor packing his bag. Sybil was fast asleep, snoring.

The doctor frowned. 'Who are you?'

In a few terse sentences Hester explained who she was and why he was desperately needed in the lounge.

The doctor snapped his bag shut, fairly sprinting from the room.

Hester remained behind for a second, staring at Sybil. She must have been given a very strong sedative to have knocked her out like that, Hester thought. She'd be all right for some hours yet.

Downstairs again, Hester found the doctor gingerly examining Violet. The policeman had stayed on in the room, but the young man was gone.

'How bad is it?' she asked.

The doctor ignored her question. 'Has that ambulance gone?' he demanded of the policeman.

'Yes, sir. It's taken the body in.'

The doctor swore. 'Then we'll just have to use my car. It's imperative we get this woman to the hospital as soon as possible.'

'I've got a Rolls outside. That'll give her a smoother ride,' Hester offered.

The doctor nodded.

In the hallway Hester found several obviously shocked servants aimlessly hanging around. She told them that someone had to stay with Sybil at all times, and that she would return after she'd been to the hospital.

They all stepped back as the doctor and policeman went past carrying the unconscious Violet.

Hester ran ahead of them to open the Phantom's back door, hurrying around to the driving seat as the doctor and policeman manoeuvred Violet inside.

'Right!' said the doctor as the back door was closed.

It was a nightmare drive of which Hester remembered little afterwards. She might have been in a dream, suddenly waking to find herself driving into the hospital's casualty entrance.

The moment the Phantom appeared, swing doors burst open and a trolley with a stretcher on top was wheeled out by a porter. After the porter came a brace of white-jacketed doctors.

Violet was taken from the back of the car and laid on

355

the stretcher. Instantly, she was covered with a red hospital blanket.

Moments later, flanked by the GP and hospital doctors, she disappeared inside.

Hester had to stay behind to park the Phantom. As she was locking the doors she glanced at the back seat. It was caked and sticky with blood. For a moment she stood with eyes closed and head bowed. Then, taking a deep breath, she hurried back into the hospital.

She waited on a hard wooden bench in a corridor, but she didn't have to wait long. Less than half an hour after she'd sat down, the GP came looking for her.

She rose to stare him in the face. He looked exhausted.

'I'm sorry,' he said.

'And Violet?'

He shook his head. 'We did all we could. She died a few minutes ago.'

'Dead? But how?'

He put a hand on her shoulder. 'It was all too much for her,' he said gently. 'The official cause of death will, I suppose, be miscarriage. But the real one seems to me to be compounded shock.'

Hester slumped where she stood, scrabbling in her pocket for a cigarette. She wasn't supposed to smoke here but she didn't give a damn. The doctor made no objections.

'Can I get you anything?' he asked.

She shook her head.

'If you're going back to the Oliphants', I'd be obliged for a lift. My car's still there.'

'Of course.'

Their footsteps echoed hollowly as they walked down the deserted corridor.

'What did Billy use to kill his father?' she asked, at last.

'An inlaid dagger.'

'A curved one?'

'That's right.' He looked at her curiously.

Hester knew the dagger he was referring to. It was a souvenir Will had kept from his army days.

'Maybe Billy wouldn't have done it if Will hadn't started grinning at him,' Hester said to herself, half-dazed.

The GP wondered what on earth she was talking about.

Although not yet midday, Hester was sitting with a large whisky in her hand. It was the fourth since the cup of tea which had been her breakfast.

Will. Violet. Violet's unborn child. All gone. And Billy. Billy in jail for the murder of his father.

She saw again Will's mutilated features. And Billy in handcuffs being led from the house in Julian Avenue.

'My Lady?'

Hester blinked and looked up. She hadn't heard Harkness either knock or enter the room.

'Mr Beat is here. Will you see him?'

'Yes. Show him in.'

'Oh, Hester, lass!' Alan said when he appeared.

'You know then?'

'Aye. The news broke this morning. The lads who cover the police stations picked it up.'

'Will you take a dram?'

'Please.'

As she poured she said. 'Have you also heard about Billy's wife and child?'

'No. What about them?'

Hester told him, passing him his drink with an unsteady hand.

'God Almighty!' Alan whispered.

They each reflected for a few seconds. At last, Alan said, 'Why did Billy do it?'

'A lot of reasons, Alan,' she replied slowly. 'He and his father have been at loggerheads for as long as I've known them. But it goes deeper than that. I suppose what it all boils down to is that Billy couldn't stand the idea of his father appearing to be the better man.'

'You mean the success of *The Scottish Daily News* and all?'

'Yes. And all.'

'I take it you're not coming in today?' Alan asked.

'I couldn't.'

'I understand. That's why I came over. You take as much time off as you need. We'll be able to cope in the meantime. I thought we might get Jim McConnochie to act up as editor-in-chief? Your uncle thought very highly of him.'

'Then do that, Alan.'

'Right. I'll get back then.' He laid down his glass. Then, on a sudden impulse, came to Hester and threw his arms around her.

At the door he paused, a glint of moisture in his eyes. 'We had a few barneys in our time. But I'm going to miss that old bugger,' he said.

Hester smiled. 'Go print a newspaper,' she ordered, blinking back her own tears.

'Aye,' he said. 'I'll do just that.'

Hester supported Sybil on one side, Christine on the other.

'Ashes to ashes, dust to dust. . . .' the minister intoned.

Hester stared out at the huge crowd who'd come to pay Will Oliphant their last respects. Many of them had the unmistakable stamp of newspapermen about them, there to say goodbye to one of their own.

This afternoon she would be going to another funeral. That of Violet who was being buried with her unborn child.

She glanced into Aunt Sybil's face and saw death there. The wife wouldn't be long behind the husband. Months at the most, she guessed. Another victim chalked up to Billy. she thought in despair.

*   *   *

It was less than a week now till Billy's trial and Hester couldn't understand why she hadn't been contacted by his lawyer. Surely, she reasoned, she was going to be called as a witness for the defence?

Her evidence regarding her previous involvement with Billy and Will would hardly get Billy off, but once everything was properly explained it would give a great deal more meaning and depth to Billy's actions. It might even gain him some leniency.

She pondered the matter further, then decided to make a phone call.

Murray McGartland was a small, fat man with a some-what seedy appearance. He sucked a front tooth as he listened to Hester's story.

When she was finally finished he said, 'I agree with you. This could literally mean the difference between life and death. What I can't understand is why Mr Oliphant didn't tell me about it himself?'

'I've no idea,' Hester replied.

'Up until now all I've been able to establish is that Mr Oliphant and his father hated one another. Hardly mitigating circumstances.'

Hester agreed.

'I think the best thing is for me to go and see him right away,' said McGartland.

Hester rose. As McGartland walked her to the door, she said, 'If there's anything I can do, and I mean any-thing, don't hesitate to get in touch.'

Outside the lawyer's chambers she wondered why Billy had engaged a lawyer like McGartland who was hardly at the top of his profession. He could easily have afforded a QC, so why hadn't he?

There was definitely something about all this which didn't add up.

★   ★   ★

Shortly after Hester arrived home from work, Harkness announced that a Mr Murray McGartland was at the door wishing to speak with her.

McGartland's face was glum as he entered the room. 'You said to contact you if you could help. And that's why I've come,' he said, without preamble.

'Surely Billy hasn't denied what I told you?'

'No, no,' McGartland replied quickly. 'But he flatly refuses to allow me to call you in Court. He says he doesn't want your involvement with himself and his father made public.'

'That's ridiculous considering what's at stake!' Hester exclaimed.

'I agree with you.'

'Did he give you a reason?'

'No.'

Hester drew in a deep breath. 'So what do you want me to do?'

'Go and see him. Convince him you must testify on his behalf.'

Go and see Billy. It certainly wasn't a prospect she relished.

'He's in Barlinnie isn't he?' she asked at last.

'That's right.'

She'd never seen Glasgow's notorious prison. Far less been inside. But she knew of its fearsome reputation. Amongst a certain section of the community, it was commonly referred to as Bar–L.

'When can you arrange it?'

'The sooner the better I would say. How about tomorrow morning?'

'Fine,' she replied.

On entering Barlinnie, the first thing that his Hester was the smell. A worse stink than even came from the slums.

God, she thought, what a nightmare.

McGartland held her arm as they passed along a

cream-coloured brick corridor. The warder leading the way was dressed in black. His face was the most hard and uncompromising one Hester had ever seen.

She shivered. This was a hellish place. She couldn't even begin to imagine what it must be like to be shut up here for years on end.

The visiting room was also painted cream. There was one small window high up on the wall; three iron bars in front of its reinforced plate glass.

There was a plain wooden table and two wooden chairs. Hester sat on one of the chairs, but Murray McGartland remained standing.

Hester lit a cigarette as the minutes ticked by. Suddenly the door swung open and Billy strode in, coming up short when he saw her.

A warder positioned himself in a corner of the room to watch the proceedings. The door banged shut behind Billy, followed by the sound of a key turning in the lock.

'What's she doing here?' Billy demanded.

'I asked her to come to try and talk some sense into you,' McGartland replied evenly.

Billy accepted one of Hester's cigarettes, which she then lit for him.

'The answer's no,' he said.

Hester glanced up at McGartland. Then back to Billy. 'Your chances of avoiding the rope are negligible otherwise,' she said brutally.

He smiled. 'I know that.'

'You mean you want to die?' she asked slowly.

'Yes,' he said shortly.

The breath sighed out of Hester. Staring down at her hands she noticed they were trembling slightly.

'Why did you never tell me about you and father?' he asked.

She groped for the words. 'It wasn't an episode in my life I was particularly proud of. You were his son after all. And at the time I loved you.'

Billy studied his cigarette as though it had suddenly

become of great interest to him. 'Were you . . . were you and he when you and I . . . ?'

'No,' she broke in. 'Your father and I were finished long before we began.'

Still regarding his cigarette, he listened to her with a bowed head.

'When you and I were together Billy, I loved you. I never felt that way about Will.'

'And yet you slept with him?'

'I was a child. I thought the alternative might be an orphanage or the ragged school. I thought he was the only person who cared about me. What else could I do?'

Billy's face was clouded with anger.

Hester shook her head. 'It wasn't just lust. There was a great deal more to it than that.' And she went on to tell him about her mother, and how that love had been transferred to her.

Billy digested all she said. 'And yet you asked him to come and work for you when you started up *The Scottish Daily News*?'

Hester shrugged. 'Time passes. Things mellow. I'd come to like your father again. We had a new relationship. We were finally friends.'

'And you never loved him?'

'Not in the way you mean. You were the only man, except my husband, whom I ever felt that for.'

Billy stared off into space. In a voice that seemed already to belong to the grave he said, 'There are only two things I've ever cared deeply about. You and *The Glaswegian*. Father made it so that I had to give one of them up. Rightly or wrongly, I chose to hang onto the paper. Can you imagine how I've suffered all these years? It was either my right arm or my left. What sort of choice is that? I think I've always hated him. I've never been able to live up to his dreams. He never allowed me to be myself.'

Hester was suddenly aware that she was crying.

Billy went on. 'Then you and he started up *The Scottish*

Daily News and completely shot *The Glaswegian* out from under me. Your *Scottish Daily News* has won hands down. I've lost.' He took a deep breath. 'I think I could just about have borne losing you and having the paper decimated. But when I found out he'd had you before me. That you'd been his mistress. That . . . *that* left me without anything. Everything I'd held dear or of value he'd either taken away or made a mockery of. I *had* to do what I did. I just had to!' His last words came out as a cry of despair.

If only she'd never dreamed up the idea of *The Scottish Daily News*, Hester thought. If only Billy had never found out about her and her father. If only Billy hadn't gone on loving her. If only. . . .

Billy ground out what was left of his cigarette, coming rather unsteadily to his feet.

'I thought I had nothing left of my own. But what you've told me today alters that. I had your love once. Which he never had. That fact makes an awfully big difference to me.'

'Then you'll let me go into court and speak on your behalf?' she asked hopefully.

He shook his head. 'No. I have to pay, Hester. Not so much for the old man, but for Violet and the baby. Can you understand that?'

Her eyes suddenly clogged with tears so that she couldn't see. Using the back of her hand, she wiped them away.

'I understand,' she whispered.

There was nothing more to be said between them.

At the door, he turned to look at her for the last time. 'Goodbye, Hester.'

'Goodbye Billy,' she whispered in reply.

There was a hint of a smile.

And then he was gone.

Hester was reading page three of the latest edition, hot off the presses, when the telephone rang.

'Mrs McNeill speaking,' she said.

'It's Peter McLennan. I've got the verdict for you.'

Hester's stomach tightened. Peter McLennan was their crime reporter covering the trial.

'Go on,' she said slowly.

'He's been found guilty and given the death sentence.'

There it was. Official now. Billy was to hang.

'When?' she asked.

'The date for execution hasn't been set yet. But it will be later on today.'

'Thank you for ringing, Peter. Now come on back and write your story.'

For a long time she stared off into space. Thinking. Remembering. Wishing the past could be changed.

She'd tried to sleep but had found it impossible. Just before 2 a.m., she got out of bed, put on her dressing gown and came down to where the Jonge Genever bottle was.

For what seemed like the millionth time, her gaze came to rest on the ticking clock which she knew to be correct to the nearest second.

Only a few moments now and it would be all over. Closing her eyes she offered up a silent prayer.

Her prayer gave way to vivid images. The last walk. Stepping onto the trapdoor. The black hood. The noose being tightened. A hand activating the switch or lever. The drop.

Ting! Ting! Ting!

Her eyes jerked open as the clock struck the hour.

Ting! Ting! Ting!

In her mind she saw it happening. The trapdoor opening. Billy falling.

Ting! Ting! Ting!

The sudden arrest as the end of the rope was reached. The snap of his neck.

Death.

★   ★   ★

364

The day after Billy's execution Murray McGartland again presented himself at Hester's house.

'I've come about Mr Oliphant's will,' he stated solemnly.

Mystified, Hester showed McGartland to a seat. She was dressed entirely in black, not only for Billy, but for all those who'd died.

She raised an eyebrow, the signal for McGartland to go on.

'After your visit to Barlinnie, Mr Oliphant made out a new will in which he left you *The Glaswegian*,' McGartland said.

Hester stared at the lawyer in complete astonishment. 'Me?'

McGartland nodded.

'But why?'

'He said you were the logical choice. He was absolutely certain his mother wouldn't want it. And the only other person was his sister Christine, and her husband, whom he was convinced would make more of a hash running it, his words not mine, than he did. He said you would find a way to build the paper back up to what it had been. He said it was to be *your* inheritance now.'

Hester was stunned. This was the last thing she'd imagined happening. But maybe Billy was right, and there was a sort of cock-eyed logic in it.

'If you'll just sign this document,' continued McGartland, '*The Glaswegian* becomes officially yours.'

Hester stared at the document laid in front of her. Out of it, faces stared back at her. Billy's. Will's. Violet's.

Memories from a dozen past occasions flashed through her mind. The first day she and Billy had started work at *The Glaswegian*. The pair of them with Alan Beat at the subs' table. Them together in the Adler. Will holding her in his arms. Will as he'd been of late, her friend and mentor. Will grinning. Violet lying on the pavement outside the house in Julian Avenue. . . .

Accepting the pen offered her by McGartland, Hester bent to sign.

Her eyes were filled with tears.

On the Monday of the week following Billy's execution, Hester entered *The Glaswegian* for the first time as owner. Beside her various accoutrements she was carrying a brand new box of cigars.

Fearful and nervous glances were cast in her direction as she made her way to what had been Billy's office and Will's before that.

The feeling in the air was one of doom. The general opinion among the staff was that she was going to close the paper down. Wasn't it her own newspaper's main rival after all?

Nothing was further from Hester's mind.

She smiled on entering Billy's office. And almost said 'Thank God!' out loud.

The room was exactly as she remembered it. The walls dirty with cobwebs in the corners. The carpet underfoot a threadbare rag, pulverized by the comings and goings of countless feet. The overall impression was complete shabbiness.

Hester drank it all in. Her eyes shone to be once again in that room.

She'd been certain Billy would have had the office totally refurbished, obliterating his father's former occupancy.

But he hadn't. She'd misjudged him. He'd been more of a newspaperman than she'd given him credit for.

Using her nail she opened the box of cigars, selected one and lit up.

Then she flipped the intercom and asked Mrs Nicholson, formerly Billy's secretary and now hers, to come through.

Mrs Nicholson's eyes opened wide with surprise when she saw that Hester was smoking a cigar.

'Tell the editors I want them assembled here in ten minutes' time,' Hester said briskly.

Deep in thought Hester began striding up and down. Every few seconds or so puffing on her cigar. She didn't know it, but that was precisely what her Uncle Will had often done there when he'd been thinking.

Ten minutes later there was a tap on the door. 'Come in!' Hester called out, taking up a position behind the rolltop desk.

The editors filed in, standing in a semi-circle facing her.

'*The Glaswegian* is a bloody disgrace, and as from this Friday will cease to exist,' she announced.

Without exception the editors sagged where they stood, their worst suspicions confirmed.

Hester waited a few seconds before continuing. 'It was Billy Oliphant's belief that I could build this paper back to what it had been. Which is precisely what I intend doing.'

Men glanced at one another, confused.

'But you just said that as from this Friday *The Glaswegian* will cease to exist?' an editor called McRae piped up.

'So I did. And so it will. Three weeks this coming Sunday a brand new paper is going to appear, gentlemen. The *Sunday Glaswegian*. Sister paper to *The Scottish Daily News*.'

A buzz ran round the room. Relief, mingled with excitement, appearing on every man's face.

'The idea wasn't originally mine,' Hester confessed. 'It was Billy Oliphant's. Only he had it the other way round. *The Glaswegian* remaining a daily and the old *Clarion* becoming the Sunday.'

She blew smoke in front of her. Giving them a few moments to let all this sink in. 'As you know, up until the appearance of *The Scottish Daily News*, this paper was the best daily in Scotland. Well, it's going to be the best again. Only this time as a Sunday. Now what do you say?'

'We're with you all the way!' a man named Simpson called out.

'It's going to mean an awful lot of hard work over the next four weeks. And beyond, I know. It's not all that long since I went through exactly the same thing with *The Scottish Daily News*. But believe me, it'll be worth it.'

Suddenly Hester was inundated with questions. What sort of format were they going to have? Were they going tabloid like *The Scottish Daily News*? Were the staff to remain exactly the same or were there to be changes?

Hester held up her hand and the babble ceased. 'Some of these questions I have answers for. Others I don't. At least not yet. In an hour I'll address the entire staff, telling them what I've just told you. Later on today, I'll visit you each in turn. We'll get to know one another. And if you'll individually put your questions to me, then I'll answer those that I can.'

She paused for emphasis. 'The first dummy of the new *Sunday Glaswegian* will be a week on Wednesday.'

A ragged cheer went up.

'Till later,' Hester smiled.

Chattering nineteen to the dozen, the editors trooped out of the office. The last one closed the door behind him.

Making *The Sunday Glaswegian* the best was going to be a lot harder than it had been with *The Scottish Daily News*. Hester had no illusions about that.

Before, she'd had the cream of Scottish journalism to help her. Now she could only rely on herself.

It would take time, therefore. A year or two at least, with perhaps a certain amount of shuffling around between the two staffs. But do it she would.

Of that she was determined.